Times and Seasons

Also by Beverly LaHaye and Terri Blackstock

Seasons Under Heaven
Showers in Season

Times and Seasons

BOOK THREE

BEVERLY LAHAYE
TERRI BLACKSTOCK

Bookspan Large Print Edition

ZondervanPublishingHouse
Grand Rapids, Michigan

A Division of HarperCollinsPublishers

Times and Seasons

Copyright © 2001 by Beverly LaHaye and Terri Blackstock

Requests for information should be addressed to:

Zondervan Publishing House

Grand Rapids, Michigan 49530

ISBN: 0-7394 2326-6

Published in association with the literary agency of Alive Communications, Inc., 7680 Goddard St., Suite 200, Colorado Springs, CO 80920.

Printed in the United States of America

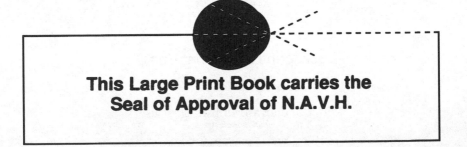

**This Large Print Book carries the
Seal of Approval of N.A.V.H.**

Dedication

This book is dedicated to parents of prodigal children, searching the horizon for their loved ones to come home.

Acknowledgments

Special thanks to Jim Woodall, who helped us get our facts straight regarding Nicaragua. Thanks, also, to Terry Bartlett, who offered valuable insights about the juvenile prison system.

He urged them to plead for mercy from the God of heaven. . . . Then Daniel praised the God of heaven and said: "Praise be to the name of God for ever and ever; wisdom and power are his. He changes times and seasons; he sets up kings and deposes them. He gives wisdom to the wise and knowledge to the discerning. He reveals deep and hidden things; he knows what lies in darkness, and light dwells with him."

DANIEL 2:18–22

Chapter One

I'm telling you, Mark, it's a sorry idea."

Mark Flaherty turned from his bedroom window and glanced back at Daniel. His best friend still wore his church clothes from this morning—a button-down blue shirt neatly tucked into khakis. The clothes made Daniel look older than fifteen as he stood with his arms at his sides, preparing to fight him if he tried to push past. "You always think my ideas are sorry."

"You've already been arrested once," Daniel said.

Mark turned back toward the window with a clear view of Cedar Circle, in full summer bloom. His mother was next door, revving up for the wedding shower the neighbors were giving her. Brenda Dodd and Tory Sullivan had been talking about it for weeks, and Sylvia Bryan had come all the way back from her mission work in Nicaragua to host it in her home. It griped him that his mom had insisted on the men in her life being there. Showers were for women, and he had better things to do. It was only early June, and the wedding wasn't until July 4th. The shower was just a lot of trouble for nothing, in his opinion.

"I'll be back before anybody knows I'm gone," Mark said. "I'd have to be crazy not to do this. It's easy money." He turned back to his friend and reached for the small bag of marijuana he'd bought from a friend at the baseball park last night. "Chill out. I won't get caught, okay?"

The words sent a little jolt of memory through him, for he had said them before. Just over a year ago—months after his mother had freaked and got Miss Brenda to home-school him. He had sneaked out of his dad's house in Knoxville and gone joyriding with a kid—in a car he didn't know was stolen. They'd been caught spray-painting graffiti on the side of a school building. Mark had been charged with car theft and vandalism, both in one night. The judge, who'd had a fourteen-year-old kid of his own, had let him off with probation.

But this time was different. He had turned fifteen last week, and he wasn't following the crowd anymore. He was in control here. He had this figured out.

"You're just mad because you won't be able to buy a concert ticket," Mark said. "But I'll be there in the front row. I'll buy you a T-shirt."

"Your mom will go ballistic," Daniel said. "She won't even let you go to that stupid concert, and you know it."

"She won't know," Mark said, stuffing the bag into his pocket. He heard a horn honk and looked out the window. Ham Carter and some other guy waited in his jeep at the end of the driveway. "Gotta go. He's here."

Daniel's cheeks were blotched pink as he tried to block the way. "Man, I'm telling you, you're making a mistake."

"I have to go," Mark said. Though Daniel was a little taller, Mark knew he could take him if he had to. "Move!"

Daniel stood there for a moment, then finally moved aside. Mark pushed past him to the stairs and bolted down, Daniel right behind him.

Eighteen-year-old Annie stood in front of the wall mirror at the bottom of the stairs, dressed like Barbie's evil brunette twin. Rick, his twenty-year-old brother, waited by the front door, tugging at his collar.

"Mom said to wear a tie," Annie told Mark. "Hurry up and get ready, or we'll be late."

"I have to go somewhere," he said. "I'll just be gone a few minutes."

"Gone *where?* We're supposed to *be* there!"

"I have to run an errand," Mark said.

"What kind of errand?" Rick asked with that tone he got when he tried to be the man of the house.

Daniel didn't wait for Mark's answer. He shot out of the house, leaving the screen door to bounce shut behind him. Mark watched him cross the street, ignoring the two guys in the jeep. That was just as well.

"If I'm not back in fifteen minutes," Mark said, "go on without me. Just tell Mom I'm coming."

"No way!" Annie cried. "Mark, you're going to get her mad at all of us. I was counting on her being in a good mood later when I hit her up for concert money—"

Mark grinned. He didn't have to hit her up. "She will be," he said, pushing open the screen door. He took off down the driveway, smiling at Ham and his friend. As he jumped into the backseat, he patted his pocket.

"Hey, guys. I'm kinda in a hurry, okay?"

"Sure, man."

Mark grinned as they pulled out of Cedar Circle. This would be the easiest money he'd ever made.

Chapter Two

Cathy Flaherty kicked her pumps into the corner of the kitchen and wondered why she'd gone to the trouble of getting her hair done this morning. Her blonde strands were already wisping out of the French twist, and the guests hadn't even arrived yet. She should have come in her jeans and lab coat, the veterinarian's garb she wore every day. She would have been more comfortable with her hair in a ponytail and sneakers on her feet.

But that would have disappointed the friends who were throwing this shower. Brenda Dodd and Tory Sullivan, her neighbors on Cedar Circle, had been working on this for weeks. And if that weren't enough, Sylvia Dodd had left her mission work in Nicaragua to come back and host it. It was as if Sylvia had to see it to believe it, Cathy mused.

"Hold still and I'll fix your hair," Brenda said, coming at her with a comb.

"I'm not used to having my hair up," Cathy said. "Shoulda known not to go fu-fu."

Brenda moved a bobby pin, catching some of the escaped wisps. "Tory, does that look okay?"

Tory turned back to them with her fifteen-month-old daughter, Hannah, asleep in her arms. Her body rocked from side to side, as if she swayed to some imaginary beat that only a mother could hear. "Looks good," Tory said in a voice just above a whisper. "I think I'll run home and put her down. Barry can watch her if she's napping."

"When your hands are free, you can help me put out these flowers," Sylvia said. She had several vases of fresh flowers, probably cut from her garden. Cathy had trouble growing weeds, yet Sylvia still had beautiful blooming jasmine, impatiens, petunias, periwinkles, and a dozen other floral varieties around her house, when she didn't even live here to care for them. But Cathy knew Brenda and Tory weeded and watered Sylvia's yard. In March, Brenda had taken her home-schooled children over to plant new annuals in the front garden. She'd considered it a science project. Cathy's son Mark, who was home-schooled with Brenda's four children, had taken great pride in his green thumb. Now, in June, the yard overflowed with blooms, showing evidence of their care.

The Gonzales family had done a good job of caring for the home while the Bryans were on the mission field. In early May, they had finished Juan's seminary training and returned to Nicaragua, so the house was empty again. It was clear Sylvia had enjoyed being back in the home in which she'd raised her children and that she loved launching Cathy's new life with this shower.

Tory was on her way out the front door when Annie and Rick burst in. "Steve's in the driveway," Annie said. "He and Tracy are on their way in."

"But Mark is AWOL at the moment," Rick said.

"AWOL?" she asked, going to the door

and waiting for Steve and Tracy. Tracy was all dressed up, and her hair had been braided with little white flowers. Steve had taken her to get her hair done this morning.

She switched her thoughts back to Mark. "So where is he?"

"Went to run an errand."

"An errand? In what?"

"In Ham Carter's jeep," Annie said. "He said he'd be back in a few minutes. Right."

Steve came up to the porch, dressed like a financier, and grinning like an Oscar winner. Cathy matched that grin and reached up for a kiss. "So we're gonna go through with it, huh?" he teased.

"I wouldn't get too excited," she said with a wink. "It's just a shower." They had postponed the wedding two other times. One was after Mark's arrest, the other after they'd realized how hard it was to blend parenting styles. This time, they had sealed their plans with work—building an addition onto her house. She let Steve go as Rick grabbed a monstrous handful of peanuts, dropping some onto the floor as he shoved them into his mouth. "Rick, please. They'll think you haven't eaten in a week!"

Sylvia came over and gave him a hug, and

Brenda bent down to pick up the fallen peanuts. "It's good to see a healthy appetite," she said. "Besides, who cares what we think?"

"That's what I was thinking, Mom," Rick said with his mouth full. "You've just got to get over this constant worrying what other people think. Are you going to wear shoes?"

Cathy tried to remember where she had left them, then hurried to slip them on. Annie was right behind her. "Your hair looks funny, Mom. It's falling on one side. Looks kind of like somebody jabbed some pins in trying to hold it up."

"Okay, so I'll never be able to work as a hairdresser," Brenda said, throwing up her hands in mock defeat. "Annie, help her."

"I'll help!" Tracy shouted, bouncing up and down. "I can fix your hair, Cathy!" The eleven-year-old was already reaching for the bobby pins.

"Tell you what." Cathy started pulling pins out and letting the hair fall around her shoulders. "Forget the fu-fu do. I'm coming as me."

Steve grinned and stroked the silky hair. "Suits me fine."

"Me, too," Brenda said. "Just run a brush

through it, and you'll look like a catalogue model."

The front door came open, and Cathy turned hoping to see Mark. Instead, Tory stood just inside the door, looking tired and slightly out of breath. "Okay, let me at those flowers," she called to Sylvia.

Sylvia handed her two vases, and the women began placing them. The smell of white roses and lilies wafted on the air. Cathy looked around at the house full of memories—gold gilded photos of Sylvia's children on the walls, an eight-by-ten of her new grandbaby, and multiple pictures of Sylvia and Harry with the children they loved in Nicaragua. A dried vine wound over and between the pictures, creating that thread of life that had never been broken. Not in this family.

Cathy wished her vine wasn't broken. There was something strange, unnatural, about having a wedding shower when you were forty-two years old. But the events of her life had not always been her decision.

"So where's Mark?" Steve's question turned her around, and she thought of lying and saying that she'd sent him to get something. She didn't want to see that look of *he's-at-it-again* pass across Steve's face, and she didn't want to start him down the *are-we-doing-the-right-thing* road again, either. She'd been down that road enough herself.

Besides, she wanted to be free to hear Mark's reasons for being late, *before* she lambasted him. Her reaction to the children was different when Steve was around. She found herself responding the way she knew he would want her to, with consistency and discipline—all the right things, but for all the wrong reasons.

But the truth would come out soon enough, anyway. "Mark seems to have disappeared with Ham Carter. We're expecting him to be back soon." She turned to Annie. "This Ham Carter. How old is he?"

"At least sixteen, I guess," Annie said. "Can you believe his parents are letting that loser drive? They ought to announce it on the evening news or something just to give everybody a chance to get out of his way. Cool! Cake."

"Annie, don't touch that. We're not ready to cut it."

Annie looked insulted. "So what do you think I'm gonna do? Just grab a handful?"

Cathy glanced at her son, who had just about finished off the bowl of peanuts. She thought of pointing out to Annie that the only thing she could expect from her children was the unexpected. She stepped into the kitchen, where Brenda and Tory were busy decorating plates of pastries. Steve followed her in and leaned against the counter. He reached for a pastry.

Sylvia slapped his hand. "The guests will be here soon," she said. "Just a few more minutes. Then, after you and Rick and Mark make your introductions, you can go watch football until we need you to help carry everything home."

"Might be a long wait, then," he said. "When did you say Mark would get here?"

"Few minutes," Cathy said.

Steve looked at his watch. "Mark knew what time the shower started, didn't he?"

"Oh, yeah, he knew. In fact, I even picked his clothes out for him and told him to get dressed before I left. Annie, he was dressed in those clothes when he disappeared, wasn't he?"

Annie shrugged. "Not his tie. Not yet."

Steve stiffened, and that pleasant look on his face was replaced with concern. "Why would he do this today of all days? Do you think this is some kind of psychological plea for us not to get married? Because every time we've set a date, something has happened."

"No, he's not lashing out. He's just being thoughtless."

"Cathy, any psychologist would have a field day with your youngest child running off *today.*"

"Well, thank goodness no one's analyzing it." She took a brownie and bit into it. "Come on, this is not a crisis. Mark's been disobedient, and I'll take care of it when I see him. But I don't want it to ruin the party. So let's not mention it again, okay?"

Steve locked looks with her, threatening to say more, when Tory walked up between them. "Why'd you take your hair down?" she asked. "Cathy, it was beautiful up!"

Grateful for the change of subject, Cathy handed her the brush.

When Tory had finished lacquering Cathy's hair, they emerged from the bathroom in time to see Tracy barreling for the door.

"Grandma's here!" she shouted, and Cathy looked out the window to see Steve's mother and sister getting out of the car in the driveway. "Let me get it!" she shouted. "Please, can't I?"

"All right," Cathy said. "Have at it." She turned to Steve and struck a pose. "So give it to me straight. How's it look?"

A gentle smile softened Steve's features.

"Like cool water in hundred-degree heat. As usual." He leaned down to kiss her. "How'd I get so blessed?"

Tracy threw the door open, and her grandmother and aunt came in with a flourish of gifts and hugs. Sylvia turned on some piano music on the old stereo system Harry had left behind. As more guests arrived, Cathy greeted each one as if they were her old best friend. It bowled her over that anyone had actually taken the time to come. When there was a lull in the number of women arriving, Cathy went to look for her children, who had retreated into the kitchen. "You guys come out here and be polite now," she whispered. "Speak to every guest, and when

I open gifts, ooh and ah over everything. And no cryptic comments about what I get."

"Do you believe this?" Annie asked Rick. "She's asking us to lie."

"I'm not asking you to lie," Cathy said. "I'm just asking you to be polite."

"So what are you going to do to Mark?" Annie wanted to know.

"I'll deal with him when the shower is over. One thing at a time, okay?"

The doorbell rang again, and she heard more guests coming in. "Come on, now. We have to get out there."

The smell of fruit punch and sugar icing hung on the air, along with that of melon balls and a dozen different pastries that Brenda had concocted. Cathy owed them big-time, she thought. She just hoped she wouldn't have to move out a couple of rooms of furniture to get all the gifts into her house.

She and Steve had thought of moving to his place, but she hadn't been able to stand the thought of leaving her little neighborhood. Sensing her reluctance, he had offered to move into hers and build a couple of extra rooms, so they would have a little more square footage in which to spread out. The foundation had been poured last week, and the contractor said it would take a couple of months to get the rooms up—not in time for a July 4th wedding. But that hadn't bothered them. They would go ahead with the wedding and move Steve and Tracy into her house, as it was. That way they could put Steve's house on the market while they waited for the new master bedroom and the extra family room to be finished, and they could take their time decorating Cathy's room for Tracy.

The doorbell rang again, and Tracy flung it open. Her excited face changed to surprise, and she stepped back and called over the crowd, "It's a policeman!"

Everyone got quiet and turned to the door, and Sylvia rushed to the foyer. "May I help you?"

"Could you tell me if there's a Cathy Flaherty here?" the officer asked.

Cathy started to the door, not certain whether this was some kind of prank her friends had played on her, or something more serious. She glanced at Tory and Brenda and saw that there was no amusement in their eyes.

"I'm Cathy Flaherty," she said. "Is something wrong?"

"Mrs. Flaherty, I need for you to come to the police station as soon as possible."

If she hadn't still been standing, she would have been certain her heart had stopped beating. "Why?" she asked. Something told her she didn't want everyone to hear this, so she stepped outside. Steve followed her out, then Annie and Rick bolted to the door.

"It's your son, Mark," the police officer said. "I'm afraid he's been arrested."

A wave of uncertainty and denial washed over Cathy, and she took a step back and bumped into Steve. His arms came around her, steadying her.

"For what, officer?" he asked.

"The charge was drug distribution."

Cathy couldn't get her voice to function, and she felt Steve's hand squeezing her arm. Tears blurred her vision, and she thought she might tip right over and collapse on Sylvia's front porch.

"No way," Rick said, finally.

"My brother was selling drugs?" Annie asked, as if to make sure everyone in the house had heard.

"He was picked up on Highland Avenue," the officer said, "after he tried to sell marijuana to a plainclothes officer."

The world seemed to grow dim. Cathy was going to throw up. Her head was going to explode. Her heart was going to give out. Her knees were going to buckle.

But she just stood, letting the words sink in like some kind of toxin, seeking out every vulnerable cell in her body.

She heard Steve taking charge, finding out where they were holding Mark, asking Rick to get the car, telling Sylvia to call off the shower. For a few moments, her thoughts remained scattered. Only one seemed to motivate her to action.

Her son needed her.

Chapter Three

What was he *thinking?*" The shock etched itself on Cathy's face, making her look older and less like a bride-to-be. She had given up on her hair and pulled the pins out again, and now it was in her way. She swept it behind her ears.

Steve clutched the steering wheel with both hands. He had been quick to get his mother to take Tracy home, as if hearing about Mark's rebellion would influence the child somehow. Cathy wondered what he would do when they all lived together. How would he shelter Tracy from Cathy's kids then?

In the backseat, Rick and Annie sat with their arms crossed, staring out opposite windows. She didn't remember their ever being this quiet before. But she wanted answers.

"Where did he get drugs to sell, for heaven's sake? I tried to separate him from all the kids who were leading him in the wrong direction. He's home-schooled! He must have gotten it in Knoxville when he was with his dad last weekend."

"Mom, he could get it anywhere," Annie argued. "You don't know if he got it in Knoxville."

"But that's where he got in trouble before! Hanging around with car thieves. He could have gone to prison!"

"Mom, he didn't steal a car," Rick said. "His friend took his stepfather's car, and the guy pressed charges. Mark didn't even know he didn't have permission."

"My son was *charged* with car theft—and vandalism of that kid's school. It should have been a wake-up call, but your father didn't wake up. I told him not to let him hang around with them . . . and now he's selling drugs!" Her face tightened, and she felt the arteries at her temples throb. She slammed her hand on the dashboard. "I thought once

you got your life right that things were supposed to fall into place! But they're not falling
into place! How can my son be selling
drugs? He just turned fifteen last week. He's
just a child!"

"Mom, he's not a child," Rick said. "He's
mobile now. His friends have cars."

"And he's not the little angel you think he
is," Annie added.

"I never *thought* he was an angel," Cathy
said, turning around in her seat. "Believe me.
I've known for years that he was far from an
angel. When I was taking him to his probation officer once a week, I knew he wasn't an
angel! When Steve and I canceled our wedding twice last year because of Mark's behavior, I knew he wasn't an angel! But I
didn't think he was a criminal, either!" She
shifted in her seat and turned her accusing
eyes to her children. "Why didn't you tell me
what he was doing? This doesn't even seem
like a surprise to either of you."

"Mom, we didn't know," Rick said. "Don't
you think we would have told you if we knew
our brother was selling drugs?"

"Then why did Annie say that about him,
that he wasn't an angel?"

"Because he's not, Mom," Annie said. "I

mean, I've known for a while that Mark was headed in the wrong direction. Even with the home-schooling and everything, he's just a bad kid."

"He is *not* a bad kid!" Cathy said through her teeth. "I will not let his own siblings label him like that!" She turned back around and glared out the windshield.

Steve reached across and gave her shoulder a reassuring squeeze. She wondered when he would jump in and agree with the kids.

"I'm just saying that he doesn't pick the greatest guys in the world to be his friends," Annie said.

"They're trouble if you ask me," Rick said. "All except for Daniel."

"*I* could have stopped him from seeing them!" Cathy shouted. "I could have made him quit going to visit his dad if his father wouldn't control him. Why would you keep something like that from me?"

"Mom, it wasn't Knoxville. It was here, too. At the baseball park . . ."

"So I was wrong to let him keep playing on a baseball league? I thought he could be home-schooled and still be athletic. I thought he could be trusted at least that far."

"Guys like Mark can get into trouble no matter where they are," Rick said.

Cathy breathed out a bitter laugh that only resulted in tears. "I will not accept that. I . . . will . . . not . . ." Her voice broke off, and she pressed a fist to her mouth. "Maybe he's innocent. Maybe it's all just a stupid mistake."

Steve didn't respond, and she knew he wasn't buying it. Everyone in the car knew Mark had probably done exactly what he was accused of. Everyone except Cathy. She still held out hope that this would all be cleared up by the time they reached the station.

Mark had been such a pure, happy little boy. He had been the one who skipped everywhere he went. He hummed a lot, little kid songs from nursery school. He brought stray animals home and nursed them back to health. She remembered the turtle he'd found dead in its bowl. He had cried for hours, then arranged a burial and a solemn ceremony, in which they'd all crowded around to pay their last respects.

Was this some sort of burial ceremony for his future? Were they all supposed to gather at the station with solemn faces and mourn the loss of the child who could feel things so deeply?

What had happened to that little boy?

She would not believe that he had turned bad, that there was no hope, that he was destined to go down the wrong path for the rest of his life. She would not believe that he had hardened into a criminal who would break a law just to make a buck.

It had to be a mistake.

Chapter Four

She found Mark sitting in an interrogation room with swollen red eyes, as if he'd been trying to cry his way out of this. It had worked when he was four, when one forbidden match had resulted in flames swallowing up the yard. She remembered that Jerry had lambasted him at the top of his lungs, and Mark had cried and cried until Cathy's focus had shifted from punishment to comfort.

But he wasn't four anymore.

She came into the room alone, because they wouldn't allow Steve, Rick, or Annie to accompany her. Instead, they sat in the waiting area for her to come back.

When she saw Mark, she followed her first instinct to pull him out of his chair into a crushing hug. He clung to her as he hadn't in years, and her mother's heart melted at the fear she felt in his embrace. "Mark, what's going on?"

"Mom, I didn't mean to," he said. "I swear I didn't mean to."

"You didn't mean to *what?*"

"Sell drugs," he said. "It's not like I'm some kind of dealer standing on the corner looking for little kids to mess up. I just trusted Ham Carter. You know, the catcher on my team. He called me and told me to meet him. And all he wanted was a bag, Mom. It's not like I keep an inventory or something. I thought I could make a few bucks so I could go to the concert next week. I knew where to get one for him—"

"Mark!" The word yelped out of her mouth, shutting him up. Had he just admitted that he'd done exactly what they said? Had he really bought drugs so he could sell them to someone else? She grabbed a chair and shoved it under the table, as if it was in her way. Trembling, she made herself turn back to him. "Where . . . did you get it?"

"Never mind," he said. "I just got it, okay?

And the reason I was going to sell it to him was because he was going to pay me real good. You know, if you gave me a decent allowance, I wouldn't have to do stuff like this."

Her finger came up level with his gaze, and her eyes snapped caution. "Don't you dare blame me for this." Her voice broke, but that finger kept pointing. Through her teeth, she whispered, "Allowance?"

The sad humor in that word made her feel suddenly weak, and she dropped her finger and turned away. Her hair seemed too hot against her forehead, so she pushed it back and held her hand there. "How could this happen?" The words came in a whoosh of emotion. "How *could* you? *Selling drugs?* They put people in jail for that."

"But I didn't think I'd get caught. I thought I could trust him. I didn't know he had some cop with him when he came to get me. The guy looked young. They set me up, Mom. They tricked me."

She dropped her hand and turned back around. He was still wearing the khaki pants and dress shirt she had ironed for him this morning. The tie was probably still hanging on his doorknob. The coat was probably on his bedroom floor. Today was supposed to have been a good day.

She leaned back against the wall and looked up at the ceiling. "That's what they do, Mark. That's how they catch criminals."

"But it's not fair. I'm *not* a criminal."

"Depends on your definition." The words didn't come easy.

"Come on, Mom. I'll make this up to you. I promise I will. I'll work every day this summer at the clinic, and you don't have to pay me or anything."

Suddenly she realized that Mark just didn't get it. He was standing there looking at her, pleading, as if she had a decision to make. "Mark, don't you understand? You've broken the law. You're sitting in a police station. *I'm* not the judge! It's out of my hands."

"It's *not* out of your hands," he said. "You can get me a lawyer."

"Of course I'll get you a lawyer, but that doesn't mean you're going home."

"But you're my mother. They can't hold me here. I'm only fifteen. It's not like I shot somebody and have to be tried as an adult."

"Mark, don't you understand what you've done? This isn't like when you broke a rule at school and got suspended. This is the law. You broke it, and you've been arrested. They have evidence."

"But it's practically my first offense."

"It is *not* your first offense. It's your *third* offense. There were those little matters of car theft and vandalism."

"But I didn't do those things, Mom. I didn't steal Craig's old man's car, and I didn't so much as pick up a can of spray paint at their school. I just got run in with them. I was practically an innocent bystander."

She wanted to break the closest thing she could reach, but since that was Mark, she pulled the chair back out and sat down. Mark slowly took the chair across from her. She sat there, face in hands, staring at her son. Was he really oblivious to what lay ahead of him?

"Mark, I don't even know any lawyers in Breezewood. I haven't needed a lawyer since my divorce, and that was in Knoxville. Steve is working on trying to get one. He knows somebody at our church. But I can't believe I'll have to hire a lawyer to defend you for selling drugs."

"Mom, I've learned my lesson, okay?"

She dropped her face back in her hands

and squelched the urge to scream. How could he treat this like it was a traffic violation? She leaned forward and locked onto his blue eyes. They looked so soft, so innocent. He was too young to be facing a charge like this. Too young to commit this kind of crime. Too young to grasp the reality involved.

Her mouth trembled. "Mark, I was so proud of you last week," she said. "You hit a home run the night of your birthday. And then just a week before that you finished the school year with Brenda and made all A's and B's. I thought maybe we were finally seeing light at the end of the tunnel, that there was hope that you'd gotten through that rebellious phase, and that now you were trying to buckle down and do the right things. I didn't know you were out buying drugs and selling them."

"So I guess now you're not going to let me go out of the house for the rest of my life."

Her eyes shot up like a backdraft blaze, and she almost dove across the table. "Mark, don't you understand? The State of Tennessee may not let you out of the house! You may be locked up in the juvenile detention center. Do you understand what you've done?"

"No!" he said. "Mom, they don't lock you up for doing a favor for one friend who turns out to be a Benedict Arnold."

She wanted to slap him, but she knew better. Holding her hands in the air, she cried, "*Yes, they do!* They caught you red-handed. You sold drugs to a police officer, Mark. It's your third offense. Don't you get it?"

"I didn't know he was a police officer. He had long hair and a goatee, and looked like a kid. Isn't there something called entrapment?"

"Mark, you did it. You did it, and that's all there is to it. They caught you."

"Okay, so you've made your point," Mark said. He looked down at his finger as he rubbed at a spot on the table. "Mom, I'm really sorry, okay? I'm sorry I messed up your shower. I'm sorry I trusted Ham Carter."

"Mark, they said the judge won't see you until the morning, so you're stuck here at least one night, and I hope that's all. For the life of me, I hope it's not going to be longer than that."

Mark sprang out of his chair, his mouth

wide open. "Mom, you've got to be kidding! No way can I stay here all night!" He got to his feet, and she saw that he still didn't get it. His ready-to-leave posture indicated that he thought she was bluffing.

He was still small for his age. He hadn't been given the height that Rick had. Even though he had just turned fifteen, Mark looked thirteen. She wondered why in the world he would think he could play among criminal types with his stature. Maybe his height was part of the problem. Maybe he was playing the part of big shot to make up for his lack of height.

"Mom, I'm telling you—you can't leave me here," he said. "Do you know what happens in these places? You took me to the juvenile center—that River Ranch place—yourself last year. *You* told me how horrible it was."

"I thought it would be a deterrent. Never, in a million years, did I think—" She closed her eyes, unable to stop the thoughts of what she had seen there. Kids with rap sheets as long as their arms had filled up those cells. Some had committed violent crimes; others had been in isolation over and over for fighting with other inmates. She shook her head as tears rolled down her face. Maybe they wouldn't put him there tonight. Maybe he'd be safe . . . in a cell alone.

The door opened and a burly police officer came in. "We're ready to take him over to River Ranch," he said. "That's our juvenile facility."

"I know what it is," Mark spouted.

Mark's reaction to the officer set off a small explosion within Cathy. "Mark, if you know what's good for you, you'll talk to him with respect," she said. "You're not in a position to go spouting off."

"Mom, please. You can't let him take me."

"I'll be back as soon as I can get a lawyer, Mark. But I can't promise anything."

"But I didn't *do* anything. They trapped me." He turned to the police officer. "It was a *trick!*" Mark insisted, as if that would make him change his mind about taking him away. The officer wasn't impressed.

"Mom, please!"

But there was nothing Cathy could do.

Chapter Five

Tory Sullivan wasn't good at keeping se-
crets, but she felt that Mark's arrest should
be kept quiet. As new guests arrived for the
shower, she tried, with Brenda and Sylvia, to
make excuses for the couple.

"They had an emergency with one of the
children," she told a group of women who
had shown up together.

"Oh. Is someone sick?"

"No, no one's sick. We're not really sure
what the problem is, but we're going to have
to cancel the shower."

"It's not Annie, is it? The way that child

runs the roads in that car of hers, she's bound to wreck one of these days."

"I really can't say." Or actually, she *wouldn't* say. If her child had been arrested, she would have wanted as little passed on to her acquaintances as possible. She tried to show Cathy the same consideration, even though she knew word would be all over town before sundown. Cathy was the most popular veterinarian in Breezewood, and everyone knew her.

When the last of them had left, Brenda started covering the food. "Maybe we could reschedule the shower," she said. "Freeze the food and try it again in a few days."

Sylvia shook her head. "I have to get back to Leon in just a couple of days. Besides, everyone left their gifts. Another shower would be kind of anticlimactic."

Tory looked around at the gifts that had filled up the table and lined the wall. Cathy would have had so much fun opening them. "So what are we going to do with them?" Tory asked.

"I have a key to Cathy's house," Brenda said. "We could just take them over and set them in her dining room."

"I'll get Spencer's wagon," Tory said. "It'll

take several trips, but we can carry the gifts over in that."

"Better yet," Brenda said. "How about if I get David's truck and back it up in the driveway? We could fill it up with the gifts, then take it to Cathy's in one trip."

"You're a genius," Tory said.

Tory and Sylvia waited outside as Brenda crossed the cul de sac to get the truck. The trellis at the front of Sylvia's yard was covered with a rose vine and jasmine, and the scent seemed to hover in the air as the warm, gentle breeze stirred it. A beautiful day for a shower.

"Poor Cathy," Sylvia said. "This was supposed to be such a happy day. I was so looking forward to it."

"So was she," Tory said as Brenda backed the truck into the driveway. "Leave it to Mark."

Brenda got out and opened the tailgate. "Why would he do this, today of all days?"

"Because he's a brat, that's why," Tory said.

"Tory!" Brenda said.

Tory realized that Brenda had a stake in Mark's life, since she had home-schooled him for the last year and a half. He had turned Brenda's peaceful, ordered life into something unpredictable. Mark's disruptive influence had forced Brenda to come up with skills she'd never thought she'd need. But Tory had to hand it to her. She had done a good job with him.

And now this.

They unloaded the truck at Cathy's, counting thirty-two gifts, which they laid on the dining room floor. Maybe the gifts would cheer Cathy up when she got home, Tory thought. Maybe it would be a good distraction from the boy's trouble.

When they were finished, Tory hurried home and burst in, expecting to hear Hannah's weary cries. But there was no wailing. Instead, she heard Hannah's giggle.

She hurried into the living room and saw Barry lying flat on the floor, with the baby draped on his calves. He was doing leg lifts with her, holding her hands and raising her up, then lowering her quickly.

The baby was gurgling with laughter.

But Tory didn't find it funny. "Barry! What are you doing?"

Her words startled the baby, and Hannah started to cry. He sat up and lifted the baby. "You scared her. Why did you yell like that?"

Tory crossed the room and took the baby from him. Hannah was still small; she looked ten months old, rather than fifteen. Her development was slow. She couldn't sit up alone or crawl yet, her muscle tone was weak, and her joints were loose.

It took a moment for the baby to realize she had changed hands, and her crying ceased as Tory kissed her and bounced her. "Barry, you can't roughhouse like that. She's too fragile. Her neck isn't strong enough."

He got to his feet. "It's not going to get strong unless she uses it. I was doing it just like the physical therapist told me. She was fine."

"But you were being too rough."

"She liked it, Tory. She's not a doll. She likes to have fun just like Brittany and Spencer did." He pressed a kiss on the baby's plump cheek. "We had fun, didn't we, Hannah? Daddy was making you fly."

Tory saw her smile, and she tried to calm down. "I'm sorry I yelled," she said. She shifted Hannah in her arms, so that she held the baby's legs together instead of allowing them to straddle her hip. They had to make accommodations for Hannah's loose hips, in hopes of avoiding a brace.

"Tory, you have to trust me. She's my daughter, too."

"I know," she said. "I'm overprotective. Tell me how to stop and I will." The hurt look on Barry's face registered, and she quickly changed the subject. "Well, the shower was canceled. Mark got arrested."

Barry's jaw dropped. "What did he do?"

"He was charged with drug distribution."

"Is this a joke?"

"No. Who knows what the real story is?" She sat down in the rocker with Hannah. The baby's mouth opened, and her tongue slipped out. Tory touched it to make her pull it back in. "Anyway, Cathy and Steve ran off to the police station, so we had to cancel." She leaned her head back. "I don't know why I'm so tired when I didn't do anything."

"You're tired because you don't sleep. You worry too much about Hannah." He took the baby out of her lap, carefully holding her legs the way the physical therapist had taught them. "Why don't you go lie down? Hannah and I were all geared up for a dad and daughter afternoon. You have a couple of hours to kill."

She didn't want him to know how uneasy it made her to let anyone else care for the child. "I'm not that tired," she said. "Besides, I need to do her exercises with her."

"She doesn't want to exercise," he said. "She wants to play."

"Well, I'll exercise her and try to make her *think* she's playing."

"That's what I was doing." He was getting angry, and Tory wondered why he had to take this so personally. They were both trying to do what was best for their child.

"Did you feed her?"

"Does she look hungry?"

"Barry, can't you just answer me?"

"Of course I fed her. And I changed her diaper twice and gave her her medicine *and* a breathing treatment, which is why she's breathing so well. If you weren't obsessing so, you might notice."

The baby yawned, and Tory took her back from him. "I'll just rock her for a minute. Maybe she's sleepy again."

He surrendered her unhappily, then headed for the door. "I'm going out to check on the kids."

Tory didn't answer. She made no apology for being a good mother. Barry was just going to have to get over it.

Chapter Six

Brenda lingered on her porch before going into the house. She wondered if Daniel knew about Mark's problems today. He had been at Mark's house when she left for the shower.

She glanced at the front door and saw the shoes lined up there. Leah's and Rachel's were missing, since they were at Mary Hogan's birthday party. Joseph's small ones were next to his father's big ones, and off to the side were Daniel's, parked toes pointed in. At least she knew he was home.

How had this happened to Mark? He was

rebellious, but deep down he was a good kid. There had to be some mistake.

A year ago, when he had first gotten into trouble with the law, Brenda had sat Mark down, looked him in the eye, and asked him what would cause him to follow those kids into trouble.

"We were bored," he said. "I was in Knoxville at Dad's house and he was playing golf. And the guys came by and we went out. There just wasn't anything to do."

"So you decided to paint curse words on the walls of the local high school?"

"I didn't know what they were painting. I was just standing guard."

"You knew they were painting," she said. "You know that was against the law. I've taught you enough about civics that you had to know what you were doing."

She was sure she saw genuine shame on Mark's face. "You gotta understand, Miss Brenda. When I'm in Knoxville there's this different me."

"No, Mark. There's only one you. You make choices wherever you are."

"But it's *like* I'm two people. I'm different in Knoxville than I am in Breezewood."

Brenda screwed up her face, trying to follow his reasoning. "So you want me to believe that the Knoxville you is not as intelligent as the Breezewood you?"

"It doesn't have anything to do with intelligence," Mark said.

"Doesn't it? How intelligent was it to go with a kid who stole his stepfather's car? How smart was it to ruin public property?"

"Well, maybe I'm just as dumb there as I am here, okay?"

"Sorry," Brenda said. "I'm not buying that, Mark. I know better than that." She had been teaching him for six months at that point and knew he was as smart as any of her own kids. "But I will believe there's an element of dumbness in the Knoxville you." She couldn't believe she had said that. She usually tried to make everything into a positive. But it was hard to make anything positive out of what Mark had done that day.

She had patted herself on the back often and told herself she was doing well with him. That the evil had been purged, and that he was maturing into a decent young man who liked to learn.

But what had gotten into him this morning? Boredom, on the day of his mother's shower? Was it another case of his friends having an idea that he thought would be fun? A case of not thinking he'd get caught? And how had Daniel been involved?

She looked for Joseph, and through the kitchen window saw that he and David were in the workshop. She hoped Joseph hadn't forgotten to wear his mask, to keep him from breathing sawdust. Ever since his heart transplant two years ago, he was prone to respiratory infections and pneumonia.

She went into the computer room and found Daniel pounding on the keyboard.

"Daniel?"

The word turned Daniel around, as if he'd been caught at something. She saw the guilt on his face. "Hey, Mama."

"Daniel, what do you know about Mark's arrest?"

He gasped so hard that he had to cough, and he got up and gaped at her. "Arrest? Oh, no. He didn't, did he? You're just kidding, right?"

He did know. She stepped toward him, her eyes searching his for a clue that might break her heart. "Daniel, tell me everything you know."

"I *told* him not to do it, okay? I begged

him. Bullied him, even. But he's so stubborn." He looked like he might cry. "Mama, what happened?"

"The police came and got Cathy. Told her he was arrested for drug distribution."

He slapped his hand against his forehead and looked up at the ceiling. "I can't believe this! He wanted money for that stupid concert ticket next week. How could he be so stupid? I *told* him!"

Brenda watched the genuine reactions passing across his face, and she realized that he had not been involved. At least, not in the actual act of selling the drugs. "Daniel, you should have gone to someone if you couldn't stop him yourself."

"I thought about it. I really did. But he was so sure he had it all figured out . . ."

"Then you were at his house when he had drugs?"

Daniel looked at her with those blotchy cheeks, as if he knew he was in trouble now. He opened his mouth to speak, then stopped and looked down at his bare feet. "Okay, yeah, I saw the drugs," he said. "It was a bag of marijuana. I should have left right then. But Mark's my friend, Mama, and I thought I could talk him out of selling it. Maybe get him to flush it or something. What good would it have done him if I'd told on him?"

"He wouldn't be in jail right now."

Daniel sank back into the computer chair and slumped over, staring at the floor. "Oh, no. What is he gonna do?"

Brenda sat across from him. "I don't know." She saw the shame in his shoulders and in the way he hung his head, and felt sorry for him. "Honey, I don't mean to accuse you of causing this. But you're not ever supposed to be in a house where someone has drugs. If something illegal or dangerous is going on, you should tell an adult immediately. You know that, don't you?"

He nodded. "Yes, ma'am. I should have called Miss Cathy or something. Instead I just let him get in that jeep and take off with those guys."

She sighed and slumped, too, pressing her forehead against his. "I've been there. I've dealt with Mark for over a year. I know how frustrating it can be."

"But I'm his best friend. I should have stopped him. Even if I had to knock him down, I shouldn't have let him go."

"I'm not sure knocking him down would have helped." She pulled Daniel's face up and looked him in the eye. "Why would he think of doing this?"

"Like I said, to buy the stupid concert tickets. He said it was easy money." He caught his breath and straightened. "Mama, it's the first time he's ever done this. Mark is not a drug dealer. They'll go easy on him, won't they? They'll see that he's just a stupid kid . . ."

"I don't know, Daniel. They went easy on him the last time."

The back door opened, and she heard the heavy sound of David's footsteps through the kitchen. He came to the computer room door and looked surprised to see her.

"Shower over already?"

"Dad, Mark got arrested," Daniel cut in.

David's eyebrows shot up, and he looked at his wife. "What happened?"

"He was charged with selling marijuana to a police officer."

David took an astonished step back. "I can't believe it," he whispered. "You would think his father would have made him sever his ties with those kids by now."

"It wasn't the Knoxville kids," Daniel said. "It was a kid from the baseball team. From around here."

David got quiet as he realized Daniel knew the story. He met Brenda's eyes, and she gave him that silent communication that husbands and wives sometimes have. It said that there was more to tell, that she was taking care of it, that she would fill him in later.

"All we can really do now is pray," Daniel said. "Maybe the judge will let him off."

David looked down at his hands. Brenda knew that he didn't believe in prayer. To him that was the same as doing nothing.

"He'll probably get off," David said, changing the subject. "The juvenile facilities are overcrowded as it is."

"But what he's done is pretty substantial," Brenda said. "I mean, they don't take it lightly when you're selling drugs."

"Could it be a mistake?" David asked. "Wrong place at the wrong time kind of thing?"

Daniel shook his head and looked back down at his feet.

"Oh." David's word brought his eyes back to Brenda, silently beseeching her to hurry up and fill him in.

"Mama, please don't start thinking that he's influenced me. You know I don't let him do that. Besides, he's not that bad when he's here."

"You're right," Brenda said. "He's come a long way. But do you remember what he said when I was talking to him about being a different person in Knoxville than he was in Breezewood?"

"Yeah, I remember," Daniel said.

"We don't know what the other Mark is like. The one that lives here can sometimes be a real handful."

"But he's gotten better, Mama. You know he has."

"I know," Brenda said, "but the judge doesn't care about any of that."

"We can be character witnesses," Daniel said. "You and I, we can vouch for Mark. Dad, too. Can't you, Dad?"

David had never cared that much for the boy who had brought so much disruption into their lives. But he shrugged. "I guess so," he said.

Brenda nodded weakly, hoping it wouldn't come to that. She wasn't sure any of them honestly *could* vouch for the boy who was so intent on messing up his life.

Chapter Seven

Cathy was silent as she rode home in Steve's car, her two teens brooding in the backseat. "He'll be okay there for one night," Steve said.

She recognized his effort to comfort her, but it was futile. "He will not be okay," she said. "He's in jail. He's fifteen and small and clueless, and he's with gang members and drug addicts and thieves."

"I meant that I think they'll keep him isolated from the others. He won't be in any danger. If I'm wrong, then they'd have lawsuits up to their ears, parents suing them for putting their children in harm's way."

"The parents are mostly powerless," she said in a dull voice. "Children get beaten up at River Ranch all the time."

"I'll bet you're wrong about that. I'll bet they have more control over things than you realize."

She didn't want him to be wrong—but she couldn't entertain a conversation that accepted that Mark was in jail. She couldn't stand the thought of his sleeping in a cell full of gang members and criminals. She couldn't stand the thought of the guards yelling at him, or of a cell mate who might be stronger or bigger or angrier. She couldn't stand the thought of him lying there, afraid, all night.

It sounded so homey and safe—River Ranch. But it was still a jail. She had toured it with Mark herself, hoping the threat of it would be a deterrent. Apparently it hadn't frightened him into good behavior. But it had frightened her.

As Steve turned his car into Cedar Circle, Cathy's three neighbors were huddled on Brenda's front porch, as if waiting for her. She wished she could have just gone into the house unnoticed, without saying a word to anyone. She wished she could just crawl under the covers and bury her face in her pillow.

But while the kids headed into the house, Steve lingered beside her as the three women headed over. Sylvia was in the lead, her face drawn and sympathetic. She just pulled Cathy into a hug. Brenda was next, searching her face for an answer about Mark. Then Tory came up, holding Hannah in her arms. "Where's Mark?" she asked.

"Had to spend the night in jail," Cathy said, leaning back wearily against the car. She was still wearing the pink suit she had worn to the shower, and the pumps were killing her feet. She wondered if they would let Mark keep his clothes, or if they had some kind of uniform for him. She wondered if she should take some clothes to him. "Steve called a lawyer," she said. "Slater Hanson from church. You know him, don't you, Sylvia?"

Sylvia nodded. "He'll do a good job. What did Mark say?"

"That he did it," Cathy said matter-of-factly, though there was nothing matter-of-fact about it. The corners of her lips trembled as she added, "He didn't *mean* to. Just wanted to make a few bucks. You know, for the concert." The sarcasm in her words left a sour taste in her mouth.

The look on Sylvia's face was as sick as Cathy's, but it seemed to Cathy that Brenda wasn't all that surprised. Maybe Daniel had said things.

Tory just shook her head. "Someone influenced him, Cathy," she offered.

Cathy shrugged. "Well, it sure wasn't me. Or Brenda, either, for that matter. The only people who have any influence over Mark are his friends."

"Some of his friends," Brenda whispered.

"Yeah, I had hoped his friendship with Daniel would make a difference." Cathy sighed. "Does he know?"

Brenda nodded.

Cathy rubbed her face, trying hard not to cry. She didn't want to look weak, beaten. Steve put his hand on her shoulder. She was thankful that he hadn't said much.

"We brought your gifts home," Tory said in a quiet voice. "They're all in the dining room. Thirty-two of them."

Cathy looked down at the concrete beneath her feet. A sprig of grass was growing up through a crack. "Thank you for taking care of that. I hope everyone understood."

"We just told them you'd had a family emergency," Sylvia said.

Cathy met her eyes. "It'll be all over town by morning, anyway," she said. She blinked back the tears. "Even if the judge lets him out, his reputation is shot. Not that it was that good to begin with." She reached for Steve's hand on her shoulder, laced her fingers through it, and squeezed hard.

His grip was strong, reassuring. It promised help and peace in the face of chaos.

She wished she could believe that promise.

She reached out to hug Sylvia, then pulled Brenda and Tory into her outstretched arms and held them for a moment. Then she let them go and took a step back. "I need to go in now. I need to talk to the kids, and . . . I have to call Jerry."

They said their quiet good-byes and promised to pray. Slowly, she headed into the house. Steve was right behind her.

When she turned back and met his eyes, he reached out. "Come here."

She went willingly into his arms and soaked in the feeling of love as he held her so tightly that she couldn't breathe. His face was rough and warm against hers, and his brown hair was soft beneath her fingers. He smelled of early summer and wind and the slightest trace of cigarette smoke from the police station. She tried to blink back her tears but became vaguely aware of how they wet his shirt.

"When Mark was a baby," she managed to get out, pulling back from him and looking up into his eyes, "and I was still married to Jerry, he had all these dinner parties and conferences we had to go to together. He insisted I go with him, but I didn't want to leave my kids so much. I spent three weeks interviewing baby-sitters before I would leave Mark with one of them."

She got a glass out of the cabinet, half-filled it with tap water, and swallowed it down. Staring at the glass, she said, "When he was old enough for nursery school, I literally toured fifteen places before I chose one. I was so careful who I left him with. Even in the last year, I've only left him with Brenda. And now he's there with a bunch of kids who stab and shoot each other."

"Maybe not," Steve said. "Maybe they're just like him."

She leaned on the counter, trying not to let herself fall apart. "He's little, Steve. He can't defend himself against some of those guys."

"Honey, this might be the longest night of your life. I don't have any Band-Aids to put on this. All I can say is that tomorrow maybe things will turn out better than you think. Maybe he'll come home and this will be the wake-up call he needs, the scare of his life that will turn him around."

"I thought that would happen when he got arrested last year," she said. "It didn't work." She stepped toward the door and looked out the screen, as if she would see Mark heading up the driveway. "If I could just go to that place and sleep outside his cell, I would. Just to know he was all right . . ."

She drew in a deep breath and stood straighter, wiped her eyes. "Well, I can't, and that's that. Meanwhile, Tracy is probably worried sick, and you need to go update her and relieve your mother." She covered her eyes. "Oh, I hate for your mother to know this about my son."

"My mother's realistic. She understands what some teenagers go through."

"And she knows Mark," Cathy said.

He didn't seem to know what to say to that, so he said nothing.

"Go," she said. "You need to take care of Tracy, and I need to talk to the kids and call Jerry. Really, I'm going to be all right."

"I know you are." He crossed the room and took both of her hands in his, brought them to his lips. "I love you," he whispered. "Call me when you can. If you don't, I'll call you. And if you need me, I can be back over in ten minutes."

As he headed out to his car, she leaned against the door and stared into the garage.

She imagined all manner of doubts rushing through his mind as he drove home. He hadn't bargained for a criminal stepson, or the roller coaster that was Cathy's life. And he hadn't bargained for a mother's confusing mix of rage and grief, self-recrimination and crushing disappointment.

What would Mark's situation do to their plans?

She couldn't think about that now. Wedding plans didn't seem so important when her son was sitting in a jail cell.

Chapter Eight

Annie and Rick came into the den when they heard Steve leaving. Rick looked slightly shell-shocked. Annie had been crying. They both sank onto the couch, sudden allies.

"Mom," Annie said. "He's just a kid. He's not ready for this."

"We really didn't know," Rick said. "Really. If we had, we would have told you. We wouldn't have let Mark get himself into this much trouble."

She sat down across from them. "I'm sorry I yelled at you in the car on the way there. It was uncalled for. I was just upset."

"We know, Mom," Annie said. "You always yell when you're upset."

She stared down at her knees for a moment, trying to get a grasp on her emotions. "Well, I need to stop it," she said. "Maybe that's part of the problem."

Rick let out a loud sigh and jammed his elbows into his knees. "I knew you were going to do this."

"Do what?" she asked.

"Blame yourself. You blame yourself for everything. It's not your fault, Mom."

She pressed her fingers against her tear ducts, but her hands trembled. "I just feel like so many things should have been different in this family."

Quiet settled around them again, and she knew they were each counting the ways things could have been different.

"Mom, somebody needs to call Dad. He needs to know."

Cathy had planned to do that, but she couldn't stand revealing her emotions to her ex-husband. "I need for you to call him and tell him, okay? Rick? Annie?"

"Why can't you?" Annie asked.

"Because I'm . . . a little volatile right now. If you think I yell with you . . ."

Rick frowned. "Mom, you're not blaming him, are you?"

She threw up her hands and felt anger quaking through her as tears spilled down her face. "Sometimes I can't help but wonder what you guys might be like if you had a father in the home. You and Annie, you had him longer than Mark did. He was pretty small when your dad left. I can't help thinking that if Jerry had just been here, just his presence in the home might have made a difference."

Annie's voice was weak. "I know families with both parents in the home and they still have kids that turn out wrong and do stupid things. Even kids who were raised with big doses of the Bible every day can still turn out bad."

"I know that's true," Cathy said, her voice wobbling. She wiped the tears with the pads of her thumbs. "I know you're right. But I'm not the most rational person in the world right now. Just please . . . do this for me. Tell him what happened, and what time Mark appears in court tomorrow," she said. "I'm going to be in my room."

She hugged each child in turn before she left the living room. As she got to her room, she sat down on her bed and kicked off her shoes. This day had started out so differently. She had gone to church, floating on an air of anticipation, then her hairdresser had done her the favor of fixing her hair on Sunday. She had been excited about the shower, had looked forward to seeing so many friends and hearing their good wishes for her future. Tonight she was supposed to be taking inventory of the wonderful gifts she'd gotten and working on the wedding that was just around the corner. Now what would she do about that?

She heard the kids on the phone in the living room, and her thoughts went back to her ex-husband. He had played such a part in this, by playing so *little* a part in their family. She knew the kids didn't want her to blame him, and she had no right to do so in front of them. But hadn't he robbed her and the kids of something critical in their lives? Something they may not even know they were missing until an event like today's occurred?

Mark was paying dearly for their father's failings, and Rick and Annie had paid, too. They had all paid.

But they were paying for their mother's failings, too.

She lay back on her pillow, staring up at the ceiling through misty eyes, and thought back to that pivotal week in the life of her family when Jerry had announced he wanted the divorce, that he was leaving her for another woman. There had been no reasoning with him. No logic could have turned his head. It was not something she had counted on in life, nothing she had expected. He didn't want to be married, so *she* had been left alone.

Ironic, that need of his to end the marriage was only to begin another one just weeks after the divorce.

She had tried to forgive him, especially in the past couple of years since she'd given her life to Christ. But forgiveness was a hard concept. It didn't come through lip service or intention. It took her heart—and whenever her heart got involved with her ex-husband, it always came out on the wrong side of Christianity.

Sylvia had said that God would be a husband to Cathy, that he was a husband to widows and orphans, and she supposed, by some stretch of the imagination, that was what she was. A widow with three orphans. She had no doubt God had sent her Steve, a man who would no more betray her than Christ himself would. But if God was ordering things in her life, why had things become such a mess?

No, it wasn't God. It had to be her own failure again. She had done so many things wrong. Prayers of repentance couldn't undo any of them.

And neither could Mark's own remorse.

Now it was all in the hands of God and the circuit court judge.

Chapter Nine

Cathy recognized the knock the moment it started. It wasn't the polite, neighborly kind of knock, which said comfort was coming, and it wasn't Steve's knock, which had a gentle eagerness about it. It was Jerry's knock, loud and hard and announcing that he was here and they'd better hurry and answer the door.

Cathy heard Annie get to it first. "Dad! What are you doing here?"

She heard muffled voices as Rick jogged down the stairs, and quickly she got dressed. She had been lying on the bed in her pajamas, trying to work the whole thing out with God. But she knew Jerry hadn't made the two-hour drive from Knoxville just to say hello to the kids.

She went into the living area of the house and saw the drawn, angry look on his face as he spoke to their children. Annie swung around as Cathy came in.

"Cool," she said. "I haven't seen you two together in the same house in years."

Cathy didn't find that particularly refreshing *or* amusing. "Hi, Jerry. Guess you heard."

Her ex-husband was sunburned, as if he'd gotten the news on the golf course. He was dressed in a white polo shirt and a pair of khaki shorts. She hadn't seen him in a long time and was surprised that his dark hair was receding. A couple more years, and he'd be as bald as his father.

"Kids, I need to talk to your mother."

Rick looked insulted. "Dad, I'm almost twenty years old."

Annie stood firm, too. "We kind of wanted to hear what you're going to do about Mark."

She recognized and understood the look of helplessness on his face. "What I'm going to do." He breathed out a laugh. "Right."

He stepped into the living area and looked instantly out of place among the pieces of furniture they had bought together. Cathy remembered how they had agonized over the couch, because they wanted something that would last for years. He looked down at it now and ran his fingers across it thoughtfully, as if to see if it was holding up better than their marriage had.

"How could he have done this?" he asked, bringing his eyes up to Cathy.

She didn't want to share this pain with him, didn't want to commiserate or mourn together. She had cut off her feelings for him long ago, had prayed for God to anesthetize her to him in spite of her vows to love him for life. Years ago, God had been merciful and answered that prayer.

"What did he say about it?" he asked when she didn't answer the first question.

"He said that he was trying to make enough money for a concert ticket," she said in a dull voice.

"A concert ticket?"

"It was Third Eye Blind," Annie said, as though that would explain everything. "They're coming next week. The tickets are sold out, but if you can get them from a scalper—"

"So he sold drugs to pay for them?" The

words came on an incredulous note of accusation, as if Annie had just condoned what he'd done.

"That's his story. Dad, don't look at me like I did it, because I didn't. I'm just telling you what he told Mom."

Cathy sank down into a chair, and Jerry took the couch. "I want to know what he said to you."

Cathy sighed. "He said that he had been set up. That his friend asked him to get him a bag of marijuana, and when he came to buy it, he had somebody in the car with him. Mark didn't know it was a cop."

"Set up." Jerry had always been a repeater, as if he had to say the words to process them. "And Mark *had* a bag?"

"He got it somewhere," Cathy said. "Bottom line, they're keeping him tonight, and his arraignment is tomorrow."

"What is he pleading?"

"I've been on the phone with the attorney trying to figure that out." It had been difficult trying to work this out herself. She had to admit that she was glad Jerry could help make the decision. "If he pleads innocent, he's lying. It's his third offense. Plus, they caught him red-handed. If he pleads guilty, maybe they'll go a little easier on him. Maybe community service. It's also possible that he could plea bargain. In exchange for a guilty plea, maybe they would reduce the charge. And if we could get him to name the person who gave it to him—"

Jerry was on his feet and laughing bitterly, hands on his hips. "How does he even know people like this?" He turned back to Cathy. "Don't you watch him?"

She sat rigid, stunned that he could accuse her of neglect when he played golf on his visitation weekends. "Yes, I'm watching him," she said. "He's home-schooled, for heaven's sake. I took him out of school to get him away from the kids who were influencing him. But I thought I could still let him play baseball. I didn't know he was at the park making drug deals!"

"If you'd been there, maybe he couldn't have. Do you even go to the games?"

Now she felt like a volcano near eruption. "Yes, I go to the games," she said, her voice rising. "Every one of them. Unlike you!"

"Hey, I live in Knoxville. What do you want from me?"

"How about a little fathering?" she said angrily. "Forget the full-time stuff! How about

every other weekend? Or is it too much to
ask that you miss a day at the golf course
just because your children want to be with
you?"

"Mom—" Annie said, trying to stop her.
She had confided those things to her
mother, and Cathy knew it was a betrayal to
use them against him. "Dad does spend time
with us."

"Don't defend him!" Cathy cried. "You told
me that there wasn't any point in your going
every two weeks anymore because you only
see him for a couple of hours. Mark and Rick
even tried taking up golf so they could
spend time with him, but he didn't want to be
bothered!"

Annie gave her father a stricken look.
"Dad, that's not exactly what I said . . ."

"If I wanted to play golf I'd play golf," Rick
cut in. "Dad didn't have anything to do with
my quitting." He headed for the stairs, his
face flushed, and Cathy knew she had hurt
him. "I'm going upstairs." Neither child liked
to admit that their father had chosen anything over them, and they didn't like for him
to know they cared. Cathy had known better
than to say that in front of them.

She was instantly sorry she had.

Annie just stood there, her eyes locked on her father's face. "Dad . . ."

"Go upstairs, Annie," he said. "I told you I need to talk to your mother."

She swallowed hard, looked back at him, then started up the stairs. "You'll say good-bye before you leave?"

He nodded and turned back to Cathy.

Cathy waited for her to disappear at the top of the stairs. "Don't you try to make it sound like *she* did something wrong," she said. "All she did was confide to her mother the fact that her father didn't seem interested."

"She exaggerates everything," he said. "You know it. And I don't appreciate the implication that my son has become a drug dealer because I'm a bad father."

"Of course not," she shot back. "He did it because *I'm* a bad *mother.* Isn't that where you were going with the baseball accusations? When have you ever seen your son play, Jerry? You could have made that drive once or twice."

"And that would have changed everything. If I'd just come to a stinking game."

"No, Jerry. If you'd just showed up *in their lives.* If I hadn't done it all myself!"

"Hey, you wanted custody. You got it. Now it's too much for you?"

"We had those children together, Jerry. I never expected to parent them alone."

"You haven't parented them alone. That's why I'm here tonight."

"And some comfort you are."

"I didn't come to bring comfort," he said.

"No kidding. Just a spotlight to shine in my face."

He started to the door. "Do you want my input on this or not? Because I can walk out of here and let you make the decision, and hope that, for once, you have clear judgment, since Mark's life is at stake—"

"Clear judgment?" she shouted. "What are you talking about? I'm the one who stayed, Jerry! I'm the one who raised these kids and nursed them through sickness and helped with their homework and drove them everywhere and went to every game—" Her voice broke off, and she kicked a chair. "*You* were the one who wanted your space! And *I* have poor judgment?"

She had seen it before. That look he got when she'd stopped getting through to him, when he'd shut down and tuned her out, like some hysterical woman. He might as well have his hands over his ears. He gave her that smug are-you-finished look, and changed the subject. "Do you want to talk about Mark's arraignment or not?"

Her chin was so tight, she thought it might pop out of place. "I think he should plead guilty and hope the judge gives him community service."

"I have to talk to the lawyer. Do you have his number? Maybe I'll even meet with him tonight."

"Of course." She tore down the hall and to her bedroom, where she got the number off the pad on which she'd been taking notes. She returned to the living room and thrust it at him.

He looked down at it, drew in a long, deep breath. "I can't believe my son needs a criminal lawyer."

"Neither can I."

"Well, he can't go to jail. That's all there is to it. No son of mine is going to jail."

She didn't answer. She wanted to believe the same thing, but somehow she knew that it could be exactly where he went.

He looked at the card again, then went to the stairs. "Annie, Rick, I'm leaving."

Rick didn't come, but Annie came quickly,

as if he would disappear if she didn't hurry to the bottom of the stairs. "Bye, Dad. Will you be in court tomorrow?"

He kissed her easily, then hugged her. The gesture surprised Cathy. She hadn't pictured any affection between him and the kids. Not since they were little.

But then, she hadn't seen them together since Rick started driving because she no longer had to meet Jerry halfway.

Annie hugged her father, kissed him again, then walked him to the door. "I'll be at the Best Western," he said. "I'll call if there's anything we need to discuss after I talk to the lawyer."

Cathy sat back down, wrapping herself in her numbness, as he headed out to his car.

Chapter Ten

Late that night, when Annie and Rick were sound asleep in bed, Cathy gave up trying to sleep. She went into Mark's room, saw the clothes thrown on chairs and across the bed. CDs lay scattered around the table, and his stereo had been left on. She turned the power off and sat down in the middle of the mess. What was Mark doing tonight? Was he in a cell alone, or in a room with others, scared to death that harm might come to him? He didn't even like spending the night away from home much. He said there was something about sleeping in his own bed.

Was he repenting of his crime? Or was he

merely looking at this with the logic of a child, wishing his mother would come and rescue him, or hoping his father would ride in on a white horse?

She wondered if a mother had any chance of getting inside River Ranch tonight.

"Oh, Lord, please don't let any harm come to him," she whispered. "Please take care of him."

She wasn't one to get down on her knees when she prayed. She'd always believed that God wanted her to be comfortable, like a child in the lap of her father, when she talked to him. But somehow the gravity of these prayers knocked her to the floor.

Her knees were cushioned on a pile of T-shirts and underwear, and she leaned up on the bed, her elbows on a pair of wadded blue jeans. She prayed morning would bring Mark's release. If she could just get him home, she told the Lord, she knew she could straighten him out. All he needed was one more chance. All he needed was an opportunity to start over.

But as night wore on and turned into morning, Cathy knew that his crime had a penalty. And she couldn't pay it herself.

Chapter Eleven

The next morning, Jerry waited for Cathy in the hallway outside the courtroom. He looked like an older version of Rick, only more comfortable in a suit and tie than Rick had ever been. He paced and perspired, cracking his knuckles as if preparing for a boxing match.

Cathy always felt awkward and uncomfortable when she came face-to-face with her ex-husband. If she smiled and acted civil, it seemed too familiar. Their relationship felt better at arm's length. Soft or fond feelings were strictly forbidden, for she had long ago counted them futile. Besides, too many bitter, hostile memories had buried themselves deeply in her heart.

Last night he had called her after a lengthy telephone conversation with the lawyer, and he'd agreed that a guilty plea was probably the best course of action. She'd spent the rest of the night second-guessing the decision and wondering if they were doing the right thing for Mark.

They both looked tired, strained, and had little to say to each other as they waited there for the attorney to show up.

"He's late," Jerry said.

Cathy looked at her watch. "He's not late. We're just early."

Annie went to stand beside her father. Rick lingered in the middle of the hall. "That him?"

They all looked up and saw the man starting toward them with a briefcase in his hand. "Yes," Cathy said. "That's him." She met him halfway up the hall.

"Cathy?" he asked.

"Yes." She shook his hand. "I recognize you from church now. Thanks for coming."

"Steve filled me in on Mark's case, and I did a little checking last night after I talked to your ex-husband."

Jerry pushed off from the wall. "I'm Jerry Flaherty."

"Slater Hanson," the attorney said, shaking his hand. "They'll be bringing Mark. We can go in this room right here."

He opened a door and ushered them in, but Cathy asked Annie and Rick to wait in the hall.

The attorney sat down and opened his briefcase, shuffled some papers around. He seemed so rushed and distracted that Cathy got the feeling he had twenty other clients down the hall waiting for him. She silently prayed that he wouldn't take this case lightly.

The room seemed so cold that she expected icicles to be hanging from the folding chairs. They should have something more comfortable, she thought, when people were awaiting the fate of their children.

By the time Slater Hanson had fished Mark's paperwork from his briefcase, the door opened and Mark was escorted in. He was dressed in a bright orange jumpsuit and wore handcuffs. His hair was greasy and hung in his eyes.

"Mark!" Cathy burst into tears at the sight of him and pushed his hair back from his eyes. When they removed his hand-cuffs, she hugged him, and he clung back. Jerry stood off to the side, looking down at the floor, fingers jingling the change in his pockets.

The attorney interrupted the hug and reached out to shake Mark's hand. Cathy stepped back.

"Mark, I'm Slater Hanson, your attorney. How was your night?"

"Horrible," he said. "Mom, you can't believe where they put me. I had a mattress that was like two inches thick. It was noisy. There were people yelling all night, cussing up a storm. You just wouldn't believe it. They had me in a little cell that wasn't any bigger than our bathroom."

"You were alone?" she asked through her tears.

"Yeah, I was alone."

"Well, maybe that was a blessing."

"*None* of this is a blessing! Mom, get me out of here." He looked up at his father. "Dad, can't you do something?"

Jerry pulled out a chair roughly and sat down. "Mark, that's what we're here for. We're trying to undo the damage you've already done."

"Dad, I didn't know. I didn't mean to do this. I just—"

"Shut up, Mark," Jerry said. "Sit down."

Cathy didn't know whether to come to Mark's defense or join in on the tough love that Jerry seemed intent on practicing. They all took their seats, and she pulled out a Kleenex and dabbed at her eyes.

"So how does it look?" Jerry asked the attorney wearily.

"You have to know that we're going up against Judge Massey today, and he's one of the toughest judges in the city."

"Oh, great," Mark said. His face looked as if his blood wasn't circulating well.

"Look at him," Cathy said. "He's fifteen years old. It's not like he was standing on a street corner selling crack through car windows."

"In the district attorney's eyes he did," Slater said. "He did it of his own free will, and no one coerced him."

"Come on," Mark said. "I just wanted to make a few dollars."

"Mark, enough with the few dollars," Jerry said. "You've dug yourself in deep enough. Just shut your mouth and don't say another word."

"But he's my lawyer! I'm supposed to talk to him."

Jerry ignored him. "He's just a kid. So he experiments with drugs occasionally, and yesterday he was going to do a favor for a friend. You're going to let them throw him in prison for that?"

"Of course not," Slater said. "I'm going to do the best I can to get him out. I'm just telling you what the possibilities are."

"So what do we need to do?" Cathy asked. "Just tell us."

"Well, neither of you has given me a clear answer on what you want Mark to plead."

"Innocent," Mark said quickly. When his parents were quiet, he looked from Cathy to Jerry. "Come on. I'm nothing like the guys they're trying to get off the streets. It was my first time to do anything like that, and I was set up."

"If you plead not guilty, there will be a trial if the judge thinks there's enough evidence. From the looks of things, I'd say there is. And you have to know that if there's a trial, there's a possibility they'll keep him incarcerated until the trial date. Frankly, that could be longer than the sentence if he pleads guilty."

Were they really talking about her child,

this little boy who had had curly hair and skipped everywhere when he was two? Were they really discussing trials and guilty pleas and convictions?

"So let me get this straight," she said. "If he pleads guilty, he's got an automatic conviction, but they may just give him probation again, right? Or community service or something like that?"

"That's a possibility," the attorney said, but seemed tentative.

"But if he pleads innocent, he'll have to go to trial, and the trial may not be for months and months, and he may have to stay incarcerated until then. Is that what you're saying?"

"But, Mom, they *might* let me out," Mark said. "I might get to go home today and then we can figure out what to do next."

Cathy leaned across the table, locking into her child's eyes. "Mark, even if they let you come home and you have to stand trial, we'd have to hire lawyers, and somehow we'd have to prove that you didn't do it. There's a big problem with that, because you *did* do it."

"What do you recommend we do?" Jerry asked the lawyer.

He looked down at the file, flipped through

a few pages, then glanced up at Mark, meeting his eyes. "Son, I want you to be straight with me. Did it happen like they said?"

"Well, yeah," Mark said, "I mean, I sold the drugs and everything, but I didn't know it was a cop."

"Did the cop who was with your friend talk you into selling the drugs?"

"No, he didn't say much at all. Just sat there, waiting to bust me."

"He didn't coerce you at all? Convince you to make the sale?"

Mark shrugged. "No . . . When Ham called, I told him I had gotten one bag and I'd sell it to him. There wasn't much conversation about it once I got there."

"Did the cop talk to you on the phone?"

"No. Just Ham."

The lawyer jotted a few notes, and Cathy wondered where he was going with this. "So you're guilty of doing exactly what they said?"

"Yeah, but it's not the way they made it out. I'm not some kind of junkie."

The man took a deep breath and looked from Jerry to Cathy, then back to Mark. "A trial would be expensive, and the chances are you'd lose, anyway. And, like I said, you still might not get to take Mark home today."

Mark slammed his hands on the table and threw himself back in the chair. "I am *not* pleading guilty," he said. "I am *not* going to go in there and say I sold drugs."

Cathy dropped her face into her hands. "But you *did* sell drugs."

"But, Mom, I've got to deny it as long as I can. People get off all the time. We can say he didn't read me my rights, that there was an illegal search and seizure. Something." He looked at Slater. "That's your job, man!"

"Mark, they have evidence. I have the police report right here," Slater said. "There weren't any of those things."

Cathy closed her eyes and, for the first time, wondered if it had been wise to get a Christian attorney. Maybe she needed someone shrewd and cutthroat who would go in there and lie through his teeth to get her son cleared. She had only wanted someone who would do the best job he could, who would care about the young boy whose life hung in the balance.

As quickly as those thoughts skittered across her mind, she banished them and whispered a prayer of repentance. God would honor their honesty. If her short time as a Christian had taught her anything, it was that.

Jerry seemed to be struggling with his own emotions as he stared down at the table. She didn't think she had ever seen him quite so distraught.

"The upside of this," Slater said, "is that he's not old enough to be tried as an adult. The juvenile detention center isn't a place where you'd want to raise your kids, but it's not the worst place in the world either. It's certainly better than prison."

"Prison!" Mark said. "You've got to be kidding! All I did was—"

Jerry's hand came down hard on the table, making them all jump. "All you did was sell drugs," Jerry bellowed. "Don't you get it, Mark? You don't have a leg to stand on. You have humiliated me and your mother and your sister and brother. You've broken the law, and they have evidence against you that we can't refute. You've acted like a juvenile delinquent, because that's exactly what you are. And that's why they're going to put you in the juvenile detention center if we don't get you off. That's where you belong!"

"Jerry!" Cathy's shock radiated through the room, reprimanding the man she had once called her husband. "My son is *not* a juvenile delinquent. He broke a law and he got into trouble, but it seems to me I remember you breaking a few laws in your day, too. Some people just never get caught."

Jerry met her eyes. She knew that he knew exactly what she referred to. Back in their teenage days he'd been known to smoke a joint or two, and she knew there'd been a couple of times when he'd even sold some of his own stash to a friend. It was no different than what Mark had done.

"I was never arrested and charged with drug distribution," Jerry said. "My father never had to come to the police station and discuss my defense!"

Slater looked at his watch, then began loading his papers back into his briefcase. "Why don't I leave you alone with this decision? I have another client to see. I'll come back before we go into court and see what you've decided."

Cathy looked up at him, stunned that he would leave them at this juncture. "Well . . . okay. If you're sure you'll be back."

"Before you know it," he promised, then hurried out of the room.

When the door had closed, Mark got up. "Great!" he said. "My lawyer cares more about some other client." He dropped back down, leaned his elbows on the table, and raked his hair back. "I can't believe they're doing this to me."

"I can't believe you're doing this to us," Jerry said.

"That's enough, Jerry!" Cathy bit out. He shot a look at her, as if daring her to speak that way to him again. The look only made her wearier. "It looks like we have a few choices, Mark. They're all equally bad. Most of them require taking huge chances with your life in the next few months, and there are no guarantees."

"So, what do we do?" Mark asked.

She let out a rough breath and looked at her ex-husband. "Jerry, do you have any constructive ideas, or just more snide comments?"

"He deserves whatever he gets," Jerry said.

Cathy wanted to throw something. "That may be true, but don't we all? Some of us never have to pay for what we've done."

Jerry cursed under his breath and got back up, striding to the window at the back of the room.

"Mark," Cathy went on, "the only thing I can suggest is that you go in there and face up to what you did. You plead guilty and we pray that the judge will have mercy on you."

"But, Mom—"

Jerry turned around. "Much as I hate to admit it, I think she's right," he said. "I have a feeling that if you do that, the judge will probably let you go home with us today. That doesn't mean you won't be on probation, that you won't have a conviction on your record, that it won't affect all of our lives. But it might be our only hope."

Mark's face burned as he stared at his dad. "You're not doing this just to save money, are you, Dad?"

The words seemed to ricochet across the room. Cathy flinched.

"Because if you're gambling with my life just so you won't have to pay an attorney, then that's pretty sleazy, Dad."

That artery in Jerry's neck looked as if it might burst, and he took a few steps toward his child, wearing that expression that suggested he could break him in two. "You really think I'd gamble with your future to save a buck?"

She held her breath, hoping Mark had the good sense to say that he didn't, so they could get on with business. Mark just stared him down, too prideful to reveal any intimidation or vulnerability.

Finally, she watched Jerry turn to a barred window and peer out. His shoulders rose and fell with seething breaths.

Cathy tried to clear her brain of accusations and inflammatory memories. "This isn't getting us anywhere, Mark."

"Then what should I do?" he asked. "Just go in there and surrender to them? Let them take me off?"

"Lots of people are in there praying for you, Mark. If you plead guilty, maybe God will show you mercy."

"The whole neighborhood probably showed up, didn't they?" Mark said, further accusation in his voice. "Best entertainment around, Mark getting convicted of drug dealing."

"You didn't hear me, Mark," she said. "I told you they're praying for you. You should be glad."

"Yeah, big hurrah."

The comment turned Jerry around. "That's it," he said. "You've gone far enough, Mark. If you don't want to help with this decision, then we'll make it for you. You're pleading guilty, you're facing up to your crime, and you're taking whatever it is the judge hands down to you. And if you go to jail, maybe you'll learn something your mother wasn't able to teach you at home. Respect."

"Dad, I do have respect," Mark said as tears came to his eyes. "I'm just scared."

"So am I." Jerry strode to the door, opened it, and looked around for the attorney. He turned his dull eyes back to Cathy. "I'll go tell him he's pleading guilty," he said. He closed the door behind him, leaving mother and son alone.

Mark looked small as he stared in the direction his dad had gone. But Cathy couldn't think of a thing to add to what Mark's father had said.

Chapter Twelve

The courtroom smelled moldy, and paint peeled off the walls. A big crack cut through the ceiling plaster, and the industrial tile on the floor looked as if it needed a good washing with Lysol.

It was a depressing place, where lives changed with the strike of a gavel.

She saw Steve sitting with Rick and Annie, and on the other side of them, Jerry had slipped in. Behind them, Brenda, Sylvia, and Tory sat together. Little Hannah lay asleep in her stroller next to Tory. The court was already in session, and those with traffic violations were quickly being processed. Quietly,

Cathy slipped into the row between Steve and her children. Brenda leaned up. "How do things look?" she whispered.

Cathy drew in a deep breath and indicated that she really didn't know. Before Cathy could respond, a side door opened, and those charged with criminal offenses were paraded in, all dressed alike in their orange jumpsuits.

Annie made a noise and covered her mouth. Her shocked eyes fixed on her mother, as if asking if she was going to allow this.

Cathy couldn't take her eyes from her son.

He sat next to a boy with a goatee and colored tattoos of serpents down each arm. The boy smiled as he saw some of his friends in the back of the courtroom, and she saw that two of his teeth were missing. He looked as if he'd recently lost a fight but hadn't learned from it.

Steve held one hand as she waited for their turn, and Annie latched on to her other one. The toothless kid next to Mark was called, and she watched as his teenaged wife got up and limped to the front of the courtroom.

After the case was read out, the judge regarded the girl. "Want to tell me what happened to your face?"

She looked at her boyfriend. He gave her a threatening leer that no one in the courtroom could have missed. But little hinged on the obvious, Cathy thought. It was all about paperwork and lawyers making the right motions.

She turned back to the judge. "I fell," she said. "That's all. I just want him out of here."

The judge gave a long hard look at the boy, who obviously had little respect for the girl next to him. "You're charged with Assault and Battery. How do you plead?"

The kid's proud chin came up. "Not guilty."

The judge gave the lawyer a look of disgust. "If she won't talk, my hands are tied. Case dismissed." He pointed a finger at the kid. "But I'd better not see you back in here. Do you hear me?"

"Yes, sir," the boy said, his chin held high. A grin cut across his face as they let him go.

And then came a case with a drunk driver who'd killed someone, and then a car theft followed by several other drug charges.

Finally, it came to Mark.

He looked like a little boy as he stood up and shuffled to the front. She thought he was about to cry. Wouldn't the judge see that this wasn't an everyday occurrence for Mark? Wouldn't Mark's young features soften his heart?

"What do you plead?" the judge asked.

"Guilty," Mark choked out, then glanced back over his shoulder at his mom. Cathy nodded her head, hoping to give him some strength. When Mark looked at his father, Jerry looked down at his hands.

The judge flipped through the pages again, studying the file. She wanted to tell him to forget the papers and look at the boy. She wanted to get up and tell the attorney not to just stand there, to do something and do it quick.

"Your Honor," Slater told the judge, as if her very thoughts had prompted him. "My client is only fifteen years old. His record will show some prior offenses, but it's worth noting that both of them occurred on the same night a year ago. There haven't been any since."

"Until now," the judge said, peering at the attorney over his glasses. "And if I let him off the hook this time, then he'll do it again. Trust me. I see these kids over and over."

"No, Your Honor!" Mark blurted out. His attorney tried to silence him, but the judge looked up as if he couldn't believe someone had dared speak out of turn in his courtroom.

"I won't do it again," Mark said. "I swear. You can ask my mom. She'll probably ground me from now till Christmas."

Cathy closed her eyes. She knew he was making himself look more naive and clueless, as if he still didn't understand that months of his life behind bars was not the same as being grounded in his bedroom. Annie squeezed her hand, and she clung to it, trembling. The judge took a deep breath, as if the very thought of what was about to happen pained even him. He leaned forward, pressing his elbows into his leather inlaid desk.

"Young man, what you did was a very serious offense. And you may have heard that in my courtroom people don't get off the hook. Not guilty people."

Mark looked over his shoulder at Cathy again, and she let go of Steve's and Annie's hands and slowly brought hers to her mouth. A feeling of terror rose up inside her.

"I'm going to sentence you to a year at River Ranch Juvenile Correctional Facility."

Mark swung around, his mouth open, and

looked at his mother. She got to her feet and looked across to Jerry. He looked as stricken as they did.

"No!" Mark shouted. *"You can't."*

The judge banged his gavel and ordered Mark to be quiet.

"Your Honor," Cathy shouted. *"Please!"*

"I will have order in my courtroom!" the judge insisted, banging the gavel again. The bailiff came to take Mark out of the room. He turned back with tears on his face, waiting for someone to run to his rescue.

When no one could, he cried, "Mom!" as if she had let him down. "Dad!"

Cathy had never felt more inadequate in her life. Jerry was standing now and looked as helpless as she.

Steve got to his feet and pulled Cathy against him, and she felt as if the world were going black. It all became shaky as he helped her out of the row of spectators and led her out of the courtroom.

Chapter Thirteen

Cathy fought her way down the hall and to the door where they had led Mark out. Annie, Rick, and Steve ran to keep up with her. She tried to catch Mark, but they had already gotten him into the processing room.

"I want to see my son!" she yelled to the bailiff who was coming back to the courtroom.

"You can't see him right now, ma'am. I'm sorry, but he's being processed."

"He is my son!" she shouted. "You can't keep him from me!"

"He's not yours right now, Mrs. Flaherty. He's a ward of the state."

"How dare you!" she shouted. "You can't keep me from talking to him!"

"You can talk to him later, but right now there are things that have to be taken care of."

She started to lash out at the bailiff, who could have picked her up and snapped her in two, but Steve stopped her.

"Calm down, Cathy," he whispered. "This man's just doing his job."

"Well, his job stinks!" she said. "They can't take a child away from his own mother."

"Of course they can," he said. "They do it all the time."

She turned on Steve, as if he had declared the verdict himself. "Not to *me,* they don't!"

She saw Jerry coming up the hall and jerked out of Steve's hands. All the rage that had built over the last twenty-four hours tornadoed toward the man who had fathered these children, then left her to raise them on her own.

"You!" she shouted as he came toward her. "This is your fault! *You* did this to us!"

"Did what?" Jerry asked. "Mark did this to himself."

"He needed a father!" she screamed. "He needed somebody he could count on. He needed a man to show him how to be a man. Do you even know how, Jerry? Do you even know what that means?"

"Quiet, Cathy. You're making a scene," Jerry spat out. "I don't have to listen to you talk to me that way."

"No, you never have to listen, do you?" she shouted. "All you have to do is walk out, just disappear, and nobody will hold you accountable. Nobody will expect anything. And then when they come visit you on weekends and you let them run wild just because you don't want to have to deal with them, then you can blame *me!*"

Jerry pointed at Annie and Rick, who leaned against the wall with tears on both their faces. "Hey, these two turned out fine," he said. "Apparently they weren't too badly warped by my leaving you, so you can't blame Mark on me."

"Well, I do!" she said. "I blame you, and I blame the divorce, and I blame that little wife of yours that broke up our marriage! And I blame every morning that Mark woke up without a father in the home. I blame every night that he went to bed without knowing what it was like to have a male role model!"

Steve touched her shoulders, trying to calm her down, but she couldn't be comforted.

"I've tried to forgive you, Jerry Flaherty," she cried. "I've tried my hardest. I thought I had."

Jerry's eyes narrowed. "I don't want your forgiveness, and I don't need it."

She opened her mouth to lash back, but Steve put his arms around her and stopped her. "Come on," he whispered in her ear. "Come on, Cathy. Just walk away. Come on."

Summoning all the strength she had, she shook out of Steve's arms and took another step toward Jerry. She was trembling and felt as if something inside her would explode, that they would have to pick up the pieces and declare the end of her. "You're going to be accountable one day, Jerry," she said. "You're going to have to face God with what you've done for your kids. He's going to ask you where you were all those years, and if your little mistress was really worth it."

Jerry shook his head and walked away. She thought of going after him, grabbing him and making him listen to what he didn't want to hear. But she couldn't make him take the blame, or the pain, or the guilt that wasn't supposed to be shouldered alone.

She leaned against the wall and wept. Steve stood just off to her side, not touching her, but quiet as he waited. "I hope I'm there when God holds him accountable," she said. "I hope I get to hear the answer, because I really want to know..." She brought both hands to her head. "I can't take 365 nights like last night! I can't live like that!"

"I know, honey."

She covered her mouth with both hands and turned to her children. Rick and Annie hugged her as she wept out her anguish. Steve was behind her again, touching her back, stroking her hair. She knew that she was distressing him as much as the judge had distressed her, but there was nothing she could do. It was not a time for comforting. It was a time to mourn.

Finally, Steve tapped her shoulder and said, "I'm going to go check on Mark."

He was gone for a few minutes, and she just stood there with Rick and Annie, desperately trying to hold herself together. She was at the end of her rope, about to let go and fall and fall and fall...

When he came back, she stepped toward him. "Where is he?"

"They've already taken him."

She slammed her fist against the wall. "Taken him *where?*"

"To River Ranch. Cathy, they said you can't see him until Wednesday night. That's the next visitation."

"No!" the word came out in horrified grief. "No, no, no!" Steve pulled her against him and held her.

"Cathy, I'm so sorry," he whispered.

Her body racked with despair. She had to stop them, she thought. She had to *do* something. She pushed out of Steve's arms and bolted up the hall. He followed on her heels. She turned a corner and ran into Tory, Brenda, and Sylvia. "Cathy, are you all right?" Sylvia asked.

"No!" she said, pushing through them. She grabbed Rick and Annie. "Come on, let's go home," she said. The two fell into step behind her as she hurried out to her car. She got into it and sat behind the wheel and looked back up at the courthouse. Steve stood on the sidewalk, hands on his hips, watching her with that helpless look on his face. She knew she was hurting him, but she couldn't help it. She just had to get away, close herself in her room, and weep and cry and pray.

Rick got in the front seat and Annie in the back, and she started the car and pulled out into the traffic.

"Mom, are they really going to keep him for a year?" Rick asked.

"Yes," she said through her teeth, "and there's not a thing in the world I can do about it."

Silence passed for the next five minutes, and finally, Annie spoke from the backseat.

"Mom, what you said to Dad . . ."

She almost couldn't see through the blur of her tears. "I shouldn't have said it in front of you."

"Why not?" Rick asked. "Everybody else heard it."

Again, silence ticked between them, and she had to force herself to drive more slowly than she felt like driving. She tried to replay the tape of what she'd said to Jerry in the courthouse. How condemning had it been? How upsetting for the children?

"I'm sorry I said those things. I've tried all these years not to talk bad about your father in front of you, and I know I haven't always been successful at that. Sometimes I've just seen red and I just rant and rave and say whatever comes to my mind. Today was one of those days."

"It's okay, Mom," Annie said. "Maybe those things needed to be said."

Cathy looked in the rearview mirror and saw that Annie had tears on her face. She was wiping them away.

"And maybe they didn't," Rick said.

She glanced over at him and saw the bitterness in his gray eyes. He hadn't let the tears fall, and she could see that the grief was eating him from the inside out.

"You know, Mom, Mark made that choice on his own," Rick said. "It's like you always say. We can make choices in our teen years that affect the rest of our lives. This one's going to affect Mark."

Her face twisted as she turned the corner to get them home. She shouldn't even be driving. It wasn't safe.

"I know you're right," she said. "Your dad didn't do this. I never should have accused him." But as the silence followed, those accusations rose in her mind again. Maybe if Jerry had been around to tell Mark to stay away from drugs, he would have listened.

Cathy had told him a million times, but sometimes a mom's word wasn't as powerful as a dad's. Maybe he wouldn't have been so willing to follow his friends, to seek their approval, if his dad had been there for him.

As she turned onto Cedar Circle and pulled into her driveway, she knew that bitterness was eating her up. And no words were going to cure the sin in her heart. It had been deeply planted and cultivated, and Jerry fertilized it every time she saw him.

Before the kids had even gotten out of the car, she got out herself, ran into the house, and hurried for her bedroom where she could lock herself in.

Chapter Fourteen

Mark braced himself against the profanity spewing from the kid behind him in line. Surely the words would erupt into action, he thought, and someone would get hurt. He stood stiff with trembling, clammy hands at his sides.

The pale, greasy kid behind him looked like he'd lost a recent fight. His orange jumpsuit, identical to the one they'd issued Mark, was dotted with blood from his busted lip and broken front tooth.

This was all a mistake, he thought, desperately fighting tears that would mark him as a loser. He wasn't like the ones in this line, with their foul mouths and fighting wounds. They'd kill him as soon as they knew he was weak. He would be an open target—the home-school kid from suburbia. His conviction was a death sentence.

A yellow school bus with bars on the windows came to the curb. A guard with the build of a bouncer began ushering them on. It had been a long time since he'd ridden a school bus, a year and a half at least since his mother had taken him out of the public school and trusted him with Brenda to educate. He wondered what Miss Brenda thought of him now. Had Daniel told her how innocent the whole stupid thing had been? That he'd never in a million years thought he'd wind up here?

It was a joke, he thought. It had to be.

He got onto the bus and took a seat on the courthouse side. He watched the door of the old building, certain that his mother would come along, point to him, and say, "Gotcha!" Then he could get off and lose these handcuffs. It had to be one of his mother's object lessons. A year and a half ago she'd been so mad at him after he got suspended from school that she had taken him to River Ranch for a tour. Maybe this was just a step up from that. Maybe she just wanted him to know what it was like to get arraigned and convicted. Maybe it was all a conspiracy and the whole neighborhood was part of it. It was a pretty cruel way to teach a lesson, but he wouldn't hold it against them.

But his mother didn't come out, and no one lingered at the curb waiting to get him off the bus. Then the doors closed and the guards got on, and the bus started moving. It was not a trick, and it wasn't one of his mother's lessons. He was on his way to the state's teenaged version of prison.

The bus smelled of body odor, unwashed hair, and stale vomit. Mark stole a look around. Some of the prisoners had been here before, and their faces held dread but no mystery or fear. They sat like powder kegs ready to ignite. Others looked as though they'd just been shoved off a cliff. One kid up at the front was so pale that Mark thought he needed medical care.

Mark thought he was going to be sick, too.

Where was his mother? Why hadn't his father done something? The bus turned down a dark, tree-covered street, moving farther and farther and farther from anyone who cared.

After a while, they came upon the facility that he had seen only as a spectator a year and a half earlier. Even when he'd been arrested last year, they hadn't locked him up. He'd had friends who'd spent a little time here. His friend Jayce from Knoxville had a droopy eye because he'd gotten in a fight in the center and it had damaged a nerve in his eyelid. They were mean here, he'd warned him, but Mark had had no intentions of ever confirming that fact.

They were taking this punishment thing too far, he thought as his lungs tightened. He wouldn't do it again if they'd just let him out. He would study and clean his room and respect his mom.

The bus stopped, and an angry guard stepped on and walked up and down the aisle. "Stand up!" he shouted, as if he'd told them a dozen times and was tired of it. "On your feet!"

Mark got to his feet.

"Hustle, now. Single file! Mouths shut!"

Mark shuffled off the bus and looked up at the Conan-sized guard waiting to take them inside. "Excuse me," he whispered. "This is all a mistake."

The man gave him a look of mock amazement, then shot another guard a look and started to laugh.

"No, really," Mark said. "I'm not supposed to be here."

"Course not," the guard said. "But till they discover their mistake, how about you just line up with all the other mistakes?"

Mark closed his eyes. "But you don't understand. My mother's going to get my lawyer to do something. She'll never let this happen. I'll be out of here before dark. There's no point in going through any more of this."

"What's your name?" the man boomed, making Mark jump.

Mark straightened and looked around. The other guys were getting a laugh out of this. "Mark Flaherty."

"Let's see," the guard made a ceremony of checking his clipboard. "Mark Flaherty, Mark Flaherty. Oh, *yeah,* here it is." His eyes widened and he looked up at Mark. "You know, you're right. It is a mistake. Good clean kid from Breezewood don't belong in no juvenile facility. Says it right here. Whadda you know?"

Mark's heart soared and he looked over at the clipboard for the place where the man pointed. Then laughter spat out, and the guard doubled over. The inmates around them snickered with bitter superiority. Mark felt like an idiot. They were playing him, he thought. They didn't understand, but they would as soon as his mother came and did something about this mess he was in. And if she didn't, his father would. He knew they wouldn't let him stay here another night.

His mother had jerked him out of public schools because he'd been hanging with people like this. If she'd known what he'd been doing in Knoxville, she would have had every lawyer in town working to keep him from going there again. No, she would never sit still for this.

But he could do nothing except go along now as they marched them into the facility.

Chapter Fifteen

Tory had neither the time nor the energy to attend Sylvia's luncheon presentation at Cathy's church—but she'd had so little opportunity to hear about Sylvia's work that she and Brenda felt obligated to go.

Tory hadn't wanted to leave Hannah at home, so she had brought her with her. She was exhausted from battling Hannah's ear infections and bronchitis the night before, but this afternoon they had sessions with the physical therapist, the respiratory therapist, and the occupational therapist.

She had brought Hannah's stroller and hoped the baby would sleep through the meeting. But before she had taken her seat, she heard her name shouted over the ladies filling the room.

"Tory Sullivan!"

She looked up and saw Amy Martin, an old friend who lived next door to her in the duplex where she and Barry lived before they'd had children. "Amy!" she said, and threw her arms around the woman. "I didn't know you went to church here."

"Six years," the woman said. "Look at you. You're so thin and perfect, just like you always were." She bent down to the stroller and smiled at Hannah. "A baby? What is this? Your third?"

Tory grew tense. "Yes, my third."

"Oh, what a sweetie!" She reached into the stroller and tickled Hannah's stomach. The child's mouth was open, and her tongue was hanging again. Tory wished she would pull it back in. "How old is she?"

Tory thought of lying, then was instantly ashamed. "Fifteen months."

"Fifteen?" The word came out a little weaker, and Amy eyed the baby again.

"She has Down's Syndrome," Tory said quietly.

Amy raised back up, her face stricken. "Oh, Tory! That's awful. I'm so sorry, honey."

Tory didn't know what she'd expected. Maybe the usual change of subject, or some benign words about how Down's Syndrome kids were such sweet children. Those things always made her angry, because she didn't like stereotypes any more than dismissal. But the sorrow was a new one. No one had expressed sadness over Hannah's birth in a long time.

Brenda stepped up to the stroller and found Hannah's pacifier. She gently put it in her mouth. "She's a precious child," she said. "Tory is a world-class mother. No child with Down's Syndrome was ever more blessed." She smiled that smile that instantly put people at ease. "I'm Tory's neighbor, Brenda Dodd."

"Amy Martin," the woman said. She turned her sorrow-filled eyes back to Tory. "We need to get together sometime and catch up, Tory. Over lunch, maybe."

There it was. The dismissal. Tory realized that Amy couldn't win. Anything she said would have made Tory angry. This wasn't her friend's problem. It was hers.

"Let's do that," she said, then looked up and saw that the chairman of the ladies' group was heading to the stage. Sylvia was about to be introduced.

Brenda took a seat near the back, but Tory felt tears choking her. She lifted Hannah out of her stroller. "I have to change a diaper," she whispered to Brenda. "I'll be back."

Brenda watched her retreat. Tory knew her neighbor read every crushing thought on her face and would have done anything to fix it. But this couldn't be fixed.

When Tory was in the hall, she held Hannah close, as if to make up for any slight the baby had faced. The pacifier fell out and rolled across the carpet. Tory bent to get it and slid it into her pocket until she could wash it. Hannah looked up at her with her mouth open. "She didn't mean it," Tory whispered to the child. "She doesn't know what a treasure you are."

As hard as she had fought to encourage Hannah's development, part of her hoped the child never grew aware enough to feel shame over something she couldn't control.

Then again, she wanted her to be normal, and be aware of everything.

She couldn't have it both ways.

She heard the group applauding as Sylvia got to the stage. Tory listened from the hallway as Sylvia told about her work in Leon, first with the orphans, then with the food program for the poor. Then she introduced the slides she had to show them.

Wearily, Tory went back in. She returned to the back row next to Brenda, Hannah in her lap, hugged back against her.

The woman operating the slide projector took her cue, and the first picture flashed on the screen. "I want to show you a few slides of the children that come to us for food," Sylvia said. The face of a starving, malnourished boy flashed onto the screen. He was dirty and had crusty mucus under his nose and greasy tangled hair. Rags hung off his body, as if his clothes had been made for someone much larger. He had a look of hopelessness on his face, and his eyes held a glint of despair. His little belly swelled above bony legs.

"This is Miguel," Sylvia said, her voice catching. "He's my little friend. His father was killed in the hurricane along with two of his sisters. His mother and he come each night hoping that we'll have food. We've been feeding him for about a month now, mostly beans and rice, since that has a lot of nutritional value and it doesn't cost very much. We figured out that we can feed a hundred to a hundred-fifty children like Miguel on $400 a month. Think about it, people," she said. "That's a little over two and a half bucks to as high as four dollars a day to feed a child like Miguel for a month. What better use can you think of for your money?"

Tory sat straighter, her arms tightly wrapped around Hannah. Another face flashed on the screen. This boy had bright, alert eyes.

"This is also Miguel," Sylvia said. "I took this picture the day I left. Notice the difference. His little belly isn't as swollen. He has a twinkle in his eye. He's actually smiling now. He connects. Not only has the food filled his hungry belly, but it's helped him physically in so many other ways. But that's not all," she said. "We had a Bible school last week in Leon, and little Miguel gave his life to Jesus. His mother brought him to church last Sunday. I have every faith that soon she'll come to Christ, too."

Applause erupted over the crowd. Tory could see that she wasn't the only one moved by the pictures. She glanced at Brenda and saw the tears on her face.

Sylvia showed several other slides, equally dramatic photos of other children she knew by name, their mothers and fathers, their baby sisters and brothers. When the slides were finished, Sylvia leaned on the podium, her eyes sweeping over everyone in the room.

"I know that Nicaragua seems a long way away," she said. "It did to me when my husband first came home and told me he wanted to go to the mission field there. And these faces, you don't know them. You've never seen them. Chances are, you'll never meet any of them. But I can tell you, they're real. They're my family now. They live where I live, and they're victims of the hurricane that has just destroyed the economy, taken away their homes and their businesses, ruined their crops. I know that the Lord sent me there to help in the aftermath of Hurricane Norris, and my husband and I are willing to make as many sacrifices as we can to help those people. But I came here today to ask you to help, too.

"Think about it. Four dollars or less will

feed one child for a month. What do you spend four dollars on?" she asked. "When I lived here, I spent four dollars a day on the sodas I drank. It was nothing to run through McDonald's and pick up a burger and fries for under four dollars. But if you think about it the next time you go through that fast food window and realize that there's a child in another part of the world, with a distended belly and skinny little arms and a look of hopelessness in his eyes, then maybe you'll choose to spend that money on him, instead."

Tory smeared a tear across her face. Sylvia was right, she thought. Here Tory sat in her perfect little world, worrying constantly about her imperfect little child. But Hannah was happy and she was healthy and she was a joy, even if others couldn't see it. What if they'd had a hurricane sweep through the land and destroy their homes and businesses? What if they didn't have enough food to eat and had to rely on the kindness of people like Sylvia to feed them? What if that was all her children could hope for?

When Sylvia asked for pledges from the people there to help support the food program in Leon, Tory wanted to fill out a card. But this wasn't her church, she thought.

"We have to get our church involved," she whispered to Brenda.

Brenda's eyes glistened, too. "I was just thinking the same thing."

They were quiet as they got back into the car and drove home. "That was really good, Sylvia," Tory said. "Really, really good."

"Thank you," Sylvia said. "I get a little nervous when I get up in front of all those people like that. But then I remember it's not for me."

"What can we do, Sylvia?" Brenda asked. "How can we help?"

Sylvia smiled. "Well, to tell you the truth, I *had* planned to hit you up for something."

Tory grinned. "What?"

"Well, when I made it known I was coming home for a few days, I started getting a lot of invitations to speak to other churches about the work I was doing. I had to turn some of them down. But I was thinking that maybe you and Brenda and Cathy could go around and do it for me. I could leave these slides for you and some of my notes. If you could just go and make a presentation, tell them about the work we're doing, maybe you could get them to raise some money, too. We need all we can get. If we don't get it, we'll have to turn children like Miguel away. We'll have to tell their mothers and fathers that we can't help them. Then they won't want to hear the gospel, and they'll never get what they need most."

"I'll help," Brenda said. "But I'm not too good at public speaking. I kind of go weak in the knees. I break out in hives."

Tory grinned. "No, you don't."

"I do," Brenda said. "I have this fear of throwing up right on the stage."

"Brenda Dodd?" Tory asked. "The woman who has it together better than anyone I know, except Sylvia?"

"Well, sorry to pop your bubble," Brenda said. She was growing pale just talking about it. "I'll do what I can. I mean, I can try . . ."

"Me, too," Tory said. "I don't know what I'll do with Hannah. But I'll figure something out. Maybe we could do it together. Brenda could hold Hannah and work the slides, and I could speak."

"I could do that," Brenda said.

"Don't forget Cathy. I want her to get involved, too. It might help her get her mind off of Mark."

"I don't think anything is going to help get her mind off Mark," Brenda whispered.

"I've never heard her yelling like she did at the courthouse today," Tory said in a quiet voice.

"She seems so well-adjusted. You'd never know she had all that anger . . ."

"She's probably been wanting to say those things for years."

"I just wish she hadn't said it where the kids could hear," Brenda said. "They need to think their father's their hero—even if he's not."

"Brenda's right," Sylvia said. "No matter what a father does—or doesn't do—the children need to see him on a white horse. If they don't, how can they believe that God the Father is their rescuer and redeemer?" She looked out the window at the hazy mountains overlooking Signal Mountain. "Some of the children in Leon are so wounded by their fathers being absent during the hurricane. Little children and their mothers had to fight to survive on their own, when the father's strength might have made a difference. I can't fathom why men don't know how important they are." She dabbed at her eyes and glanced from one friend to the other.

"I'm glad I came home for the shower,

even if it wasn't what we planned. But to tell you the truth, I can't wait to get back. I miss the children, and the eagerness in their faces, the sweet expectation when they look at me."

"Then it *was* a calling," Brenda said. "A couple of years ago you fought it tooth and nail."

"Yeah, but the Lord changed my heart. And now I don't think I could ever come back."

"Don't say that, Sylvia," Tory said. "Let us go on thinking that someday we'll have you back to sit with us on Brenda's porch and mentor us into women of God."

"You're already women of God," Sylvia said. "But who knows what the Lord had in mind?"

Chapter Sixteen

After a lunch of plain ham sandwiches, the guards herded Mark and the others into a room they facetiously called the beauty shop. The sound of buzzers startled him, and he saw three of the inmates sitting in the chairs. Burly guards, who looked as if they had no barber experience, shaved the hair off the inmates' heads. Mounds of blonde, brown, black, and red hair lay on the floor around the chairs.

Mark thought his heart was going to burst through his chest.

"No way, man," he bit out to the boy in front of him.

The kid turned around. "Shut up," he whispered. "Don't get us all in trouble."

"I'm not getting anybody in trouble," he whispered harshly, "but they are *not* shaving my head!"

"Watch them," the kid said.

This was too much. Mark had done everything else they had required. He had filled out all the paperwork they had requested and taken the obligatory shower complete with lice shampoo. He had listened quietly through the rules as they were read out to him and had kept his mouth shut while they'd gone over the schedule. He couldn't believe any of this was constitutional. He made a note to look it up in his civics book when he got out of here. He was an American citizen. He had rights. They couldn't treat him like he was some subhuman, just because he'd made a mistake.

His frightened, angry gaze fixed on the foulmouthed boy who had been causing so much trouble since they'd loaded him onto the bus. But there wasn't anything even that kid could do about the hair being mowed off his head. He looked like an Army recruit.

To Mark, this seemed a more binding act than riding the bus here, putting on the clothes, using the lice shampoo. If they shaved his head and his mother still came and got him out, he'd have to return home like that. He didn't want to look like a doo-fus—and he didn't want to have the mark of a convicted criminal.

The guard called his name, and Mark backed away. "No, man, they're not shaving my head."

"Oh, yes, they are, pal." The guard grabbed his arm and jerked him toward the barber, but Mark resisted. Two more guards came to help, and Mark finally realized that he didn't have a chance against these peo-ple. He had to do what they said or suffer the consequences. He gave up and let them put him in the chair. He closed his eyes and, as the buzzer moved across his head, swore to get even.

It was his mother's fault. She should have been here sooner. It served her right to have a son who looked like this. It would show her. Every time she looked at him she'd remem-ber what he'd been through.

Yes, maybe it was all right after all. He could get a lot of mileage out of this. But as he got down from the chair and rubbed his hand over his head, he realized what had been taken from him. Then he looked ahead into the hall—and saw that more was yet to come. It dawned on him with vivid clarity that he had lost all control of his life.

The guards moved the newcomers into what was called Building A. They had been issued special outfits: orange striped pants, like something the Cat in the Hat would wear, and white pullover shirts. They all looked alike with the stupid clothes and their heads shaved. None of them looked cool, and they were anything but tough. As they lined up on a yellow line drawn on the cement floor, he realized he was a clone of all of these other kids who had come in here with him. His life was not his own anymore.

Building A was a huge room with fifty beds lining the walls. At one end, high above the floor, was a wall of windows, behind which was an elevated room like those you see in drugstores. From this room, the guards kept close watch and took care of business. Mark realized that his days of privacy were gone. He had forty-nine roommates now. Even showers were not private.

They handed him a schedule of daily activities, and as his eyes ran from the five o'clock wake-up to bedtime at nine-thirty, he realized that he'd also lost control of his time. If he had thought Brenda was bad, giving them so little free time during her school day, he realized this was much worse. Not more than thirty minutes at a time was given for one to think. Even the school schedule was more grueling than what he'd had in either public school or at Brenda's house. He supposed it was all designed to make him miss what he'd left back home.

But instead of wishing for what he'd had, he fed the anger festering inside of him, making him angrier at his mother for failing to fix the situation. It was her job to get him out of this mess. It was the height of neglect for her to leave him in here, and he would never forgive her for it.

He only hoped he would see her soon so he could tell her.

Chapter Seventeen

Cathy drove slowly down Pinewood Boulevard, searching the numbers on the houses for 352. She was so tired that her muscles ached, for she had lain awake all night, trying to picture where Mark was being kept, how frightened he must be, how full of remorse . . . and worrying about the arraignment and Mark's future.

Though he had confessed to selling the bag of marijuana to his friend Ham Carter, he hadn't told her much else. She had questions, like why the kid had picked Mark to set up. Why he'd seen fit to get a police officer involved. Whether it was really the first time Mark had done such a thing.

She found 352 and pulled into the driveway. A Jeep and the blue Lumina she had seen his parents drive to ball games sat in the driveway, so she knew she had the right house.

Her face hardened as she got out of the car and looked up at the yellow house with navy shutters. She hoped Ham was home, so she could look him in the eye and find out what he knew.

She stepped up on the porch and rang the bell, then knocked hard. The house shook with footsteps as someone crossed the floor, and the door came open.

"Yeah?" His face changed as he recognized her, and he started to close the door.

She stuck her hand out, willing to have it crushed to keep him from shutting the door. "No, you don't," she said. "I have to talk to you. Stand there like a man and look me in the eye."

Reluctantly, he stepped outside and pulled the door shut behind him. She wondered if his parents were inside. Why didn't he want them to know of his heroics in getting such a reprobate arrested?

Her mouth quivered as she looked up at Ham, who was taller than she. "I understand you had something to do with getting Mark arrested," she bit out. "I want to know what happened."

He shrugged. "Look, I'm sorry about Mark going to jail. I didn't know . . ."

"You didn't know *what?*"

"That he'd get a year. I didn't know he had two other offenses. He's a good guy. I don't have anything against him."

She realized she wasn't following him very well. Maybe her mind was too tired. Maybe her senses were dull. "Explain this to me," she said. "Did Mark or did he not sell you marijuana?"

"Yes, he did."

"And was it the first time?"

"Yeah."

"Then why did you call him and ask him to sell you some? What made you think he'd do it?"

"It was just a guess."

"A guess? What? You were bored that afternoon? You thought you'd spice up your life a little by putting Mark together with an undercover cop?"

"It was a deal we made, okay? I had to deliver *somebody.*"

She still couldn't understand. "A deal who made? You and Mark?"

"No." He got quiet then and looked through the windows into the house. Satisfied that no one could hear, he whispered, "Me and the cop. He nailed *me* first, okay? It was my first offense, but I knew my dad would kill me if he knew. I mean, he'd *kill* me. He can't find out about this."

Cathy's eyes narrowed as the words sank in. "So why aren't *you* in jail?"

"Because the guy . . . the cop . . . he said that he wouldn't book me if I could give him somebody bigger. A dealer."

"A dealer." Cathy repeated the words in a monotone as her eyes grew wider. "Are you telling me that you gave him Mark?"

"I didn't *have* a dealer, okay? At least, not one I could name. I got mine from this guy who was at the ballpark one night. I didn't know if I could find him again. I had to come up with somebody. I knew Mark would have some . . ."

She thought she might throw up. The air seemed stagnant, useless, and perspiration dotted the back of her neck.

"I figured Mark would sell us a joint, he'd get arrested, and they'd let him off since it was a first offense. Nobody told me Mark stole a car last year!"

"He didn't steal a car," she said in a metallic voice. "His delinquent friend took his stepfather's car without asking." She didn't bring up the other charge. It didn't matter now. All that mattered was that this kid had been trying to get himself out of trouble, and Mark had taken the fall.

She knew she should be rabid with rage. She should slap the kid and parade him in the house before his parents, let them hear what he had done. "My son is going to spend the next year of his life in a juvenile prison," she managed to get out. "A year. Do you know how long that is?"

"Yes, ma'am."

"Well, I hope you're sleeping well. I hope you're able to look yourself in the mirror."

He looked down at the boards beneath his feet, and she turned her back to him and started down the porch steps. Her knees wobbled and her hands shook. Finally, she turned back to him. "This can't be legal," she said. "I'm going to the police. I'm going to tell them what this cop did. Trading you for my son."

The kid got a pleading look. "Getting me thrown in jail isn't going to make up for what happened to Mark," he said.

"Maybe not," she whispered. "But it would sure make me feel better." Slowly, she made her way to her car.

By the time she reached the attorney's office, her anger was at a red-alert level. She stormed in, demanding to see him.

Slater heard the commotion and came to the door of his office.

"My son was set up," she said. "I just found out that he was a trade. A minor possession charge against his friend was dropped if he could lead the police to a dealer. Since the kid didn't know any, he figured he could turn Mark into one. Doesn't that constitute entrapment? Isn't this deal-making illegal?"

Slater took her into his office and sat down behind his desk. "Cathy, I know this must be upsetting. But the bottom line is that the police do make deals to catch bigger fish."

"If this isn't entrapment, then what is? I thought that entrapment was when a police officer tricked someone into committing a crime."

"Not exactly. I thought it might be entrapment, too, when I first heard about it. I even spoke to the arresting officer and got the lowdown, then talked to that Ham Carter kid to get the other part of the story."

"When did you do this?"

"The night Mark got arrested. Right after I got Steve's phone call, I started working on it. I didn't want to mention it to you when I interviewed Mark before the arraignment, because I had already figured out that it didn't fit the definition of entrapment. There's no entrapment unless the officer persuaded Mark to commit a crime he ordinarily wouldn't have committed."

"But he did!"

"No, he didn't. The Carter kid called Mark and asked him to sell him the bag. Mark never spoke to the police officer. Even when he got in the car with them, the cop never asked him to sell him the drugs. The Carter kid did all the talking."

"But it was planned! It was part of a deal. It wasn't Mark's idea. He never would have done it if it hadn't been for the deal."

"But the police never coerced Mark, so we

don't have a leg to stand on there. All they did was give him the opportunity to commit the crime."

"The cop lied to him about who he was!"

"Yes, but that's legal. Police officers are allowed, by law, to operate undercover."

She got to her feet and rubbed her forehead, blinking back the tears in her eyes. "My son would not have done this on his own." Her voice cracked. "It was *their* idea, not his. You could, at least, have tried."

"I would have if I'd had the proper evidence," he said. "Instead, I had lots of evidence to the contrary. Mark was more than willing to make this transaction, he worked it out with one of his peers instead of a cop, and he anxiously took the money. It was his third offense, which didn't help matters any. Believe me, Cathy. If I could have used the entrapment defense, I would have. But they had Ham Carter's statement, and Mark confirmed it in his own statement to the police. They asked him point-blank if the cop persuaded him to sell the bag, and he said no, that the guy was pretty quiet."

"There *must* be a way. There has to be something we can do."

"If he hadn't already had three offenses . . . if it hadn't been a violation of his probation . . . maybe . . ."

"If he were *your* son . . ."

"If he were my son, and he had the same record, and made the same transaction, he'd be right where yours is tonight. As badly as I'd want to, there wouldn't be anything I could do. I'm sorry."

She drove home, feeling the pain of fatigue and frustration, and the ache of those tears that had swollen her eyes. Her son had been betrayed by a friend. Despite his own behavior, she knew the fury he must feel right now.

He was counting on her to get him out.

But there wasn't a thing she could do.

She went home and headed for her bed, fell to her knees beside it. She began to pray, the deepest, most earnest prayers she had ever prayed.

But there was a wall between her and God, keeping her from connecting. Sickness rippled through her stomach, and fatigue pulled at her body like metal weights.

Why wasn't God answering?

Had she constructed these walls, or had he? She remembered what Steve had said about her not being able to trust her emotions. She tried to run through what she knew for sure about God.

He would never leave nor forsake her.

So why wasn't he helping?

He was just.

So why had he allowed Mark to be tricked?

He was merciful.

So why couldn't she get another chance for her son?

Maybe she wasn't righteous enough. Maybe she had been too hate-filled, too angry, too unforgiving. Maybe he was punishing her for the way she had talked to Jerry today.

The bitterness and anger and hatred that she had harbored for Jerry had spilled out when she was tipped over, and now she realized that if she was to be forgiven, she was going to have to forgive him. If she wanted her prayers heard, prayers for protection of Mark in this dark time of his life, then she was going to have to agree with God that her words and her behavior with Jerry had been sinful, that the blame she tried to cast on him was not helpful either to him or to the children, or to herself for that matter. Christ had forgiven her so many times, and now she was being called to forgive Jerry. Again.

She took the bitterness and bundled it up like a package. Mentally, she laid it on the altar for God to consume. Along with it, she bundled up the anger she felt toward Ham Carter. She hoped she'd gotten it all. She could only surrender it through the power of Christ. She wondered if he knew how hard this was for her.

When she finished praying, she sat back on her bed. Her eyes ached from the weeping she had done that day, and her lips felt dry and raw. She hadn't learned about the pathology of tears in veterinary school, but she knew there was something cleansing about them, something comforting in their aftermath.

She took a deep breath, feeling as if she were a little child being prodded along by God to do the right thing. She picked up the phone and dialed Jerry's number. His wife answered, and Cathy breathed another prayer of deliverance from the bitterness directed at her.

"May I speak to Jerry, please?" she said.

The woman recognized her voice and didn't answer, just gave him the phone.

"What do you want?" he asked.

She closed her eyes. Her hand was shaking as she clutched the phone.

"Jerry, I just wanted to apologize to you for the way I spoke to you today. It was uncalled for."

"What happened? Did the kids hear it and get angry? Is this apology because you want to show them you're really a big person?"

"No," she said, "they're not here. I'm apologizing because I'm a Christian now and I'm supposed to be more aware of what God has done for me. I'm not supposed to go off half-cocked and rant and rave against people who have hurt me. I'm supposed to understand that there are plenty of people I have hurt, too."

"Your point?" Jerry asked.

"My point is that I'm sorry for the things I said. It didn't help anybody. It only upset the kids."

"So you're admitting that it wasn't true, that it wasn't my fault that Mark turned out the way he did?"

"Mark hasn't turned out any way," she bit out, her voice rising. She closed her eyes and prayed that God would help her through this. She just couldn't do it on her own. "He's only fifteen. We don't know how he's going to turn out yet. I haven't given up on him, and I'm not going to. I will not surrender my child to the world."

She heard a deep sigh on Jerry's end. "I'll ask you again, Cathy. What is it you want?"

"I told you," she said. "I wanted to apologize. It's up to you. You can accept it or not. Your call. I just wanted to offer it."

She heard the click on the other end and knew he had hung up. She knew she shouldn't feel this way, but the severed line of communication gave her relief. She lay back on the bed and looked up at the ceiling, wishing she could see God's face there. Was he nodding that she had been obedient and done the right thing, or was he shaking his head because she still didn't get it?

"I'm trying, Lord," she whispered. "I'm trying, but I need your help."

Wednesday she could go and visit Mark. She wondered if he'd had anything to eat today or if he was too upset to choke anything down. Sometimes when he pouted, he went for days without eating. She remembered when he was much younger, when she and Jerry had told the kids they were getting a divorce, she had heard Mark a little while later throwing up in the bathroom. She wondered if he was throwing up now.

She heard a knock on the door and called, "Come in." Annie opened the door.

"Mom, I was just wondering. Can I go with you to see Mark Wednesday?"

Cathy saw that she had been crying, too. Her eyes were as red and swollen as Cathy's. The thought surprised her. Besides apathy, Annie's main emotion concerning Mark was disgust. She never missed an opportunity to insult him, and one of her favorite pastimes was making him feel like an idiot. Why would she cry for him now? She supposed that was the paradox of siblings. They loved each other, even when they didn't act like it.

"Annie, I think I need to go by myself the first time. There are going to be plenty of times when Mark's going to need to see you, but I think right now he's probably too upset."

Annie swallowed hard and looked at her mother with misty eyes. "Mom, what am I going to tell people?"

"I guess the best thing would be the truth. It's going to come out anyway, if they don't know already."

"But when I think about having a brother

who's been convicted of a crime, I just think of scumbags and sleazeballs. Not Mark. He's just some little mixed-up kid. He doesn't know any better."

"He knows better," Cathy said. "He absolutely knows better. Don't ever fool yourself into thinking he doesn't."

"But, Mom, he's just dumb, that's all. He does stupid things. He always has. He shouldn't have to pay with a year of his life."

"Well, maybe if I'd made him pay a little more when he broke those little rules, the government wouldn't have to make him pay now."

Annie wiped her eyes. "Well, I guess that means you're going to really crack down on Rick and me now. Turn into some kind of Hitler."

The thought had crossed Cathy's mind. "No, honey, I'm not going to do that. You don't have to worry. You haven't done anything wrong, and neither you nor Rick is headed for prison."

"Well, thank you for that, at least," Annie said, falling onto the bed next to her mother. "I'm glad you agree. As a matter of fact, I've spent most of the day patting myself on the back 'cause I'm not in jail."

Cathy almost laughed, but the humor quickly melted into despair. Annie hugged her. It was something the girl rarely initiated, and it moved her. "I can't believe he did this on the day of your shower," Annie said. "That was really low."

Cathy laughed without humor. "There's really no good time to break the law and wind up in jail."

When Annie went back to her room, Cathy went to bed and stared at the ceiling, wishing for sleep. But it wouldn't come. Peace was a gift that God had withdrawn from her. She didn't know if she'd get it back in the next year.

Chapter Eighteen

Wednesday finally came, and as Cathy prepared for her first visit with her son in prison, she took great pains with her appearance. She knew that her grief would be apparent on her face, but at least she could look like someone who knew how to get along in society. She didn't want anyone mistaking her for the mother of a houseful of criminals.

How would they process the visitors? Would they take her purse and search her clothes? Would she have to pass through a metal detector? Would she be able to sit side by side with Mark, hug him, kiss his cheek, cry with him? Or would they have them separated by glass and make them talk on telephones? How was a mother to behave when she visited her son in juvenile detention?

All of those questions would be answered soon enough. And she knew Amy Vanderbilt hadn't covered them in her etiquette book. Steve had asked to go with her, but Cathy had felt it was best if she went alone this first time. Mark would want to vent, and she didn't want anyone there to interfere with his freedom in doing so. But she had to admit, the thought of going alone terrified her.

She would just have to feel her way through this, and pray that God would accompany her every step of the way.

Because it wasn't a maximum security prison, the guards only made the visitors walk through metal detectors and asked them to leave their bags in a holding room. Anything they wanted to bring to the inmates had to be approved, and to get it approved, they were forced to stand in a long line in a poorly ventilated room.

But Cathy hadn't brought Mark anything, so she went into the visitation room and took a table. She was the first one there, and she looked around, thankful that she would be allowed to sit at a table with her child and hug him, even though the guard had given them each a stern warning about public displays of affection. That *couldn't* apply to mothers—if so, the guard would just have to call her down.

She sat fidgeting at the table as other visitors came into the room to wait for the inmates to come in. A teenaged mother of three took a chair at the back of the room. The baby cried a hungry cry, but the girl ignored it as she tried to keep her two- and three-year-olds corralled.

Next to her table, a grandmother came in with a stack of books she had gotten permission to bring. At another table, two boys who looked like they might belong here themselves slouched in chairs tipped back on two legs.

The door opened, and a guard began escorting inmates in. She watched their faces, watched them head for their families. When Mark stepped into the doorway, she almost didn't recognize him. She hadn't been prepared for the shaved head. It startled her, and she knew her surprise showed on her face.

She got up and waited for him to approach

her, and all the emotions of the day he'd been arraigned came rushing up again. She reached out for him, but he shook her off.

"Don't touch me."

Without waiting for her reaction, he stormed to the table, scraped a chair back, and dropped into it. Wearily, Cathy accepted his rebuff and sat down.

"Mark, how are you?"

His eyes bored into hers. "Look what you got me into."

Cathy sat back. "*I* got you into? What are you talking about?"

"I'm talking about the guilty plea. You're the one who made me do that, and if I hadn't, maybe I would have gotten off. A year, Mom! I'm in here for a year! Do you have any idea what this place is like?" He lowered his voice as he looked around. "These other guys, they'd just as soon slit my throat as look at me. The same kind of people you wouldn't let me hang around with before, now I've got to live with them. They put me in this big room with like a hundred other guys. I'll never have any privacy. I can't keep any stuff because they'll take it. I have this tiny little locker where I can keep my shoes at night when I sleep. And a change of these stupid orange pants. I can't believe you did this to me!"

"Mark, I didn't do this to you," Cathy said. "You did this to yourself. You broke the law. The guilty plea was a gamble. You're right. We didn't know what we should have done. Nobody had any answers or guarantees. We did the thing that we thought was best."

"So are you going to appeal this or what?" Mark asked.

Cathy's head was beginning to throb. "Honey, there's nothing to appeal. You got caught red-handed. You pled guilty. The prosecutor has lots of evidence. The judge has made a ruling."

"But I can't stay here, Mom!" He burst into tears and grabbed her hand. "Mom, please. If you'll just get me out of here, I swear I'll never do it again. I'll never see those guys again. I'll just hang around with Daniel 'cause he never gets into any trouble. And I'll study hard and I'll make straight A's with Miss Brenda. You'll see. I'll start helping you in the clinic every day for free. And I'll keep my room clean and I'll even start supper sometimes. Please, Mom!"

As hard as she tried, Cathy couldn't hold

back her tears. "Mark, there's nothing I can do. Don't you understand?"

"Of course there's something you can do," Mark said. "You're my mother. They can't decide where I live. I have the right to live with my family."

"You don't have any rights when you break the law," she said. "You gave up those rights when you decided to sell those drugs."

He pressed both fists against his temples. "If this is one of those lessons where you're trying to teach me something, trying to scare me to death so I'll straighten up, it's working, okay? You can stop it now. You can just go tell the guy that I'm finished, I'm changing. I'll do anything I have to do, but please get me out of here."

"Mark, this is not something I've chosen for you. You're stuck here for a year, because of what *you* did, not because of anything else. And, honey, I know it's horrible. I know you never even dreamed that this could happen. But it did. And I'm not able to do anything about it."

"I wish they had the death penalty for something like this," he said. "Maybe I'll just kill myself and get it all over with. Then I won't be a bother to you or Dad or anybody, anymore."

"Mark, don't talk like that."

"Why not?" he said. "Why should I care? If I've got to spend the next year of my life in this place, I might as well be dead. A year is practically an eternity."

"No, it's not an eternity," Cathy said. "Do you want to know what eternity is? Eternity is a billion times longer than the sentence you're serving in here, and then some. And, Mark, when you do die you're going to stand face-to-face with God. Whether it's sooner or later, I'm not going to be able to stand there with you any more than I was able to stand with you in front of that judge."

"Don't talk to me about God," Mark said. "If God cared about me, I wouldn't be here in this stupid place."

"God does care about you, Mark," Cathy said, "and he's a better parent than I am. If I had any power at all, I'd jerk you out of here so fast these people wouldn't know what hit them. But I don't have that power. I don't have any power at all."

She rubbed her face and tried to calm herself down. "Come on, Mark, can't you just tell me about the place? What's it like? Who are the people in that room with you? What are they here for?"

"Want to know what it's like, Mom?" he asked. "They treat me like dirt, that's what. And then they put me in the room with more dirt. And what are those guys in for? For acting like dirt. And for the next year that's all I'll be. Dirt. And when I come out, I'll still be dirt."

"You're not dirt, Mark," Cathy said. "You are my son."

"Well, enjoy it, Mom, because your house will be empty as soon as Annie goes to college. Then you won't have me to kick around anymore. It'll be just you and the empty house. Oh, and yeah, your new husband and his perfect kid. This is pretty convenient, isn't it? Get rid of the kid who's probably going to make the most problems in your marriage. Then you don't have to be bothered."

Cathy felt as if he had struck her. She sat back hard in her chair and gaped at him through her tears. "Mark, I know you're upset," she managed to choke out, "but you can't possibly think for a minute that either of us wished this on you. I did everything I could to keep you away from kids like that, to keep you from walking down the wrong path, but you went anyway, Mark. It wasn't my fault, and it wasn't Steve's fault."

She felt that tugging on her heart and obeyed it. "And it wasn't your father's fault either," she added. "It was *your* fault, Mark. And if you don't own up to it, you're never going to get over this. Never. It will be the longest year you've ever lived."

Mark drew in a deep breath as if filling himself with strength, then pushed himself up out of his chair. "I guess I'll just have to do what I can to get along here," he said.

"What does that mean?" Cathy asked.

"That means I'll act like dirt. I'll be what everybody expects." Then he turned around and headed back to the guard.

Cathy tried to stop him. "Mark, don't go. Come on back. We can talk." Some of the others turned and looked, and she sank back down, trying to be less conspicuous.

"I don't have anything left to say to you, *Mom*." His emphasis on the word was filled with sarcasm.

As the guard took him back through the metal door, she looked around at the other families visiting at the tables. They looked very much like her. Some were having pleasant conversations. She supposed they were the ones who accepted their plight. Others were crying, just as she was. How had she wound up here? This wasn't how her life was supposed to turn out. This wasn't where her son was supposed to be at age fifteen.

Feeling nauseous, she headed to the door, anxious to get out of this place, but devastated that she had to leave her son behind.

Chapter Nineteen

When she got home that night, Steve was sitting in his car, waiting in her driveway for her. As soon as she pulled into her garage, he got out and came to meet her, a look of caution on his face.

"How was your visit?"

She was too tired to cry any more tears, and as she reached out to hug him, she let herself lean on him for the first time since the arraignment. "It was about as bad as you could expect," she said. "Mark's blaming everybody, even you."

"Me?" Steve asked.

"Oh, yeah." She took his hand and led him

inside. She dropped her keys and purse on the table with a clash. "He even had this scenario in his mind that you and I were secretly delighted that this had happened, because when Annie goes off to college it will leave my house empty, then you and I will be free to get married with no problems. The only child in the house will be Tracy. Where is she, by the way?"

Steve seemed momentarily confused, as If he couldn't concentrate. "Oh—I got a baby-sitter to come stay with her after she went to bed. I wanted to come over and see if you needed me. He actually said that?"

"Yeah, but I think it just came to his head as he was talking," Cathy said. "He also blamed his friends . . . and God. And, of course, he blamed me from several different angles. Just one wouldn't do." She tried to stop her tears. "I don't know how I'll get through this, Steve. I really don't."

"I'll help you," he whispered. "I'll be here for you."

She breathed a laugh and pulled herself away from him. "Steve, you can't be thinking that we can still get married, can you?"

She saw that look of dread coming across his face. "Of course I am, Cathy. What do you

think? That *I'm* going to call it off just because of what's happened?"

"No," she said. "Maybe you should be
thinking that *I'm* going to call it off. I mean, I
can't think about getting married when my
son is sitting in a prison."

"It's not a prison, Cathy," he said. "He'll be
all right."

She knew he didn't mean to downplay her
grief, but the comment made her angry, anyway. "That's easy for you to say," she told
him. "It's not your child that's in there."

His face instantly softened, and he
stepped toward her. "Cathy, I didn't mean
that you shouldn't grieve. And I hurt when
you hurt. I love Mark, too."

That made her even angrier. "You can't
love him," Cathy said. "You don't love somebody just by saying it. His own father doesn't
even know how to love him."

He dropped his hands to his sides, frustrated. "What do you want me to say, Cathy?"

"I don't know," she said. "I guess maybe
we ought to just call off the wedding for now."

"Until when?" Steve asked. "Cathy, it's
time. Please don't do this again."

"It can't be time," she said. "Not when my
son is in trouble. I can't *think* right now,

Steve. I can't plan. Everything feels like it's just hanging in limbo somewhere, like it's all going to come crashing down on me."

He breathed out a laborious sigh, then dropped into a chair and stared at the wall for a moment. Finally, he slapped his hands on the armrests. "All right. We can postpone it, but I won't call it off. I'm going to marry you, Cathy."

"Fine," she said. "We can postpone it. That's all I want."

"And you'll keep wearing the ring?" Steve asked.

She looked down at the diamond he had given her for Christmas over a year ago. It was beautiful and had been such a sweet surprise. Neither of them had known just what they were getting into at the time. The ring sealed the promise they had made to marry each other when the time was right. But she wondered if it ever would be.

"Yes, I'll keep wearing the ring," she said. "I just need some time right now. I need for you to understand."

"I do understand," he said, and she saw the emotion battling for control of his face. "I'm disappointed. Tracy will be disappointed. *Everybody* will be. And I don't really see how waiting will make things easier for you. If we could just combine our households and become man and wife, I could be here with you night and day to support you and be with you when you're upset. I could help you through this."

"Won't you, anyway?" she asked.

"Of course I'll help you." He got up and crossed the room and looked into her eyes. "I'll do whatever I can, but it's not the same. I won't be in your bed at night to hold you when you cry." He tipped his head to the side and gazed down at her. "Cathy, I love you. It's hard to wait."

"I know it is," she whispered. "But I just need more time."

"How much?" he asked.

She shrugged. "How long will you wait?"

He sat down on the couch and leaned his head back, thinking. She wondered what was going through his mind. Was he wondering if it was even worth hanging on?

"I guess I'll wait as long as it takes," he said.

"Well, if he's going to be in there a year . . ."

He looked up at her with that look of dread again.

"I don't want him coming home to a whole

different family, to a household that's not what he left. I don't want to jolt him like that, make him feel like he lost a whole year out of his life. Or give him the feeling that he's not a part of things here."

"If he feels *that* way, Cathy, it has nothing to do with you. He's losing a whole year out of his life no matter what you do. There's no way around that."

"But if we could just wait until he got out, set the date for some time after that. We could do it, Steve. I know it'll be hard. It's been a hard wait already, but we can wait. Can't we?"

He looked like a child who had just been told Christmas wouldn't come until July.

"Steve, look at it this way. If you marry me now, you marry all my problems. You marry my kids. You marry the smart-aleck remarks and the screaming fights. And you marry this prison sentence that I can't even deal with yet. You and Tracy are so much better off without us right now. This is not what you bargained for when you gave me this ring."

"I bargained for you, Cathy," he said. "I wanted you, and I knew everything that came with it."

"You didn't know about jail."

"No, but neither did you," Steve said. He grabbed her hand and pulled her down next to him. Framing her face with both hands, he looked into her eyes. "We're going to get through this together whether we're married or not, Cathy. Okay?"

"Okay," she whispered.

"Will you count on me?" he asked. "Will you lean on me? Will you let me help and stop being such a tough guy?"

"I'll try," she said.

He held her with his eyes a moment longer. "I'm not promising to wait a whole year." He smiled then, and she saw the mist swelling in his eyes again. "That doesn't mean I'm walking out on you. What I mean is that I'm going to try my best to talk you out of waiting until Mark gets out. I don't think waiting that long will do him *or* us any good. Maybe the time will come before then when you'll feel more peace about it. Maybe when you see light at the end of this tunnel. Besides, if we break up, we have to return all those gifts."

She smiled. "I can't open them, you know. I don't know whether I should return them now or not."

"You don't have time," he said with a grin.

"Just leave them right where the neighbors put them. They're not in the way. And since the wedding was going to be so small, we don't have a lot of planning to undo. My mother was going to make the cake, so that will be easy to cancel. I'll call our guests and cancel the florist. Meanwhile, I'm going to go on acting like a man about to get married."

He stayed a while longer. By the time he left, she felt a little better. But depression quickly fell back over her.

She walked aimlessly around the house, trying to straighten things up. Rick and Annie were out, and her every movement seemed loud and hollow. She avoided Mark's room, knowing that there wasn't comfort there— only more recriminations.

The blinking light on her answering machine told of stored messages. She dreaded hearing them. Most of them were probably shocked reactions from friends as they heard about Mark's mess. But what if his lawyer had called with a new idea for getting him out?

She pushed the button and cringed at the first pity-filled platitude from the women's minister at her church. She pressed fast-forward, and made her way through several more. When Sylvia's voice came on, she sat back and listened.

"Honey, it's me, Sylvia. I came by before going to the airport, but you weren't home. I hope you're all right."

She could hear Sylvia pause to control her voice.

"Tory and Brenda are taking me. I have a 9:00 red-eye flight, so I can get there in the morning. I don't know when I'll see you again. But I love you, and I'll be praying. Hang in there, honey."

Cathy pulled her knees up on the couch and closed her eyes. Tears squeezed out. She felt lost, as if she'd let her life raft slip out of her reach.

Sylvia was leaving, and she didn't know when she'd see her again. It could literally be years.

She looked at the clock, saw that it was only eight-thirty. If she hurried, she might make it to the airport before Sylvia left.

She grabbed her purse, stumbled into her shoes, and bolted out to her car.

It had begun to rain, and the scent of wet summer was heavy on the air. Darkness fell over Breezewood like a good-night blanket tucking them in.

Mark slept hard when rain pattered against his window. She wondered if he could hear it tonight.

She reached the airport and parked at baggage claim, then checked the monitor for Sylvia's gate. Then dashing up the escalator without waiting for it to carry her to the top, she checked her watch.

Nine o'clock.

She ran down the wide hall, checking gates, until she came to one overflowing with people. Her eyes fell on Sylvia, Brenda, and Tory, huddled in the corner.

She was breathing hard when she got to them. "I thought I'd missed you!"

Sylvia sprang up. "Cathy! Oh, honey, you didn't have to come!"

"Yes, I did. I couldn't let you leave without saying good-bye." She pulled Sylvia into a crushing embrace.

Brenda laughed. "Well, this just couldn't be more perfect. Sylvia's plane is late because of the weather."

"Looks like a God-thing to me," Tory said.

Sylvia pulled Cathy down into the chair

next to her. "We can sit here and visit and pretend it's one of our porches. Did you see Mark?"

Cathy sank into the seat and leaned her head back against the wall. "I saw him. He's angry. Blaming me. I don't know what to do."

"It could be a long year," Sylvia said. She looked down at her knees. She was wearing a pair of shorts, and Cathy noticed that her legs were thinner than they'd ever been. Sylvia was working too hard in Nicaragua, she thought. She wasn't getting enough to eat.

"I was thinking about how awful this was today," Sylvia said, "and then I started thinking back on Joseph's illness, and Tory's pregnancy. We thought both of those were horrible crises, too."

"They *were* crises," Cathy said. "No way around it. Don't try to sugar-coat it. They were awful."

"Yeah, they were," Tory said.

"But remember when they were all over?" Brenda cut in. "That night in the hospital, when we all sat around and talked about the best moment of the crisis, the pivotal ones where we learned something and grew?"

"I'm tired of learning things and growing," Cathy said.

"Well, aren't we all?" Sylvia agreed with a smile. "I was tired of learning and growing in the fourth grade when we started doing multiplication tables, but I still had to learn them." She gave Cathy a thoughtful look. "We did it again with Tory, you know. After Hannah was born and all was well, we were able to look back and think of the best moments. There were lots of them."

Cathy knew what she was getting at, but she rejected it. "Sylvia, there aren't going to be any best moments when my son is in jail. I'm not going to grow from this. I'm not going to learn from it. I'm just going to grieve for a very long time."

"That's what I thought," Tory said, "but Barry came back . . . and we have Hannah. As hard as things have been with her, I wouldn't undo any of it."

"If we learned anything from those days," Brenda said, "it's that sometimes God uses crises to bless us."

"Thanks, guys, but this isn't just your run-of-the-mill crisis."

"No crisis is run-of-the-mill," Sylvia said.

"And we know you're in pain. I'm not trying to make it sound easy. I'm just saying that I think some day, maybe not so far away, we'll all be able to sit around and think back on this year and what happened with Mark, and we'll see some things that we can't see now. Who knows, Cathy? Maybe this will be a wake-up call for Mark."

"I wish I'd taught him better," Cathy said. "I should have taught him responsibility. I should have taught him consequences. I shouldn't have waited for the state to do it."

"You tried," Sylvia said. "Don't kid yourself. You haven't been sitting around letting him off the hook."

"You haven't, Cathy," Tory said. "Every time I'm at your house, Mark's been grounded for something. And for the last couple of years he's been home-schooling with Brenda because of what he did in the public school. You did the best you could to keep him away from the friends who were a bad influence."

Brenda nodded. "He's building a testimony, Cathy, and you have to let God finish the work that he started on him."

Cathy wanted to believe that God had a plan in all of this, that things were going to turn out well, but she knew Mark's heart was not where it needed to be. She wasn't sure he was going to allow God to work in him.

The ground clerk's rapid-fire voice amplified across the terminal. "Ladies and gentlemen, Flight 531 from Memphis has arrived at Gate 15. We will begin boarding momentarily."

The reality of Sylvia's departure hit Cathy in the heart, and she grabbed Sylvia's hand. "Don't go," she whispered.

Sylvia smiled. "I have to. I have work to do."

Tory pulled a tissue from her purse and dabbed her eyes, and Brenda struggled valiantly to hold back the tears welling in her own eyes.

"But there's a mission field right here in your own neighborhood," Cathy said. "You don't have to go to Nicaragua to find people who need help. All this time you had a criminal living right next door and you didn't even know it."

"Don't say that," Sylvia scolded. "Honey, don't ever say that about your son again. You need to learn to bless Mark, not curse him. The words that come out of your mouth, even if he doesn't hear them, are more powerful than you think."

Cathy wondered if there was a cave

nearby she could crawl into for the next year. "Maybe my words are exactly what got him to this point," she said. "Maybe without even knowing it, I've cursed his entire life."

"There you go again," Sylvia said, "blaming yourself. You've got to stop that. All you can do is say that from this moment on things will be different."

"But how?" Cathy asked. "How do I make them different? Sylvia, you don't know how many times I've gotten on my knees and prayed and asked God to make me a better mother, to make me stop finding reasons not to teach them the Bible, to stop letting the television dictate our evenings. I've prayed that God will empower me to do that and make me want to when I'm lazy. But I'm still me. I still say things I wish I hadn't said. And I still do things wrong. How do I change? How do I make myself the kind of parent that would raise godly children? None of this is working for me."

"Do you remember the story Jesus told about the vine and the branches?"

Cathy was thankful that was one part of the Bible she was familiar with.

"Jesus said that we should abide in him

and that through him we could bear fruit. Do you understand what that means, Cathy?"

"I think I do," she said. "It means that we get our power from God."

"Don't you know that a branch that's not attached to the vine is going to die? The leaves wither, and it doesn't bear anything. There's no fruit."

"So you think I've fallen off the vine?" Cathy asked.

"No," Sylvia said, patting her knee. "I think you're still on the vine. I just don't think you're using the vine for your power. You see, in a vine all the branches get all their energy and all their life from that vine. Every piece of fruit, every leaf on the branch, comes from that vine. The branch can't do it alone. There's no way. If it falls on the ground it just withers up and dies. That's what Jesus was trying to tell us. All you have to do is abide in him. You have to soak up the life that he gives you. You have to soak up the power. You have to use it."

"And how do you do that?" Cathy asked. "By reading your Bible every day?"

"Not just reading it," Brenda said. "By soaking it up. Studying it. Meditating on it, thinking about it, turning it over in your mind, living with it, breathing it."

"That takes a lot of effort and a lot of time," Tory said. "It's not so easy when there are kids running through the house demanding your time and attention."

Cathy allied herself with Tory. "Or when you've got a clinic to run and people who need things done, when you're trying to keep a fiancé happy. Life just wears me out. I'd love to spend all day every day reading the Bible, but that's just not realistic. I really do want to feel that power and authority that comes from Jesus. But I'm new at this, and I'm slow growing. I guess I should be a lot further along by now, but I'm not." She shoved her hand through her hair. "I guess God's pretty disgusted with me."

"He's not disgusted," Sylvia said. "He'll feed you milk as long as you need it. But eventually you've got to take solid food."

"If I'd taken it sooner," Cathy said, "then maybe Mark wouldn't be in this position."

"And maybe he would," Brenda said. "Do you believe that God is a good and loving parent?"

"Yeah," Cathy said. "And a wise one, too. He always knows what's best. When I just parent in fits and starts, trying and failing and trying again, God gets it right."

"You have to trust him with Mark," Sylvia said. "He's coming of age, Cathy. He's at the point where there's very little that his mother can tell him. God's got to get his attention. And he's in a place right now where he can."

"How can you say that?" Cathy asked. "He's in there with criminals and thieves and drug addicts!"

"Maybe he needs to look around and see what he could turn out to be. Or maybe God has just strategically positioned him there for a very important reason. Maybe he's going to use him."

"Yeah, right."

"Just wait," Sylvia said. "Just wait and see what God can do. I can't promise that everything will turn out exactly the way you want, but I can promise that you'll be amazed at the way God works through this."

Cathy stared off into space for a moment, trying to picture it, but she failed. Finally, she reached out to hug her friend. "I'm going to miss you," Cathy whispered.

"And I miss you already," Sylvia said. She turned back to Brenda and Tory, and they all got up and hugged.

When they separated, Sylvia smeared her tears across her face. "I wish I could come back for the wedding."

"Well, maybe you can," Cathy said. "We postponed it again. Indefinitely."

"No!" Tory cried. "Cathy, you can't."

"It's just not a good time," Cathy said. "But it's okay. We're still in love. I'm still wearing the ring. And according to him, he's still going to act like a man about to get married."

The boarding call piped across the terminal, and Sylvia framed Cathy's face. "Don't you throw everything away because one bad thing happened," she said. "Steve's a good man. An answer to prayer."

"I know," she said. "I won't forget that."

Sylvia picked up her bag. "And if you need me . . . any of you . . . I'm just down the continent."

They laughed through their tears and hugged again, none of them in a hurry to let go.

That night, unable to sleep, Cathy got out of her bed and knelt down beside it. She put her elbows on the mattress and folded her hands in front of her face.

"Lord," she whispered, "I know I don't even

have a clue what it means to abide in you. I can say I'm doing it—but when I try to read the Bible . . . the words just rattle around in my brain, and ten minutes later I forget what I read." She hated admitting that. "Change me, Lord. I'm talking a major makeover. I want to be able to pray for Mark the right way, in a way where you can hear me and honor the prayers and answer them. I don't think I've been taking prayer seriously enough, especially not the prayers about my children." Her voice wobbled.

"I need you to put me back on the vine, Lord, and give me that life that I know you have. Pump it through me and help me." She wiped her tears. "And, Father, be a parent to Mark, so he has at least one good parent who knows what he needs. Because I sure don't."

The words tightened her throat, and she sat back on her heels and leaned her face into the mattress.

There were no more words, no more petitions. She had nothing left to say, but she hadn't finished praying. She felt as if God's hand touched the back of her head, stroked her hair, like a daddy comforting a hurting child. He was here with her, her father and her husband. He was her provider and her sustainer, her teacher and her comforter. He had revived her branch on the vine.

Neither her church nor Steve, nor Sylvia, nor any of her godly friends could do that for her. Only Christ could. And he could do it for Mark as well.

Time passed without any marking. She never looked at the clock nor yearned to get back in bed. She was still praying, even if the words weren't coming. This time, she was listening, receiving. And God was not locked away somewhere in some inaccessible throne room, silently registering her prayers. Instead, he was sitting here with her, holding her in his lap, loving her like the child who had finally come home.

Chapter Twenty

After changing planes in Atlanta and San Salvador, Sylvia arrived in Managua at ten the next morning. Weary and stiff, Sylvia got off the plane and ran into Harry's arms. He looked tired, as always, but his eyes danced with the joy that he'd found since coming to Nicaragua. His work here was effective, she thought. People were impacted and lives were changed.

Her life most of all. An hour hadn't gone by back in Breezewood that she hadn't wondered what the children in the orphanage were doing, and if they missed her. Their lives were already so uncertain, and sometimes so tragic, that she dreaded causing them any more sadness.

"Did you bring the pictures?" Harry asked.

She knew he wasn't asking about the shower, but rather about the grandbaby Sylvia had stopped off to see before she'd gone to Breezewood. "I took six rolls of film," she said. "She's the most beautiful baby you've ever seen."

"And the shower?" he asked.

She sighed. "Well, there's bad news. Mark got arrested. He's going to serve a year in the juvenile facility."

"Cathy's Mark? What did he do?"

"Drugs," she said. "He was selling them."

Harry touched his heart. "I don't believe it."

"Believe it. Cathy's a wreck. She postponed the wedding again."

"After the shower and everything?"

"There was no shower. We had to call it off. Everybody still left gifts, but Cathy hasn't even opened them."

Harry quietly took the news in as he escorted her to the secondhand car they had bought when they'd first gotten to Leon. It was a 1975 Fiat Berlin. Half the time it wouldn't run, but somehow it had gotten Harry to Managua today. A piece of plastic was duct taped to where the back window should be, since it had fallen out shortly after they'd gotten it. They hadn't been able to replace the glass. He'd had an order in for a year now, but they despaired of ever getting it replaced.

She got into the old car and sat on the torn vinyl seat. As they drove the distance from Managua to Leon, she told Harry everything that had happened with Mark. When they reached Leon, instead of getting him to drive her home, she asked him to let her off at the orphanage. She needed to see the children.

She hurried in, and some of the kids spotted her and screamed, "Mama Sylvia!" She fell to her knees and hugged them all at one time, kissing them and exclaiming how she had missed them.

Cindy, the other missionary wife who ran the orphanage, hurried into the room, as glad to see her as the kids were. Sylvia could see from Cindy's tired eyes that she was in need of a reprieve. Sylvia got to her feet and hugged her.

"Thank goodness you're back," Cindy said. "Little Juan is sick. He's been crying for you."

"What's wrong with him?" she asked. Juan

was a four-year-old who had been abandoned by his mother, and he was continually
struggling through an illness of one kind or
another.

"Dr. Harry said strep throat. He gave him a
shot this morning, but he's still sick. I've had
to try to keep him isolated from the other
kids, but it isn't easy."

"Where is he?" Sylvia asked. "I want to
see him."

"He's in the sick room," Cindy said.

She went into the room and found the little
boy lying limp on his side. There were dark
circles under his eyes, but his eyelids were
swollen from crying, and a pink flush mottled
his cheeks. She pulled up a chair, sat beside
him, and stroked his hair until his little eyes
came open.

"Mama Sylvia," he whispered weakly. She
reached down and gave him a hug so tight it
lifted him into her lap.

"I missed you," she told him in his language. "Tell me what feels bad."

He didn't have much energy to talk, but he
gave her a rough sketch of his ailments,
probably embellishing just a little. She could
feel that he was burning up with fever. Harry
had already given him Tylenol and had tried

to cool him down, but now all they could do was wait until the fever broke.

She felt him relax in her arms, and she started to sing a hymn. "Jesus, name above all names, beautiful Savior, glorious Lord . . ." His eyes came open and he focused on hers for a long moment, then finally they closed, and she felt him drifting off to sleep. Poor child. Cindy had undoubtedly been so busy with the other thirty kids in the home that she hadn't been able to give him much attention. But now Sylvia was here, her heart almost bursting for this child who had been feeling so poorly, with no one to attend to him personally.

When she got to the end of the song, she pressed a kiss on the little boy's forehead. "Get well now, Juan," she whispered. "Mama Sylvia is here."

Chapter Twenty-One

Incarceration was nothing like Mark had envisioned. He had pictured himself lying in a cell alone, flat on his back on a bunk bed, listening to the radio with nothing to do all day but read and watch TV. Instead, he had to rise at five A.M., clean up his sleep area, and wait for a ruthless inspection. Then, like enlisted men in the military, they walked single file into the shower, bathed, dressed, then headed for breakfast—at which there was no talking allowed.

At seven A.M., they headed for their first meeting of the day, an affirmation meeting that Mark dubbed "spill-your-guts time." Mark usually sat there with his mouth shut, listening to his cell mates talk about their drug addictions and their withdrawal, the babies they had fathered by several different girls, the foster homes they'd grown up in or the grandparents who had raised them, and Mark began to feel more and more different . . . even while he felt the same.

All their pasts were different, all their addictions and their demons. Mark found himself fighting the realization that everyone here had made choices that had landed them right where they were . . . including him. He didn't want to admit that yet. He still wanted to blame his mother. She wasn't going to get off the hook that easy.

He glanced at the kid named Lazzo, who slept in the bunk next to him. He was trembling more than usual today. He kept rubbing his hands on his pants legs and jerking his head as if to sling his greasy hair back . . . except that he didn't have any hair anymore.

Mark looked over at him and whispered, "What's the matter with you, man?" Lazzo didn't answer. He just kept fidgeting.

The counselor leading them noticed that Mark had spoken. "Mark, do you have something to say?"

Mark shrugged. "No, not really. I was just watching Lazzo. He's kind of freaking out over here."

"What do you mean, freaking out?" the leader asked. He looked at Lazzo and saw the sweat dripping down his face, the trembling in his hands. "You having withdrawal, man?" he asked.

Lazzo just stared at him for a moment, then said, "Man, you gotta help me. I ain't gone this long before."

So Lazzo was an addict, then. Mark had no idea what kind of drugs the boy was addicted to, although he knew Lazzo would tell him if he asked. "It's going to get worse before it gets better, man," one of the guys said.

Mark didn't know why everyone just accepted this. "Isn't there something you can do? I mean, don't they have some kind of medication or something?"

"He'll be all right," the leader said with a dismissive shrug. "Time to line up for movement to the school, everybody."

Mark got up and watched Lazzo push himself to his feet. His face had a look of desperation on it, and Mark wondered how he was going to get through this dark tunnel if it really did get worse before it got better.

"I need to go to the infirmary," Lazzo said.

The leader shook his head. "Sorry, kid."

"But I ain't feeling good," Lazzo said. "My heart's pounding. I need some help."

Mark looked up at the guard blocking the door, wondering what he would do if Lazzo had a sudden heart attack and dropped right there. "Man, let him go to the infirmary," Mark said.

"We'll keep an eye on you, Lazzo," the guard said. "If you get really sick we'll take you, but you don't get to go just for the jitters."

"But I can't study like this, man," Lazzo said, wiping his hands on his pants legs again. "Come on, you gotta help me."

"In line, Lazzo!"

"Man, I'm telling you. I can't go!" he shouted. "I have the right to go to the infirmary."

"Buddy, you ain't got no rights," the guard said. "You in jail now. Did you forget? You give up your rights when you come through those doors. Now get back in line or you really *will* need the infirmary."

Lazzo spat at him and uttered a profanity,

and suddenly there were three guards on him, throwing him down on the floor as he fought and kicked and screamed for help.

Mark backed away, watching with horror as the closest thing to a friend he'd found in this place was subdued by three huge guards with weapons and handcuffs. But Lazzo didn't stop. He just kept yelling and cursing and spitting and kicking with all his might as they wrestled him out of the room. It got quiet, as the remaining inmates lined up.

"Where are they taking him?" Mark asked the kid in front of him.

"To disciplinary, probably," the kid said. "He ought to know better than to act like that even if he is withdrawing. Ain't nothin' worse than disciplinary."

Mark frowned, wondering if Lazzo would be locked in a room that Mark had seen a year ago when he'd come here with his mother. Everything was steel and bolted down, and there wasn't even a mattress on the bed. Maybe the guards feared that the inmates would tear off the cloth in strips and use it to hang themselves.

"I'm not going to make it here," he whispered under his breath. But he didn't dare say it out loud, for he feared that the guards would descend on him as well and teach him a lesson about the trouble his mouth could get him into.

But the altercation had given him an idea. Maybe if he was sick, they would let him go to the infirmary, and then he could sleep all day and just hang around and get out of school and work and all these stupid meetings. Maybe then life would be a little more tolerable.

As he sat in class that morning, studying the work that the prison teacher had given him, he tried to figure out some kind of illness he wouldn't have to prove. Then he'd have easy street, at least for a day or two, before he had to get back to work.

Mark could vomit if he needed to. When he was little, he'd used that talent against his mother when he wanted her to feel sorry for him. She had thought he was just a sensitive child, when all along he'd just been pulling her strings.

He choked back a whole cup of water when they had their break, and when nobody was looking, he spat it out on the floor with a retching noise that drew the guards.

"I'm sick," he said, on his knees and clutching his stomach.

"No, you ain't. Get up and clean up this mess."

"But I'm sick, man!" he said. "You don't throw up unless you're sick."

"He ain't sick," a kid named Miller shouted. "I saw him gulping down his water and looking around to see if anybody was looking."

Mark didn't know what it was inside him that exploded, but he looked at the little snitch and decided he could take him. Without warning, he launched across the floor and head-butted him, knocking him down. The kid yelled and got back up, and his fist flew into Mark's face.

Before he knew what hit him, Mark was beneath the rabid boy, fighting for his life. The guards broke it up before the kid could kill him.

"All right, that's enough! Both of you, to disciplinary."

Mark felt as if he was really going to be sick now, as he dabbed at his bloody mouth and let the guards drag him out.

Chapter Twenty-Two

As soon as Sylvia was able to leave Juan, she hurried to the food kitchen where one of the ladies from town was already engaged in making the beans and rice they would serve for that evening's meal. Maria was thrilled to see her, for she had been trying to do the work alone for the length of Sylvia's vacation.

When the children and their parents began to arrive for the evening meal and Sylvia saw how many more now there were than when she'd left, she wondered why she had ever decided to stay away that long.

She dripped with perspiration and her

heart was pounded with panic as they spooned out the last of the food—long before the line had ended. How was she going to tell these people that they couldn't be fed tonight?

She looked into the eyes of the little boy who was next in line and realized she couldn't do it. She would not turn him away. She tried to formulate a sentence in her mind, but her Spanish was too confusing, so she looked at Maria. "Tell them they're going to have to wait a little while," she said, "until we can make another pot."

Maria looked up at her. "But there's no more," she said in Spanish. "That was all we had."

"I have some at home," Sylvia said. "I'll go home and get it." Even as she spoke, she wondered if she had enough. There were at least twenty more people in line. She knew this was the only meal some of them would eat all day.

Harry was in the kitchen when she got home. "I just came home to get something to eat," he said. "Do you want me to make you something, too?"

"No!" she said. "There're too many people at the kitchen. I've got to feed them—but we've run out of food. I didn't realize we were out. I should have gotten some in Managua while I was there. I should have spent every penny I had . . ."

Harry rubbed his eyes. She wondered how long it had been since he'd slept. When she wasn't there to nag him into taking care of himself, he never gave himself much thought. "I'll send somebody back tomorrow to see if they can get some more supplies."

She went to their pantry and started unloading the bags of rice and dried beans that she had stored there in case of another emergency. "I'll feed them this," she said. "They have to eat. You should see these children. They're skin and bones."

"I know," he said. "I've treated most of them." He went to the doorway that led to the little garden in the backyard. Sylvia hadn't had much time to work in it, so she knew Harry was looking at more weeds than blooms. She doubted, though, that that was causing the sadness she sensed in his slumping posture. "What's wrong, Harry?"

He turned back, leaning against the casing. "Sylvia, we've got to find a way to get the cash to buy more food."

"I brought back a little," she said, "but most

of what I got from those churches was pledges. The money should be coming in soon, but we've got to find a way to get by until it does."

"I was thinking . . ." He paused. "Maybe it's time to sell our house."

Sylvia almost dropped the groceries she'd been gathering in her arms.

"The Gonzaleses are out, and it's empty," he went on. "I know you probably left it spotless. We could call a realtor and have it listed."

"Oh, Harry. I just don't think I can do that! You should see it. It's exactly the way we left it. You wouldn't even know the Gonzaleses had lived there. Brenda and Tory took care of the flowers. And all the memories . . ."

"Our life is here now."

"But I wanted to keep it in case we ever went back," Sylvia said. "I just don't feel right cutting off that connection."

"Sylvia, think how many children that house could feed. And we don't intend to ever go back, do we?"

Sylvia looked down at the food in her hands that represented the needs that had brought her to this country. She knew the Lord was using her here and would use her as long as she was willing. "No, I don't intend to go back, either," she said. "Being back just made me miss this place, and all the children . . ." She closed her eyes. "I can't think about it right now. I have to get back to the kitchen and cook for those families."

"Yeah, I'm going to go back to the clinic as soon as I eat," he said. He reached up and touched her face. "Think about it, honey. The kids are all grown and settled. We're here. There's no point in keeping that beautiful home when we could sell it and raise enough cash to keep the pantry stocked for several years. And with the money coming in from the churches, we'd never have to turn anybody away again. Maybe we could even hire people to work in the kitchen. These people need jobs."

"We'll see," she said. Then she scurried out of the house and back to the kitchen to feed the starving children.

Chapter Twenty-Three

Cathy still felt God's presence Sunday afternoon as she went to visit Mark again. Though the visit had ended badly the Wednesday night before, somehow her prayer time had convinced her that she could handle it today. Maybe the interval had mellowed Mark and made him realize that he needed his mother.

But the moment he came into the visiting room and she saw his busted, swollen lip, she knew that her hopes were in vain. She tried not to look shocked as she stood up and met him halfway across the room.

"Mark, what happened to you?"

"I got in a fight with some jerk who thinks he owns the place," he said. "They're animals here, you know. I'm the only human being in the whole place." He threw himself down in a chair at the table.

She found she was having trouble breathing, and it was suddenly very hot. "Mark, I want you to tell me what happened."

"I told you. The guy had an attitude problem and he thought I was in his way just because I breathe and exist."

She wanted to scream out that an injustice had been committed against her son, that someone had to *do* something. "Did you tell the guard?"

"He was standing right there. He saw the whole thing."

"He didn't stop it?"

"Of course he stopped it, but by the time he did, I was already like this. I'm telling you, Mom. Animals. That's who I'm living with now."

He leaned forward, his eyes entreating her as he went on. "Mom, can't you go to the lawyer today and explain to him that I got beat up last night, that I'm not going to make it in here? Because I'm really not. I'm going to die in here. If I have to stay here for a whole year, somebody will kill me or I'll starve to death."

She tried not to let him know how affected she was. "I know they feed you, Mark."

"Yeah, but do you know *what* they feed me? I mean, we're not talking pizza and hamburgers here. Who needs Weight Watchers? They ought to just send fat people here and they'd lose weight in a few days. My stomach's been nauseous since the first thing I ate."

"That's because you're nervous."

"No, it's because the food makes me gag."

She closed her eyes. She had to keep this in perspective. They were playing by a new set of rules. "Mark, there's nothing an attorney can do. I've tried."

Mark slammed his hand on the table. "Then try something else! Wake up! Look at me. You're walking around like you're in some kind of daze, like you have to accept everything that comes down. You don't accept other things. You didn't accept it when Joseph was dying, and when Tory and Barry split up, you didn't accept that. You didn't accept it when the school system was passing out condoms. You fought like crazy that time. Why can't you fight for me?"

She wanted to tell him that she *would* fight for him, that she would fight anyone she could, that she would gladly trade places with him to get him out of here. But the fight was over, and Mark had lost. "There comes a time, Mark, when fighting is not appropriate and accepting your guilt is."

He opened his mouth in astonishment and banged his hands on the table. "Great, Mom. What about *your* guilt? How come you never have to pay?"

She knew this line of accusation. It came as no surprise. "Mark, I'm not gonna sit here and take this. I want to see you, talk to you, but I'm not gonna take your abuse. So you can stop throwing your accusations at me. I haven't done anything wrong."

The words angered him more, and his face turned crimson. "Why don't you just get out of here?" he asked.

She drew in a deep breath. "What?"

"I said get out of here. If you're no good to me, then don't come. I don't want to see you."

Her eyes flashed. "Mark, you don't mean that. Later today, you're going to regret saying it."

"I'm not going to regret it," Mark said. "I hate you. You don't love me, and I don't love you. If you can't help me, then get out of here." He got up and headed back to the guard who stood at the door.

"Mark!" she called.

"I mean it," he told her, swinging around and pointing a threatening finger at her. "Unless you have something good to say to me, don't even come in here. I don't want to hear anything else."

The guard took him out of her sight and the door swung shut behind them with a clash. Cathy just sat in her chair, staring at that metal door and wondering where she had lost her little boy.

After a moment, she realized he was not coming back, so she headed back to her car, feeling as if every ounce of energy had bled right out of her. She drove home in a fog of numbness.

When she pulled into the cul de sac, she saw that Brenda was in the car across the street, with Daniel behind the wheel. Tory sat on her porch with Hannah, watching. Cathy wondered whether either of them had anything better to do than sit outside while their children romped and played around them.

And here she was, grieving the loss of her child, while a child across the street—exactly the same age—did the things that fifteen-year-old boys were supposed to do.

It was as if Mark had died a week ago, and something or someone else was occupying his body. She didn't know how to relate to him or how to reach him, and his anger reached much deeper than the love she could show him.

She got out of the car and started inside, unable to talk to the friends she knew cared about her. She had no energy left to vent right now. She just needed to lie down and cry about her lost son.

Chapter Twenty-Four

As frightening as the prospect of speaking in public was to Brenda, she would have taken on a coliseum full of hostile hecklers rather than ride in the passenger seat when Daniel was driving.

It wasn't that her fifteen-year-old was a terrible driver. She couldn't have said that for sure, since he hadn't yet made it more than a few feet without slamming on the brakes.

Her hand gripped the door of her minivan, and she silently thanked the Lord for their anti-whiplash headrests. Her knuckles were turning white, and she was beginning to get a rare headache.

But she didn't want to discourage him.

"Daniel, your spatial skills just amaze me," she said.

Daniel grinned over at her. "Sure you won't let me off the cul de sac?"

"Not yet, honey," she said too quickly. "You need a little more practice."

He let his foot off the brake and stomped on the accelerator, thrusting the car forward again.

"Not so hard, Daniel!" she shouted. "Let off the gas a little!"

He took his right foot off the gas and slammed his left one on the brake, making the car jerk again. She checked the street for children in harm's way.

"Honey, you can't drive with both feet. You have to drive with your right one."

"But I'm left-handed," he said. "I drive with both foot."

Brenda closed her eyes and leaned her head back, wondering where she could buy a neck brace. "You can't drive with both feet, Daniel," she said, "not with an automatic transmission. Only people who drive standard transmissions can drive with both feet. And then they only do it because there's a clutch."

"What's a clutch?" Daniel asked.

"Something we don't have." She glanced

back at the house. "You know, maybe your father ought to be the one teaching you to drive. He doesn't get to spend enough time with you and—"

"But I'm doing a good job," Daniel cut in. "I haven't hit anything yet."

She thought about how much money her van had cost and wondered if the insurance would cover her son. He had just passed the written test and gotten his learner's permit, and it wouldn't look good if he totaled the car on his first day out. She looked out the window and saw Tory sitting on her porch with baby Hannah in her lap. Spencer and Brittany were standing in the yard, jumping up and down, cheering for Daniel. She was glad the van was pointed away from them.

"If I agree to drive with my right foot will you teach me?"

She cleared her throat and wondered if these palpitations could do serious damage to her health. "Daniel, don't do it for me. Do it because that's the way it's done."

There she went, getting negative. She should have learned more patience after dealing so long with Mark. "But go ahead and drive to the corner. Nice and smooth."

He shifted the car into overdrive and gave it gas again. They thrust forward.

"Why did you put it in overdrive?" she asked. "You can't do that."

"Dad does that sometimes."

"Only when he's going up a steep mountain. We don't need to do that right now. Stop, Daniel! Stop!" They were coming up on the stop sign, and his foot was nowhere near the brake. "Daniel, I said *stop!*"

He slammed on the brake, and the car jerked again. Her head was beginning to throb.

"Daniel." She wished she had a paper sack to breathe in. "I think maybe we need a bigger space to work in, some place where there aren't houses and other cars and mailboxes and little children."

Daniel was injured. "Mom, you think I'm going to hurt somebody," he said. "I made 100 on the learner's test."

"But driving is different on paper than it is in real life," she said. So much for being positive. "Honey, I want you to keep your foot on the brake and put the car in reverse. Then slowly let off the brake and back up until you get to our driveway. *Very* slowly."

Daniel breathed out a defeated sigh and did as he was told. The car inched back until it was right in front of their yard.

"Now," she said, "just put it in park and get out. I'll pull it in the driveway."

"No, Mom," he said. "I can't let everybody see me handing it over to you for something as simple as parking. I can do it. Just let me try."

"Spencer and Brittany are little children. They don't know the difference."

"Well, Joseph and Leah and Rachel do. They'll make fun of me, too."

"They're your brother and sisters. They always make fun of you. You've never let it bother you before. Come on, honey. You're not ready."

"But how am I ever going to learn if you don't let me try?"

She looked at his hands clutching the steering wheel, his foot on the brake, and glanced back at the driveway. It couldn't be that hard, she thought. Maybe he could do it, after all. She didn't want to destroy his confidence or give him the idea that she didn't expect the best of him. So her head would hurt, and she'd wear a neck brace for a few weeks. Mothers had to make sacrifices. "All right," she said, fearing that she would regret this. "I want you to put it in drive and slowly turn the car in a circle, and then pull into the driveway very carefully with your foot on the brake the whole time."

"Score!" he shouted, as if he'd just made a touchdown. "I wish Mark was here to see this." He put the car in park and carefully gave it some gas. She was pleased as he gently turned the car around and pointed it toward the driveway. Maybe he could do this after all. Maybe he wasn't as bad a driver as she thought.

The front bumper scraped the concrete as he took the pitch of the driveway too quickly. "Slow down," she said. "On the brake, Daniel! On the brake!"

But instead of the brake, his foot pressed the gas. The car bolted up the driveway, dragging the back bumper as it went over the gutter.

"Daniel, that's the gas! The gas!"

Panicked, he stomped the accelerator.

"Look out for the truck!"

Brenda threw her arms over her face as the van crashed into the truck—an awful sound of metal smashing metal and thousands of dollars' worth of vehicle being crunched like empty Coke cans. The impact flung them forward. Seat belts jerked them back.

When she had uncovered her eyes, Brenda surveyed the damage, her heart still in panic mode. Daniel froze, clutching the steering wheel and staring at the smoke rising from the van. "Oops," he said.

"Daniel, are you all right?"

"Yes, ma'am," he said. "At least, until Dad sees."

Brenda tried to open her door, but it was jammed. She thrust her shoulder against it, forcing it open.

Leah and Rachel came running across the lot next door, bouncing up and down as Brenda got out.

"Daniel wrecked the van!" Leah shouted. "Go get Daddy!" Rachel dashed around the house.

Having heard the crash, David was already out of his workshop and halfway to the driveway. He stopped at the sight and stood with his hands hanging at his side as his face betrayed his shock.

"What in the name of all that is good happened here?" David asked through his teeth.

"Dad, I'm sorry," Daniel cried, getting out

of the van. "Mom said to hit the brake and I accidentally hit the gas."

"I can see that," David said. "Son, this is our *family* van. I've had that pickup truck for twelve years. How could you do that the *first* time you got behind the wheel? Don't you know the difference between the brake and the gas?"

Brenda touched his arm to calm him down. "He didn't mean to, David."

"Didn't mean to?" David asked. "Daniel, didn't you learn anything when you were studying that handbook?"

"Dad, I was trying, okay? I did really well when I was turning the car around. Didn't I, Mom?"

Her head hurt so badly that she didn't know if she had enough Tylenol to get rid of It. Joseph had come around the house now and was laughing his head off at Daniel's plight. Daniel looked like a little boy as he walked around the van, assessing the crumpled metal, as if he could fix it somehow.

"I'm really, really sorry."

"Just go in the house, Daniel," David said. "Just . . . go."

Daniel walked up the front porch steps.

That old protective maternal instinct kicked in, and Brenda's heart surged with compassion for the boy.

When the front door closed, she turned back to her husband. He was still gaping down at the van, as if wondering if he could fix it.

"It's my fault," she whispered. "He wasn't ready."

"It was not your fault," he flung back. "How could he ram the truck in the *driveway?*"

"At least no one was hurt." She knew the statement was weak, that it didn't really help matters at all.

"I don't believe this," David said again. He started into the house. "I'm going to call the insurance company."

"It's Sunday," she said. "They won't be open."

"Right," he said. "Well, let me go in and look up our deductible. We may not even be able to afford to get it fixed."

She followed him in. Daniel was waiting just inside the door. "Dad, I'll pay for it myself," he said. "I'll get a job and I'll pay every penny back."

David wasn't in the mood to hear. "Daniel, go to your room."

"But I didn't mean to—"

"Just go upstairs. Your mother and I are going to need a little time here."

Leah and Rachel had their hands over their mouths and were muffling their laughter, and Joseph was running along beside Daniel like a paparazzo trying to get the dirt.

"Joseph, Leah, and Rachel—go to your rooms, too!" David yelled.

"But we didn't do anything, Daddy," Leah piped in.

"Just do as I said."

Slowly, they all climbed the stairs and retreated to their bedrooms.

"Go easy on him," Brenda whispered. "He really didn't mean to do it. This is not a punishable offense. It's just really bad driving. Really, *really* bad. Why do they even let teenagers drive?"

"Do you think we could get the state to take back his learner's permit?" David asked. "You know, just because the law allows it doesn't mean *we* have to."

She drew him into the kitchen and got them both a glass. As she poured David some ice water, her hand came up to touch her aching head.

David took her wrist and brushed her hair

back from her forehead. "Did you hit your head?"

"No. Just a headache. I had it before the wreck."

He kissed her forehead, then let her go, and she poured her glass and sat down. David followed.

"So what do we do now?"

David shook his head. "I guess we call the insurance adjuster to come look at it tomorrow, and we see if it can be fixed. Let's hope it can, because we can't afford another car right now. Maybe I *should* let him get a job and help pay for it."

"No," Brenda said, "he's too young to work. He's just barely turned fifteen."

"Hey, I was working at fifteen."

"Yeah, but that was different. He has a lot to do, and I don't want him having that kind of commitment right now."

"You just don't want him having to go to work and be surrounded by people who aren't Christians."

Brenda wished they could talk about this later. "David, you know that's not true."

"Of course it's true," he said. "You're used to sheltering him."

"What is wrong with that?" Brenda asked.

"Would you rather he hung around with drug dealers and wound up in jail like Mark?"

"No," he said, "I'm not saying that you've done wrong. You've done a good job with him. But I'm telling you that it's not going to hurt him to be exposed to other types of people. Especially when he just totaled our car and we need help paying to get it fixed."

She ran her fingers through her hair and looked out the window at the two damaged vehicles. "Well, the truck's not in bad shape. Maybe it still runs."

"We can't transport six people in a pickup truck," he said.

"Well, maybe we won't all need to go somewhere at the same time. I'll just have to hold my driving down a little."

"Brenda, it won't hurt him to pay for what he's done."

"But it's not like he broke the rules or was disobedient," she said. "He just doesn't know how to drive."

"We'll talk about it later," he said, heading to the computer room where they kept the file cabinet. "I've got to find the insurance policy and see what our deductible is."

Brenda lowered her face into her hands as she awaited the verdict.

Chapter Twenty-Five

Spencer played fast and hard with a friend who had come home from church with him, and Tory wondered if she should coax them from the front yard into the back. It seemed somehow disrespectful to have her son playing out in the open, where Cathy would see and be reminded of her own child, locked in a jail.

The thought of forbidding her children to play in public seemed a little overreactive, but she had no clue how to make things easier for her grieving neighbor.

And just across the street, both of Brenda's vehicles sat crumpled and possibly disabled. Tory wondered if the strain this put on the family finances might send Brenda back into the workforce. Again, she wished there was something she could do.

Sylvia would have known exactly what to do. She would have shown up at Cathy's doorstep at the perfect time, would have known when to hug and when to speak and when to be quiet. She would have known whether to cook a meal or call on the phone or send a note.

And she wouldn't have spent a moment wondering if she was doing all the wrong things. She would have known that it wasn't about her.

Tory was still learning, but she would have given almost anything to have Sylvia still here to teach her.

And the first thing Sylvia would tell her was that she didn't need to borrow trouble from the neighbors up the street, because she had enough of her own.

The physical therapist was on her way over for a rare Sunday visit, since she was going to be out of town the next day and couldn't come to work with Hannah. Every visit carried potential for progress, and Tory took it seriously, each time praying and hoping that Hannah would have a victory on that day.

Tory moved from her rocking chair to the floor of her porch, and bent down until she was face-to-face with her daughter. "Today's the day you're gonna sit up for her, isn't it, Hannah? We're going to surprise Melissa and show her what a big girl you are. That you're very high functioning."

Hannah smiled and shoved her fist into her mouth. Tory ran her thumb along the baby's chin.

"What if Mommy let you go, and you had to sit up by yourself? What if I did that?" She asked the questions in a soft, teasing voice, and Hannah's eyes locked onto hers.

Tory opened her fingers and started to let her go, but Hannah fell back and let out a wail. Tory caught her and scooped her up. "It's okay," she whispered, angry at her own disappointment.

"What'samatter with her?" Spencer yelled from the street. He abandoned his little bike with a clatter and stepped through the impatiens to get to the porch.

"Spencer, use the steps, not the garden," Tory said. "She was trying to sit up but she fell over. It scared her. No big deal."

But it was a big deal to Tory. She told herself that it didn't matter, that she'd had no reason to think Hannah would be able to hold herself up this time.

Spencer's friend, Andy Holloway, dropped his bike with a crash on the sidewalk and clomped up the steps.

"How come she's so scared?" he asked. "My brother's walking and climbing now."

She looked down at the boy whose mother had been pregnant at the same time as Tory. His brother had been born two months after Hannah.

"Babies develop at different rates," she said, as if that would mean anything to a six-year-old.

"Ain't Hannah crawling yet?"

"Crawling?" Spencer shouted. "Duh. She's not even sitting up yet. Her back's not strong."

Andy just stared at Hannah as if he didn't understand, and Tory wanted to take her inside so she wouldn't have to answer any more questions. But the child meant no harm.

"Miss Tory, how come Hannah doesn't do nothing?"

She tried to smile. "Andy, Hannah does

plenty. She's just having a little trouble sitting up."

"But my brother did that a long time ago,
and he's younger than her."

"Not that much younger." She was getting
defensive now, and she reminded herself
that he was a child.

"I know how to make her crawl," he offered. "You put her down on her hands and
knees and rock her back and forth. Want me
to show you?"

She swallowed back the retorts that came
to her mind, retorts that she might have
given to an older person who wouldn't leave
her alone. "No, Andy, I don't. Hannah's got
some problems with muscle tone, and her
backbone isn't as strong as your brother's.
She'll sit up and crawl and walk when she's
ready. We just have to be patient."

Andy considered her pensively again.
"What if she doesn't?"

Tory wanted to scream that she would,
that she *had* to, that they still had every hope
that Hannah would be one of the Down's
Syndrome children who was high functioning. The physical therapist had predicted
that, as soon as she sat, other things would
quickly follow.

She realized that her idea about sending the kids to the backyard was a good idea, and not for Cathy's emotional state, but her own. "Spencer, why don't you take Andy and play in the sprinkler?"

Spencer let out a whoop and took off running around the house, wiping out the marigolds and periwinkles on his way. Andy forgot his concerns about Hannah and followed.

Tory went back to the rocking chair and leaned back with Hannah on her lap. Her heart ached for the baby . . . and for herself. "Please help her sit up today," she whispered to God. "Please give us that."

She saw the little yellow Volkswagen Beetle pulling into the cul de sac. The physical therapist, Melissa, putted up to the front of their house and, dodging Spencer's bike, parked and cut the engine off.

Melissa, in her early twenties, had perky eyes and an expressive face that Hannah responded well to. Tory tried to point Hannah's gaze to the car to see how long it took the child to recognize her visitor.

The young woman got out of the car and bounced up the yard. "Hi, Hannah!" she said in a voice dripping with baby delight.

Tory answered for the baby and made her wave. It didn't yet appear that Hannah had recognized her.

"Thanks for letting me come on Sunday," Melissa said.

"That's okay," Tory told her. "Hannah's ready to work. I think she just might sit up to-day." She turned her pleading eyes up to Melissa. "She just has to, doesn't she? Soon?"

Melissa took Hannah from Tory's arms and headed into the house. "We'll see what we can do, won't we, Hannah? But we don't want to get our expectations too high."

Tory followed them in and closed the front door behind them. Brittany was sitting at the kitchen table, drawing a cartoon picture of a puppy she had copied from a magazine. "See my puppy, Mommy?"

Tory muttered that it was nice, then went into the den where Melissa was setting up. "If you don't expect anything, you won't get anything," Tory said. "I've always found that to be true."

Melissa handed Hannah back and opened the mat they kept in the den for her work. She spread it out on the floor. "Well, with Down's Syndrome, all the rules change." She said it as though it was a little thing that wouldn't affect Hannah's entire future. Tory laid Hannah on the mat. The baby kicked her legs up at her. "Look how aware she is today," Melissa said. "She knows me. Look at those smiling eyes."

Hope fluttered back to life in Tory's heart. "Really? I'm around her all the time, so sometimes I think it's my imagination. Some of the babies at the school aren't aware of anything yet. They just stare at their mothers without any real response. But Hannah seems pretty aware to me. Wouldn't that indicate that she was high functioning?"

"High functioning is a relative term," Melissa said. "Let's just take one step at a time. How have her exercises been going this week?"

Tory's heart sank again, on the downhill spiral of that roller coaster she rode. No one would tell her that Hannah was high functioning, primarily because they didn't know. But Tory *needed* to know.

"They were fine," she said.

She glanced out the back window and saw Spencer and Andy dancing in the water of the sprinkler, while Barry read the paper on the swing. She thought of Andy's hurtful words about his own normal baby brother, who was developing the way babies were supposed to. She longed to see Hannah do some of those things . . . to pull up and climb and walk and run from her mother.

She longed to hear her talk. She longed to know that everything was going to be all right with the child.

But there were simply no guarantees in life.

Not about anything, it seemed.

Chapter Twenty-Six

Rain set in with as much force as the depression in Cathy's heart. She curled up on her bed, listening to it pound against the roof and the bare foundation behind her house, where they were supposed to build the addition—blending houses as they blended families.

But the house addition wasn't a source of joy or excitement anymore.

The doorbell rang. It was probably Steve. She had promised to call him after her visit with her son. But Mark's attitude had knocked the wind out of her.

She got up as the bell rang again, and

went in sock feet to the door. She felt small, weak, as she opened it to let Steve in.

"Cathy, are you okay?" he asked.

"I couldn't call you," she said. "I was upset." She looked around the house and realized how cluttered it was. Dishes filled the sink, and shoes littered the den. She didn't know they had that many shoes.

"Did your visit with Mark upset you?"

She nodded, grabbed a wadded paper towel off the counter, and tossed it into the trash can. "It was awful. He told me he hated me. Doesn't want to see me again."

Steve's face changed. "He said that? That he hated you?"

"He meant it, too," Cathy said. She curled up on one end of the couch, her arms around her knees. "He does hate me. In his mind, I've let him down. I've betrayed him by making him plead guilty, and now he's stuck there and I'm not doing a thing to get him out. But I've tried, Steve, and there's nothing I can do."

Steve sat down next to her and closed his hand over one sock foot. "He shouldn't have talked to you that way."

"Well, he did." She looked curiously at him, noting the crinkles next to his eyes where laugh lines had carved character into his face. But those eyes looked angry now.

"I've felt sorry for him, and I've prayed for him," he said. "I've lost sleep worrying about him. But I've got to tell you, I don't like it when anybody treats you like that. He had no right."

"He had every right," she said, hugging her knees tighter. "I'm his mother. I'm supposed to be abused."

"Actually, you're not. And Mark needs to learn that his own frustration and discomfort aren't grounds for disrespect. I can't even imagine saying those things to my mother."

"But you were raised by Mrs. Cleaver," she said. "Why would you say it?"

"So you're saying that you deserved it because you're not Barbara Billingsley?"

"Well, let's face it—"

"Cathy, you are a devoted mother, and if you don't think so, it's because you've been buying into Mark's attitude. How dare he treat you that way after what he did!"

"He's more concerned with what I did . . . or didn't do."

"Well, don't let him throw stones at you."

Sighing hard, she got up and went back to the kitchen. "This isn't about me, Steve. It's about him. I'm not real concerned with my feelings."

Steve followed her. "That's *because* you're a good mother. But look at you. You're a wreck. He has no right to put you through this."

"I'd like to see what kind of shape you'd be in if Tracy was taken away from you and locked up for a year. You wouldn't be trying to make a point about disrespect. You'd be wringing your heart out."

"I'd be in terrible shape," he agreed. "I'd be just like you. But I guarantee you she wouldn't talk to me like that."

It was the same old argument they'd had many times over the past year. He always thought her children were disrespectful. He tried to defend her, only to make her feel more torn apart. Nothing new.

"You know, I really can't deal with this right now," she said, "and since you and I have called off the wedding, there's no use in you trying to change my kids now. This is not the time. I'm trying to deal with a crisis in my family, and I don't need your criticism about my parenting skills. I've had enough of it. I've given *myself* enough of it all night."

"I'm not criticizing you," he said. "I'm criticizing Mark. I think you need to nip this in the bud early, let him know that your visits are a privilege, and if he can't treat them like that, you won't come."

"No, I will *not* do that," she said. "I'm going to be there for him if it kills me. The state is teaching him about disrespect and rebellion. He's locked up in jail for a year. What do you want from me?"

He stood quietly for a moment, then got up and came around the counter and took her hands in his. "What do I want from you?" he repeated. "How about a smile? I want to see joy back in your face again. I want to hear that laughter that lights up my heart."

She didn't want him to be soft and sweet. She wanted to lash out. She needed to be angry. But his fingers came up to caress her face. "I love you, Cathy, and for the rest of my life I'm going to defend you from any unnecessary pain."

"I don't need defending from my son. He's upset, okay? Give him a break."

"I'm not trying to bully you, Cathy. I'm not trying to force you to do anything you don't want to do with your children. But I take it real personally when you're mistreated."

"And I love them and take it real person-

ally when you try to stifle my maternal in-
stincts. I have to be free to love them the way
I need to. The balance is off here. You're not
Mark's father. You didn't change his diaper
when he was little, or hear him say his first
word. You don't have that image that I have
in my mind . . . of him chewing on a biscuit
when he took his first step. One hand clutching that piece of biscuit like it was holding
him up, crumbs all over his face, curly hair
flopping all over his head . . ." She choked off
the words and swallowed. "You can't love
him as if you were there. You never will. So
how can you tell me how to treat him? How
can you know what he needs?"

He backed away, slid his hands into his
pockets. "You make it sound so impossible."

"It is impossible. I mean, isn't it?"

"No. I think with God's help we can be a
family. Nothing is impossible with God."

"You say that so confidently, until the first
time I criticize Tracy and tell you to do something that contradicts your parenting in-
stincts. And then you'll be torn between
keeping peace with me and loving her the
way you need to."

"I'm not trying to get in your way, Cathy. I
just want to be your protector."

"I don't want protection," she said. "I just want to have the freedom to bless my children. Like you want the freedom to bless yours."

"Okay," he said. "I'm sorry I said anything."

"I'm sorry you did, too."

That guarded look returned to his eyes, and he went to the door, opened it, and gazed through the screen door into the rain.

"I've got to get on back to Tracy," he said quietly. "I left her playing at Shelly's house. I just wanted to see if you were okay. I'll call when I get her to bed. And I was thinking about going to visit Mark myself Wednesday."

"Steve, please don't give him more to be upset about. If there's ever any hope for us, I want you to build a relationship with him, not make a bigger rift."

He looked helpless as he stood at the door. "I want to help you, Cathy. I just don't know how. I want to be there for you and comfort you, and I also want to be there for your kids, all three of them. And that means going to visit Mark and doing what I can while he's in there. He's not a lost cause, Cathy. You can't give up on him."

"*Me* give up on him?" she asked. "What makes you think *I've* given up on him?"

"I think if you start letting him get away with everything, you're giving up on him. Acting as if it's too late to change anything about him. You've got a captive audience there, Cathy. Use it."

As she heard his car pulling out, she plopped on the couch and stared at the door. She hoped that, when he went to see Mark, nothing erupted. She didn't know how much more Mark could take. And frankly, she didn't know how much more she could take, either.

The old axiom that this, too, would pass seemed unlikely. She was locked here in this nightmare that was destined to go on, and there wasn't a thing she could do to stop or change it.

Chapter Twenty-Seven

It was still raining on Monday when Tory took Hannah to the Breezewood Development Center for the class she took with other mothers of Down's Syndrome babies. The class, originally supposed to have been such a comfort for her, had become something she dreaded. Some of the babies in the class had surpassed Hannah, and that fact depressed her more each time they came.

One child, a little younger than Hannah, had started walking just last week. Another one, only ten months old, was starting to crawl.

Most of the mothers were struggling to get

their children to do simple things like sit up and reach for or hold a spoon, and Hannah seemed more functional than a few, who lay limply on the mat, never making any progress at all.

She had considered quitting and just taking all her therapy at home, but the benefit of belonging to a group like this outweighed any downside—at least as far as Barry was concerned. Barry had warned her that she needed to stop comparing Hannah to babies outside the class who were normal, *or* babies within the class who might be doing things differently or better. Hannah was Hannah, and she had her own pace and would not be pushed.

But Tory felt it was her own personal challenge to make her baby everything she could be. And if Hannah didn't sit up, Tory considered it her own fault. She hadn't exercised Hannah enough to strengthen the muscles in her back or hadn't held her right, enabling the joints to do their job.

Tory hadn't bonded much with the other mothers because of that sense of competition. She looked jealously at the mothers whose children were walking and crawling and had bitter thoughts about how superior they thought they were. The truth, of course, as Tory dimly realized in her best moments, was that those mothers, like her, were simply grateful for any progress at all. Their children still had Down's Syndrome, no matter what they were able to do in class.

Tory tried to concentrate on the day's classroom activity—guiding their children through a series of exercises to music as the physical therapist who worked with them wandered through the room, encouraging and offering advice.

Tory heard a tap on the hall window and looked up. Barry stood there, smiling in. Hannah caught his eye, and he waved at her. Her mouth came open in delight. Tory looked around, hoping one of the other mothers had caught that. It meant that Hannah was aware of her daddy, that she responded appropriately to the sight of him. She allowed the thrill to alter her mood and picked up Hannah's hand to make her wave at her daddy.

"Don't you want to do a trick for Daddy?" Tory whispered to Hannah. "Come on, baby. You can do it."

She sat Hannah up in front of her and tried to make her balance. The child raised her hands in excitement at her daddy's face, apparently forgetting that she was making the effort. Tory balanced her on her little rump, sat her up, then tried to let her go. Always before, Hannah had gone limp and fallen back against her. But this time Tory could feel that there was a little muscle tone there, a little balance. Her heart rate quickened, and slowly she let Hannah go. Barry's smile faded and his eyes widened as he saw what she was doing.

Slowly Tory pulled her hands away. Hannah was sitting up on her own, waving her arms and laughing up at her daddy in the window!

Tory held her breath as the child sat there for ten, fifteen, twenty seconds. Tory wanted to scream out that Hannah had done it, but she knew it would startle her. So she sat there, frozen, counting off the seconds.

Finally, Hannah seemed to realize what she was doing, and wilted back against her mother. Tory snatched her up and let out a loud whoop. Everyone in the room turned around and Barry burst through the door.

"She did it!" she said. "She sat up! Did anybody see her? She sat up! Barry, did you see it?"

He came into the room and took Hannah from her, swung her around, and the baby laughed.

"She did it!" he said. "That's my girl!" They were both crying and laughing at the same time.

Other mothers in the room cheered for Hannah and made their babies clap along with them. Joy danced in Tory's eyes, until she saw the looks in the eyes of the mothers whose children were older, yet had not passed that milestone. She knew how it felt.

But this was Hannah's time. Her baby had sat up! That meant she was progressing, developing. Next, she would crawl—and then walk. Maybe there was hope. And as Barry clung to his youngest child, Tory threw her arms around his neck and hugged them both.

Chapter Twenty-Eight

Tory couldn't wait to tell Brenda. She didn't even go inside when she got home, just let Spencer and Brittany out and hurried over to the Dodd's house. The wrecked minivan still sat in the driveway, along with the dented truck. She went to the door and gave a light knock, then stepped inside, carefully carrying Hannah.

She found Brenda in the kitchen. "Brenda, you'll never guess what she did. Hannah sat up by herself!"

Eyes wide, Brenda clapped her hands. "Hannah, you're such a big girl! You sat up for your mommy?"

"It was so great," Tory said. "Barry was there, and she was laughing and reaching up at him, and it was like she just forgot I was trying to make her do something. You know, sometimes I think she just doesn't want to do it for me. Like she's tired of the constant exercises and just doesn't want to work. But today she forgot she was working."

"See? I told you she'd do it in her time. Relax, Tory. Hannah's gonna be all right."

Tory let out a breath and looked down at the food covering the stove. "You're cooking supper already?" she asked. "I don't even know what I'm going to fix tonight. I was thinking pizza sounded good. I want to celebrate."

"I'm actually making this for Cathy," Brenda said. "You know how it is. When you don't know what else to do, make food."

Tory picked a cut cucumber out of a bowl and crunched on it. "I didn't know what to do either. I thought of food, but didn't know if she'd even feel like eating." She shifted Hannah in her arms. "How do you do it, Brenda? How do you always know what to do?"

Brenda dropped a fork in the pan and turned around to Tory. "I hate it when you make me out to be some kind of angel,"

Brenda said. "I'm not like that at all, and you know it. We're supposed to love our neighbors and that's what I'm doing. Just trying to love my neighbor."

"I love her, but I don't know whether to show up at her door or take her food or write her a card or visit Mark or what."

Brenda put aluminum foil over the fried chicken piled up on a platter and covered a Tupperware dish full of mashed potatoes and a little Cool Whip container of gravy. "You know what Sylvia would say. If you err, err on the side of too much food. It's sustenance, energy. It's also sometimes comfort." She stacked another Cool Whip container of green beans and a bowl of corn on the cob. "Could you help me carry this over?"

"Sure," Tory said, shifting Hannah again. "Is she home?"

"I don't think so. I saw Annie and Rick drive up a little while ago. We'll just leave the food."

"I'd love to tell her about Hannah," Tory said. "I know she'd be excited. She knows what a step this is."

"You'll have a chance soon. Cathy's not the type to wallow in depression. If I know her, she'll be over here laughing and praying with us again soon."

"I don't know," Tory said. "We haven't watched Cathy deal with anything this serious. All the rules might change. The pain from our children's hurts can really do us in. They can be downright debilitating."

"But God doesn't leave us," Brenda said, "and he won't leave her. He'll tell us what to do."

Chapter Twenty-Nine

Steve had struggled between anger and compassion all week long, and Wednesday as he sat in the visitation room at River Ranch, waiting for them to bring Mark to him, he told himself that he needed to go easy on the kid. By now, Mark was probably pretty shaken up at what his own actions had cost him.

The door opened. Steve looked up and saw the guard standing a foot taller than the kid he ushered in. For a moment Steve didn't recognize Mark. His lip was cut and swollen, and his head was shaved.

Mark searched the room, then caught

Steve's eye. Steve saw the look of profound disappointment pass across his face. He got to his feet and reached out to shake Mark's hand as the kid came closer.

Mark ignored the outstretched hand and sat down. "They told me my dad was here."

Steve gave the guard a frustrated look. "I didn't tell them I was your dad. I don't know why they'd think that." Steve put his elbows on the table. "So, how you doing, buddy?"

Mark shrugged. "How do you think?"

"Well, you don't look so good. How's the other guy look?"

Mark didn't find that amusing. "He looks just fine, okay? He's had more experience than I have."

"I talked to one of the guards while I was waiting," Steve said. "They said you threw the first punch."

"There's only so much a person can take before he snaps."

"I'm sure that's true," Steve said.

Mark looked surprised that Steve would agree with him. Suspicion narrowed his eyes.

"What do you want from me?" Mark asked. "Why are you even here?"

The sudden question surprised Steve. "I'm

here because I care about you," he said. "I
don't like to see what's happening to you.
You're too good for this."

"You don't think I'm good. You're probably
glad to get me out of the way."

"You're wrong about that," Steve said. "I'd
take your sentence myself to keep your
mom from going through this."

"My mom? I'm the one going through it."

"Actually, she's trapped in prison, too.
She's impacted by this more than you'll ever
know. I worry about her."

"You're not even married to her yet. What
are you trying to do? Score points with her
or something?"

Steve swallowed back the retort that
flashed into his mind. "I love her, Mark. I
can't stand to see her heart breaking."

"My mom can stop this. She doesn't have
to leave me here. If her heart is broken, it's
her own fault."

"Wrong again, Mark. Your mom feels completely helpless. And you should have seen
her when she came home last week, after
you told her you hated her," Steve said. "She
doesn't deserve that, Mark."

Their eyes locked and held each other off
for several moments, and finally Mark looked

away. "Well, thanks for this visit," he said, getting to his feet. "Feel free to come any time, but next time don't make them think you're my dad."

Mark headed out of the room. Steve sat still for a moment until his heart rate settled. It was going to be a long year. And it was going to take every resource he had to get through it without doing any serious damage.

Chapter Thirty

The food that Brenda had brought over was a godsend. Cathy hadn't thought as far ahead as supper, and now, as Rick and Annie sat down with her to eat, she wondered if any part of the day could be salvaged.

It was getting warm in the house, but just before they sat to eat, Rick had opened all the windows and left the door to the garage open, as if they needed fresh air to blow out the cobwebs and the sadness from their home. They all ate in relative quiet. Finally, Annie spoke up.

"This is the worst day I've ever had in my life."

Cathy tried to look interested, but Annie was prone to exaggerations and melodrama. "Any special reason?"

"Yeah, a special reason," Annie said. "The fact that my brother's in prison."

"It's not prison," Cathy said. "Don't call it that."

"Jail then," Rick said.

"It's not that, either. It's a correctional center. A school, really."

"Oh, yeah, that's a lot better," Annie said. "It was all over town. Everybody's heard about it by now. Even at the church, that was all they could talk about."

When Annie had taken a job at the church helping with the summer day camps, Cathy had seen it as an act of God. The jobs were coveted, and the fact that they'd chosen Annie had given Cathy hope that the girl would enter a deeper level of commitment to God. Would Mark's situation change all that?

"Well, you'd better just get used to it," Cathy said. "There's no use hiding."

"They act like *we're* convicts," Rick said. "I had a date with Rebecca Farmer for Saturday night, and would you believe, her mother made her break it!"

Cathy looked up. "Why?"

"Because she found out about my brother and figured I was the same way. She told Rebecca she doesn't want her going out with a druggie."

"A druggie?" Cathy said, throwing her fork down on her plate. "I have a good mind to call her myself and tell her that no one in this family is a druggie."

"It's ruining our social lives, Mom."

Cathy sat back in her chair. "Well, I'm sure Mark is devastated to have a part in that, Annie. And if the judge had only known, I'm sure he would have given Mark a lighter sentence."

There it was again. The sarcasm. She didn't know where it came from or why it seeped into her tone so quickly. She thought about being on her knees the other night and repenting and asking God to put her back on the vine. Why was it that she kept falling off?

She rubbed her face. "I'm sorry. I'm just under a lot of stress right now, Annie, and I have a few more things to worry about than your social life."

"Hey, Mom, people kill themselves over their social lives, okay?"

"Well, I'm just going to have to trust that you're not planning to do that."

"Well, you wouldn't care if I was."

Cathy got up from the table, trying to keep herself calm.

"Annie, I don't have the patience for your games right now." She took her plate to the counter and left it in the sink. "Since you have so much energy to keep pounding me, why don't you just clear the table when you're finished and come do the dishes?"

"Mom, that's not fair," Annie said. "Rick never has to do anything."

"Yes, I do," Rick said. "I do more around here than anybody else does. Why do you have to be such a jerk?"

"Don't call me a jerk," Annie said. "I'm sick of you calling me names. Mom, make him stop calling me names!"

"Rick, why don't you go out and mow the yard when you're finished eating?"

"Mow the yard? I just mowed it a few days ago."

"It grows," Cathy said, and she threw her dish towel down and started out of the room.

"What is it with you, anyway?" Rick demanded. "You're acting like Annie and I are in jail ourselves. We haven't done anything wrong."

"She's not acting any different than she always does," Annie pouted.

"Annie, go to your room," Cathy said.

"How can I if I'm supposed to be doing the dishes?"

Cathy was getting confused now. She brought her hand to her head. "Get up and do the dishes and *then* go to your room."

"Well, I'm still eating and so is Rick. I can't very well take his plate from him when he's still eating, can I?"

"Annie, why don't you shut up?" Rick asked. "You're making it worse for both of us. She's going to jump all over us no matter what we do."

"I don't jump all over any of you. I respond to the things you say to me!" Cathy shouted.

"Well, why don't you just respond to somebody else!" Rick returned. "I'm sick of taking the heat for what everybody else does around here."

It was at that moment that the screen door flew open and Steve stepped inside.

Cathy was startled. She hadn't heard his car pull up, hadn't known he was standing there listening to the exchange. "Steve, I didn't know you were here."

"Obviously," he told her, "and neither did they."

"Oh, great! Here it comes," Annie said. She got up and took her plate to the sink and turned on the water, as if to drown out whatever Steve might have to say.

He just stood there, hands in his pockets, looking down at the floor as if he had lots to say but was restraining himself.

"I'm sorry you heard that," Cathy said. "I lost my temper."

"No problem," he said in a strained, quiet voice.

She just stood there, looking at him, wondering if he was judging her, condemning her. She stepped outside with him and closed the screen door behind her. In the garage, she turned back to him with her hands on her hips. "So just say it. I'm a terrible mother because I talked to my kids that way."

"No, that's not what I was thinking."

"What then?"

"I was thinking that they shouldn't talk to *you* that way. You're their mother, not a paid servant. Not an equal. They're supposed to respect you. All of them—Annie, Rick . . . and even Mark. But if you don't require it of them, if you don't *expect* it of them, then they're not going to do it."

He started back out to his car.

"Wait!" she said. "Where are you going?"

"Home," he said. "If I go back in there, I'll say something that won't be constructive." He got into his car and drove off.

Feeling as if the wind had been knocked out of her, Cathy went back in.

"You know, Mom, I heard what he said out there," Rick spoke up. "If you ask me, he's gotten way too power-hungry. He's not our father, and he has no right to tell you how to treat us."

"Go to your room," Cathy said. "Now."

Annie just threw her hands up. "The dishes? Excuse me?"

"I'll do the dishes myself," she said. "Go to your room, both of you. I don't want to see you again until I tell you you can come out."

The kids scurried off as if they were getting away with something, instead of taking punishment. As Cathy began to clean the kitchen, she felt as if she had failed again.

Chapter Thirty-One

Steve was pensive and still nursing his anger when he picked up Tracy from her friend's house that afternoon. He fixed them a light supper and tried to pay close attention as the little girl rambled about her day, and all the friends who had done silly things, and the way Matthew Rutledge had made fun of Susan Murphy until everyone on the playground had been cracking up. It all seemed so simple, he thought, when he listened to Tracy talk about her grade school problems and her friends who were too young to break their parents' hearts.

He realized that he and Tracy had it pretty

easy. Yes, they had had trauma in their lives when his wife died of cancer. It was the worst two years of his life, but they had come through it together.

That night, he sat on her bed, brushing out her braids and thinking how precious she was to him. What would it be like when they were all living together as a family? Cathy's three kids and Tracy. Some part of him felt as if he was sacrificing his own child on the altar of that family life. That instead of her children becoming more respectful and better behaved, Tracy would be the one to decline.

"Daddy, why did Mark have to go to jail?"

He brushed her hair and stroked the silkiness of it, wondering how much longer she'd let him do this. "He's not really in jail, honey. He's kind of in a home. It's a place where they're going to teach him not to do the things he did."

"I already know what he did, Daddy," Tracy said. "He took drugs and he sold them to somebody."

"How do you know that?" he asked.

"I heard everybody talking at the shower after the policeman came. And then Annie told me. Why do people take drugs if they're going to go to jail for it?"

He didn't know how to explain to his child that not everyone went to jail, that only the ones who got caught did, that many, many others got away with the act to the detriment of their own bodies. He hated for his daughter to be exposed to such things. Would there be any preventing it, once he and Cathy got married?

"I don't know, honey. Sometimes people do pretty stupid things."

"Are you still going to marry Miss Cathy?"

"I hope so," he said.

"I want you to," Tracy whispered. She crawled under her covers and lay flat on her back, looking up at her dad. "She's really sad right now, isn't she?"

"Yeah, she's worried about her son."

"I don't like for her to feel like that," Tracy said.

Steve's heart melted. "I don't either."

"Then we'll just have to cheer her up, won't we, Daddy?"

He swallowed the emotion in his throat and leaned down to kiss his little girl. They prayed for Cathy together, then for Mark and the others, and finally he left her alone and went into his own bedroom. He lay on top of the bedspread, staring at the ceiling.

Was he doing the right thing even wanting a marriage to Cathy? Wasn't he just taking on a whole barrelful of problems? He would forever be at odds with her children, biting his tongue and cringing every time they spoke to her in the tone that suggested that she was a subordinate. And then she would be mad at him for his anger at them. It would be an endless cycle, like so many other stepfamilies he'd encountered.

He didn't know if he had the constitution for it. But then he thought of life without her, and he realized the alternative was no better.

Sleep came hard that night, but finally he dozed, still wearing his clothes. Sometime in the middle of the night, he heard Tracy crying. He got up and ran to her bed.

"I had a dream, Daddy," she cried. "He was in there trying to get me! I saw him in the kitchen!"

"Saw who?" Steve asked her.

"Somebody," she said. "He was coming to get me!" She was crying and trembling, so he lifted her up out of bed and held her. She wrapped her arms around him, clinging with all her might.

"It's okay," he whispered, "Daddy's here."

He sat down in the rocker across the room

from her bed, and slowly rocked her back to relaxation. He could feel the tension seeping out of her, the fear dripping away. All was well, he thought, because he was here.

He realized that Mark hadn't had his father to comfort him when he was afraid. Annie and Rick hadn't had their dad to guide them with a firm hand. But he knew it was too late for him to fill Jerry's shoes. They wouldn't have it, didn't want it . . . and he wasn't certain he had enough love in his heart to bridge those gaps their father had left.

As he rocked his daughter to sleep, he closed his eyes and tried to imagine whether he had the strength to enter into this marriage when Cathy said it was all right.

But wouldn't it take even *more* strength to walk away from the woman he loved?

He put Tracy back to bed, tucked her in, kissed her good night, then went back to his own bedroom. His picture of his wife sat on the table beside the bed, and he picked it up and gazed down at it. Why had she died and left him to make such decisions? Why was he in the position now of having to take a family that was broken and lost and blend it with his? Could two families ever really blend?

He wasn't sure. But he was committed. Living with Cathy and being her husband might outweigh the hassles and dread of living with her children, and maybe God would teach him something in the process. Maybe he would actually make a difference in their lives. Maybe they would make a difference in his.

He took it to God before he went back to sleep, laying all his concerns and feelings on the altar, asking for God to show him what he was to do, how he was to help. Before he said "amen," Steve was hit with the overwhelming sense that there *was* one thing he could do. He couldn't be Mark's father, but he could help Mark's father give him what he needed. It was a start.

Tomorrow he would go and see Jerry in Knoxville and try to get him to visit his son in jail. Maybe then Mark could start his road to recovery. Maybe then Steve could help him fill the empty places that no stepfather would ever be able to fill.

Chapter Thirty-Two

Steve didn't tell Cathy he was going to Knoxville. He didn't want to give her another source of worry today. He had business of his own to handle in Knoxville; then, when he'd finished what he needed to do wearing his account manager's hat for the telecommunications company he worked for, he navigated his way to Jerry Flaherty's office, hoping he was there.

He stepped up to the secretary's desk, hands in his pockets.

"May I help you?" she asked.

"I'm here to see Jerry Flaherty. Is he in?"

"Do you have an appointment?"

He shrugged. "No, I was just in town and thought I'd stop by and talk to him. I won't take long."

She picked up the phone and dialed a number, then told Jerry that he was here. "Could I get your name, please?" she asked.

"Steve Bennett."

She said the name into the phone, then glanced at him again. He wondered if Jerry had asked her if it was the Steve Bennett who was his ex-wife's future husband.

Hanging up, she said, "You can go on back. It's that door right there."

He went to the door she was pointing toward, knocked, then opened it. Jerry was on his feet coming toward him.

"Steve," Jerry said, shaking his hand. "Didn't expect a visit from you. I saw you at the courthouse the other day, but it didn't seem like a good time to introduce myself."

Steve gave him a weak smile. "Cathy doesn't know I'm here."

"I see," Jerry said, dropping down into his own executive chair. He leaned back, tapping his fingertips together in front of his chest. "So, did you come here to get advice on how to handle her?"

Steve shifted in his seat. "Actually, no. Cathy and I get along just fine. It's about the kids."

Jerry's eyebrows came up as if he finally understood. "I see." He laughed and set his arms on their rests. "Well, I might have expected this."

Steve frowned. "Expected what?"

"I should have known you didn't want to marry Cathy and all her kids, so you thought you'd come here and make a little deal with me, maybe to have them in Knoxville a little more often."

The remnant of Steve's smile vanished. He got to his feet and looked down at the man who had broken Cathy's heart. He had never liked him, but he disliked him more intensely now.

"No, actually, that's not what I want. Cathy would be brokenhearted . . . devastated . . . if she didn't have her kids with her. I would never do that to her."

"Well, it hardly matters now, since Annie and Rick will be going off to college in a few weeks, and Mark's otherwise detained."

"You don't have to worry about my relationship with the family," he said. "We're doing just fine."

Jerry grinned, as if he knew better. "Then what brings you here?"

Steve sat slowly back down. "I came here to talk to you about Mark. Have you seen him since he's been at River Ranch?"

Jerry's face hardened. "No, I haven't."

"Well, Mark's really angry right now. He's very upset. He's at a turning point in his life, and he doesn't know which way to turn. I think he needs your support."

Jerry stiffened. "You have a lot of nerve, coming here and telling me how to be a father to my son."

"I'm not telling you how to be anything," Steve said. "I'm just telling you what Mark needs. I saw him yesterday, and he's right at the end of his rope. He's rabidly angry about what's happened. He desperately needs to know that he's still loved, in spite of what he did." He stopped and leaned forward, setting his elbows on his knees. "Look, I'm not divorced. I'm new at all the dynamics that go on in a divorced family. All I know is that when I went to see him, they told him his father was there, because they thought that was who I was. You should have seen the look on his face when he saw me, instead of you. He was crushed."

Jerry glared at him for a long moment. "You know, your fiancé—my beloved ex-wife—made it out to be all my fault," he said. "She claimed that if I had been there in her home as Mark was growing up none of this would have happened. Like Mark did all of this to get my attention or something. But I'm not buying it. Mark did what he did because he's a selfish, bratty kid, and he's been getting away with murder. His mother has no backbone and no discipline and no consistency."

Steve felt his hackles rising. "And you do?"

"I have more than she has."

"Well, what exactly are you consistent *about?*" Steve asked. "Your golf game? Because the kids claim you don't spend time with them even on your weekends. So where do you get off criticizing how Cathy has brought them up?"

Jerry got to his feet, dismissing him. "Glad you could come by," he said.

Steve was happy to leave. He started for the door, then stopped before walking through it. "You know, it doesn't really matter if Cathy was wrong or right about your part in this," Steve said. "The bottom line is that your son is in trouble. He needs you, and I came here to ask you to go to him and be what he needs for you to be. One time in your life."

Jerry pointed to the door, as if Steve had lost his way.

But Steve didn't leave. "Just tell me one thing. Are you going to go visit your son or not?"

Beads of perspiration dotted Jerry's upper lip. "As long as my son wants to humiliate and disgrace my family, he can't count on my support. Respect and approval have to be earned, and he hasn't done a thing to earn it."

"A child needs respect and approval whether he's earned it or not," Steve said. "Maybe your attitude is just what's wrong with this picture."

With that, Steve left the room and went back to the elevator. He seethed all the way down.

Chapter Thirty-Three

Steve was troubled all the way back to Breezewood, and it took the whole two-hour drive to cool his anger. No wonder Cathy had such trouble dealing with her ex-husband. Some part of Steve had expected him to be a good guy deep down. After all, Cathy had chosen him once. She had been in love with him. She'd had children with him. Steve had expected him to have some redeeming qualities, and maybe he did. If so, they were pretty well hidden on first impression.

He thought of Mark and the disappointment on his face yesterday when he realized that Jerry hadn't come after all. The kid might go through the whole year of his sentence without one visit from his father. It wouldn't surprise Steve a bit. He wondered how a father could turn that cold against his son. The thought made his heart swell with compassion for the boy.

If he was going to marry Cathy, then he had a responsibility to Mark. He had an obligation to help him as much as he could. Cathy deserved it. She couldn't do this alone.

He racked his brain, trying to find a way that he could have more of an impact on Mark, build a relationship with him, mentor him while he was in jail. But Steve was limited by the visitation hours—and by Mark's attitude.

Maybe he could mentor Mark through the mail. Mail call was probably an important time for the inmates. Maybe Steve could use the mail to do a Bible study with him or something. Maybe Mark would read it.

Then again, maybe he wouldn't. It was no substitute for a father. And as hard as Steve tried, it wasn't in his power to give Mark that.

Chapter Thirty-Four

The kids were gone, Rick to work and Annie to a movie, and Cathy found that the house was quiet. She paced from one room to another, straightening here and cleaning there, wondering why she hadn't heard from Steve today.

Part of her wanted to reach out and lean on him, but another part of her, the pride-filled part, wanted to handle things herself. She had done it for years.

She walked around the house aimlessly, cleaning up little bits of clutter, wiping counters, folding laundry. Suddenly, she had a sense of how purposeless her life had become. She went to work every day to take care of people's pets, animals who couldn't say thank you or pass her kindness on to others. And then she came home early to be there for her children. But being there wasn't all they needed, and now she wondered if she might as well have worked longer hours and made more money, for all the good coming home early in the afternoons had done her.

When the doorbell rang, she ran to answer it. It was Steve. "I tried to call you," she said. "Where have you been?"

"Long story," he said, coming in. "I went to Knoxville."

"Knoxville? Was it last minute? You didn't say you were going." She closed the door. "You want something to drink?"

He went to the couch and sat down. "No. I'm fine. And I didn't tell you I was going, because I didn't want you to stop me."

She stood looking at him for a moment, then slowly lowered into a chair.

"I went to see Jerry."

"You *what?*"

"I went to see Jerry. I wanted to tell him how hurt Mark was that he hasn't visited. I thought I could appeal to him father to father."

She only gaped at him, her mouth open. "I can't believe you did that." She got up. "Why didn't you tell me? Why didn't you *ask* me? What did you think? That you'd pop in and have a nice talk over lunch? Find out that my ex really isn't such a bad guy? Solve all of his problems with his children?"

He looked down at his clasped hands. "Well . . . yeah. I hoped. But it turned out not to be true." He looked up at her, registering the anger on her face. "Cathy, I was trying to help. I wanted him to know how disappointed Mark was when I came instead of his dad yesterday. I thought if he heard that—"

She turned away and crossed her arms. "This is incredible. You and Jerry . . ."

"It's not like we talked about you behind your back," Steve said. "Come on, Cathy. I'm going to be your husband. I'm going to be your children's stepfather. I wanted to do the most effective thing for all of you. I thought visiting Jerry would do it."

She turned back around. "And what did he say? Was he receptive, or did he have security escort you out?"

Steve got up, fighting the slight grin on his face. "Well, he did get a little hot."

She didn't say anything, but her eyes changed, as if she tried to picture the scene.

"He's not going to visit Mark," he said softly. "At least, not soon. He said that Mark hadn't earned his respect."

"Perfect," she said. "Well, at least we know where we stand."

"Yeah. Guess we can prepare Mark. Let him know not to look for his dad."

She shook her head and dabbed at the corner of one eye. "I can't do that. I'm not going to tell Mark to give up on his father. He's just going to have to figure it out."

Steve reached for her hand and pulled her next to him. Then he pulled her into a hug. She closed her own arms around him, laying her head against his chest.

"Mark was hateful to me again last night," she said. "You think he was disappointed to see *you?* He ranted the whole time I was there."

He moaned. "Why didn't you call me when you got home?"

"I was too upset, and I didn't want to hear what you would say about it."

He touched her chin and made her look at him. "Cathy, you know I'd be right."

"You're confusing me, Steve. One minute

you're his knight in shining armor, defending him to his dad. The next minute you're telling me I need to come down harder on him."

"To me, it's all about you," he said. "I want you to be okay. I want you to be treated with respect. And believe it or not, I want him to grow up to be a good, productive citizen. Not a smart-mouth who treats his mother like pond scum."

"What do you want me to do? Abandon my child just like his father has?"

"No. I think you should withhold your visits until he apologizes."

"He won't know why I didn't show up!" Cathy said. "I can't just not come."

"I can go and tell him. Make him understand that your visits are a privilege. They have phone time. He could call and tell you he's sorry. Or he could write you a letter."

"A letter will take three days to get here. And what if he doesn't write it right away? What if he waits a week? He's a stubborn kid. He doesn't do anything anybody expects. Not until he absolutely has no choice."

"Just try it," Steve said. "Let him miss you; let him realize that he's blessed to have a mother who comes faithfully. You've got to show him, Cathy. You've got to teach him that he can't talk to you that way, that he has to treat you with respect along with every other adult who makes an effort to come see him."

"He's just angry, Steve. He's been through a trauma."

"You don't think he's put *us* through a trauma?"

"Yes, but we're adults. We can handle it. He's just a kid."

"He's a kid who needs to learn some things. He's a kid who needs to suffer some consequences."

The word made something snap inside her. "Consequences?" she said. "He's going to be in jail for a year. You don't think that's enough of a consequence?"

"Not yet," he said. "Not when he's still throwing things in your face like he has."

She paced the room, looked down at the floor, shaking her head frantically. "Steve, what you're asking me to do is to punish him for being punished. Make him pay another penalty when he's already paying the dearest one of his life."

"No, I'm asking you to teach him to treat you with respect."

"But this isn't about what I need, okay? This is a critical time for Mark. He needs someone. Jerry has abandoned him. I won't do it."

"Cathy, you can't sacrifice yourself on the altar of Mark. You can't let him treat you like you're some subordinate that he can kick around."

She ran her hands through her hair, unable to believe what he was asking her. Part of her knew that he was right, that she had to teach Mark these lessons sometime. She didn't like being treated the way she'd been treated the last couple of times she'd visited him, but in her mind, it was a sacrifice she had to make for her son.

"Steve, when I was first divorced, I made myself a promise," she said. "I promised myself that I would never choose a man over my children. I promised myself that I would never let a man's influence cause the destruction of my relationship with them. And I'm not going to start now."

He looked as if she had struck him. "So what about when we're married, Cathy? Is my opinion never going to count? Are you never going to take my advice about parenting?"

"Steve, we're not married, and the reason we're not married is because of this. I'm not willing to give the reins of my children over to you. I'm still their mother. And no matter how long we're ever married or what we ever mean to each other, you are not their father."

"Their father has abdicated his seat."

"Then I'll be *both* parents like I've been for the last few years," she said. "I can do that."

"You don't have to," Steve said.

"Oh, yes, I do. I do have to when you issue ultimatums like this. I'm not going to turn my back on my son, Steve. Not because you tell me to. Not for any reason. Mark is not going to get the impression from me that he can blow it with his mother. Because he can't. Never. Not ever. Just like Tracy could never blow it with you."

"Tracy wouldn't treat me that way. She wouldn't rebel this way and then blame others for it."

The comparison slashed across Cathy's already-open wounds. "That was low, Steve. The lowest yet. Tracy's a great kid. I'll give you that. But I don't need for you to hold her up like some standard by which I measure mine. I love my children as much as you love yours. And I'm committed to them above my work, my friends, and my love life. If you can't see that—if you can't allow me that—

then I don't see much hope for marriage with you." She took off her engagement ring and handed it to him.

He took it, cleared his throat, and rubbed his face hard. "Do you mean that?"

"Yes, I mean it. I'm not finished being a mother yet. And that's enough of a fight."

Staring at the ring in his hand, Steve let out a deep, broken sigh. "I love you, Cathy. I'm not finished with you, unless you're finished with me."

She couldn't answer him or even look at him.

Then, without another word, he walked out the door and headed to his truck.

Cathy waited until he was out of the driveway and had turned from the cul de sac before she let herself burst into tears.

Chapter Thirty-Five

Cathy had hoped Mark's disposition had improved, but the moment he was ushered through the door into the visitor's room, Cathy knew that he was in a worse mood than he had been the time before. She got up and reached out to hug him, but he shrugged her away.

"What do you want?"

Too weary to fight, she plopped down in the chair. "Mark, don't treat me like that. I've worried about you all week, and—"

"You know what the guy in the bed next to me did?" he butted in.

She tried to follow his change of subject. "What, Mark?"

"He's a thirteen-year-old kid who stabbed his brother."

She felt the blood draining from her face.

"And he's out to get me."

She tried not to respond the way he was hoping. "He's just bluffing."

"Well, you know, he's used to people calling his bluff."

She wondered where the closest bathroom was. She felt an urgent need to throw up.

"I used to think I was different from the kids in places like this," he bit out, "but now I know we have something in common."

She shouldn't egg this on, she thought. It wasn't healthy. But she wanted to have a conversation with him. If she didn't engage, she didn't know how she would maintain a relationship with him.

"What do you have in common, Mark?"

"We all have scummy mothers."

The urge to swing her hand as hard as she could and slap him across the face overcame her, but she stopped herself. Suddenly, the blood was pumping back through her face again.

She got up. Clutching the back of the chair, she bent down. "Mark, do you want me to keep visiting you or not?"

"I don't care," he said. "Why don't you just stay home from now on?"

He was bluffing, she knew, but if that was the game he wanted to play, she suddenly felt she had the strength to play it. She got to her feet. "Mark, I'm leaving, and I'm not coming back until I'm strong enough to handle these visits. I don't know when that will be."

He didn't say anything, just looked down as if he didn't care. Her throat constricted, and she found herself unable to speak again. Tears sprang to her eyes.

"Annie and Rick are coming later. Try not to abuse them, okay?" Without saying another word, she left him sitting there and headed out of the visitation room.

Cathy wept as she drove to Steve's house, hoping she would find him at home. He had every right to go out and find something else to do. What made her think he would be sitting around pining over her? But when she got there and saw his car in the driveway, she was grateful.

She knocked hard at the door. After a moment, he answered. "Cathy!"

All the emotion she'd been trying to contain in the visitor's room at the prison just came pouring out. "I don't want to hear I-told-you-so. I just miss you and realize that you're the one I want to run to when I have to run somewhere."

He pulled her hard into his arms and crushed her against him.

"He called me scummy. He said I was just like all the other mothers. He hates me. I left him there, just sitting at that table. He didn't care."

He slid his fingers through her hair. "I'm sorry, Cathy. So sorry."

"And I told him I'm not going back until I shore up strength for those conversations. I don't know how long I can stay away, and I'm not playing games, trying to make him think I could turn my back. I just . . . don't know what to do."

"I know. I understand." He kissed her forehead and wiped her tears. "Whatever you do . . . I'm behind you. Not criticizing, Cathy.

Not comparing. I'm sorry for what I said about Tracy not acting like that. I don't know how she'll act when she's fifteen."

"It's okay," she said. "This can't be easy for you, either. None of it."

He took her hand and pulled her into his kitchen. "Have you eaten?"

She tried to think back and realized she hadn't eaten since the half bagel she'd had for breakfast. "No."

"Then our first order of business is for me to feed you," he said. "Sit down."

Then he began preparing a meal that she had no appetite for. But something about eating it and having him care for her gave her a warm sense of comfort. She found the tension leaving her body, though the grief kept its foothold. She wondered if she would ever get over it.

When she'd finished eating, she found that she felt better. "I didn't realize how much food could help. I've had a headache for days. I think it's finally going away."

He touched the lines on her face as if his fingertip could erase them. "But those lines are still there," he whispered.

"They're going to be for a while, Steve," she said. "I hope you can get used to them. I can't feel good when Mark is there."

And she was thankful he didn't demand that she did.

Chapter Thirty-Six

Mark brooded as he sat in the schoolroom off the main room of Building A, waiting for mail call. Mail call was one of those privileges that you had to earn. Some of the kids only got mail once or twice a week because they hadn't worked hard enough to earn the privilege on the other days.

Since they claimed he hadn't been "cooperative" at his job in the cafeteria, they'd taken his mail privilege away for the past couple of nights. It qualified for cruel and unusual punishment, he thought. Since his mother hadn't visited Wednesday night, he really felt the need for some mail, some contact with the outside world. He must have several letters saved up from her, Rick, and Annie. Maybe even Brenda and her kids. He wouldn't be surprised if Sylvia had written from Nicaragua.

He waited as they called out the names one by one, and people cheered as they got their letters from home. He watched as Lazzo, who had the bunk next to his, scrambled up to get the letter from his girlfriend. Even Beef, who seemed like a guy who would mock anyone who foolishly wrote him, got two or three envelopes. But they never called Mark's name.

As the other inmates shuffled out of the room, Mark sat stunned. He had been *cheated* out of his mail! They were holding out on him. How else could this have happened? How could no one in his family have written, none of his friends, none of the neighbors?

"Nothin' for you, man?" Lazzo asked him, slapping his own envelope against his palm.

Mark got up and started out of the room. "I hate mail. I didn't want it, anyway."

Lazzo followed him in and pulled his bed

covers back. With a groan, he dropped onto the bed, propped his feet up, and began reading his mail.

Mark lay down and stared at the ceiling. "My mom's boyfriend probably talked her out of writing. He can be a jerk."

He heard Lazzo folding his letter back up, cramming it into the envelope. "So what has that dude done to you? Beat you up?"

Mark gave him a sour look. "No, he doesn't beat me up."

"Beats your mom up, then?"

"No!" he said, getting angry. "He doesn't do anything like that."

"So why is he a jerk?"

"I don't want to talk about it, okay?" He kicked his covers away and turned on his side, wishing they'd turn the lights out.

He shouldn't have been so hateful to his mother. That had been a mistake. He had to admit that he missed her. He hadn't gone a day in his life without her, except for the weekends when he was at his dad's. And now here he was, locked away from everyone he was used to.

They were forgetting all about him, and he didn't blame them. Some people could only take so much before amnesia set in. It was how they stopped hurting, like painkillers or alcohol.

He wished he could forget. But he was stuck here, with no one but himself . . . and the other forty-nine convicts in his room.

Chapter Thirty-Seven

Brenda sat—weak and dejected—on the steps of the front porch,watching the insurance adjuster's car pull away. Behind her, she heard the front door open, and Daniel stepped out. "What did he say, Mom?"

"Deductible is what we thought," she said. "A thousand dollars for each vehicle. Thank goodness the truck still runs. I can drive it beaten up."

He looked sincerely distraught. "I'll get a job," he said. "I'll pay for fixing both of them."

"I don't want you to get a job," Brenda said, reaching for his hand. She pulled him down next to her. "You're too young."

"Why am I too young? It's summer and I don't have anything else to do, anyway."

"Daniel, do you know how many hours you'd have to work to make two thousand dollars?"

"I'm willing, Mama," he said. "Please. Dad's never going to let me learn to drive if I don't take responsibility for what I've done. I don't want you to give up on me."

"I haven't given up on you," she said.

"Then why did you ask Dad to teach me to drive?" Daniel said. "I don't want him to. He's still mad about the wreck. Besides, you're a lot more patient than he is."

It was one time when Brenda wished she didn't have that gift. She didn't have the patience to get back in a car with Daniel, and putting him behind the wheel of their only running vehicle seemed crazy.

"Look, Daniel, I think we all need a little more time before we get you behind the wheel. Why don't you just stop worrying about it for a while? Your dad and I will take care of the thousand dollars to fix the van. We can wait on fixing the pickup." She kissed his cheek and stroked his hair back. "At least neither car is totaled. But we can't get the van fixed until we have the deductible." She patted his knee and got up. "We'll figure something out, honey."

Feeling very tired, she went into the house.

Chapter Thirty-Eight

Daniel opened the driver's side door of the wrecked minivan and sat behind the wheel. He felt like a failure. He couldn't believe he'd done such a terrible job of driving his first time out. He had always pictured himself driving flawlessly with one elbow out the window and his wrist on top of the steering wheel. He had pictured the radio playing and himself turning corners as smoothly as a Nascar driver. He had even pictured himself getting his own car and driving Joseph, Rachel, and Leah around when his mother didn't have time. Maybe even going on a date or two.

His dreams were shattered now.

"What's up?"

He turned and saw Rick, Mark's older brother, crossing the grass.

"Hey," Daniel said.

"Looks pretty bad." Rick stepped to the front of the van and evaluated the damage. "I saw some man over here. Was that the insurance guy?"

Daniel moaned. "He said we have to come up with a thousand dollars for each."

"Tough luck," Rick said. He came around the van, dragged the passenger door open, and slid into the passenger's seat. "You know . . . I was watching out my bedroom window when you were driving, and I could see right off what you were doing wrong. First off, you were nervous, and it was showing."

"It was my first time." He should have known Rick would see him. He should have waited until the older boy had gone to work.

"You have to have a light touch," Rick said, demonstrating with his hands, "just barely touch the accelerator until you get used to it. Just ease into the accelerator and the brake, real slow like." He nodded to Daniel. "Go ahead. Put your foot on the accelerator. Just push it down real slow."

Daniel did as he was told. "Man, if I just hadn't punched the accelerator when I meant to punch the brake."

"Yeah, big mistake," Rick said, "but I bet you won't do it again."

"I won't have the chance," Daniel said. "My parents will probably never let me drive again. I'll be forty-two years old and still riding my bike. I'll have to get my mother to come drive my kids to school."

Rick chuckled. "Come on, it's not that bad. We've all had our wrecks."

Daniel glanced over at him. "You?"

"Sure," Rick said. "My mom tried to teach me how to drive, and you've never heard such yelling in your life. The first day I got my driver's license, I scraped a pole on my way out of the parking lot."

"No way," Daniel said, a grin illuminating his eyes.

"I did," Rick said. "I did great through the driving test and he gave me my license. Man, I was all proud, struttin' around. And then we got back in the car, and I took off driving a little too fast and took a corner too close. Next thing I knew, there was this terrible sound—concrete scraping metal. My mom almost had a heart attack. And then there was that time I ran into the garage and busted my headlight. That was back when I just had my permit."

Daniel was captivated. "You hit your own garage?"

"Yeah, there's still a black mark there to this day," he said. "I thought Mom would never let me drive again. And then she turned me over to my dad, and he never had time to teach me. When he did, he had this idea that he could do it in three easy lessons. When I didn't learn just like he wanted me to, he went ballistic."

"How'd you finally learn?" Daniel asked.

"Dr. Harry," Rick said. "Miss Sylvia told him all the problems I was having, and he took me to the parking lot at the city auditorium for several Saturdays in a row, and we drove around there until I got the feel of things." Rick's eyebrows shot up. "Since Dr. Harry's not here, you and I ought to do that."

Daniel gaped at him. "Really? You would teach me?"

"Only if your parents said it was okay. But

in the parking lot, you couldn't do too much damage. And you could drive my car."

"You would trust me with your car?"

"Sure," Rick said. "I'm supposed to be teaching Mark how to drive anyway, and since he's not here, I might as well teach you."

Silence settled like bereavement between them. "How's he doing?"

"Not so good," he said. "He got beat up the other day. They busted his lip. You know Mark. He's going to fight this kicking and screaming. If he settles in there before a year is up, it'll be a miracle." He looked out the cracked windshield. "Man, I can't believe he would be so stupid."

"Yeah, me either," Daniel said.

"I can't stand the thought of people knowing that my kid brother's in jail. Makes our family look like a bunch of losers."

"You're not losers. You didn't do anything."

As if he didn't want to talk about it anymore, Rick opened the door and got back out. Daniel followed and met him in the yard. "So when are you going to take me driving?"

"I don't know," Rick said. "Talk to your folks about it. Then I'll talk to them, and we'll see."

Daniel slid his hands into his pockets. "I was thinking that maybe I could get a job, and then the state would give me my hardship license so I could drive there and back. That way I could make the money to fix the minivan and maybe buy my own car."

"A job, huh?" Rick asked, a thoughtful grin creeping across his lips. "You ever thought of bagging groceries where I work?"

"Are they hiring?"

"Sure, they're always hiring. And I have a little clout. I've been there three years. I can get you hooked up."

Daniel looked up at the house. "I don't know if my parents would let me."

"Talk to them," Rick said. "You can convince them. You're a smart kid. You know, you're gonna want to date sometime soon, and a car would help things out."

Daniel's face blushed pink. "Where am I ever going to meet a girl?"

Rick shot him a grin. "We have some cute ones checking groceries," he said.

Daniel's eyes widened. "Yeah, I've seen some of them."

"Talk to the folks about the driving and the job, then get back to me. I can work you in," he said. "And if you want an application, I'll bring one home from work."

"Yeah," Daniel said. "Bring one. That way I can fill it out and have it ready to turn back in as soon as they say it's okay."

"All right." Rick held out his hand, and Daniel slapped it. "It's pretty fun most of the time. And sometimes you get tips."

"Tips?" It sounded too good to be true. "Thanks, Rick. I really appreciate it."

"No problem, man," Rick said as he went back across the street.

Chapter Thirty-Nine

Everyone had forgotten Hannah's triumph by Thursday, when Tory returned to class. Cynthia Harrison's year-old baby had said the word *Da-da,* and everyone was lauding him as if he'd just recited Lincoln's Gettysburg Address. Elisa Marshall's baby was walking as securely as any of the adults in the room, and Peg Jenkins's baby had started crawling. Hannah still lagged behind.

When the occupational therapist met with them for their twice-a-week appointment after the class, Tory proudly demonstrated Hannah's progress. "This is a great sign, don't you think? I mean, don't you think she'll be crawling soon, now that she's got the muscle strength to sit up?"

The OT was a woman in her fifties, built like a linebacker. Her name was Tilda, and she was compassionate and sweet to the babies, but stern and demanding with the mothers. She was trained in neurodevelopmental treatment and was never as concerned with what Hannah was doing, as much as she was with *how* she was doing it.

"I don't really like the way she's sitting," she said, studying the positioning of the baby's back, hips, and legs. "This could cause problems when she starts to crawl and walk. You need to check these joints when she sits up. Make sure her posture is right, that her legs aren't too far apart . . ."

Tory's heart rate went into overdrive. "She's sitting, okay? That's major progress! I've been working with her to do this. Can't you say anything positive?"

Tilda's smile seemed condescending. "I know this looks like a big step . . . and of course, it is. But if you don't watch her positioning, the rest of her development could be slowed."

Tory tried to bite back the rest of her reactions to Tilda's instructions, and her weariness and frustration nearly brought her to tears.

But on the way home, she stewed and told herself enough was enough. She wasn't going back to that class, and if the doctor insisted that she keep seeing Tilda, she would have to come to the house like the rest of the therapists did. Tory couldn't stand comparing Hannah to other Down's Syndrome babies. She couldn't stand knowing that she was always a little behind, even in a class of children like herself. She couldn't stand seeing the joy on the faces of the moms who saw more progress than she.

No, she and Hannah could do this alone. She would just work harder with the baby, exercise her more, spend every waking moment trying to stimulate her into talking and reaching and crawling.

If she just worked hard enough, she could make Hannah as close to normal as it was possible for her to be.

Then they would all see what a high-functioning baby she was.

Chapter Forty

The next few days crept by for Cathy like the
long, empty days following a funeral, when
grief gets its foothold. Because both Rick
and Annie worked afternoons, she stayed at
the clinic instead of rushing home at three
o'clock, as she had done when Mark was
home. She tried to concentrate on the animals in her charge, but found herself calling
her answering machine every fifteen minutes, just to see if Mark had used his telephone privilege to repent of his treatment of
her. At lunchtime, she rushed home to check
her mail, hoping he had written her a re-
morseful letter.

But nothing ever came.

Sunday, she decided to go back and suffer whatever abuse he had for her, but a storm of tears assaulted her in the parking lot, and she couldn't go in. The words "scummy mother" played through her mind like a broken record, and disappointment and anger turned her back.

As she drove home, she couldn't honestly say whether she was following Steve's advice to teach her son respect or simply nursing her wounds. Whatever her motives, she prayed that Mark would miss her and regret the things he'd said.

But as soon as visiting hours were over, she was sorry she hadn't gone. She hurt for him. He must feel abandoned, forsaken. But there was nothing she could do except wait for Wednesday.

She ran purely on nervous energy, trying to get through the days without breaking down. She spent a lot of time on her knees asking God to do a mighty work in Mark, asking him to enable Mark to take the blame for his own actions, asking him to show her what she should do.

Wednesday dawned like the bright morning after a long, miserable night, and she prayed once more about whether to see him that night.

The call came at the clinic just before noon, and her receptionist answered and called her to the phone. "I think it's Mark," the girl whispered.

Cathy attacked the phone. *"Mark?"*

"Uh . . . Mom?" His voice cracked on the word.

"Honey, are you all right?"

There was a moment of silence, as if he struggled with every syllable. "Mom, I'm sorry."

Relief flooded over her. "Mark, it's okay."

"I didn't mean to be disrespectful," he went on, as though he'd practiced the words and had to say all of them. "I was just so mad. I felt like everybody was against me, and I hated the world. I still do. But not you, Mom. I don't hate you."

"I know, honey," she whispered. "I know."

"Will you come back and see me tonight?"

"Yes, honey, I'll be there tonight, as soon as visiting hours start."

She could hear the relief in his voice, and she would have given anything to reach through the phone and hug him. "Thanks, Mom. I gotta go now. There's a line waiting behind me."

"See you later, baby," she said. "Can I bring you anything?"

"Maybe my Bible," he said. "The one I used at Miss Brenda's. It's got notes in it and stuff."

She closed her eyes and tears pushed out. "Sure, I'll bring you your Bible. Anything else?"

"If you can find any books you think I might like. It gets pretty boring in here during free time. And maybe some paper to write on."

"I'll do it, honey. I'll bring them tonight."

He said good-bye, and she heard the click. Then, collapsing against the wall, she held the phone against her chest for a moment. "Oh, Lord, thank you," she whispered. She covered her face and wept.

Her spirits soared as if they were lifted by angels, and she went through the rest of the day watching her clock. She couldn't wait to put her arms around her son again.

Chapter Forty-One

Annie begged to go with Cathy that night, so Cathy acquiesced and took her along. It took her a while to get through the checkpoint with the books, Bible, and paper, but finally, she and Annie made their way to the visitation room. She would never have believed she'd be happy to see it again.

When Mark came in, she saw that his countenance had changed. The defiance was gone, and in its place was a wide-eyed vulnerability that told her he was on the edge of tears. Cathy hugged him first, and he clung to her in a way that reaffirmed his remorse.

Annie got up and patted him roughly. "How's it going, kid?" she asked.

Mark patted her back and sat down. "Okay, I guess."

"Have you made any friends?" Cathy asked.

"Mom, he's in jail," Annie cut in. "It's not like he's the new kid in school."

"I've made some friends," Mark argued. "There are fifty of us in the same building. You'd have to be a real dork not to make any friends."

Annie leaned up with great interest. "So what are they in for? Did anybody kill anybody?"

Mark grinned. "Yeah, there's this kid who killed his teenaged sister."

"Mark!" Cathy said.

But Annie laughed. "Don't lie." She pointed to a guy talking to his family in the corner. "Like, what's he in for?"

"I don't know, Annie. Probably drugs, too."

"Anybody you know in here?" she asked.

Again, he rolled his eyes. "Yeah, Annie, three kids from my kindergarten class, and a guy from my English class last year."

"Really?" Annie asked on a shocked whisper.

"No, not really," he said, mocking her tone. "They're all new faces."

"Are any of them—"

"Nice?" Cathy butted in.

Again Mark grinned, and she could see that he was getting more comfortable in the place, that it wasn't as much of a horror as it had been the first few days.

"Some of them haven't tried to beat me up, if that's what you mean."

"Oh," she said, trying to sound enthusiastic. "Well, good."

His grin crept broader. "Mom, you don't have to worry," he said. "The guards sit up above us in this little room with glass all around it, and they watch us 24–7. If anything ever happens, they're on us like flies at a picnic."

"Then how come you got beat up the first week?" Annie demanded.

"Long story," he said. "I know what not to do now."

He sat back in his chair and looked around the room. "So, have you heard from Dad?"

Cathy exchanged looks with Annie. "No, not since court."

"Me, neither," he said quietly. He looked down at his clasped hands on the table.

"Guess he's pretty hot about what happened. I tried to call him yesterday, but he wouldn't take my call."

Cathy felt that flame rise up in her chest again. "Wouldn't take it? Are you sure?"

"Well, they said he wasn't there. I told them to leave him a message I had called. It probably embarrassed him."

"Do you blame him?" Annie said, and Cathy kicked her under the table. She didn't want any confrontations today. Nothing negative.

"So . . . I brought you some books," Cathy said, changing the subject. "And your Bible, and some paper. Boy, they really check things out in here. It takes an act of congress to get them through."

He glanced down at them, and Cathy got the impression that he didn't care much about them. She wondered if he'd just asked for the Bible to make her feel better about things.

Annie looked at her watch and got up. "Well, I've got to go. I have a date."

"What else is new?" Mark asked.

"The guy," she said, lifting her eyebrows. "It's Jimmy Donovan."

He feigned shock, and she laughed. Cathy knew he was glad Annie had come. His sister leaned down and kissed his cheek. Cathy hadn't seen that in years, and her heart jolted. "Hang in there, kiddo," Annie said. Then she straightened. "See you later, Mom. Don't get mugged in the parking lot."

"Annie!"

She watched her daughter prancing out and shook her head. Then she turned back to Mark. She saw the pleasure in his eyes. Annie's visit had done him good. "Mark, do they have chapel in here?"

"Yeah," he said. "I went Sunday."

Her eyes brightened. "You did?"

"Yeah. There's no TV or anything. When we do have free time there's nothing to do."

"What do you do with your time?"

"Well, during the day they work us to death," he said. "If we're not doing schoolwork—which, by the way, is a lot worse than what Miss Brenda used to teach, and a whole lot less interesting—then they've got me in the hot kitchen helping with the cafeteria food."

"That's the job they gave you?"

"Yeah. It's not so bad. You get to munch on snacks once in a while."

She sat back. She should be grateful that he wasn't out on a highway median picking up trash like she'd seen adult prisoners do.

He looked down at his hands. "Mom, I want you to know that I'm not one of those guys that's going to keep coming back here. I'm never going to do this again. I mean it. I'm not just saying that."

"Well, good, Mark. I hope that's true."

"And when I get home, I'll appreciate my room and my privacy, and I'll keep my clothes picked up. Really. These guards in here, they watch us constantly. You can't burp without getting into trouble."

"Well, be glad for the guards, Mark. They just might save your life."

"Tell me something I don't know," Mark said.

Cathy leaned forward and took his hand, kissed it and squeezed it, and Mark squeezed back. Then she started telling him about some of the animals she'd recently treated at the clinic, what the score of the ball game had been the other night, and the letter they'd gotten from Sylvia and Dr. Harry.

Before she knew it, visiting time was up.

Choking back tears, Mark initiated the hug this time. Cathy tried not to cry as she watched her son being taken away from her again.

Chapter Forty-Two

When Annie came in that night, she climbed onto the bed next to Cathy. "Feeling better, Mom?"

Cathy smiled. "I feel more relaxed than I have since this first happened."

"Yeah, it was a good visit."

"I've been thinking a lot about all this." Cathy fluffed her pillow and sat up in bed. "About my part in Mark's being in jail."

"Mom, you didn't *have* a part in Mark being in jail. You did everything you could to keep him from getting involved with those kids. It's not your fault."

"I know, but I still keep thinking that maybe . . ."

"Mom, you can't do that to yourself. Rick and I didn't wind up in jail, did we?"

"It's not over yet," Cathy said with a grin.

Annie slapped at her playfully, and Cathy laughed.

"You have to have faith in us, Mom," Annie said. "Rick and I, we make good decisions all the time."

"You do?" Cathy asked. "Like what?"

"Like, don't you realize we've had ample opportunity to go out and get drunk on Saturday nights?"

Cathy's stomach knotted again. She realized this conversation wasn't going to help her stay relaxed. "I had a hunch that you might have the opportunity."

"Well, we don't do it. Even Rick doesn't. I mean, most of the time he's hanging around with some of the straightest kids in Breezewood."

"He is?" she asked. "Really?"

"Yeah. The ones he works with at the grocery store. I mean, there are some partyers in the group, but they're not the ones Rick hangs with."

Cathy decided this was good news. "Well, what about you, Annie? Who do you hang with? I don't know enough about the guys you date. And some of your girlfriends, well, I can only judge them by what I see. I don't quite like the way they dress. But then I haven't always been real crazy about the way *you* dress, either."

"Big surprise," Annie said. "But really, Mom, some of the kids I hang with are partyers, but that doesn't mean I do it."

"Are you ever in the car with them when they're drinking?"

"Not if they're driving," Annie said.

Cathy closed her eyes, wishing her daughter had simply said no. "Honey, why do you want to be in their presence if they're drinking? Why can't you just hang around with people from church?"

"Well, I do a lot," Annie said. "A lot more than I ever thought I would. I mean, you know me. A couple of years ago, I wouldn't have gone near that place, and now some of my best friends are from there. I just don't feel like dropping my other friends like hot potatoes. I mean, aren't we supposed to make a difference in our world?"

"Yeah, but first I think we need to be

grounded in our faith. I'm not so sure you are."

"Well, I'm working on it, Mom. I mean, I'm better off than I used to be. All that Scripture memorizing you used to make us do."

Cathy moaned. She was embarrasssed and ashamed that, a couple of years before, she had routinely made her children memorize Scripture when she was mad at them. Brenda had pointed out that that was no way to make them fall in love with the Bible. She hadn't done it since.

"You know, they do make us memorize some Scripture in youth group. And it comes in handy every now and then."

"Really, Annie?" Cathy asked. "Are you serious?"

"Sure," she said. "When I took the SAT test I was really nervous. I thought I was going to blow it. And I started quoting to myself, 'Peace I leave with you, my peace I give to you. I do not give to you as the world gives. Let not your heart be troubled and do not be afraid.' It's from John 14:27. Mike taught it to us in a song. I remember the tune and everything." She sang a line of the song, and Cathy smiled.

"And then last week when all this happened with Mark and we were all so upset, I kept quoting to myself over and over, 'Consider it pure joy, my brothers, whenever you face trials of many kinds, because you know that the testing of your faith develops perseverance.' That's from James 1."

Cathy's eyes filled with tears, and she rolled over and hugged her daughter. "Annie, I can't tell you how much this means to me."

"Well, Mom, why do you always assume that I'm out on the street somewhere emptying beer bottles and making drug deals?"

"I don't assume that," Cathy said. "I have never assumed that."

"Well, I'm just saying you should quit making yourself out to be this horrible neglectful mother who's done everything wrong. Because apparently you've done a few things right. And if you had to weigh which one of the three of us you've done the most right with, I'd have to say it was Mark."

Cathy sat up and looked down at her. "Why?"

"Because look what you did. The minute you saw signs of trouble, you took him out of school, got him in with Miss Brenda, and had her teaching him Scripture. And, Mom, let's face it. Ever since you became a Christian, you've had us in church every time the doors open. A person doesn't have a chance to reject the gospel when you put it in front of us every time we turn around."

"Oh, people have plenty of chances to reject the gospel," she said. "Just because people are sitting in church doesn't mean they're Christians."

She had been worried about Annie, because none of her children had made a profession of faith or walked down the aisle and joined the church. Yet she had seen subtle changes in both Annie and Rick.

"I know that. I'm just telling you that you've done a good job."

Cathy lay back down, considering that. "Annie, have you got a personal relationship with Jesus? I mean, more than just knowing about him and quoting Scripture?"

The lamplight cast dark shadows on Annie's face. "Well, yeah. I use it in my life, okay? I put it into practice."

"But have you accepted Christ? Do you understand about what he did for you?"

Annie sat up and hugged her knees.

"Mom, you don't have to preach to me. I'm not Mark, okay?"

"The gospel isn't just for Mark. It's for you, too."

"And I have," she said. "One night at a youth rally. I talked to Jesus that night for the first time, and he and I have had a thing ever since."

Cathy couldn't have scripted a better answer. "Annie, I thought I was going to worry about you when you started college this fall, but now I know you're going to be all right."

Annie flopped back down and looked at the ceiling. "Oh, yeah. College."

She had noticed a coolness in Annie's voice whenever the subject of college came up. She had enrolled at the local community college for the fall, but Cathy knew she was looking for a way out. "Annie, why aren't you excited about college?"

"Well, I just don't know what I want to do yet. It seems like such a waste of time."

"An education is never a waste of time."

Annie slid off the bed. "Can we talk about it later? You need to sleep."

Cathy wasn't fooled. The college conversation could wait, but she sensed that it would be a difficult one when it came. She sat up and kissed Annie good night, then watched as her daughter left the room. She slid to her knees and whispered a prayer of tearful thanks for the night of affirmations.

Chapter Forty-Three

Tory couldn't wait to open the package that came from Leon, Nicaragua. She wondered what Sylvia had sent her. She tore into the package and pulled out the little rolls of film in plastic cylinders. Frowning, she pulled out the letter that came along with it. One short note was addressed to Tory individually, and the other was to all three neighbors. At the top of the letter were explicit instructions not to read it until they were all together.

She folded the long letter back up and stuck it in her pocket, then skimmed through the short one that was addressed to her.

Dear Tory,

It cost too much to get film developed here so I was hoping you wouldn't mind if I sent you the film. These are pictures of other children who have come here to get fed. I thought you and the girls could use them in your presentations if you wouldn't mind getting them made into slides. Give your precious little Hannah a kiss for me, and Brittany and Spencer, too.

I love you,
Sylvia

Tory looked down at the cylinders. Here, she knew, were priceless pictures that would move people into helping. But how would she work this around her schedule with Hannah? She supposed she could give up a little more sleep.

"Spencer, Brittany," she cried. The two kids came running from the back of the house. "Get in the car. We've got to go get some film developed."

"Can we get candy?" Spencer asked.

Tory checked Hannah's diaper. "No, no candy."

"Potato chips?" Brittany asked.

"It's too close to suppertime." Cradling Hannah, she headed out the door. "Come on, kids."

"Where are we going?" Brittany asked.

"To the mall, to that one-hour photo place. Miss Sylvia sent us some pictures, and I want to see them as soon as we can."

Tory paid extra to have the pictures developed quickly, and as soon as they walked out of the photo shop, Brittany begged to see them. Tory put little Hannah in her stroller, then sat on a bench with Brittany and Spencer on either side of her, and started flipping through the pictures. One by one, she saw the faces of hungry children with glazed looks in their eyes, swollen little bellies, toothpick legs.

"What's wrong with them? Are they sick?" Brittany asked.

Tory shook her head. "They're hungry. They don't have enough food to eat."

"Why not?" she asked.

"Because they're poor."

"Why don't they just go to the grocery store?" Spencer asked.

"Because they don't have them there. At least, not like we have. Miss Sylvia said that the stores there have a whole bunch of one thing but not enough of everything."

"One thing like what?" Brittany asked.

"Like hats or something," Tory said. "But not food."

"Hats?" Spencer asked. "Why aren't they wearing them?"

"Well, I didn't mean hats, for sure," Tory said. "I was just using that as an example."

Spencer grabbed the next picture and studied the little boy. "He's not wearing a hat."

"I know. I was just telling you . . ."

"None of them are wearing hats."

She couldn't help laughing. "I was trying to explain that, instead of having a lot of different things on the shelves of the grocery stores, they only have a few things. Those things are usually things they don't need."

"Well, why don't they just get food?"

"It's a long story," she said, "but we're trying to help Dr. Harry and Miss Sylvia get money so they can buy it and feed these children. It's real important."

She looked into the envelope; yes, the box of slides was there too. They would need them for their presentations.

"Why are there children who don't have

food?" Spencer asked. "Why can't we give them some of ours?"

"That's a good question," Tory said, "and that's exactly what we're going to try to do. We're very blessed, you know. We never have to go hungry, and we have those wonderful grocery stores with everything in the world."

"You don't think they're wonderful," Brittany said. "You always hate to go."

"I always say I hate a lot of things, but then I find out that somebody is worse off than I am, and I feel really bad about it."

As she loaded her children back into the car, she resolved that she was going to stop whining. There were people with genuine problems, much worse than hers. Even Cathy's problem was monumental compared to Tory's. She had been a terrible neighbor. She needed to do what Brenda had done and take Cathy a meal.

She changed her mind about heading home and pulled into the parking lot of the grocery store she frequented.

"What are we doing here?" Spencer asked. "Getting candy?"

"No," Tory said. "I need to pick up a few

things. I'm going to make a casserole for Miss Cathy tonight."

"Is she hungry, too?" Spencer asked.

"Probably," she said. "But that's not why I'm doing it. Food is a good way to tell her I love her."

Brittany and Spencer pondered that as she unloaded them again and headed into the grocery store.

Chapter Forty-Four

Sylvia was exhausted by the time she had fed all the orphans in the school and all the families that had come to eat that day. It was way past dark when she finally made it home. She found Harry sitting quietly in his recliner, reading his Bible through bifocals in the light of a lamp.

She went to stand in front of him. "Okay," she said. "I'm ready."

"Ready for what?" he asked, looking up at her.

"I'm ready to sell the house," she said. "There's no other way. We've got to do it to raise the money. More and more families are hearing that we've got provisions, and they're coming to get food. Harry, we're going to run out, and there's no way on this earth that I can tell those people I can't feed them."

He closed his Bible and dropped his feet. "Sit down," he said. "You look really tired."

She sat down and realized how little energy she had left. She'd been on her feet most of the day. "So what do we do? What's the next step?" she asked.

"I guess we call the States and get a realtor to put a sign up."

She thought about that. "I have to tell the girls first."

"Okay. When?"

"Soon," she said. "We can't wait. We have to do something quick."

Harry took her hand and pulled her onto his lap. Holding her, he said, "I'm really surprised that you would come to this decision on your own. I didn't think you were going to agree to it."

She put her arms around his neck and laid her head on his shoulder. "I don't know," she said. "I should have been willing to turn it over in the first place. There are so many things we need here. It was my last hold on home, almost like a lifeline to Cedar Circle. But I don't need the house. I still have the girls."

"Yes, you do," he whispered. "They're not going to cut you off just because you're not a property owner in the neighborhood anymore." He kissed the top of her head. "I'm proud of you, you know. This means you're totally committed to your work here. Completely, unequivocally, without looking back."

"What was it that Jesus said?" Sylvia asked. "'He who puts his hand to the plow and looks back is not fit for the kingdom of God.'"

"He did say that," Harry agreed.

"Well, I've got both hands on the plow," she said, "and all I can see is a field of children who are starving to death. I might as well send that treasure to heaven. There's no sense in holding onto it."

"All right," he said. "I'll get the ball rolling with the realtor as soon as you've told Brenda, Tory, and Cathy. Now you go on to bed."

With that decision made, Sylvia dragged herself to their room and fell into the bed.

Chapter Forty-Five

Cathy could count on her kids for overlapping crises—after all, she had three of them, and they had each vowed not to let their mother's life get dull. So when Annie walked into Cathy's clinic just before it closed and announced that she wasn't going to college that fall, Cathy wasn't all that surprised.

Her daughter made the announcement as calmly as if she were telling Cathy that she was going to a friend's house or getting her hair cut. She stood there happily, her hair pulled up in a flip ponytail, and big dangly earrings slapping against her face. She was chomping on a piece of gum.

"Annie, you're already enrolled. What do you mean you're not going?"

"I'm going to get a real job and skip college."

She blew out her impatience. "Annie, a full-time job is no picnic. And I'm not going to let you loaf. A few months of having to support yourself and you'll be begging to go to school. You'll hate the routine of a job."

"Well, *you* don't hate your job," Annie challenged.

"No, I don't," Cathy said, "but I happen to have college degrees, so I'm able to do something I love. What are you able to do, Annie?"

"I don't know," she said. "I could get a job at the mall."

"And do you ever intend to move out and get an apartment of your own, maybe get married, have a family?"

"Well, yeah, sure. Someday."

"And how do you plan to support yourself?"

She twisted her face and leaned back against the wall. "I don't know. I haven't thought that far out. All I know is I hate school and I don't think I can stand it for four more years. This thing with Mark has just reminded me how precious my freedom is. I don't want to be institutionalized."

Cathy rolled her eyes at the melodrama. "Institutionalized? Annie, school can hardly be compared with juvenile detention."

"But I bet it *feels* the same. Mom, I just don't want to go to college."

Cathy was getting flustered. She hadn't prepared for this. She raked her fingers through her hair, feeling her spirits sinking again to their level before the breakthrough with Mark. "Look, could we talk about this later? I'm really kind of busy right now."

"Sure," Annie said and popped her gum. "How 'bout we talk about it in September after I've already missed registration?"

"No," Cathy said, "I meant that we'll assume you're going to college this fall until I'm miraculously convinced otherwise. You see, it's like this. You live in my house and you do as I say. I'm not sacrificing another child to the world. You either go to college or you find a way to support yourself, period."

Annie looked at her as if she'd disowned her. "You would think I came in here and told you I was pregnant."

"No, Annie, if you came in here and told me you were pregnant, there would be a marked difference in how I responded. Trust me."

Annie smiled, as if she wished she could pull that particular string. "So when are you coming home?"

"In a few minutes," Cathy said. "I just need to finish up some paperwork."

"Well, Miss Brenda left a message at home for you to call her. She said that Miss Sylvia is going to call tonight, and she wants to talk to all three of you."

"About what?"

"She didn't know," Annie said.

Cathy shuffled the papers on her desk and got up. "Well, okay. I guess I'd better get home. I don't want to miss that." She took off her lab coat and hung it up. "Annie, I'll meet you at home."

"After the big phone call, can we talk some more about college?"

"We'll see. But I'm not changing my mind, Annie. You're going to college."

"What if I get a job? I could get one tonight, you know. Between now and sup-pertime, I could join the military or get into a management program at the mall. I could be earning more than you before the day's out."

Cathy retrieved her purse from its hook on the wall and dug for her keys. "Tell you what, Annie. If you get a job making more than I make, you can skip college. But it has to be legal and moral."

"Oh, right," Annie teased. "There you go laying down a bunch of conditions."

Cathy escorted Annie out of the clinic and locked the door behind them.

Chapter Forty-Six

Cathy and Brenda gathered at Tory's house at seven that night, when Sylvia had promised to call. Tory laid out the pictures of the Nicaraguan children on the table, and they tried to organize them into the right order for a slide show. Cathy would take the first speaking engagement for the following Sunday afternoon, since Brenda went weak in the knees at the prospect, and Tory had committed to speak at another church that evening.

They were certain that was what Sylvia was calling about. It was probably a pep talk,

Cathy thought, or she was making sure that they got all the details right. They'd kept in touch by e-mail about the requests coming in for them to speak, and she supposed Sylvia was afraid they would blow it.

When the phone rang, they each picked up on a different extension in Tory's house. "Hello?" Tory said.

"Are you all together?" Sylvia asked. Her voice sounded so clear she might have been next door.

"Yes, we're here." They each gave their greetings, and she spent a few valuable minutes asking about Mark and Hannah and the wrecked cars in Brenda's driveway. Then she got to the point.

"I wanted to talk to you girls and let you know something before you heard it from someone else."

Cathy didn't like the sound of that. Her chest tightened. "What is it, Sylvia?"

"It's the house."

Cathy glanced at Tory, who stood across the room holding another phone to her ear.

"The house? What house?"

"My house. The empty one?"

All three women got quiet.

"Girls, we've decided to sell it."

"No!" Tory's cry carried through the house. "Sylvia, you can't."

Cathy sat down, and Tory leaned back against the wall.

"Sylvia, this is a big step," Cathy said. "Are you sure you've given it enough thought? This is your *life.* It's your history."

"No, *this* is my life now," Sylvia said. "And I'll have my history no matter what I do with the house. It's the future I have to think of now—of these children, and the fact that we don't have enough money to keep feeding them. I have to think of the starving parents and the medicine Harry needs for these people."

"But we're raising money, Sylvia," Tory said. "Both Cathy and I have speaking engagements Sunday. We were just organizing the slide show. We're on it, Sylvia."

"I know you are," she said. "And I need for you to go ahead with that, because it might be a while before the house sells. But Harry's calling our realtor tomorrow, and she's going to list the house and put up a sign. I just wanted you to be prepared. I wanted you to understand."

Cathy looked at Tory and saw the way the

light caught the tears in her eyes. Brenda came out of the back room with a cordless phone to her ear. "Sylvia, please don't," Cathy said.

"We were hoping you could come back when you retire," Brenda said in a cracked voice. "It's your house. Nobody else can fill it."

"That's sweet." She could hear the tears in Sylvia's voice. "But I have to do what I've been called to do. And we need this money. It would do so much for the children. And I can come back there and visit and stay with one of you."

"But you won't," Tory said. "Your own kids don't live here anymore. You'll go to see them when you're in the States. You won't have time to come here, if you don't have your house to bring you back."

"It's not the house that makes Cedar Circle my home," she said. "It's you. Your families. I love you and I *will* come back to see you. And I'm going to keep in touch as if you were all still my next-door neighbors."

Silence weighed heavily over the line. Finally, Brenda spoke again. "We understand, Sylvia. You do have to follow God's leading. We're just a little sad for us. But how wonderful that you've come from not even wanting to go to Nicaragua, to being willing to sell your house for those people."

"That's how you can know it's God," Sylvia said. "It's not like me at all."

Later, when they'd gotten off the phone, Cathy, Tory, and Brenda sat around the pictures on Tory's kitchen table, staring at each other with smudged eyes. "It was one thing to have the Gonzales family living there," Tory said. "They were temporary. Just house-sitting, sort of. I always thought Sylvia and Harry would come back."

"What kind of people do you think will buy it?" Cathy asked. "Retired people? People with children?"

"Maybe they'll have kids the ages of ours," Brenda said. "Maybe they'll fit right in."

"And maybe they'll be antisocial and let their grass grow to their hips," Tory brooded.

"Maybe it'll be an axe murderer," Cathy said, and as her eyes met Brenda's and Tory's, a slow smile broke out on her face. The others smiled, too.

Brenda took both of their hands. "We've got to support her in this," she said. "Sylvia's being obedient to God. He never said it wouldn't hurt."

"Maybe the house won't sell," Tory said.

"Yeah." Cathy grinned again. "Maybe we could put up roadblocks. Make the neighborhood look less attractive. Hey, I'm willing to let *my* grass grow."

"I'm doing my part," Brenda said. "I have two beat-up cars out in the driveway."

"And I'm the mother of a convict," Cathy said. She tried to smile at the flippant remark, but it didn't feel funny.

"And I could always sic Spencer on them," Tory said. "Let any lookers know that Dennis the Menace comes with the neighborhood."

They all laughed, then wiped at their tears again. "At least we still have Sylvia, no matter how far away she is."

"But I don't look forward to seeing someone else's furniture being carried into that house," Tory said.

"Or hers out," Cathy added. "Boy, will that be painful." She set her chin on her hand. "Feels like a new era. Like things will never be the same again."

"They won't," Brenda said. "But maybe they'll be better. Maybe God wants us to turn this corner. Maybe he has something special waiting. And if he doesn't, the house won't sell."

"We can hope," Cathy said. "And raise

money like crazy while we're waiting. Then maybe she won't need to sell it anymore."

That was the best idea any of them had come up with yet, so they set about organizing their photographs and planning speaking engagements.

Chapter Forty-Seven

As Cathy crossed the cul de sac to return home, an old pickup truck pulled up to her curb, with an elderly weather-beaten man behind the wheel. Annie was just pulling into the driveway, and she got out of her car and met Cathy in the yard before the man got out.

"Mom, I know you and Steve are kind of on hold, but really, you can do better than that."

Cathy elbowed her daughter in the ribs. "Who is he?"

"Like I know?"

Cathy crossed the yard to meet him as he got out of the truck. He smiled at her, flashing a decaying front tooth. "May I help you?" she asked.

"Yes, ma'am," he said. "Sorry to come by so late, but I just need to scope out the backyard and make sure everything's ready for tomorrow."

"Ready for tomorrow?" Cathy asked. "What's happening tomorrow?"

"We're starting work on the new addition on the house, that's what," the man said. "Ain't nobody told you?"

She frowned. "Well, no. I mean, I thought we postponed it."

"Can't postpone it," he said. "You got a contract."

Cathy thought back to the document she and Steve had signed with the contractor weeks ago. The man had so much business that he'd put them on a long list and promised to get started at least a month before the wedding. He had the slabs poured weeks ago, but he was late beginning the construction. Neither Cathy nor Steve had thought to tell him the wedding had been called off.

"Well, your boss has so much business it won't matter to him. He can tear up the contract, can't he?"

"No, ma'am," the truck driver said. "Never heard of him tearing up one yet. He's got him a lawyer, though, that presses pretty hard when it comes to breach of contract."

Cathy gaped at him. "Are you telling me that you're going to start work on my house tomorrow whether I want you to or not?"

"All I'm doing is following orders, ma'am. He told me to come and make sure everything was ready to start."

"How do you mean, 'ready'?" Cathy asked. "Apparently it's not 'ready,' since I don't want it done—at least not yet."

"Take it up with him. Mind if I walk around to the back and look at the foundation?" He started around the back before she could answer.

"Excuse me!" She trotted behind the man. "Do you have your boss's phone number on you? I need to talk to him immediately."

"Yes, ma'am," he said. He pulled a leaky ballpoint pen out of his ink-stained pocket. "Got something to write on?"

She didn't, so she stuck out her hand. "Here, just write it on my hand. I'll go in and call him right now."

He seemed amused that he was writing on flesh, but he jotted the number down. Then scanning the work that had already been done, he said, "Tell him it looks okay. Won't be no problem starting in the morning."

"There definitely *will* be a problem starting in the morning," Cathy said, "but I'll take care of that right now."

She went into the house and dialed the number. A man yelled hello into the phone, and she could hear something like a jackhammer buzzing behind him.

"Mr. Barksdale?" she asked.

"Yes, ma'am."

At least he was polite. "This is Cathy Flaherty over on Cedar Circle."

"Yes, ma'am," he said. "Sorry it took us so long to get to your house, but I sent my man out there tonight to check to make sure we could start in the morning."

"Well, that's just it. He's here," Cathy said. "Look, about that contract. I was wondering if there was any way we could just cancel it. We'll do another one later when we're ready to build."

"Cancel it?" he asked. "What happened? Your boyfriend dump you?"

She caught her breath. "No, he didn't dump me!"

"You dumped him, then?"

"No! Nobody dumped anybody. We've just postponed the wedding for a while."

"Well, I'm sorry, ma'am. After the foundation was poured and everything."

"Yes, well . . . We'll build eventually, but I just can't handle it right now."

"I understand completely," he said, though that jackhammer buzzing in the background made her wonder if he could even hear her. "No problem, ma'am."

"Then you can refund our money?" she asked.

He hesitated. "I'm sorry. Come again?"

"I asked if you could refund our check," she yelled.

"Well, now, nobody said anything about that."

"I just did. I said it. If we're not having the work done yet, then we shouldn't have to pay."

"But there's a contract, ma'am."

"But you just said we could get out of that. You just said—"

The jackhammer on his end stopped. "Oh, I'll postpone the building," he said. "Even cancel it entirely, if you want. But I can't return the money." He chuckled, as if the whole concept was absurd. "If I did that, I'd have folks pulling out on me left and right. Contracts are binding, ma'am."

"But you have business coming out your ears! You're already weeks later than we agreed. It won't hurt you to let this go. I've been having some personal problems. If you have any compassion at all . . ."

"Ma'am, if my business hung on people's love lives, I'd be bankrupt in a month."

"My personal problems have nothing to do with my love life!" She wadded the roots of her hair in frustration. "Look, would you call my fiancé and let *him* explain this to you?"

"Fiancé? Thought you said you weren't getting married."

"I don't know what we're going to do. Just call him, will you?" She spouted out his number at work, then hung up the phone.

"Mom, that man's out there spray-painting the yard," Annie said.

"Spray-painting it?" Cathy asked. She ran to the back door and flung it open. The man was painting lines on their grass with bright orange neon paint.

"Why won't they listen to me?" She swung around to Annie. "Am I invisible? Can people not hear me?"

"I hear you, Mom, loud and clear," Annie

said. "I've never had any trouble hearing you."

Cathy looked back in the yard again. "Okay, if he wants to paint up our yard, that's fine. I'll just go rinse it off as soon as he leaves. I don't have the energy to fight with him again."

She sat down at the kitchen table, her fingers threaded through her hair.

"He's leaving," Annie said, still peering out the window.

Cathy listened until his old truck started up, vibrating the neighborhood.

"Crisis passed," Cathy said with a sigh. "Steve will take care of it. That was all I needed. A construction project in the middle of everything."

"Maybe I could get a job doing construction," Annie said thoughtfully as she stared at the backyard. "Instead of college, you know? I can paint lines in neon."

"Yeah, and you're sometimes just as deaf as those guys are." She got back up and went to the box she'd brought home with the pictures of the Nicaraguan children. "I'm just going to forget about it. Steve will take care of it. I have to organize these pictures. Annie, will you help me?"

Annie looked at her watch. "Right now?"

"You weren't doing anything," Cathy said. "You've been hanging around talking about construction work." She went to the closet and got out the slide projector, set it on the coffee table, and focused it on the wall.

Annie shrugged. "Well, I guess I could help for a little while," she said. She sat down on the couch next to Cathy and started flipping through the papers that were stacked under the slides. "So what are these?"

"They're Sylvia's narratives," Cathy said. "I've got to figure out which thing goes with which slide and make sure everything's in order. It's for the presentation I'm doing Sunday."

"Cool," Annie said. "Yeah, I'll help." She put the first slide in, and they saw the group of orphans who lived at the school where Sylvia helped. It looked like any other class of children, only the kids' clothes were less elaborate, more faded.

Cathy ran through the narrative that Tory had given her about the picture. Annie changed slides—a close-up of three children who didn't look quite as healthy as the ones in the previous picture. Their hair was dirty and messed up, stringing in their eyes.

They were barefoot and dressed in clothes with holes and dirt.

"Who are these?" Annie asked.

Cathy searched through her notes. "These are kids from the community who come to get food," she said. "Look how skinny they are."

Annie's eyes grew serious. "They are skinny," she said. She turned to the next slide: a little boy with toothpick legs and a distended belly. His eyes were dull.

"Says here his name is Miguel," Cathy said.

"Miguel?" Annie asked. "What about him? Is he an orphan?"

"No, he's got a mother, according to this. But they don't have food. His father was killed in the hurricane, and his mother hasn't been able to make a living. It says she brought him to the orphanage for Sylvia to keep until she could get on her feet." Annie stared at the little boy who looked no more than four. "Mom, that's awful. Don't they have, like, welfare or something?"

"No, Annie, they don't. That's an American thing. Besides, the Bible tells us that we're supposed to help people in need, not wait for the government to do it. So that's what

Sylvia is trying to do, and that's why we're trying to raise money. So little boys like Miguel won't have to suffer."

She changed slides and saw Sylvia holding the little boy on her hip. He had his arms around her neck and was kissing her on the cheek.

Annie smiled. "He looks better here, doesn't he?"

"Yeah," Cathy said. "Go to the next slide."

Annie switched slides, and a picture of the same little boy came up on the screen. His eyes had a twinkle in them now, and his stomach wasn't swollen. His little legs had fattened up to normal proportions.

"Oh, look," Cathy said. "This is after they've been feeding him for a month. He looks so much better. Look at his eyes."

"He's in there now," Annie said. "He just looked like a little shell, before."

"He's just one example," Cathy said. "Go to the next one."

They went to the next one and saw another "before" picture of a little girl with stringy hair, dirt on her face, and a chipped front tooth. She was wearing a smock dress that was too little for her. In the next picture, she saw her with Sylvia, playing with some other children. Then there was a picture of her eating beans and rice out of a bowl . . . then an "after" picture a couple of months after they had been feeding her. She looked normal and healthier and had that same sparkle in her eye that Miguel had had.

"Mom, that's amazing," Annie said. "I always thought of Sylvia being over there just preaching to people, standing on street corners and passing out tracts or something. I didn't realize she was really helping people."

Cathy gave a dry laugh. "Annie, how can you say that? Sharing Christ with people *is* helping them!"

"Oh, I know it is," Annie said. "I mean, in theory. But the truth is she's doing more than that. She's filling their little stomachs."

"Well, not for long," Cathy said. "If we don't get people to send her money, she's not going to be able to fill anybody's stomach. She and Dr. Harry have decided to sell their house to raise it."

"No way! Mom!"

"I know. It makes me sick. But maybe if we raise enough money through the churches, they'll reconsider."

Annie switched slides, and Cathy came back to sit down beside her. They saw Sylvia and some of the other missionaries working in the orphanage, teaching school to the children who were grouped according to their ages. They were all clean and well cared for.

"They didn't come to her like this," Cathy said. "Look at the next one."

Annie put the next slide in and flashed it on the wall. It was a shot of some of the same children she had just seen, only they were in rags and covered with dirt and mud, sores and scrapes. Some of them were crying, and their noses were crusted with mucus. They were all hopelessly skinny and looked desperately afraid.

Cathy swallowed. "That was when they came to her after the hurricane," she said. "Her friends, the other two missionaries, thought they were going down there to build a school. They couldn't get any students to come to it, but then the hurricane hit and orphaned children started showing up, brought by people who had no way to care for them. And they finally realized that God hadn't sent them there to build a school at all. He sent them there to build an orphanage."

Annie's eyes rounded as she looked at

her mother. "Mom, that's awesome," she whispered.

"Yeah, only they need lots more workers. They don't have enough. And they need money."

Annie looked back at the slide. "And we're sitting here so fat and happy."

Cathy grinned. "Annie, what do you weigh?"

"A hundred ten pounds." She giggled. "Well, I didn't mean literally fat. I just meant that we have everything we need. And even most of the stuff we want."

"Sylvia said they can feed 100 children—maybe even 150—on $400 a month," Cathy said. "One child, for four dollars at the most. For a *month*. Isn't that amazing?"

"Yeah," Annie whispered. "Awesome."

Cathy saw the tears in her daughter's eyes as she flipped through the slides, watching the images on the wall as if these people were coming to life before her. It moved Cathy to see that Annie could be touched this way.

"So do you want to come help me at the luncheon Sunday?" she asked. "I'm going to need help with the slide projector, and since you've already been through the slides, you'd know what to do."

Annie dabbed at the tears dotting her eyes. "Sure, I can do that," she said. "It's the least I can do, I guess. I have a date with Jimmy, but I can get out of it." She considered the next slide. "You know how I've been saving for that new CD player?"

"Yeah," Cathy said.

"I don't need it," Annie said. "What if I just send the money to Miss Sylvia? Would it help much?"

"How much is it?" Cathy asked.

"I've got about $100 so far."

Cathy smiled. "Annie, do you think feeding twenty-five kids for a month is 'doing something'? Because that's how many kids a hundred dollars would feed. Maybe even more."

"Well, yeah, but I mean, is that really true, or is that just a figure Miss Sylvia made up to make it sound dramatic?"

"It's true, honey," she said. "Send her the money, if you want to. It'll give you a lot more satisfaction than the CD player."

"I will," Annie whispered. Her face softened even more as she watched the images Sylvia had sent of the rest of the children.

Chapter Forty-Eight

Saturday night, Annie got dressed for her dinner date with Jimmy Donovan, one of the most sought-after guys at the community college. She had pined after the "older man" her entire senior year of high school, but it wasn't until she'd graduated that he'd finally asked her out.

When he showed up in a pair of shorts and tennis shoes and announced that they were going to the soccer field to meet his friends rather than to the restaurant, she was a little miffed. Still, he was the most eligible college guy she knew, so she figured he was worth changing clothes for.

It also made her feel a little better about canceling her Sunday afternoon date with him.

"Jimmy," she said, trying to get his attention as he tossed the Frisbee toward his friends. "Could you give it a rest for a minute? I need to talk to you."

"Yeah? What about?" He caught the Frisbee and spun it back.

"Would you be terribly mad at me if I don't go to the swimming party tomorrow afternoon?" Annie asked.

Jimmy turned to her as if she had slapped him.

"What do you mean, you can't go? You have to go. You *said* you would." He missed the Frisbee as it flew back to him and gave it an annoyed look.

"Well, I know, but something's come up. My mom needs me to help her with a luncheon. We're trying to raise money . . ."

He set his hands on his waist, looking disgusted. "If you couldn't go, you could have told me earlier so I could have gotten another date."

Annie grunted. "Well, excuse me. I didn't think it was that big of a deal."

"Well, it is, okay?"

"Come *on,* Donovan!" his friend J.J. shouted from across the field.

Jimmy retrieved the Frisbee and threw it back. "So does this have something to do with your jailbird brother?"

Fire ignited in Annie's eyes, and she intercepted the Frisbee before he could grab it and held it at her side as she turned her furious face to his. "No, it is not about my brother," she said, "and if you ever call him a jailbird again, you're going to regret it. It just so happens that I'm going to help my mother speak at a luncheon about our friend Sylvia's missionary work in Nicaragua."

He rolled his eyes as if he couldn't believe she would come up with such a lame excuse. "You have got to be kidding. You'd choose that over a swimming party at Sara Beth Simpson's house?"

She wondered if he could really be that shallow. "Jimmy, Sylvia's working with these little kids over there and they're starving to death. They're malnourished; they have bloated bellies and toothpick legs. And she's got to raise money so she can feed them. Sylvia's already gone back to Nicaragua, but my mother's going to stand in for her at a church that invited Sylvia to speak. I'm going to help with the slides. I'm going to show pictures of sad little children who have nothing. And, yeah, I'm glad to say that I consider that a little more important than splashing around in Sara Beth Simpson's pool."

"Hey, your mother can do this without you. She's just trying to keep you away from me."

"She doesn't even know you," Annie said. "Why would she do that? My mother didn't force me to cancel this date. I'm doing the slides, and I sure would like to think that you had enough depth to understand."

"Fine!" He grabbed the Frisbee out of her hand and ripped it back with all the anger he felt. "You just go ahead. And I'll see if I can find another date to go with me to Sara Beth's."

Annie set her hands on her hips. "Well, you just do that, Jimmy. Have fun."

He looked at his watch. "Wonder if Karen Singer's home? Maybe she still doesn't have a date."

"Karen Singer?" she asked. "You're going to take Karen Singer to the swimming party?"

"Hey, I've got to take somebody. I'm not going to show up by myself."

"Heaven forbid," Annie said. "That might

ruin your reputation as a player. You know, I don't think I wanted to go with you, anyway. You'd probably just be watching all the girls in their bikinis and ignoring me, anyway."

"Hey, you're lucky I even give you the time of day, little high school twerp."

"Little high school twerp?" Annie repeated. "I can't believe you said that. Take me home."

"No," he said, "I'm playing Frisbee with my friends."

"Fine," she said. "Then I'll walk."

She heard him laugh as she started off over the hill and back down the road that would lead down Signal Mountain. Maybe there would be a pay phone somewhere along the way, so she could call her mother and have her come get her. If not, she could get home on pure fury. She was sorry she had invested so much time in Jimmy over the past year, pining away for him and dreaming of the day he would ask her out. When he had, she had felt so privileged. But not privileged enough to forsake hungry kids to show up like a trophy on his arm. *How dare he?* She wiped her tears away, determined not to cry another one for him. There were other guys. She was better off.

But as she stormed down the street, the

tears pushed into her eyes again. She smeared them away and told herself this was a small price to pay.

The thought of the little boy Miguel propelled her faster, each step giving her new purpose. There were other little boys like Miguel, other little girls with sick stomachs and dull eyes who didn't even know that they needed help. It was the least she could do. The very least.

Chapter Forty-Nine

Cathy was nervous during church the next morning, wondering why she had agreed to speak at the luncheon that afternoon. She had enough stress in her life. She was a veterinarian, not a spcaker. If those poor Nicaraguan kids were depending on her, then they were in deeper trouble than they knew.

But true to her commitment, she left her church after the service and hurried over to the church where the luncheon was being held.

"You can do it, Mom," Annie said as they pulled into the small parking lot.

"I'll be glad when it's over," Cathy told her. "I just hope I'm not wasting my time and all of theirs."

"You're not," Annie assured her.

They pulled into a parking place. Cathy's hands shook as she gathered up the stack of things on the seat next to her. Annie got the box on the floor at her feet.

A wave of dizziness washed over Cathy, and she leaned back in her seat. "I've got to stop a minute," she said. "I need to calm down."

"Okay," Annie said. "Just take a deep breath. You'll be all right."

Cathy looked up at the front doors of the church. "I don't know anybody in there. Do you think they know about Mark?"

"I don't know. Did you tell them?"

"No, but most of the people in this area know me. I treat their animals. Mark's arrest was in the paper, and everybody in town is talking about it."

"Well, they probably do know then, Mom," Annie said. "But that doesn't mean they won't listen to you."

Cathy forced herself to get out, but she leaned against the fender of the car and closed her eyes. She heard Annie's door close and sensed her daughter coming to stand beside her. "I don't know why I ever agreed to do this," Cathy said. "They don't care about any of this. They just have this luncheon once a month, and they needed a speaker. That's all."

"You agreed to it for little Miguel," Annie said. "That's all the reason you need. And if they don't care now, they will. Now come on. Let's go. I didn't miss that swimming party for nothing."

Cathy opened her eyes. "What swimming party?"

Annie shook off the question and shifted the box with the slide projector. "Just some stupid swimming party at Sara Beth Simpson's house. I was supposed to go as Jimmy's date."

Cathy's eyes widened. "That was the date you cancelled? For me?"

"Not for you, Mom. For Miguel, and for Sylvia, and all those other little kids."

Cathy's heart rate settled, and she stood straighter. "Annie, I'm so proud of you."

"Don't be," she said. "It's really a pathetic trade-off. They're starving, so I miss a swimming party. It's not a big sacrifice, Mom; I wouldn't get excited about it."

"But just the fact that you would do something like that. It's unselfish and mature. I'm just so surprised."

Annie grinned and looked up at the sky. "Come on, Mom. You're making me sound like a heathen. You raised me to be a decent person, okay?"

"Well, decent people sometimes choose swimming parties over slide shows."

"I know," Annie said. "But I made my choice. Now come on. Let's go in. I'm sweltering."

"Wait." Cathy grabbed her hand and stopped her. "Let's pray. I don't think I can go in there without it."

"Okay, Mom," Annie said. "Whatever you say."

Cathy closed her eyes, and Annie followed suit. Cathy asked God to help her through this, to give her the words, and to work on the hearts of those who heard and watched. When she said "amen," she felt peace wash over her where dizziness threatened just a moment ago. It was going to be all right.

"I'm ready now," she said. Annie was quiet as she followed her inside.

An hour later, Cathy stood at the front of

the room, amazed as the hundred people in attendance began passing their checks forward, along with pledge cards and notes of encouragement for Sylvia. She stood at the front as, one by one, they came up and told her how much the slide show had moved them, and how much her scripted words had convicted them.

She looked through the audience to find Annie. There she was—over to one side, talking animatedly to a group of people as if she, too, were selling them on the idea of helping Sylvia. It amazed Cathy that her daughter could have an intelligent conversation with adults concerning something other than herself or her social life. Maybe Annie was growing up.

It was over an hour more before the fellowship hall emptied of the guests. As Cathy gathered up the slides she had so carefully laid out for Annie, she saw Annie flipping through the stack of checks.

"Mom, you're not going to believe this," she whispered.

"What?"

"Well, if I'm counting right—it looks like we have almost three thousand dollars here."

"Really?" Cathy eyed the stack. "Are you sure, Annie?"

"Yeah, I'm sure. Mom, you did great. In fact, one of these checks is mine. I had planned to give it to you so you'd feel like you raised something, even if no one else gave." She laughed. "Guess you did okay without me."

Cathy grinned. "You decided to give them your CD player money?"

"Decided?" she asked. "How can anybody decide not to? I was thinking of selling my clothes and all my shoes just to raise more. That's how good you were."

"That's how good the Holy Spirit is," she said. "Annie, you don't know how much this is going to mean to those kids."

"I think I do," Annie said.

Cathy hugged her, then gathered up the rest of her things and loaded them into a box. "So, is there still time for you to make that swimming party?"

Annie looked away. "No, I don't think so."

"Come on, they're probably still there. It's early."

"Yeah, but I don't want to go. Jimmy's a jerk, and I don't want to be around him. Besides that, he's got another date."

"Are you kidding? He got another date just because you backed out?"

"Yep. That's the way he is," she said. "But it's good I found out now. I don't want to invest any more time in him. He's definitely high maintenance."

Cathy smiled. Prayers were being answered about her children. She hoped God was answering the ones for Mark as powerfully as he was the ones for Annie.

Chapter Fifty

Tory was already busy when Barry got up for work, giving Hannah a breathing treatment to break up the phlegm in her lungs. As the child lay in her seat with the breathing mask strapped on her face, Tory held her feet and made pedaling motions.

"Do you ever stop?" Barry asked, standing rumpled and groggy at the living room door.

Tory glanced back at him. "She was up and rattling. She has to breathe."

"I'm not talking about the breathing. I'm talking about the exercising. Aren't you afraid she's overdoing it? Won't you get her worn out before her class?"

Tory hadn't told him of her decision to quit the class. She knew he wouldn't understand, and she couldn't risk having him insist. "She'll be okay," she said.

He bent over her and moved his face close to hers. "It's you I'm worried about."

"Me? I'm fine."

"I never see you when you're not working with her. You need a break. Just wait and do it in class today."

She thought of telling him, but the words lodged in her throat.

"Tell you what." He straightened up. "I'll take my lunch hour during her class, and I'll take her so you can have some time off."

She looked up at him, knowing she'd been caught. "Well, uh . . . ordinarily . . . that would be fine . . . but to be perfectly honest . . ." Her voice veered off, and she searched for the right way to say it so that he would agree with her.

She laughed. "It's the funniest thing. See, that class—" The medicine attached to Hannah's mask began slurping, and she cut the machine off. "I was planning to keep her home today because of her cold."

"She always has a cold." He took off Hannah's mask and lifted her out of her seat.

"But today it's worse than usual. I just thought it wouldn't hurt to miss."

He kissed Hannah's fat cheek. "Well, I guess that's reasonable. Isn't it, Hannah?" He cradled her and kissed her belly, and the child smiled. "Here, go to Mommy," he said. "Daddy has to shower for work."

Tory took her, and as Barry left the room, she felt that familiar surge of guilt that she hadn't been honest about quitting the school. But by the time he found out, Hannah would have progressed so far that it would be clear she'd done the right thing.

Then, instead of protesting, he'd praise her.

As she took Hannah to the kitchen to feed her before she got Spencer and Brittany up, she told herself she was doing the right thing.

Chapter Fifty-One

Thursday morning Cathy woke to the sound of voices in her backyard, loud hammering, and a drill that sounded as if it were boring right through her bedroom wall. She leaped out of bed and ran for her robe, pulled it on, and dashed to the window. She bent the blinds down and peered out. The yard was full of workers.

"What is *this!*" she shouted. "I *told* them!" She rushed out of her room to the back door and stepped barefoot out into the yard.

"What are you doing?" she shouted. No one seemed to pay much attention to her.

"Excuse me!" she yelled, clutching her robe tight. "Where is Mr. Barksdale?"

"He ain't here," one of the workers said. "He's over at another site."

"No! This is not acceptable!" she cried. "I want everybody to stop what they're doing. Just freeze, okay?"

Most of them stopped their work and looked up at her, but a drill continued to clatter. She looked around, following the sound. The worker who ignored her wore headphones. He was drilling into the bricks on the back of her house.

She ran barefoot across the yard and pulled his headphones off. The grinding stopped, and he looked startled. "I told him we weren't going to build yet! I told him we wanted to postpone it! My fiancé spoke to him and told him!" She turned back to the crowd of men gaping at her. "Hold it right here. Don't hammer one more nail. Don't chip off one more brick. I'm going into the house to make some phone calls."

She bolted back inside and dialed Steve's number. He sounded too perky for six-thirty.

"Hello?"

"Steve, *they're here!*"

"Who's here?"

"The workers," she said. "They're banging holes in my house, breaking down the bricks, digging up the yard."

"Oh, no," he said.

"You said you would take care of it!"

"I did take care of it," he said. "Barksdale told me he'd check his schedule to see if he could shift us around. He never got back to me, so I assumed that he had."

"But I didn't want to be shifted around. I wanted to cancel it until we were ready."

"But if we cancel, we'll lose the money. Cathy, I borrowed money for this. I was trying to find a way to keep from forfeiting it."

"Do you mean to tell me that I have no choice in this? They're going to start tearing up my house whether I want them to or not? We're broken up! I gave the ring back."

"But I don't plan to keep It," Steve said. "I was waiting for the right time to put it back on your finger."

"What were you going to do? Drug me and make me set a date?"

"Maybe." She could hear the smile in his voice. "Something like that. So I was thinking it wouldn't be the worst thing in the world if they went ahead and got started."

"*Steve!*" she shouted. "You tricked me."

"No. It's not a trick, Cathy," he said. "And if, for some reason, things don't happen, and you meet Mr. Casanova and decide to dump me—"

"Does Mr. Casanova have a contractor?"

He laughed, then quickly cleared his throat. "Cathy, I'm paying for the renovation, and if for some reason you refuse to marry me, you'll have a nice house that's worth a lot more than it was when we started. If you think about it, I'm the one who might get taken here."

"Right," she said. "This is all my clever ploy to get a bigger house."

He laughed again.

"Steve, it's not funny. I don't want contractors here. I have too much going on."

"Just ignore them. Act like they're not there."

"But I can't. They're digging up my backyard and banging down my walls."

"They're not banging down the walls," he said. "They're just taking off the bricks. They're not going to make doors into the house until they've almost finished everything else. We talked about that."

She let out a frustrated scream.

"Mom, what's going on?"

Rick was standing, groggy-eyed, in the doorway to the den.

She put her hand over the receiver. "My life is out of control," she said. "That's what's going on!"

"What time do you go to work?" Steve asked.

She looked at the clock. "Well, I have to be there at eight."

"Fine. Just put on some headphones or something, turn the hair dryer on, do anything you can to get your mind off the men in the backyard. They'll be gone before you get home from work today. They get started early so they can knock off early and miss the hottest part of the day. You can pretend they were never there."

She opened her mouth to give him a retort, but nothing came out.

"I love you," he dared say.

She wanted to break something.

"Cathy, I know you're under a lot of stress right now, and I promise to make this as easy as we can. Most of the mess will be in the backyard, and except for early mornings, I really think they'll stay out of your way."

"Do I have a choice?" Cathy asked, falling back onto the couch.

"Of course you do. You could call it all off and let me eat that fifty-thousand-dollar loan. Hey, it's only money."

She threw a cushion off of the couch, then kicked it. A horrible noise erupted in the yard, making it impossible for her to hear. "I can't hear you!" she shouted. "I'll call you back later."

She hung up the phone and let out a frustrated yell again. The noise stopped before her voice did.

"Mom?" Now it was Annie, standing in her gown.

"Go back to bed," she said. "They're just destroying our house. Don't worry about it."

"You're letting them?"

"Unless you have fifty thousand dollars on you." She flung the cushion again, then started back to her room. "I have to get ready for work."

Chapter Fifty-Two

Cathy heard from her children a dozen times that day, complaining about how the workers sounded as if they were tearing the house down, how they were digging up the yard and blocking the driveway with their trucks. Each time, Cathy told them to call Steve at work and let him handle it.

A sense of dread crept over her as she doctored the animals that came to her for attention. She had postponed the wedding because of Mark—or had she? Was it really Mark's situation, or was it a much broader fear? If Mark could bring this much stress on them, she couldn't imagine what it would be like to be married and still dealing with the frustrations of smart-mouthed kids and attorney bills.

The thought that she would have so much responsibility for Tracy, a child at the very age where she had probably started making the most mistakes with her own children, frightened her to death. The constant comparisons that she knew were inevitable for Steve frightened her even more. How would the love she and Steve had for each other endure such hard times?

Then again . . .

It would be nice to have a partner in life, someone who had a stake in what happened, someone who could grieve with her and for her, someone on whose shoulder she could cry. And Steve was more than that. He was someone who made her laugh and brought joy back into her life.

The thought of losing Steve frightened her even more than the thought of marrying him. If he gave up and went his own way, she doubted that she would ever get over it. Yes, she was strong. Yes, she had been through grief before and come out on the other end. But she didn't want to do it again—not alone.

She went into her office and pulled out the

file that held the blueprint they'd made of the addition on to her home. It would be a beautiful home when they were finished. Steve had thought of everything.

This would be the first time she'd have a master bedroom with bookshelves. She'd always wanted that. And their bathroom would border on luxurious. They needed that family room, especially with four kids and all their friends coming and going in the house. Even when all the kids had left home, the family room would come in handy for grandchildren and visits back home.

The thought that she had a future like that and someone to share it with filled her with warmth. Maybe it was a good thing the builders had gone ahead. Maybe God was intervening with her postponement, telling her that it wasn't necessary.

Yet how could she get married when Mark was behind bars?

She decided not to deal with any of it today. She would wait until she got home and see what happened. Maybe this was a good thing. She would try to hang on to that thought.

Pulling into her driveway that afternoon, Cathy saw that the trucks were all gone, just as Steve had promised. Some supplies had been left behind, but at least they were all stacked in a pile on the side of the house. That was probably as good as she could expect.

She went into the house and put her things down. Annie was sitting in front of the television. "They finally left, Mom. But you should see what they did to the backyard."

She closed her eyes. "Should I even look, or should I just pretend I don't know anything about it?"

"I think you should look," she said.

Cathy headed to the backyard. At first sight, she was torn between feeling a thrill that her house was going to turn into something wonderful, and a little kernel of dread that this was going to get worse before it got better. In the early stages of drawing up the plans, she had asked the architect for things she had never thought she could have. With two incomes, there would be room in her life for a few luxuries . . . and more contributions to Sylvia.

She looked at the lumber stacked at the side of the yard and the other supplies that would soon be made into part of her home.

She was surprised to see Rick at the edge

of the yard, squatting in the dirt where she had spent last spring planting a garden on her weekends. Her heart sank again as she saw what had been done to it.

"They dug up my flowers," she said.

"Sure did, Mom." Annie was behind her, egging her on.

Rick looked up at her. "I was thinking of maybe putting them in some pots before you got home. I didn't want you to go crazy."

"Good idea," she said. "Maybe it's not too late. Are they dead?"

"No, they still look alive and kicking," he said.

"Come on, Annie," she said. "There's some potting soil in the storage room. Drag it around here and get some pots."

As they worked together to get the flowers into pots, she realized that no real harm had been done. The workers had been more respectful of her property than they had been of her schedule.

"So, Mom, I was thinking," Annie said. "About this college thing . . ."

Cathy gave her a warning look. "Annie, you're going to college."

"But Mom," Annie said. "I told you, I can't stand the thought."

"Then get a full-time job that will support you," she said again. "Annie, education matters. You can't do anything in life unless you're educated for it. It's worth the hard work."

"I know," Annie said, "but my problem is that I don't know what I want to do, okay? I don't have a clue. And I don't want to just float through college like Rick's doing, taking all those classes that don't mean a thing to me."

"Hey, I'm not doing that," Rick said. "I'm about to declare a major."

"Yeah? Well, what is it?" Annie challenged.

Rick shrugged. "I'm going to come up with it by the end of summer, okay? Get off my back."

"That's just my point," Annie said. "Why should I go spend all this money at college and take all these classes and keep studying for four more years when I don't even know what I want to do?"

"Annie, I'm not going to let you skip college," Cathy said. "I told you how it's going to be."

"Well, I had another thought," she said. She abandoned the pot she was working on and sat back on her bottom, not even heeding the dirt stains that she was going to have to deal with later. "Mom, listen to me," she said. "I have a plan. A really great idea."

Cathy looked up at her and braced herself. "Okay, shoot."

"Well, you know those pictures of those kids that Sylvia's working with? You know, they really moved me. The truth is that Sylvia needs help from *people,* I mean, another pair of hands, more than she does money."

"She needs both," Cathy said.

"Well, I was just thinking about what I'd be giving if I went to college. I mean, what I'd really be accomplishing, especially since I don't know what I want to do yet. And I was thinking that maybe if I went to Nicaragua . . ."

"Wait a minute," Cathy said. She got to her feet and dusted off her hands and rump. "Annie, if you're going to start asking me to send you to Nicaragua on some glorified vacation, I'm just as sorry as I can be. I don't have the money for it, and I don't have the patience to talk about it."

"No, wait," Annie said. "I don't want to go on a vacation. I'm not interested in seeing the landscape. Oh, I mean it'll be cool and all, but that's not it."

"Then what do you want, Annie?"

"I want to help those children."

Rick started to laugh. "Here it comes."

"Shut up!" Annie said. "I'm serious."

Rick snorted.

"Mom, that little boy, Miguel. The way his eyes came to life after they'd been feeding him . . . it really surprised me and made me think. It takes so little to meet somebody's needs."

"But it's not just about meeting their physical needs, Annie. It's about meeting their spiritual ones."

"I know, Mom. But I want to help with both."

She had never heard Annie talking this way before, and something inside her stirred in gratitude. She gazed in surprise at her daughter. "Annie, are you serious?"

"Mom, I was thinking that if I could just lay out of school for one year and go over there and help Sylvia with the orphans and the children who need to be fed, the hundred dollars I was going to give to help her buy food could help pay for sending me. And don't worry, Mom. I know I'd have to raise my own support, buy my own airline tickets, get over there myself."

"Annie, have you really given this any serious thought?"

"Yes," she said, "ever since I started looking at those pictures. I thought how bad I want to go over there and pick those children up and hold them and work with them."

Cathy looked at Rick. He was leaning against the fence, his mouth stretched into a huge grin as if he couldn't believe his ears. "Annie, a missionary? You've got to be kidding me."

"Hush, Rick," Cathy said. "She sounds serious about this."

"I am serious, Mom," Annie said. "Why would I make this up? Most kids are anxious to go off to college. You know me. I love the social part of school, and I love camp and I love being with the youth group and I love hanging out with my friends. That's part of what college is all about. But I don't want it."

"I know, Annie, and I really don't understand it."

"Well, maybe this is why. Maybe God wanted me to do something else this year. And then when I come back, I can go to college, and by then maybe I'll know what I want to do. It'll give me time to think, and time to get out of Cedar Circle where everything's nice and pat. I can get over there and actually help people. I don't think I've ever helped anybody before, Mom."

"But, Annie, for you to really be able to help people the way they need to be helped, you have to have a certain spiritual maturity. I'm not sure you've really grown into that yet."

"Mom, how am I going to if I never stretch? Let me go."

Cathy sat back down in the dirt and realized that tears were stinging her eyes. "Annie, I'm not ready to send you halfway across the world on a whim."

"It's not a whim, Mom."

"She's gone insane," Rick said. "It won't last a week."

"It will, too," Annie said. "Shut up, Rick. If I get over there, I can't afford to come back until it's time."

Rick chuckled and went back to his potting. "Let her go, Mom. It's about time she got out of my hair. And then you could just give Tracy her room and not worry about fixing up yours."

"No!" Annie said. "I'd be back. It's still my room."

"Of course, we'd keep it, Annie," Cathy said.

"Then you're going to let me go?"

She felt broadsided, unprepared. "Annie, I have to think about this. It needs a lot of prayer."

"Well, we have time before school starts, Mom. I don't have to go right now. I can go whenever Sylvia thinks it's best."

"That's another thing," Cathy said. "I've got to talk to Sylvia. She may not want you to come."

"Why wouldn't she? She needs help."

"Well, I know, but she remembers you as this teenaged kid floating around from social event to social event. She might not actually believe that your heart is right in this."

"Mom, let me talk to her," she said. "I can convince her. When I raise the support, she'll know I'm serious."

"And how are you going to do that, Annie?"

"I've got lots of plans," she said. "I've learned a lot from you. When you fought with the school board, and last year when you collected clothes for the clothing drive. I know how it works, Mom. I'm willing to go door-to-door if I have to and ask people to sponsor me. Trust me. If I can't raise the money, then it's not meant to be."

"You'll understand that?" Cathy asked. "You'll believe it?"

"Yes, Mom."

"Because I'm not willing to spend your college money on this. I'm not giving up on that."

"That's fine, Mom. I promise, I'll come up with the money. And if I don't, I won't go." She laced her hands together. "Just say you'll talk to Miss Sylvia."

"I will. And I have to talk to Steve."

"Why Steve?"

"Because," Cathy said, "my future's tied up with his, even if we've postponed things."

"It doesn't look like you've postponed it much," Rick said, looking around.

"No, it doesn't." She sighed and dug into the dirt. "All I do know is that I want to spend the rest of my life with Steve. You and Annie, you'll be out of here before I know it, wherever you decide to go. And Mark, well, he's where he is. Steve is for me. He's mine. He's someone that I believe God sent me to make my life more complete. And I want to consult him about things going on in my life."

"Fine," Annie said. "Consult him. I think

he'll probably be glad to get rid of me. Two down, one to go, if you can ever get Rick to move out."

"Hey!" Rick said, no longer amused. "I'm leaving in August."

"I know the time is coming," Cathy said, "and I know God has a plan in both of your lives. I don't want to cling. But I've got to know it's right, Annie. I've got to consult God and make sure it's his plan and not yours."

"Okay, Mom," she said. "Just know that I'm praying, too, and my prayers might cancel out yours."

"Thank goodness it doesn't work that way." She touched Annie's face with her dirty hand. "I'm very proud of you, Annie, for even considering this. Even if I don't let you go."

Rick stepped toward them but didn't commit by touching either of them. "It is pretty cool, Annie. If you really do it."

It was the most tender moment they'd had as a family in a very long time. Cathy only wished that Mark was here to share it.

Chapter Fifty-Three

Brenda was starting across the street to see Cathy when Rick began carrying the potted plants to the front yard. "Hey, Miss Brenda," he said.

"Hey, Rick. What's going on with the construction? Did your mother change her mind?"

"They kind of changed it for her."

The front door of the Dodds's house slammed, and Daniel bolted out. "Hey, Rick," he called. "Did you get that application?"

Brenda turned back to her son and watched him loping across the street. "What application? Daniel, did you—?"

"I got you one," Rick said. "And guess what? There's an opening right now for a bag boy at the store. I talked to them about you, and I think if you go by there tonight they'll hire you."

Daniel looked as if he'd just won a lottery. "Thanks, man."

"What?" Brenda asked. "Daniel, we didn't say—"

"Come on, Mom," Daniel said. "I need a job so I can pay the deductible on your car. I can do it, Mom. I promise I can. Then you can get the van fixed."

"Daniel, it'll take months for you to save up a thousand dollars."

"Still, it's something I can do, Mom. And I need some spending money. After I pay the deductible, I could save for a car, and then you and Dad wouldn't have to come up with extra cash. I can even help buy groceries and maybe make part of the house payment."

Brenda looked a little embarrassed that he would say such things in front of Rick. Daniel had no idea just how little minimum wage really was. But his heart was right. He was trying to take responsibility, and she didn't want to stomp it out. "Honey, they don't pay *that* much."

"But it's not bad for a first job," Rick said.

"Oh, Mom, please!" Daniel said. "*Please* let me do it."

"I'll talk to your dad again," Brenda said. "That's the best I can do right now."

"But I have to go up there tonight. If I don't, they'll hire somebody else."

She looked at Rick, wishing she had never walked over today. "I'll think about it, Daniel. If your dad says it's okay, we'll drive you there ourselves."

"That's okay," Rick said. "I can take him."

"Yeah, Mom," Daniel said. "I don't want my parents hanging around when I'm applying for my first job. It wouldn't look good."

"Well, don't you think they know that a fifteen-year-old boy has parents?"

"Mom, please."

Brenda closed her eyes and decided she was entering a new phase of life that she hadn't counted on quite so soon. "I'll go talk to him right now," she said.

But as she walked back across the street, she tried to formulate her argument so that David would agree with her that Daniel wasn't ready to enter the workforce just yet.

Chapter Fifty-Four

It took a couple of days for Cathy to get Sylvia on the phone, but when she finally did, she told her what Annie wanted to do. "So, what do you think?" she asked Sylvia. "Do you think you can use her?"

"It's an answered prayer, that's all there is to it," Sylvia said. "We need her, Cathy. She'll be a big help to us."

"Are you sure?" Cathy asked. "Let's face it, she's not the most spiritually mature person in the world. She's a little self-centered, as we both know. She's never done anything for anyone on this scale."

"Neither had I, when I came here," Sylvia said. "She'll be fine. She can stay right here in our house with us. Harry will be thrilled to have her around."

"She doesn't have to stay the whole year if you don't want her to."

"Well, we'll leave that open. If she can get herself here and home, then we'll take care of her while she's here. Don't worry about a thing. I think it's the best way she can spend this year before she goes to college, anyway. You'll see. It'll change her life."

"For the better, I hope," Cathy said. She heard the pounding outside. The workers seemed to be in a demolition phase, but she couldn't think what they were destroying. She propped her chin on her hand, wondering why her life seemed to be moving so fast these days. "I seem to be going through a lot of transitions right now, but I'm not sure it's all going to be for the best."

"This one will," Sylvia said. "Trust me. And trust God. If he's put this on Annie's heart, you know it can't be from any selfish motive. Let her come, Cathy. You'll be glad you did."

Later that evening when Steve came over, Cathy sat with him on a stack of lumber. "I feel like my life is out of control," she told him.

"How so?"

"Well, I have no control at all over what's done with Mark. He's a ward of the state now, and they're calling the shots. I only get to see him twice a week. I don't know what's happening to him in between. Rick's moving to campus this fall. And now this with Annie."

"This with Annie is a good thing," Steve said. "It's the best thing that could happen to her. You wait and see."

"Yeah, well, that's out of my control, too, pretty much. I may be sending her off to Sylvia for a year, and she'll be the one taking care of her."

"Don't you trust Sylvia?"

"Well, of course, I do. I trust her parenting a lot more than I do my own."

"Annie's not a little girl anymore," he said. "She's eighteen. Technically, her childhood is behind her."

"Technically, maybe," Cathy said, "but we both know there's still a lot of immaturity there. I don't know if she can take this. I'm almost worried that Rick is right, that she'll want to turn around and come home after she's gotten a good look at the sights."

"Maybe not," Steve said. "Maybe she'll surprise you. Maybe this is God's way of showing you that the same parent who could raise a child who would wind up serving time could also raise a missionary."

She looked up at him, her eyes glistening with the tears that seemed to come too often these days. "You know, I've thought of that myself. Isn't that amazing?"

"Sure it is, and we don't even know what will happen to Rick yet. It could be anything."

"He's really been sweet with Daniel," she said. "Almost like he's doing penance for all the mean things he did to Mark. He's going to teach him how to drive, and he's trying to get him a job."

"There's a lot of good in your kids, Cathy. You just need to have a little more faith in them."

"I know," she said.

He drew in a deep breath and looked at the work being done on the house. They'd gone too far—there was no turning back.

"This is costing a lot of money," he said, "and I know it's one of the other areas where you feel out of control."

Cathy sighed. "Even the good things seem out of control. The house, and Annie's plans. But I don't know why I'm so worried about her. She may not even raise the money."

"I was thinking maybe I could help her."

Cathy looked up at him. "Steve, I can't ask you to do that."

Steve shrugged. "It's no problem. I hocked your engagement ring today. I'll just use that money—"

"Steve!" Cathy sprang to her feet. "How could you?"

He doubled into laughter then and stood up. He dug into his pocket and pulled out the ring. "See? I knew you still wanted it."

She swung at him, and he ducked and leaped over some piping.

"Oh, no! I dropped it," he said.

She stopped chasing him and looked down at her feet. "Where?"

"Just kidding," he said, and held the ring up as he came back toward her. Amazed that she had fallen for it, she grinned and took the ring, gazing down at it. "That was low, Steve."

He took her shoulders and touched his forehead to hers. "Maybe so. But if you don't put that back on your finger right now, I'm going to the pawn shop. Annie needs that money."

She grinned and slapped playfully at him. He caught her hands, took the ring back, and held it up, as if he needed a finger to put it on.

She provided hers. Steve's smile faded, and his eyes grew serious as he slid it on. "Thank you," he whispered, then his hand came up to cup her face. He kissed her, making her melt like a candle.

"Nicaragua is a good cause," he whispered, "but marriage to you is a better one."

"Annie'll get over it," Cathy said.

"Maybe she won't have to." He pulled her back to sit next to him on the lumber. "I'm still going to help her. I won't give her all of it. I think it would be good for her to try to raise it on her own. That way we'll be able to gauge her level of commitment. But I was thinking maybe I could pitch in a few hundred dollars. Maybe that would go toward half of the airline ticket or something."

"She'll be grateful."

"I know she will," he said, "but I don't think I'm going to mention it to her until after she's raised the rest. Let's just keep watching to see how she does."

"I've been thinking, too," Cathy said. "At first, I told her I wouldn't use any of her college money to help her pay for the trip. I thought this was just a ploy to get out of going to school. But now, I'm thinking that if I did dip into it and help her, I could work a little extra to help her out with this. Maybe stay open all day on Saturdays and stop knocking off at three. What do you think? Would that be spoiling her?"

"Like I said, see how much she raises before you do that. And I'm sure there'll be times when we'll be sending money while she's over there."

"We?" Cathy smiled. She touched the diamond. It felt good on her finger. "I like the thought of 'we.' "

He slid his arm around her and pulled her close. "I love you, lady," he said. "I'm going to marry you. I'm going to move into your house. And you're going to have a beautiful bedroom and a huge family room, and we're going to live happily ever after. And your daughter is going to be a missionary, and your son is going to be a successful executive somewhere."

"And Mark?" she asked.

"And Mark's going to come out of jail a stronger person. Who knows? Maybe he'll even find Christ in there."

"Do you think so?"

"I do," he said. "And we have to make sure

during this down time in Mark's life that Christ is exactly who he's thinking of. I'll help with that."

Her eyes filled with tears again as she touched his face. She loved the way his stubble felt against her palm. It was amazing how much she loved him and even more amazing that he could love her through all this.

"Marry me, Cathy," he whispered.

"I will," she said. "I'm just not sure when."

"Marry me on July 4th, just like we planned," he said. "Let's go in there right now and open all those presents."

She smiled. "Oh, so that's what this is all about? You just want to open your presents."

He grinned back. "Well, some of them did look pretty interesting."

Her smile faded, and she gave a great sigh. "Steve, July 4th is just a few days away. You know that's too soon. It's just a bad time. And I don't want to open the presents until we've set a date. I may have to wind up returning them all."

"I'm not going to let you return them," he said, "and I'm not going to let you stop work on the house. And I'm not going to let you cancel our wedding. Not until you convince me that you don't love me and you don't want to spend your life with me."

"I could never convince you of that," Cathy said, "because it wouldn't be true."

It was clear he already knew that. "I'll wait for you. I know you're going through a tough time with Mark. I'll even be here to help you. But make no mistake. This is *we,* not *you.* It's our problem, not your problem. I'm here for you, okay?"

"Okay," she whispered.

"And, like I said, if you get sick of me and want out, then you'll have this great big nice house and you won't have to pay for any of it."

"I didn't mean for you to have to pay for everything," Cathy said. "I was really going to help."

"As far as I'm concerned, it's all about to go into the same pot, so it really doesn't make any difference," Steve said.

The feeling of warm relief washed over her like an ocean tide, and she realized that God had sent her one of the most precious gifts in her life the day she'd looked up at a parents' meeting and seen Steve standing at the door.

"Be patient," she said. "I'll marry you as soon as I know the time is right."

"That'll have to be good enough, then," Steve said. He pressed a kiss on her lips, then on her forehead, then pressed his forehead against hers and combed his fingers through her hair. Cathy knew that, no matter how bad things got, she wasn't alone this time. God had sent Steve, and he was standing beside her.

Chapter Fifty-Five

Brenda and David sat in their car at the end of the coliseum parking lot and watched as Rick taught Daniel to drive.

"I should be doing that myself," David said. "I shouldn't have overreacted to his wrecking the car."

"Don't be so hard on yourself," Brenda said. "There are some things that other people can teach your children better than you can."

He looked over at her and grinned. "I can't believe this is you talking, the definitive mother hen."

She grinned back at him. "I'm not a mother

hen, just because I home-school. At least I admitted that I can't home-school him in driving. Look at him! He just made a U-turn."

David squinted. "Are you sure that's him driving?"

They both broke out laughing, but Brenda's mirth quickly faded. "There's a lamppost coming up." They both braced themselves, breath held.

He easily swerved around it. They both breathed.

"Rick's a miracle worker," Brenda said.

David leaned back in the pickup truck and started to relax. "I say we let him take the job."

Brenda closed her eyes. She didn't want to hear this. She had decided on her own that it was too soon, and there were too many reasons not to let Daniel work. "Why, David? He's too young to go to work. When we start school again he needs to study."

"Come on. He's doing great," he said. "You've already got him at an eleventh-grade learning level. He needs a little time to socialize."

"He does socialize. He socializes at church. He plays baseball."

"I know, but he needs to learn responsibility. He needs to learn what it's like to earn money. And it sure won't hurt him to have to pay off this deductible. I guarantee you, once he learns to drive, he'll always be careful if he knows how much the insurance is going to cost. And, hey, if he's able to save up for a car . . ."

"Come on, David. At minimum wage? How much do you think he'll be able to save?"

"Don't underestimate him," David said. "He can do it. I did it when I was young."

"But what if he starts going overboard with it? How do we draw the line? What if he starts working nights and weekends and overtime?"

"We can put our foot down anytime we want to. Besides, it's not going to be such a novelty for that long. After a while, he's going to get tired of it and want to work less, not more. Mark my word."

Her gaze drifted back to the car creeping along the edge of the parking lot. "I'm just not ready for this," she whispered.

"Well, be glad you're not Cathy sending him off to prison."

"Oh, don't even say that," she said. "David, I've been sick about Mark. It's made me want to cling even harder to Daniel."

"I know it has," David said, "but we've got to let him go."

The car screeched, and Daniel jerked to a halt. Brenda threw her hands over her face. "I can't look," she said.

"Oh-oh, he's coming toward us," David said.

She opened her eyes again and sat straighter, grabbing David's hand. "He's coming too fast!" But almost as soon as the words were out of her mouth, Daniel slowed, then inched forward toward them.

"I'm too old for this, David," she said.

He nodded his head slowly in agreement. "That's why we have Rick."

Chapter Fifty-Six

Cathy took Rick and Annie with her when she went to visit Mark Sunday afternoon.

When Mark came into the visiting room and greeted everyone, Annie made her announcement with a flourish. "I've decided to be a missionary in Nicaragua. I'm going to spend a year with Sylvia in Leon."

"No way," Mark said. "Mom, is she?"

"Maybe," Cathy said. "If she raises the money to get there."

"I'm going," Annie said. "It's practically a done deal." She reached into her purse and pulled out snapshots of the children in

Nicaragua. She flipped through until she found the picture of little Miguel.

"You think *you* have problems," she said. "Look at this little boy. See how swollen his stomach is, how vacant he looks?"

"Vacant?" Mark asked. "When did you start using words like *vacant?*"

"Since your room became vacant, okay?" Annie said irritably. "Look at him, how sick and miserable he looks. And in this one, after he's been eating at Sylvia's kitchen for a while, he's gotten healthier. Do you see that?"

Mark leaned up and looked at the picture again. "Yeah, I see it."

"Sylvia's making a difference in people's lives, and I'm going to go help her."

"Don't they have, like, rules? Standards? That sort of thing? They let just anybody go to the mission field?"

"They're letting her," Rick said. "Go figure."

Annie smiled. "Hey, I'm called by God."

"You sound like Dan Aykroyd in the *Blues Brothers,*" Mark said. "What is it with her, Mom? Does she know some guy that lives there or something?"

"Hey, I'm going for the children," Annie spouted.

"No way," Mark said again. "There's something in this for her, Mom. Better figure out what it is before she costs you a fortune."

"It's not costing me anything, Mark," Cathy said. "Annie's raising her own support."

"I've already raised three hundred dollars," Annie said.

Cathy shot her a look. "Are you serious?"

"Yeah, Mom. I went to the families of each of my friends from my youth group and I told them what I was doing, and they wrote me checks on the spot."

"Why didn't you tell me?"

"Because I've been so busy doing it I haven't had a chance." She turned back to her brother. "So, see? I'm not going for any mercenary reason. I'm seriously doing this because I want to help the children."

Mark just stared at his sister for a moment, as if waiting for her to get to the punch line.

Annie rolled her eyes. "Just forget it. You'll see, when I'm writing from Nicaragua."

His eyes finally changed, and he regarded his sister with a serious look. "Well, if it's true, I think it's pretty cool. But, Mom, what are you going to do with both me and Annie gone?"

Cathy looked down at her hands. "Rick and I will get along somehow, until he leaves in August."

"The house will keep her busy," Rick said. "They've started building."

Mark looked at his mother. "Really? You're going ahead with it?"

Cathy's heart sank. She didn't want Mark to know of all the changes being done without him, anticipating how depressed he would feel after they left, when he went back to his cell and sat staring into space, aware that the world was revolving at full speed without him.

"We had sort of a run-in with the contractor. I wanted to postpone it, but we would have lost the money."

Mark didn't say anything. He just looked down at the table. "So you two are going to go ahead with the wedding?"

"No," Cathy said, "we're not. We're postponing it until you get out, Mark." She watched his reaction, hoping he would say that waiting was ridiculous, that they should go ahead. Instead, he just kept looking down at his hands clasped in front of him. She wondered what was going through his mind.

"So, tell us how it's going in here," she said

finally. "Are you getting along with the other guys?"

"Yeah, they're okay, some of them," he said. "You just figure out who to avoid."

"Have you been going to chapel?"

"Yeah. The Christians love us. We're a captive audience. They can't pass up the opportunity to preach to us every time we turn around. Of course, the Muslims and Hindus and Buddhists have chapels, too, but I don't go to those."

Annie brought her gaze back to Mark. "You talk about Christians like they were another group. I thought you were one."

"Yeah, I am," Mark said with a shrug. "I mean, I'm not a fanatic or anything like Mom, but, hey, I believe there's a God."

To Cathy, those did not sound like the words of someone who knew Christ. But lectures from her weren't going to change what was in his heart. That would take prayer—and a work by the Holy Spirit.

Later that night, as Cathy and Steve sat out on the pile of sheetrock in the backyard, looking at the new work done by the construction crew, Steve came up with an idea. "I think I'm going to do a Bible study with Mark on my own," he said.

"How?"

"Well, I can do it through the mail," he said. "Mark likes to get mail. I can just write him letters, give him things to look up, kind of disciple him like a correspondence school or something."

"I think that would be great. But prepare yourself. It may all be a waste. He may not even read it."

"Maybe not now," he said, "but at some point he might pull them out and study them. And with the Christian groups coming to him a couple of times a week, it could turn out to be really good, you know? Maybe I could supplement what they're doing somehow through the mail and then work with him one-on-one on visitation days. I don't want to take away from your time with him, but I think it could work out."

Emotion assaulted her, and tears sprang to her eyes.

"Did I upset you?" he asked.

She smiled and shook her head. "No. I was just sitting here wondering why God's blessing me so with you."

"July 4th will be here before you know it," he said. "The church is still free. The pastor's still available."

She smiled. "Not yet. It's just not time."

He didn't say any more about marriage for the rest of the evening, but she knew her delay was costing him. Even so, she couldn't think of marrying him until things had fallen more into place. Things were just too rough, too rocky right now. She was on the downward slope of a steep roller-coaster ride, and she didn't want to bring two more people into that. No, there had to be a better time to get married, a time when the problems were fewer and the path seemed straighter. Second marriages brought enough problems. She just hoped Steve wouldn't give up.

Chapter Fifty-Seven

Brenda didn't sleep at all the night before Daniel started his new job, and then she got him up early and fixed him a healthy breakfast before dropping him off at the grocery store. She found it hard to do anything that day, because she kept thinking about her baby entering the work world, earning his own money, getting to know people she didn't know, taking orders from bosses whose motives she couldn't predict.

Around noon, she decided she needed a carton of milk.

"Where you going, Mama?" Joseph asked her.

"To the grocery store," she said, distracted as she gathered her checkbook and truck keys. "I need some milk."

"But Daniel's there," he said. "Don't show up at the store on Daniel's first day! He'll be embarrassed."

"He will not be embarrassed. I go to the grocery store all the time, anyway. I'm not going to quit just because Daniel's working there."

"Okay," he said, "but I want to go with you. I gotta see this."

They both got into the pickup truck and headed off to the store. As Brenda went in, she searched the checkout counter for Daniel, hoping he would be up front where she could find him. When he wasn't there, she went down the meat aisle, then the produce, then the canned soup.

"Mama, this isn't where the milk is," Joseph said.

"I know."

"You're looking for Daniel, aren't you?"

"Why would you say that? I was just trying to remember a couple of other things I need to pick up." She peeked around a stack of cereal and still didn't see Daniel.

"Mama, what are you going to do? Go search the back for him?"

"Well, where is he?" she asked. "He's supposed to be in here bagging groceries. Why isn't he up front? He's not supposed to just disappear like this."

"Mama, he's working."

"I know he's working, Joseph," she said. "And it's wonderful that he's got a job here, but when he gets a job bagging groceries, he should be up front bagging groceries."

"Mama, you know I'm okay."

Daniel's voice came from behind her, and she swung around as if she'd been caught stealing a ham. "Daniel!"

His cheeks had that mottled, burning look. "Mama, I can't believe you're here on my first day on the job. You'll embarrass me to death. Please don't let anybody know you're my mom."

Brenda's heart crashed. Her children had never uttered those words before, and she hadn't been prepared for them. It sounded like something Mark would say to Cathy— something insensitive and ungrateful. Maybe she'd made a dire mistake in letting Daniel spend so much time with Mark.

"Daniel, I just wanted to make sure everything was going—"

"Mama, it's going fine," he whispered. "I

was stocking canned goods on aisle four. You can't check on me. It's just not right."

"Daniel, I shop here. I'm not checking on you. I needed a carton of milk."

"Well, the milk is in aisle thirteen," he said.

She started toward it, as if she didn't have time for chit-chat. A man who looked like he had a little authority was standing at the end of the aisle, looking to see what Daniel was doing.

She suddenly wanted to cry. "Joseph, let's just get the milk someplace else."

"Good," Daniel whispered. "You can shop at the Jitney on Monroe Street."

Brenda tried to blink back the tears pushing into her eyes. "I'll pick you up at three," she told Daniel, then hurried out of the store with Joseph running to keep up.

"Mama, I know he didn't mean that," Joseph said.

She touched the back of his neck and tried to smile. He was her most sensitive child, the one who seemed to read her thoughts most clearly. He would never speak to her the way Daniel had. "I know he didn't mean it," she said.

They got into the dented truck, and she sat for a moment, staring at the steering wheel.

"You're not going to cry, are you?" Joseph asked in a soft voice.

"No, of course not," she said. "I'm so proud of Daniel I just don't know what to do. Working, having so much responsibility . . ." Despite herself, she felt her mouth quivering. "It just chokes me up."

"You're not crying because you're choked up, Mama. You're crying because he said that to you."

"No, no, it's fine," she said. "He's right. I embarrassed him." She started the engine and pulled out of the parking space. "I think this is going to work out just fine. This is a good job for Daniel." But as she drove to the other grocery store, she wondered what this job would do to her son. Would he start treating her more like an embarrassment than a protector? Would he dread seeing her, instead of calling for her?

She had always known her children would grow up, but she hadn't expected for it to come in such a painful way.

Chapter Fifty-Eight

July 4th came without a wedding, and as Cathy made an effort to celebrate with barbecued chicken and sparklers in the cluttered backyard, it was clear that she was melancholy about what the day could have been. Steve tried to be festive for Tracy's sake. But that night, after he'd put her to bed, he sat at his desk in his spare bedroom and asked God to help him with the feelings of loss. There would still be a wedding day, he vowed. And in the meantime, there were things that had to be done.

He felt a clear calling to do something for Mark, so he searched through his Bible for just the right study to begin sending to him. He racked his brain for something that would get through to the boy and make him really think about the messages God had given him. Steve thought of starting with the parables. Did Mark have the ears to hear or eyes to see?

Or he could start with the gospel of Matthew. But would that just seem like a history lesson that didn't apply to him?

No . . . no, he needed to start with a baby step, something simple yet profound, something Mark could relate to.

He sat back, thinking of Jerry Flaherty, and Mark's disappointment that his father still hadn't come to visit. That was it—the perfect story: the prodigal son, a father searching the horizon each day for his child, waiting for him to return home.

Yes. That was it. Mark would be able to understand and relate to it, and maybe it would make a difference in his life.

He turned to the passage in Luke 15, then closed his eyes in prayer. He pleaded with the Lord to let the Holy Spirit work in Mark's heart through these words. Then he got out a piece of paper and started to write. "Dear Mark . . ."

Two hours later, he signed the letter and sat back and looked at it, wondering if he had just wasted his time. No, God had promised that his Word would never return void, and Steve believed it.

He addressed the envelope and applied postage. He would mail it on his way to work tomorrow. Maybe Mark would have it by Tuesday. But that wouldn't be the end of it. Steve had a lot more to teach Mark, a lot more than he could put into letters. And when Mark went to mail call, he'd be glad to get something. He would probably take the time to read it, no matter what it was.

Before he went to bed that night, Steve prayed again for the boy who was spending time in jail without a hint of real repentance in his heart.

Chapter Fifty-Nine

By Tuesday, Tory's fatigue was like an alien invading her body, turning her into a cranky shrew so irritable that she couldn't even stand herself. Her schedule for Hannah had every fifteen-minute segment of the day filled in, but the work she was doing to make her child progress kept her from time with Brittany and Spencer.

As a result, both of her older children spent most of the day whining and misbehaving.

Hannah screamed every time they began a new exercise. But there were too many things that needed to be done if Tory was to make up for the classes they weren't attending anymore, and she was determined not to wilt under the pressure.

She could do this.

Over Hannah's cries, she heard the garage door open. The kids weren't supposed to come in that way, so she prepared to call them down as soon as they stepped over the threshold into the kitchen.

But it wasn't Brittany or Spencer who came in. It was Barry.

She looked at him like a child caught running in the street. "Barry," she said in a weak voice. "You're home early."

He crossed the kitchen, came into the living room, and leaned in the doorway as he looked helplessly at his screaming child lying on her exercise mat. "Tory, what are you doing?"

"Her exercises," Tory said.

He came into the room and scooped Hannah up. She stopped crying instantly.

The sudden quiet washed over Tory like a hot bath.

"I skipped eating lunch so I could go to the school and watch Hannah's class," he said.

Tory dropped her face in her hands. She had known he'd find out. She had planned to tell him before he did.

"Tory, why didn't you tell me you'd quit?"

"Because I knew what you'd say. You would tell me to take her back, that it's good for her. But it's not, Barry. The competition is ridiculous, and the babies that are doing better . . ."

"You think *she* cares who's doing better? Tory, Hannah's not having a problem with the school. You're the one who's in competition. She's just a little baby, doing the best she can."

"She can do better," Tory said, "if I just work harder with her and don't have all those other babies distracting her. I can do it. I have a schedule, and the way I've figured it, she's going to progress much faster this way."

"Tory, Hannah needs that class. *You* need that class."

"No, we don't." She took Hannah out of his arms, and the little girl laid her sleepy head on her shoulder. "We're going to do fine, Barry. It's just been a bad day, but this is no big deal. I've already seen progress."

"She's miserable," Barry said. "Brittany and Spencer are miserable. *You're* miserable."

He saw her schedule on the end table and picked it up. "I should have known you'd schedule it out like this. You've broken her life down into fifteen-minute segments. There's not one break for you, Tory, and there's not a break for her. She'll start hating her therapy."

"You're exaggerating," Tory said.

"Yeah? Then lay her back down on that mat and see how she reacts."

Tory had to accept the challenge. She slowly approached the mat, got down on her knees, and laid the baby down.

Hannah began to wail.

Barry picked Hannah up. "Honey, you're turning our house into a developmental laboratory, and it's not right."

Tears filled Tory's eyes. "What do you want me to do? Go to that class and wallow in the frustration? Some of the babies her age are walking now. Some are talking. All she can do is sit up."

"Well, a month ago, she couldn't do that. I'll take sitting up," he said. "Let's enjoy that for a while before we start to panic."

"It's not panic, Barry. I just want her to be high-functioning."

"Well, what if she's not?" He sat down on the recliner and cradled Hannah in his lap. Her eyelids were heavy, and Tory knew she was about to drift off to sleep. It wasn't time for her nap. A nap now would throw the whole schedule off. She fought the urge to take her from Barry.

"What if she's low-functioning?" Barry asked. "Just like Nathan?"

They had been all through this during the pregnancy. Nathan was Barry's autistic brother, who sat in a wheelchair all day, staring into space and whistling. He had never been able to walk or talk, hold a job, or connect with another human being. At least, not on a level most people would recognize.

"If she is, that's fine," Tory said. "If I know I did every single thing I could to push her to her full potential, then I'll accept whatever level she reaches."

"And how will you know if you've really done everything?" he asked. "When will enough be enough?"

She looked at the mat, trying to think of a stopping point.

"I'll tell you when," he said softly. "Never.

most miserable child ever born with Down's Syndrome, because you'll never accept anything less than normal."

She got up, went to the couch, and dropped wearily down.

"I'm not criticizing, Tory. I know you're doing what you think is best. But I'm one of Hannah's parents, too. I need a say in this. If you plan to drop out of the school, you need to talk to me. If you just need a break from the competition, maybe I could arrange my schedule so that I take Hannah for a while. But she needs to stay in the school. She's really going to need it later, when she gets older. And the work they do there is good, Tory. You know it is."

"Then how come I feel so crummy every time I leave there?"

"It's pride, Tory. You want your baby to be the best. The smartest. But God didn't give us Hannah to pump up our pride. Maybe he gave her to us to *teach* us about pride."

Tory wiped her tears. She couldn't remember ever being this tired. "Barry, I don't want her to *be* the best. I want her to *have* the best."

"So do I! And I happen to think that class

and those therapists up there *are* best for her. Look what they've done so far. They've shown us what to expect, how to handle things, how to cope. They've helped her get over milestones that might have taken a lot longer."

"But I can't stand it, Barry. Tilda didn't even celebrate Hannah's sitting up. She just criticized her positioning. Said her legs were too far apart, that her hips weren't right . . ."

"Tory, she's trying to keep Hannah from having to wear a brace some day. Even if it rains on your parade, it's best for Hannah. That's what we pay her for."

"I know. I was just so mad . . . I thought I could do it." She got up and crossed the room and kissed Hannah's forehead. Hannah looked trustingly up at her, and Tory took her again and hugged her tight. "I didn't hurt her," she said. "I would never hurt her."

"Of course you wouldn't." Barry got up and stroked Tory's hair, then kissed her temple. "It's not Hannah I'm worried about," he said. "It's you. You're missing everything, Tory. Hannah's miserable, you're exhausted . . . Brittany and Spencer are bouncing off the walls . . . You haven't even been to one of Spencer's ball games this summer."

"I have Hannah," she said. "She's had ear infections and bronchitis. Besides, I don't want her to get sunburned."

"The heat won't hurt her ears, and she's over the bronchitis. And we can put up an umbrella over her stroller. She'll be all right. She'll love it."

"But . . . people stare at her. I hate that."

"People stare at all babies," he said. "They're cute and soft. Hannah's no exception to that."

"They look at her like that at first," she said, "but then they see that there's something wrong . . . and they get this sad look on their faces and start getting nervous. I always get so defensive . . ."

"You've got to get over that," Barry said. "We have a long way to go with Hannah. She's going to have people stare sometimes. You can't shelter her from that."

"But I don't want her hurt. I don't want her to know she's being talked about, made fun of . . ." She hiccuped a sob and wiped her face.

"We'll teach her to forgive. But you have to learn to relax and enjoy her. No baby wants to grow up in a laboratory. I say throw the mat out, and get rid of that schedule, and just try to get our family back to normal. The therapists are still coming, the classes still go on, but you don't have to be Hannah's constant teacher/therapist/speech pathologist/doctor. All you have to do is be her mother. And that, I know you can do."

His words brought a healing balm that Tory desperately needed. She leaned into him, and he pulled her into his arms and held her.

Maybe it wasn't all up to her, she thought as she wept against him. Maybe she could relax a little, after all.

Chapter Sixty

Tuesday afternoon, Mark scored big at mail call. He got letters from Rick, Annie, Tracy, Steve, and his mother. When he got to Steve's letter, he saw that it was a Bible study from a passage in Luke. He rolled his eyes and folded the envelope back up, crammed it into his pocket, and turned, instead, to the letters from his sister and brother.

When he got back to his bunk, he shoved Steve's letter into the Bible in his locker without reading it. He was bored, but he wasn't that bored. Grabbing his textbooks, he headed to the classroom for another hour of cruel and unusual punishment, in the form of a math class.

Steve joined Cathy, Rick, and Annie Wednesday night on their visit to Mark. On the way to River Ranch he told them of the Bible study he planned to provide for Mark.

"He probably got the first one yesterday," he said. "Don't expect any overnight changes, but you can be praying that something I wrote will reach him."

Cathy gave him a skeptical look. "It wasn't anything theological, was it? Nothing real complicated?"

"No. I knew better than that. I just started with the Prodigal Son. I thought he could sink his teeth into that."

"He won't read it," Annie said, leaning to see into the rearview mirror. She twisted her hair and clipped it. "He probably threw it away. You're wasting your time, Steve."

He glanced at Annie in the mirror. "Well, maybe he'll surprise you. Don't forget how bored and lonely he is."

"Pretty cool that you'd do that," Rick threw in.

Cathy smiled and took Steve's hand. "Yeah, pretty cool," she said. "With work and

Tracy and church and everything, I don't know how you found time."

"I'm taking time," Steve said. "Mark's too important to let fall through the cracks."

The kids got quiet in the backseat as he drove, and Steve figured they didn't buy a word of it. Once before, he'd been accused of using the kids to score points with Cathy. Rick and Annie were so young to be so cynical.

Then he told himself that Annie had come a long way in the past few months. She had chosen to go to the mission field, and had done a valiant job of raising money. Maybe she had stopped jumping to the wrong conclusions. And Rick was growing up, too.

Maybe they saw that he was honestly concerned about Mark.

Since he couldn't stand the heavy silence, he changed the subject.

"I was thinking about a swimming pool."

Cathy shot him a look. "What?"

"A swimming pool, in the backyard. I mean while they're building and everything. What do you guys think about putting in a pool?"

"All right, Steve!" Annie shouted. "We *need* a pool, Mom. We've always needed a pool!"

Cathy looked like he'd just suggested getting a pet elephant. "Steve, we can't put a pool in. It's too expensive."

"Sure it is, but it's worth it. I mean, wouldn't it be nice to come home from a hard day's work at the clinic and take a nice cool swim?"

"Sure, it would be nice," Cathy said, "but I have enough things to take care of without having to complicate my life with keeping a pool clean."

"I'll take care of the pool," Steve said. "Don't worry about it."

"Yeah, Mom," Annie cried. "We'll take care of it!"

"What are you talking about?" Rick said, laughing. "You're not even going to be here. You're about to hit some third-world country for a year."

"But when I come back I'll want to swim."

Rick shook his head. "She's insane, Mom, but no kidding. We could use a pool. I could invite my friends over."

"Yeah, maybe he'd finally get a girl," Annie said.

"And how do you guys think Mark would feel about that?" Cathy asked. "It's bad enough that he knows the house is changing and he's not there to see it, and that the family may change before he gets out, that his sister's going off to another country and his brother is moving into the dorms. How do you think he'd feel if he knew we were building a pool?"

"He'd probably be anxious to get out so he could swim," Annie said.

"No," Cathy said. "We're not building a pool. I don't want to hear any more about it."

Steve shrugged. "Oh, well, it was worth a try."

"Don't give up that easy," Annie said. "You're the man. You've got to stand up for yourself."

"Well, since I don't own your mother's house, I'm thinking I'd better defer to her on this."

"Hey, you are going to own it," Rick said. "When you get married, what's hers is yours and what's yours is hers, right?"

Cathy couldn't believe they were switching sides just for the sake of a pool. "You guys are priceless, you know that? Not *once* have you encouraged us to go ahead and get married. In fact, you both seem pretty content with the status quo. But the minute there's something in it for you . . ."

"Well, sure, Mom," Rick said. "That's human nature. There's something in it for you, too. Think about it. A cool swim after a hard day's work . . ."

"It's only you we're thinking of, you know," Annie added.

"Yeah, right." Cathy smiled at her kids in the backseat. "Sorry, no enchilada. We're not getting a pool."

"Man!" Annie slapped her hand on the seat. "I should have known it was too good to be true."

"Sorry I brought it up," Steve said.

They reached River Ranch and pulled into the usual parking lot. The visitation room was crowded tonight, full of mothers and sisters and brothers, and several children fathered by the teenaged boys.

When Mark stepped into the room, he looked around and quickly found them at the table. His face lit up.

He looked pale and had dark circles under his eyes. Steve wondered if he'd been sleeping.

Mark greeted them all with hugs for the

women and handshakes for Steve and Rick, then sat down and bantered with his sister and brother for a while.

Finally, Steve saw an opening. "So did you get my Bible study?"

Mark frowned. "Your what?"

"You know, the letter I sent you with the Scripture verses to look up?"

Mark looked down at his hands. "Oh, that. Yeah, I got it."

"Well, did you read it or did you make paper airplanes out of it?" Rick asked.

Steve wished Rick hadn't said that. It might have given Mark a new idea.

"I skimmed it," he said. "It's in my locker."

Cathy looked embarrassed. "Mark, Steve went to a lot of—"

"I'm doing it, too, you know," Rick cut in, propping his chin.

"Doing what?" Mark asked.

"The Bible study."

Steve gave him a confused look. What was he talking about?

"Steve's about to start working with me on it, too," Rick said. "I'd hate to get so far ahead of you that we had to stop and wait for you to catch up."

Steve saw the interest pique in Mark's face. "No way," Mark said. "You're doing a Bible study with Steve?"

"Yeah. It might be over your head, though."

Mark was insulted. "It's not over my head."

Steve decided to seize the moment and hold Rick to his word. "Yeah, we're going to start with the Prodigal Son, which is what I sent you. Then we'll go back to some of the more exciting events in the Old Testament."

"Yeah, that Jericho's pretty cool," Rick said.

Cathy looked shocked, but she rallied well. "Yeah, it's one of my favorites."

"Those walls falling down and all," Rick said. "And God telling them to march around the city and blow the trumpet. And they never had to fire a shot."

"Mark, you remember," Cathy said. "Didn't Brenda talk about the walls of Jericho with you?"

"Yeah, I remember," Mark said. "I know all about Jericho. But the trumpets are a little fuzzy."

"Look it up," Rick said. "I'm not doing your work for you."

"It'll be in the next installment of letters," Steve promised. "I'll mail it tonight."

"Then I'll get it tomorrow?" Mark asked.

"Or the next day," Steve said.

Mark considered his brother, and Steve could almost see the spirit of competition coloring his face.

"So what kind of schedule are you and Rick on?" Mark asked him.

"We'll work together twice a week," Steve said, and Rick turned and gave him a surprised look. Steve only grinned.

"But if that's too fast for you . . . ," Rick said.

"No, it's fine," Mark said. "I can do that."

Steve sat back in his chair and decided he owed Rick a big one. Who would have thought a challenge from his brother would have piqued Mark's interest this way?

As the bantering went on, Steve's mind reeled with possibilities. He would have to make it something that Mark could discover on his own. He'd give him Scripture to look up, ask him hard questions, get him thinking. This could work even better than he'd expected. And even if it didn't, the time he'd get to spend with Rick, bonding and mentoring him, would be well worth it.

It gave him hope for the first time in a long time that this group of separate individuals might some day actually blend into a family.

On the way home from the jail everyone

was quiet until Annie erupted with her latest idea. "Mom, I've got an idea to raise a lot of money for my mission work."

"Does it have anything to do with a pool?" Cathy asked with a grin.

"No, for real. I was thinking of having a party, maybe renting the church's family life center or something, have music and food and let it go all night like one of those junior high lock-ins."

"Well, how's that going to raise money?"

"I could charge everybody twenty bucks. If I invited twenty people, that would be $400 right there. Forty people would be $800. Fifty people would be $1000. I'd have the money I needed before the party was over."

Cathy twisted to look at her daughter in the backseat. "Back in my day we used to work for our money."

"Well, I'm in a hurry, okay?" Annie said. "I want to get there before August so I don't have to go to school."

Cathy shook her head. "And here we were, thinking you were anxious to get there and help the children."

"Well, that, too," Annie said. "But, come on, Mom. If I don't go by August, you know you're going to make me enroll. I really want to do this. Will you help me with it?"

"I'll help," Cathy said, "but I'm not planning it, Annie. I'm not doing this *for* you. If you want to do it, you can call the church and ask them if the room is available. You find out what the rental is. You invite everybody and you buy the food and line up the music and all that. I'll be there as a chaperone. I don't mind that, even though going without sleep is definitely not on my list of fun things to do."

"It's for a good cause, Mom."

"I know," Cathy said, "but I'm telling you, I'm not planning this for you. This is part of your money-raising efforts, and if the Lord wants you to go, he'll help you with it."

"That's fine," Annie said. "I can do it."

"All right, but don't be surprised if people don't want to come. Twenty dollars is a lot of money for a kid to pay."

"Watch," Annie said with a satisfied grin. "You'll see. They'll come."

Chapter Sixty-One

Days later, Mark heard about the party his sister had planned in record time, and a letter from Daniel suggested that everybody in the world was going to be there. It was turning out to be the party of the year. Annie had all sorts of things planned, and she was calling it the "Help Me Help the Children" party. Mark figured his household was abuzz with activity right now as they made the final arrangements. He was missing it all. He wondered how many more events like this he would miss before he got out of jail.

He had trouble sleeping that night and lay on his back on the thin, lumpy mattress.

Around him, the other guys slept, and through their glass booth, he could see the guards watching TV as they kept their eyes on the room.

He wondered what was on.

He stared up at the ceiling, wishing he could fall asleep so he wouldn't be dog tired the next day, but dreary thoughts of his life passing him by kept him awake.

A tear rolled down his face. He wiped it away quickly, hoping no one would see. Others cried, sometimes, at night. He could hear sniffles from across the room, but never could identify exactly whose they were. If anyone ever did, they made fun of the guy mercilessly. A lot of the guys in here were too hard-core to shed a tear.

Another tear came, and he wiped it away.

He wished he could sit up, turn on the light, and get those letters from Steve out of the locker. He'd already read them each once, but they were the kind of things you had to think about a while. Steve had asked him questions and challenged him to find answers through his own search of the Bible. He just hadn't done it, even though he knew Rick was getting ahead of him.

But he couldn't sit up now and work on it,

because the guards wouldn't allow it. Everyone had to go to bed at the same time. They had to get up together and work together and study together, and there was never a moment's privacy, none at all. He didn't look forward to the thought of paging through a Bible in front of those guys.

No, the only time he could do that was in Bible study or chapel where others were doing it at the same time. Then, it was understood that they all did it to get out of the building.

He turned to his side and tried to get comfortable, closed his eyes and tried to fall asleep, but the thoughts just kept circulating through his mind like a repeating tape on a reel.

He was a coward, he admitted. If not, he wouldn't have cared what the others thought. He would have searched the Bible as much as he wanted to. Maybe it could really offer him help. Maybe God did care.

Loneliness wrapped him in its cold cocoon, making him more miserable than he'd been before. In the bunk next to him, Lazzo snored. Beef, across the room, mumbled curse words in his sleep. J.B. wheezed and coughed. So many around him, yet he was so alone.

Finally, he reached out to the only person who could hear him at the moment.

"Help me get out of here," he whispered to the Lord. He didn't know if God heard, if he cared, or if he listened, but Mark said it nonetheless. It was the first time he'd prayed in a long time. He wasn't sure he'd ever prayed from his heart. It had always been mechanical before, the "Now I lay me down to sleep" kind of prayer, or "God is great, God is good." None of it ever really sank in, but now his plea came from his heart. He hoped God was listening. He hoped he had the power to answer.

Chapter Sixty-Two

Somehow, Annie had conned Tory and Brenda into helping with the food for the "Help Me Help the Children" party. Annie had set up a screen as part of the decoration so she could flash pictures of the children on it all night, so that everyone could see the ones she would be helping.

At first, she told Cathy that fifty kids were coming, mostly from their youth group and school, but when Friday night arrived and they opened the doors, dozens more came. Friends had brought friends, and *they* had brought cousins and acquaintances and people they'd met at the mall. Word had gotten out all over Breezewood that this was the party of the year.

The church had agreed to let Annie pay for the family life center from the proceeds. They had also given her the condition that there would be no alcohol and no secular music on the premises, so she'd spent the whole week trying to find good Christian contemporary songs that could be played. One of Rick's friends from college played disc jockey and kept the music going.

Cathy thought the music selection was a God thing in itself, for Annie had discovered some Christian groups that she might never have noticed otherwise. Cathy couldn't have been prouder of Annie as the night wore on.

By two A.M., she and Steve were exhausted, and they left the gym and went into the game room where it was cooler and quieter. They plopped onto the couch there and dropped their heads back on the cushions.

"It's going well," Steve said.

"Yeah, I'm really proud of her," Cathy said. "But you know what this means, don't you?"

"It means she's going to be leaving soon."

"Yes. Soon. Like in the next week or two, maybe. A month, tops."

"That's right," Steve said. "How are you going to handle it?"

She looked at the ceiling. "I don't know. I guess I never really thought it would happen. I mean, Annie raising her own support? No way. But then she came up with this ingenious plan, and look at her. She's made money hand over fist tonight."

"She's let a few people in free."

"Yeah, but most of them have brought the money. And some of the parents even wrote bigger checks. It's kind of unbelievable."

"Maybe she'll be an entrepreneur."

"And all this time, I thought she'd be a con artist."

Steve laughed. "You did not."

She grinned. "No, but I never thought God would use her like this. I mean, I was just hoping she would walk straight and do right. I never expected her to bear fruit."

"Well, you should have expected it," Steve said. "She's God's child, too. That's what he wants from her."

"But I never dreamed it would happen this young. Look at her," she said. "She's in there, more concerned about the kids seeing those slides of the children than she is about how she looks. That's always been her first concern, before."

"You raised her right, Cathy. It finally kicked in."

Cathy gave a harsh laugh. "Hey, I don't think I had anything to do with this."

"Yes, you did," he said. "I want you to open your eyes and look, Cathy. God's giving you rewards."

Cathy touched his face, and her eyes glistened with tears. "I think you're one of those rewards."

"You bet I am." Steve slid his arms around her. "I've been waiting for you to notice."

"Oh, I noticed," she said.

"Then when are you going to marry me, Cathy?" he asked close to her lips.

"I don't know, Steve." She kissed him, but he pulled back.

"I don't want you to marry me until you're thrilled and excited about it, until planning it is fun. I don't want you to do it until you're ready to open those gifts and giggle over every single one."

She thought about those gifts still stacked

on her dining room floor. She had gone back and forth between sending them all back and tearing them open. "I don't want to get married until I feel that way either, Steve," she said. "I did feel that way until Mark got arrested. Everything's changed."

"I know it has," he said, "and there's not a lot I can do. But I want you to think about it, Cathy. We don't have to wait a year. God's not requiring that of us. And I don't think Mark is, either."

"I'm going to have to hear that from him," she said.

"So you need permission from your child before you make a life-changing decision?"

"Not in every case," Cathy said. "In fact, not in most cases. But in this case I'd have a lot more peace about it if I did."

He let her go and sat back on the couch, closing his eyes. "Okay," he said. "Then I'll just have to be patient."

"You'll wait, won't you?"

He smiled and threw her a frustrated look. "I can't break up with you now," he said. "I've got way too much invested."

She grinned and poked him in the ribs, and he grabbed her hand and pulled her close. As his lips descended to hers again, he whispered, "And might I add, it would break my heart in two?"

Cathy pulled him back into a kiss and knew that hers would break, too, if Steve wasn't in her life.

Chapter Sixty-Three

Mark spent the little free time he had for the next few days digging through the Scripture that Steve had sent him. The first day, he'd hidden the Bible under a stack of papers, and no one had noticed. The second day, Lazzo had seen it.

"Man, what you doin' with that Bible?" he'd whispered. "You let ole Beef see you with that, you'll be an open target."

"I'm not scared of Beef," Mark lied.

Lazzo gave him a long look, and Mark could have sworn there was admiration in his eyes. It gave him the courage to uncover the Bible. Even when Beef, the gang leader who could have been a bouncer or linebacker, headed his way, Mark kept reading.

"Man, you trying to impress the guards?" he asked. "They don't believe it when nobody gets religion. Been done."

Mark looked up at him. "I'll take my chances."

"Well, let me know if it works. I might get me one."

Mark didn't say anything, just went back to reading. When Beef ambled away, Mark looked up and saw Lazzo grinning at him as if he'd just performed some heroic feat.

Mark went to bed feeling better about himself that night. And when he tried to pray this time, he felt more of a familiarity with the Creator of the universe.

Wednesday night, Annie's appearance alone at visitation surprised him. His mother would be coming later, Annie said, but Annie had been anxious to share her pictures of the party with him. She told him of everyone who had asked about him, and he felt that familiar sense of shame.

"But I wanted you to see these pictures from Nicaragua, too," Annie said. "Miss

Sylvia sent them to me the other day. She just wanted me to have more of a taste of what I was in for. Look at these." She showed him some of the children who lived in the orphanage, whose parents had been killed in mud slides and tornadoes, or structural collapses when the hurricane had come. Others had parents, but they were starving and hung around the orphanage hoping to get a meal.

Mark looked at the snapshots one by one, trying to picture his sister among them, working with the children, showing responsibility, thinking of someone other than herself.

"This is pretty cool, what you're doing, Annie," he said.

Annie smiled. "Yeah, I think it's pretty cool, too. Who would have ever dreamed?"

"I guess Mom's pretty proud of you."

"Says she is."

"One kid in jail and another who's a missionary. Thank goodness she has Rick to keep things balanced."

Annie's serious gaze locked with his. "You're going to get out of here some day, Mark," she said. "You're not going to be a convict all your life."

"No, after this I'll be an *ex*-con."

She gave him an apologetic look. "Well, you know what they say."

Mark frowned. "No, what do they say?"

He could almost see the wheels in her mind turning as she tried to think of something compassionate to say. "Well, I don't know," she said finally. "But they must say something."

He couldn't help laughing, and she grinned.

"I'm sorry, okay?" she said. "It's just a bummer all around. I'm fresh out of Band-Aids."

For some reason, he didn't feel so bad about it. Annie had cheered him up, in her flaky kind of way. "So tell me about your love life." The question surprised even him.

"You never cared about my love life."

"Hey, it's entertainment. Who's the guy of the week?"

"Well, if you have to know, nobody. I'm scared to go out with anybody. Knowing me, I'll fall in love and it'll mess up all my plans. Besides, the guys all seem like such jerks right now. Nobody understands what I'm doing. It's kind of hard to explain."

"Yeah, I guess." Mark tipped his chair back

and looked down at the stupid striped pants they made him wear. "You think I'll ever have a shot at doing something like that?"

"Sure you will," she said. "It's your choice, Mark."

"Yeah. I made stupid choices before. Trust me," he said. "When I get out of here, I'm never touching a joint again."

"I believe you," Annie said. "And I think by the time you get out, you'll really mean it."

"I really mean it now," Mark said.

"Well, if you do, then maybe you'll do that Bible study Steve gave you."

He brought his chair back to all fours. "I have been," he said. "So do you know how far Rick is on it yet?"

"I don't know. I think they're still talking about Jericho," Annie said.

"No," Mark said. "We're finished with Joshua. We're studying David now."

Annie looked shocked. "Cool."

He was glad she didn't make a big deal over it. He stacked the pictures and handed them back to her. "So, when are you leaving, anyway?"

Annie's face lit up again. "Two weeks from tomorrow."

"No way," Mark said.

She smiled. "Yep. There's no use waiting. I've got all the money I need to get there and back, and even a little bit to keep me going in between. Mom's a little freaked out that it's so quick, but she'll get over it."

"It's going to be a hard year for her."

"Yeah," Annie said. "I really kind of wish she was going ahead and marrying Steve. That way I could wait and leave right after the wedding, and she'd have him to keep her busy. You know, we'll all three be gone come August," she said. "I'll be in Nicaragua, you'll be here, and Rick will be moving to campus. You know why she's not marrying Steve yet, don't you? It's because of you."

"Hey, I didn't stop anything," Mark said. "That's her choice. If she doesn't want to marry him . . ."

"She thinks you'll be worried the family is changing too much, that everything will be different when you get home."

"Well, everything will be different. They're already working on the house."

"But your room will be the same, Mark, and everything is still in place. It's just going to be bigger, better."

"Well, maybe I don't want our family to be bigger and better."

"I wish you'd think of Mom instead of yourself," she said. "Steve's really good for her."

"Well, I'm not so sure about that," he said. "She thought Dad was good for her. She was wrong about that."

Annie looked down at her hands. "So, has Dad been to see you yet?"

"No."

She shook her head. "I don't get that."

He glanced around the room, trying to look like it didn't interest him. "So have you seen him?"

"Yeah, I've seen him some. He's real touchy when the subject of you comes up."

"He's really mad at me," Mark whispered. He leaned his elbows on the table. "I totally blew it."

"You blew it?" Annie asked. "Mark, he's our dad. You're not supposed to be able to blow it with your dad."

"Well, it's not like he's an ordinary dad. I mean not like Mr. David or Barry, always home. I wouldn't even know what that was like," he said. "If I don't do everything right, he just pretends he doesn't know me."

"That's not true," Annie said. "He's our father."

"Well, he's not acting much like it. I mean, where is he when I need him?"

"He'll come around," Annie said. "He's just having a hard time."

"Well, so am I!"

"I know," she told him. "And Rick and I have tried to talk to him, but you know how stubborn he is."

"Yeah," Mark said. "I guess that's where I get it."

"You get your fair share from Mom, too," Annie said. She glanced at her watch and slid her chair back. "Well, I've got to go. I'm supposed to meet some people. Mom will be here in a little while."

He stood up as she did and crossed his arms awkwardly. "So . . . are you coming back before you skip the country?"

"Sure I am." But something about the way she hugged him and waved good-bye told him that this was the last time he would see her for a while. Annie wasn't into long good-byes, and she didn't like crying in front of others. He hoped he was wrong about that, because he wasn't ready to say good-bye to his sister for a whole year.

He watched her leave the room, then

turned back to the table. She had left the pictures. He picked them up and took them back to his building with him.

Lying down on his bunk, he looked at them more carefully, studying the faces of the hungry children, seeing the difference the food had made in their lives.

He felt sick that he would never be able to do anything as good as what Annie was doing. He had messed up his life and ruined any chance he'd ever have of making a difference.

He didn't know why a real God would spend any time with him. He supposed that God, like his father, was turning his back on him, unwilling to pay attention until Mark had somehow made up for what he'd done. For the life of him, he didn't know how to do it from in here.

He pulled out his Bible and read back over the parable of the Prodigal Son again. He couldn't imagine the father searching the horizon for the kid who had messed up so bad. He looked up some of the verses Steve had given him again, and tried to understand what kind of father God was.

When he'd exhausted all the Scripture verses in the Prodigal Son letters, he turned to the next letters about the walls of Jericho and tried to imagine the walls of this place falling down. Rick was right. This Jericho thing was pretty cool. This God was pretty cool. Mark still wasn't sure he believed, but there were smart people who did. He supposed they must know something.

That night, when it was time for lights-out, and he lay on his bunk staring at the ceiling again, he went to God. It was starting to become a habit.

"If you're really the God from the Bible," he whispered, "then show me how to get my dad's love back. He's not like the father in the story. He's not looking for me at all, 'cause he knows right where to find me."

He felt as if the words fell on deaf ears, and he turned onto his side and wiped a tear away again. He wished his father could be more like Steve, writing him letters every day and worrying about his soul. Steve was even coming to visit him at almost every visitation, but his father hadn't contacted him once. Mark knew he might not hear from him for the rest of his sentence.

It wasn't like his dad was used to having him around and missed his sudden absence. In his dad's eyes, Mark was always absent.

For most of Mark's life, he'd only seen him every other weekend. There was nothing to miss. Not from where his father sat.

Mark didn't know why all of this suddenly mattered so much to him, but it did.

He fell into a restless sleep, dreaming of his father standing at the edge of the horizon, watching it and looking for him as he came, muddy and clothed in rags, tromping up a hill toward home. But just as his eyes connected with his dad's, he saw Jerry turn and walk away.

The Prodigal Son was not welcome home. And Mark couldn't say he blamed his father.

Chapter Sixty-Four

Tory threw away her carefully calculated schedule and immersed herself in prayer about her pride and her expectations for Hannah. Forcing herself to relax, she went back to the school on their next assigned day. This time she made a conscious effort to see the class as a support system she sorely needed, and laughed and played with Hannah as if they were in no hurry to reach that next milestone.

They both came home happier.

That evening, Barry brought home a bouquet of roses. She gave him a suspicious grin as she took them. "What are these for?"

"I just thought you deserved flowers," he said, kissing her. "And a date for the first time in a very long time. We haven't been out without the kids since Hannah was born."

Tory's face changed. "Barry, you know how I feel about leaving her with baby-sitters. Her chest is rattling again, and there isn't a baby-sitter who knows how to hold her right. Her neck still isn't strong . . ."

Barry brought his finger to his mouth, shushing her. "It just so happens that there are a few people who do know how to hold Hannah. And I've paid one of them big bucks to baby-sit."

"Who?" she asked.

"Melissa."

Tory caught her breath. "Her physical therapist? Barry, she's a professional. You can't ask her to baby-sit!"

"I can, and I did. For a hundred bucks, she decided to come. I'm taking you to dinner and dancing, so go get ready. You have two hours before she'll be here."

The shocked look on Tory's face slowly gave way to a smile as the information sank in. She could leave Hannah with Melissa. After all, she was the one who'd taught Tory how to hold Hannah. She was the one responsible for much of the baby's progress. She had been a twice-a-week fixture in their lives since Hannah was born, and the baby knew and enjoyed her.

"Come on," he said. "You can't back out. I've paid her in advance." He took Hannah from her and guided her toward the bedroom. "Take a long hot soak in a bath, and then put on that black dress I like. Our reservations are at seven."

She laughed aloud with relief that everything had been done for her. The baby-sitter, the reservations, even the decision about what to wear. Reveling in the orders to relax, she took advantage of the quiet to soak in the tub.

Chapter Sixty-Five

The day Annie was to depart for Nicaragua, most of her youth group from church gathered at the airline gate with her, as well as all of the neighbors from Cedar Circle. Cathy had moped for the last week as she anticipated this day, and she had deliberately put off saying good-bye. She had been on the verge of tears the whole day as they'd packed, pulling together all the things Annie would need for a year's stay in Leon.

But now she wished she'd had a talk with Annie before they'd headed to the airport, that she had sat down and told her how proud she was of her, how hard she would be praying for her, what high hopes she had for Annie's future now that she was following the Lord's path. But all of that went unsaid as Annie went from friend to friend and from neighbor to neighbor, hugging each one and saying good-bye.

When the boarding call finally came, Annie grabbed up her carry-on bag, and Cathy saw her big, misty eyes rapidly seeking her out in the crowd. When she found her mother, their eyes locked in dread. Cathy burst into tears and pushed through the people, got to her daughter, and threw her arms around her.

Annie clung a little longer than she'd expected. "I'll miss you, Mom." Her voice cracked.

"I'll miss you more," she said. "Honey, I'll be praying for you." She took a step back and looked into Annie's wet eyes. She felt self-conscious with everyone's eyes on them, but she couldn't let anyone deprive her of this moment. She wiped the tears on Annie's face, then her own, and pulled her daughter close again.

"I'm so proud of you," she whispered in her ear.

"Don't be, yet," Annie told her. "I might turn into a wimp and come running back home."

"And you might not," Cathy said. "You might make a difference in a thousand children's lives."

It was all she could do to let Annie go, and she stood on the other side of the rope as her daughter stepped across the threshold to the jet bridge all alone. Annie paused and turned back, looked at Cathy again, then swallowed hard and disappeared down the hallway.

Brenda and Tory came to Cathy's side, putting their arms around her while she waved good-bye. She felt Steve's hands on her shoulders from behind.

Annie was gone, but she was in good hands. God would get her there, and Sylvia's arms would be waiting on the other side of the trip.

She had to learn to let her children go and trust God to take things up where she had left off. He, after all, was a better parent than she.

Chapter Sixty-Six

Cathy couldn't sleep that night. She put off going to bed, and instead, walked from room to room in her house, looking for evidence of her children. Rick was out late with friends, and the house felt empty. She went to the back window and peered out onto the construction work, on the foundation that had been laid weeks ago and the boards that were going up to form the framework of her new life.

She tried to picture her new bedroom with Steve, him sitting in the rocker pulling on his shoes, combing his hair, shaving over the sink. It had been a long time since she'd had a husband. She wished she could just marry him and bring him into the family, with his strong hands of support, his broad shoulder to cry on when she thought of her empty nest. She wished she had Tracy's little-girl laughter filling up the silence.

But she couldn't marry him yet. Not until Mark felt better about things.

She went to the cabinet and found the old home videos that she and Jerry had made when Mark was just a little boy, and she chose one of Christmas when he was only three. She popped it into the VCR and sat down across from the television, intent on finding the little boy her son had once been, the little girl to whom she had just waved good-bye, and the firstborn who was preparing to move away in just days.

She watched Mark skipping along, holding his father's hand . . . and Jerry waving at the camera. That skipping had always made Jerry smile.

She watched as the father picked up the child and put him on his shoulder, then acted as if he was going to buck him off. Mark screamed and squealed with laughter. Annie bounced up and down next to her dad.

"Do me next, Daddy!" she cried. "Do me."

Rick, only seven, tried to act cool while awaiting his own turn.

Then the picture changed, and Cathy saw herself at a younger age. She tried to imagine what she had felt like when she'd had a man in the home, a father for her children, an intact family unit. It had been a very long time.

She put in another video, shot when Mark was a little older. Cathy studied it for his facial expressions, the bounce in his step, the smile in his eyes. He had stopped skipping when his father left. The twinkle in his eye had dimmed then, too. Was that where his life had turned? Had he been headed, ever since then, toward the prison that now held him? She couldn't say for sure, didn't even want to try. But he had lost his innocence a long time ago.

At just after midnight, she heard the car door slam in the garage. She looked up as Rick came into the house and closed and locked the door behind him.

"Mom, what are you doing up? You have to work tomorrow."

"I know," she said. "I just couldn't sleep."

He studied her as if he had caught her at something, then glanced at the TV screen. "What are you watching?"

"Just an old video," she said, "of when you and Mark and Annie were little. I was just watching Mark's face. It's hard to remember him that young and carefree."

Rick smiled at the picture on the screen. "He used to skip," Rick said. "Do you remember?"

"Yeah," she whispered. "I was just thinking about that."

He sat down opposite her and regarded her for a moment. She recognized the concern on his face. "Why didn't Steve come over tonight?"

"He had to get Tracy to bed," she said. "We talked on the phone, but he has to get up early, so he went on to bed."

Rick looked from her to the video, then back again. "You okay about Annie?"

She smiled. "Yeah, Annie'll be fine."

He sat there a moment, letting silence fall like wet dew between them. In a weaker, more doubtful voice, he asked, "You okay about Mark?"

Her smile faded. She frowned slightly and looked at the video again. "I'm getting there."

He tipped his head and gave her another gentle look. "You okay about me?"

She thought about that for a moment, then took in a deep breath. "I don't think I've told you how proud I am of you, Rick. I mean, with Annie going to the mission field and Mark getting a lot of the attention, I've just mostly been grateful for you. But I haven't said it enough."

"Why? What did I do?"

"You're just a good kid," she said. "I'm proud of the way you're helping Daniel learn to drive, and how you got him that job, and how you're mentoring him."

"Mentoring?"

"Yeah, you know, the big brother kind of thing. He needed that, I think."

"Well, I just kind of felt like it was a way to help, since I couldn't help Mark."

"I know," she said. "It was a good thing. You're a sweet boy. You're going to make somebody a wonderful husband. And some day you're going to be a great father."

He looked at her as if she were crazy. "Me?"

"Yes, you," she said. "I raised you. I know what you're like. Why would that surprise you?"

He shrugged and looked back at the screen. "Well, it's not like I've had a great role model. For being a father, I mean."

Rick rarely said anything negative about his father, so the observation surprised her. "You don't think so?"

"No. I'm disappointed in him," Rick said. "The way he's acting toward Mark. I just don't get it. I think he might just not want to be bothered. And he's acting funny to Annie and me, too. He doesn't want us to bring up Mark's name because he knows we're going to hound him about visiting. And then he didn't even show up today to see Annie off."

"She told me they said their good-byes last weekend," Cathy said. "It is kind of awkward, you know, having the ex-husband and ex-wife there alongside each other."

"Get over it, Mom," Rick said. "That's the way things are. You'll both be at our weddings. When my first kid celebrates his third birthday I'm going to invite both you and Dad. You're going to have to learn to get along with each other."

"I know," she said, "and I will."

He stared down at his feet for a long moment, and she wondered if he was trying to

picture it. His own home with a wife and children. His mother and father standing across
a birthday cake from each other. "Why don't
you go to bed, Mom?" he asked finally.
"You're going to be wiped out in the morning."

She nodded, clicked off the television, and
wearily got up. "Guess I will."

She kissed him good night. As she
stepped into her bedroom, she heard him
turning on David Letterman. The bedroom
felt big and lonely and cold, and she longed
to have Steve there beside her, helping her
to relax in the safety and security of his
arms, knowing she wasn't alone, that someone who loved her dearly was there beside
her and would be there when she woke up.

She got into her bed and lay on her side
for a moment, knowing sleep wasn't going to
come easily. She looked at the phone and
thought about calling Steve, just talking to
him into the night, as if they were teenagers
in love. She knew it would wake him up, and
that wasn't fair. But the longer she lay there,
the lonelier the room became.

Finally, she picked up the phone and dialed his number.

He answered with a hoarse, groggy voice
on the third ring. "Hello?"

"I woke you up," she whispered. "I'm so sorry."

She heard sheets rustling, as if he was sitting up. "Cathy. You okay?"

"Yeah, I'm fine," she said. "Just lonely for you."

"You sure, for me?" he asked, and she could hear the smile in his voice. "Not for Annie, or Mark?"

"Them, too," she whispered. "But mostly you right now."

"Then I'm glad you called."

"You sure?" she asked. "Because it was really selfish of me, waking you up. I should have just laid here and toughed it out."

"No, you shouldn't," he said. "You never have to tough it out again, Cathy. Your lonely nights could come to an end real soon. All you have to do is marry me. Then you can just turn over and nudge me in the side, and I'll wake up."

"I know," she whispered. She turned on her back and pulled the phone with her. "I was just watching videos of Mark, thinking back to when he was a little boy. Trying to figure out where the road turned."

"Don't do that to yourself, Cathy."

"I had to remember," she whispered. "I had

to see it, so I'd know I hadn't just made it up in my mind."

"I love you, Cathy. I wish I could give you back all the years Jerry took away from you."

She smiled. She knew he would do that if he could, no matter the cost. Just the knowing made her feel better. "You're a good man, Steve Bennett. I'm going to let you go back to sleep now."

He sat there a moment like a teenaged boy who didn't want to cut the connection, and finally he whispered, "Good night. Call me back if you need me, okay?"

"Okay," she said.

"Promise?"

"Promise."

"'Cause I'm just seven digits away. You know that, don't you?"

"Yeah," she whispered, and quietly hung up the phone.

The calming balm of Steve's voice helped her fall asleep, and she rested despite the images of her kids as young children, skipping and begging for their turn . . .

What was Mark thinking right now?

Had Annie landed yet?

She thanked the Lord that one of her chicks was still in the nest, even if he wouldn't be there much longer. The knowledge that someone was in the house gave her great peace, and finally she drifted into a restless sleep.

Chapter Sixty-Seven

Annie's stomach tied itself in knots as her plane touched down in Managua. For the last few weeks, her life had revolved around her preparation for *getting* here. She hadn't given much thought to *being* here. She tried to swallow the knot in her throat as she clutched her duffel bag and stood in the aisle, waiting for the passengers to move off the plane.

Spanish conversations were exchanged all around her. She'd heard them all the way here, and it had seemed like a novelty at first. Now she realized that *she* was the foreigner, in a country where she didn't speak the language. She should have paid more attention in Spanish class. Or at least bought tapes and brushed up before she came.

A tear dropped to her cheek, but she brushed it away. She thought of little Miguel and the other children she would get to know. She didn't feel much older than they. What on earth did she have to offer them?

She followed the passengers up the aisle and off the plane. As she walked through the jet bridge, she wondered what she would do if Sylvia wasn't waiting for her? How would she call her? How would she get to Leon?

But as soon as she entered the terminal, she saw her favorite neighbor across the crowd, laughing and waving as if she bubbled over with delight at the sight of her. "Annie!"

Annie's fears melted away, and she ran to Sylvia and threw her arms around her.

"You're here!" Sylvia cried. "Bless your heart, you're here!"

Annie's tears vanished as her purpose returned.

When Sylvia pulled her car up to load her bags, Annie thought she was putting her on. "Sylvia, this is not your car!"

Sylvia gave an amused look at the beat-up Fiat they had bought when they'd first come here. "Sorry, but it is. I told you there were no frills here."

Annie tried not to look shocked as she pulled on the passenger door handle. It stuck.

"I'll get it," Sylvia said. She got in on the driver's side and gave the passenger door a good kick. It jolted open. "You just have to know how."

Annie stood there a moment, looking into the car as her dignified older neighbor ducked slightly in the front seat to avoid the dented roof. She struggled to get her feet back in front of her.

Annie didn't mean to, but she started to laugh. She tried to stop it, tried to get serious, but the harder she tried, the funnier things seemed. Sylvia began to laugh, too, and Annie leaned against the car to support herself.

"You used to drive a Cadillac!" Annie screamed with laughter. She took a deep breath and tried to stop. "I'm sorry, Sylvia. I just can't picture you driving this."

"You're about to, honey." Sylvia wiped the tears her laughter had produced and came around the car. She picked up Annie's suitcase and crammed it into the backseat. "You should have seen me when Harry came home with it. I laughed, too. Thought it was one of the best jokes he'd ever played on me. Then I cried, until I realized it really was all we could get. And it runs okay. We haven't had many problems with its engine."

Still laughing, Annie tried to help her wedge the suitcase behind the seats, but Sylvia had some bags piled up, and they were in the way. They fell against each other laughing.

Sylvia let go of the suitcase and put her arms around the girl. "Oh, it's going to be good to have you here. Harry and I need more laughter." She let her go and shoved at the suitcase again.

Annie sighed and let her laughter die. "What's all this stuff?" she asked.

"Bags of beans and rice," Sylvia said. "I picked some supplies up before I came to the airport. It should get us through a few days. I wish I'd had more room. I thought of tying some on top but I was afraid we'd have to do that with your luggage." She pulled the seat back. "There. It's in."

Annie eyed the car again. The thought of riding in it didn't seem quite as amusing as it had at first. "Will this get us all the way to Leon?"

"It'll have to," Sylvia said. "Don't worry. It has every time before."

Annie got into the car and stuffed her carry-on bag in front of her. She sat with it at her feet, trying to get comfortable.

"That door may not close well once you get it open," Sylvia said. "Here, let me do it."

She came around and slammed it several times, trying to make it click. When it finally did, she warned her not to lean on it. She got in and started the car, then looked over at Annie. "I told you it's not like Breezewood."

Annie just grinned. "I was about to say that the bags and the suitcase are keeping you from seeing out the back window . . . but you can't, anyway, with the plastic taped on like that."

Sylvia chuckled and started to pull out into traffic. Annie felt as if she needed to swing her body forward to help give the car some pickup. "That window was one of our biggest frustrations the first few months we were here. Someone smashed our window to steal something out of the car. We ordered a replacement window, but it never came. Still hasn't come, to this day." She patted Annie's leg. "It's no Cadillac, but it gets us where we need to go."

"So the place where you live, is it kind of like the car?" Annie asked, bracing herself.

"Oh, no, honey. Don't worry about that. We have a nice place to live. We make our sacrifices where we have to, but sometimes they're not required."

"Thank heaven," Annie said, leaning her head back on the torn seat. "I was picturing an adobe hut with plastic windows duct-taped on."

Sylvia burst out laughing again and patted Annie's hand. "No, our windows are real glass," she said, "and they're all in one piece so far. It's not Cedar Circle, but it's home."

They chattered all the way to Leon, about Mark and Rick and Daniel's accident and Cathy and Steve.

But as they reached the city of Leon, Annie got quiet and looked around at the red-roofed houses up on the mountains on one side of the town, and the lush green vegetation coloring the landscape.

"We're not going straight to the house," Sylvia said. "We have to go by the clinic to let Dr. Harry see that you made it okay, then we've got to go over to the food distribution center and start cooking for the evening meal."

Annie shot her a look. "People are coming tonight?"

"You bet they are. They heard I was getting fresh supplies in Managua, so there'll be more tonight than usual. We've been real low on supplies lately, and we've had to turn people away."

"That's awful."

"I know," Sylvia told her, "but we're working on selling the house, and as soon as we do, we shouldn't have that problem anymore."

Annie got quiet.

"What is it, honey?"

"Well, it's just my mom. She's lost an awful lot lately. I hate to see her lose you, too."

"She's not going to lose me. Heavens. She'll never lose me."

"Well, I know, but your house sitting there was kind of a symbol of you. Once you sell it, it's not going to be *you* anymore. I don't know how she can handle that on top of everything else."

"Well, as soon as you write home and tell her about all the great work you're doing with the money we make on the house, she'll know it was the right choice," Sylvia said.

They ran by the clinic, and Dr. Harry made a big fuss over Annie, taking her around to meet all the people who worked there with him. Then they got back into the car and headed over to the food center. Since it was in a building adjacent to the orphanage, several of the orphans helped to cook the evening meal.

Annie's heart broke when she saw the real faces of the children she had only seen in pictures. Again, she wished she'd spent more time trying to learn their language.

They had barely started preparing the meal when the children from the community began showing up. She saw the hungry faces, the skinny little children with their ribs showing and their bellies distended. She felt as if she was in over her head as Sylvia and the Nicaraguan women who helped her hurried to make enough food to meet everyone's needs.

As the crowd of hungry people grew, Annie was overwhelmed. She counted two hundred children and at least a hundred adults. She watched their faces as they devoured the only meal some of them had had that day.

The children didn't change before her

eyes, and she didn't receive accolades or applause for her work. But that night, when Sylvia finally took her to the home that would be hers for the next year, she realized it had been the most rewarding evening of her life. She had fed the hungry, and it felt pretty good.

She only hoped she'd have a little beach time before she had to go at it again.

Chapter Sixty-Eight

Steve went with Cathy to visit Mark at the next visitation, and Mark floored them both with his question.

"So what's this stuff about the loot in Jericho?"

Steve tried not to look shocked. "The loot in Jericho? I thought we were studying David."

"I finished that and started over," Mark said. "How come they couldn't take the loot there after the walls fell down and they took possession of the city? But in the next city they could?"

Steve glanced at Cathy. Was this a sign that Mark wasn't just doing it out of competition with his brother? Had the Scripture itself drawn him back?

"I think it had to do with giving God the first of what they had," Steve said. "God calls that 'firstfruits.' Like the farmers when they have a harvest, he wants them to give the first bit of it to him. It's kind of a sovereignty thing— God's way of reminding them that they wouldn't have any of it without him."

"Well, they sure wouldn't have any of Jericho," Mark said. "But then how come they got to take loot in the other cities?"

"Because those weren't the firstfruits," Steve said. "God wanted Jericho, and he gave them the rest. But sometimes we're so anxious to take all we think we deserve, that we lose out on the better things he has in store for us."

"Well, that guy who got killed sure did. I mean, all he did was steal a few things, and the next thing you know his whole family is paying for his crime."

"God means business," Steve said. "What can I say? He wanted to show them that when he gives them an order, they'd better follow it. He wanted to show them who was in charge. Somebody's always in charge, you know."

"Tell me about it," Mark said. He looked around at the guards.

Then Mark changed the subject to Daniel's job and the letters he'd gotten from him about his work and his driving. Steve sat back in his chair, listening to Cathy's exchange with her son and trying not to look as excited as he felt. Mark's interest was a giant leap forward. He'd actually been studying his Bible, thinking about it, and now he was asking questions.

He wanted to jump out of his chair and leap for joy, wanted to pull the kid up and swing him around. But he knew that if he made a big deal out of it, Mark wasn't likely to do it again soon. So he played it cool and didn't make a scene. But in his heart he was dancing; God was already answering his prayers.

Later that night, when Cathy and Steve had gone home, Rick came by to see Mark for the last thirty minutes of visitation. They made small talk about baseball season and who had made All-Stars. Then Rick got serious.

"Hey, Mark, I was thinking about Mom the other day," he said. "About how lonely she is, what with Annie gone and you gone and me getting ready to move out. She's there all by herself. I came in the other night after midnight and she was up watching videos of us when we were little kids."

Mark tried to picture it. The thought of his mother sitting up alone in the middle of the night, strolling down memory lane, disturbed him.

"Mark, I think you need to tell her to get married."

"*Me* tell her?" Mark asked. "Why do I have to tell her? She's not waiting for me."

"She is too," Rick said. "She feels like it would hurt you if the family changed that much while you're in here. She doesn't want to do it without your approval. But, Mark, you need to start thinking of her. She never deserved to be alone in the first place. It wasn't her idea to get a divorce all those years ago. You were little, but it's no secret that Dad left her for Mary."

Mark shrugged. "I'm not stupid."

"So how come Mom's the one that had to be alone all these years? It's not fair, Mark. And now there's a man who loves her and wants to take care of her, and she won't marry him."

"She will marry him," Mark said. "Or else they wouldn't be adding onto the house."

"But she won't marry him as long as you're in here, not unless you tell her to."

"Yeah, like she'd really listen to me."

"She'll listen to you if you say *that,*" Rick said. He looked around at the visiting families at other tables, then lowered his voice and leaned in closer. "Mark, I'm asking you to do something for somebody else for a change. Think about what Annie's doing, going down there to feed all those kids. Come on, I know there are times when you sit there and think, 'I ought to be doing something like that.' Because I sure do."

Mark looked astonished that Rick had those same feelings.

"Well, you *can* do something like that," Rick said. "You can give Mom her freedom to marry Steve. You can tell her that you want her to. It's not even that big of a sacrifice for you. Not like going off across the world or something. Just say the words."

"But they would be a lie," Mark said.

"Then make it be the truth," Rick told him. "Just work on yourself until you really feel it. Mom's been through a lot. She deserves happiness."

Mark's face grew hot, and he glanced at the door where the guard stood, wondering if he should just get up right now and walk out of there. He didn't have to listen to this.

But he didn't. "You think I don't know what Mom deserves?"

"I think maybe you don't care," Rick said. "Sometimes things are all about us, you know? This time let's make it about her."

Mark leaned on the table and looked around the room with angry eyes. "So you really want Steve walking around in our house in his underwear with his little twerp girl running around like she owns the place?"

Rick shrugged. "I'm hardly ever there, anyway. What difference does it make? And it's kind of nice to have Tracy in the house. She's real upbeat, you know? Everything's an adventure to her. Mom's always in a better mood when she's around. And Steve's a good guy. He'll take good care of her."

"I never said he wasn't a good guy."

"Then think about it," Rick told him. "Maybe you'll have to work on yourself a while, sort of psyche yourself up. But do it, okay? For Mom's sake."

Mark rubbed his eyes. "I'm not promising anything."

Rick snorted. "I didn't expect you to."

Later that night, as Mark lay in bed, he turned the words over and over in his mind and wondered what it would really cost him if his mother got married. Would it really hurt that much? Was it his feeling of being left out of the family that bothered him most? Or was that just an excuse, one more way of manipulating things to his advantage?

He didn't want to be like that anymore. He wanted to be thought of as one of the good kids, not the criminal that everyone had to work around.

But he just wasn't ready to tell her to do it. Not yet. He needed more time.

Chapter Sixty-Nine

Annie didn't get near the beach for the next several days. Instead, she spent time working with the children at the orphanage, playing games with them, holding them when they wanted to be loved. In the evenings, they would assemble at the food distribution center, where she would sweat over a hot stove of beans and rice, then feed it to the children, the same thing day after day. Sylvia said it was nutritious and had everything they needed, and she could see as the days progressed that some of them really were improving.

But newer, scrawnier children showed up each day.

The fact that Sylvia took every chance she got to share the gospel of Christ surprised Annie, especially when they were working hard to get things done. Sylvia was never too busy to stop and have a one-on-one, heart-to-heart talk with anyone who would listen.

Just that day, one of Sylvia's converts had come by to tell her that he had decided to give his life to ministry. Sylvia had almost danced for joy.

"See this, Annie?" she asked. "This is how it works. You lead someone to Christ, and before you know it, they're leading others, and the next thing you know there are hundreds and thousands of people who know Jesus. That's more important than the food we're giving them. Do you understand that, Annie?"

Annie stopped stirring and wiped the sweat from her forehead. "Actually, no. It seems to me like the food is more important right now. I mean, the spiritual stuff is good and everything, and yeah, they need Jesus. But I guess I don't see it as first in importance."

"Jesus said he was the Bread of Life,"

Sylvia said. "He's the Living Water. We can feed their bellies all we want to, but we've got to feed their souls, or it doesn't do them any good."

Annie thought about it that evening when she dropped exhausted into bed. Just before she fell asleep, she realized that Sylvia was right. There were millions of people in America who had full bellies . . . but they still seemed hungry. It wasn't until they knew Christ that their focus shifted and they were finally filled.

Just before she drifted to sleep, she asked the Lord to help her to make a deeper commitment to him, so that she would have the nerve and the courage and the enthusiasm to distribute her faith among the needy, just as she was helping distribute the food.

She wanted to be as excited about that part as Sylvia was. She knew the children of Nicaragua needed the Bread of Life. And maybe she was the one to give it to them.

Chapter Seventy

David Dodd hadn't been to the grocery store in years. Although he considered himself an equal partner with his wife and didn't necessarily hold to traditional roles for men and women, he always let Brenda take care of the food in their house. There always seemed to be everything he needed, so he never had reason to shop for groceries.

But today he found reason.

He needed bread, he told himself, and if Daniel happened to be working at the time, so be it. He wasn't a father checking up on his son. He was just a customer who had a purchase to make.

He came, glanced at the cash registers, and saw Daniel at the end, bagging groceries as fast as he could. Pride swelled in David's heart. His son was a hard worker, just like he had taught him to be.

He slipped on past the cash registers and went down the produce aisle, searching for the bakery. Thirteen aisles later, he found the bread aisle. He stood there for a moment, looking at the wide array of breads. Whole wheat? White? Rye? He grabbed the wheat, because he recognized the wrapper. Then he headed to the cash register.

He tried to pick an aisle where his son wasn't working, hoping that maybe Daniel wouldn't notice him. But their eyes met as he reached the line. Daniel's face fell, just as Brenda had described the other day. David just lifted his hand in a wave, trying not to embarrass his son.

Daniel looked relieved and turned back to his work. David made his purchase, then gave his son a wink. Daniel smiled.

David grinned all the way out to the car.

For the rest of the day, David couldn't stop thinking about his son working hard at his first job. Despite Brenda's protests, he had allowed Daniel to work almost every day. At this rate, he would have the insurance deductible paid soon. Within a couple of years, he might even be able to save for a car.

He hated to make Daniel wait. Maybe there was some way he could help out. They didn't have much money, but maybe a little could be allotted for a car for the boy, now that he was learning responsibility.

David didn't mention it to Brenda; he just turned the idea over and over in his mind, wondering how it could be worked out. He worked with his budget for several days, trying to see if a hundred dollars could be spared here, another hundred there, a couple of hundred somewhere else. The car didn't have to be that good—just reliable enough to get him to work, church, baseball practice, and back.

He was out cutting the front yard one night when Steve drove up at Cathy's. They waved at each other and, as he often did, Steve stepped across the street and shook his hand. "How's it going, David?"

"Pretty good," David said. He cut off the lawn mower and leaned on it, taking a breather. "So how's this wedding thing going with you and Cathy?"

"Well, right now it's not," Steve said.

"Oh, yeah? Well, then why all the construction?"

"Going out on faith," Steve said. "But I'm hoping we're getting closer."

David chuckled. "You know, Rick's been a real good kid, helping Daniel the way he has with driving and all."

Steve smiled. "That's good to hear. I'll tell Cathy you said it."

David glanced across the street and saw that Steve was driving a newer model pickup than the one he'd last noticed him in. "Get a new truck?"

"Sure did," Steve said. "I have a friend who owns a used car lot on the other side of Breezewood. He gave me a good deal, so I decided to upgrade."

David studied the truck. "Gave you a good deal, huh? Did he have any older model cars that might be good for a teenaged boy?"

Steve lifted his eyebrows. "Sure. Had a bunch of them."

"I wonder if I could get a deal. I can't afford much, but I sure would like to get something for Daniel. He deserves some wheels, as hard as he's been working. Maybe we could take out a little loan, let him pay the notes."

Steve grinned. "Tell you what. I'll take you

down and introduce you to my friend. Maybe he can work you up a deal, too."

"Sounds good," David said. "When do you want to go?"

Steve looked at his watch. "Couple of hours?"

"He's open at night?"

"Sure is," he said. "That's the only time I have to look."

David couldn't believe his luck. "Sounds good to me, Steve. That'll give me a chance to finish what I'm doing and get showered. Then we can go take a look."

"All right," Steve said. "I'll see you then."

David grinned as he finished mowing the yard.

Chapter Seventy-One

There were at least two cars on the lot that would work well for Daniel, and that night as Steve drove them home from the car lot, David seemed excited. "He'd be thrilled to have either one," he said.

"Can you convince Brenda?" Steve asked. He knew how worried Brenda always was about money, not to mention her worry about Daniel driving on his own.

David sighed. "Well, I'm not sure. The money will set us back a little each month, but as hard as Daniel is working, he could pay the notes. I could work a few more hours a week to finish up the kitchen cabinets I'm building. If I get them installed for the customer before my deadline, that could pay for it right there." He looked out the window. "I don't blame Brenda if she doesn't go for it, though. I'm always telling her how we're having trouble making ends meet. But sometimes a father just needs to reward his son, you know?"

Steve nodded. "Yeah, I guess I do." He glanced over at David. "Wish Jerry Flaherty felt that way."

"Cathy's ex?" David asked.

"Yeah. He hasn't come to see Mark yet. He's completely written him off. So I've been trying to fill the void, best I can. I've started doing a Bible study with Mark and Rick, and it's given us something to talk to each other about." He glanced at David, wondering how he'd react. He knew David didn't put much stock in Christianity, much less Bible study.

But David's response surprised him. "I guess it's something."

"I figured it was a good way to bond with them, you know?" Steve said. "I mean, it's not so easy to blend as a family. When we get married, there are going to be enough problems. And this was a great way to bridge the gap. We're bonding. They need a dad, and I'm trying to be there for them."

David shot him a look. "So how does their dad feel about that?"

The question surprised Steve. "He couldn't be less interested."

David frowned. "Are you sure?"

"Well, there's plenty of evidence," Steve said. "In the beginning, I went there one night to visit Mark by myself, and he comes out all expectant, thinking it's his dad. When he saw me, you should have seen the look on his face."

"Does his dad know Mark is looking for him?"

"Oh, yeah," Steve said. "I told him myself. Went all the way to Knoxville to confront him. He didn't appreciate it one bit. He can be a real tough case sometimes. Meanwhile, Mark still looks for his dad every visitation and every mail call, but he hasn't so much as written him a note. The last conversation they had was angry, and Jerry made it clear that he was ashamed of Mark. That he had disgraced him."

David's gaze drifted back out the window.

"I'm just trying to take up the slack," Steve

said. "I really feel like I'm supposed to do the best I can to fill Jerry's shoes when I marry Cathy and be what he's supposed to be in this family."

"I don't think you can."

The quiet declaration hit Steve like cold water. He tried to rally. "Well, technically, it's probably impossible, but I can at least shoot for it, you know? I believe that, with God's help, I can do anything."

David looked skeptical. "Maybe you're jumping the gun, Steve. I don't mean to downplay your faith or anything, but you know I don't share it. And even if you're right, and God could help, I don't know if he'd really want you taking their dad's place."

They came to a red light, and Steve looked over at him. "Why do you say that?"

"Sometimes fathers get mad at their kids. They say things they don't mean. Sometimes they *mean* things they don't mean. Later, anyway."

Steve tried to think that over, but he found it hard to fathom. He'd never gotten that mad at Tracy, not mad enough to tell her that she had disgraced him and made him ashamed.

But then again, Tracy had never sold drugs or stolen a car or vandalized a school.

"Like when Daniel crashed the car," David said. "I was so mad at him I could have bitten his head off. I yelled at him, said some things that I meant at the time, but now I wish I hadn't said them."

"Well, don't you think after the number of weeks Mark's been in jail, that Jerry would have had a chance to feel some remorse and come around to make up with his son?"

"Yeah, you would think," David said, "but don't jump to conclusions. That won't help."

"And what conclusion would I be jumping to?" Steve asked.

"The conclusion that his dad doesn't love him."

"That's not *my* conclusion," Steve said. "I think it's Mark's. And what else is he supposed to think?"

A horn behind them honked, and Steve realized the light was green. He stepped on the accelerator.

"I know it's a natural conclusion," David said, "but the truth is that Mark needs his dad, and you'd be making a mistake to try to push him away."

"Hey, I haven't pushed him away," Steve said, trying not to sound as aggravated as he felt. "I've tried to pull him in. *He's* the one pushing away."

"That may be," David said. "And maybe I'm way out of line. But I'm speaking as a kid who grew up without a dad."

The anger in Steve's heart faded. David had never shared that with him before. It made all the difference in what he was trying to say. Steve tried to hear it without letting his pride get in the way. "How old were you when you lost him?"

"He left when I was eight," David said. He swallowed and looked out the window, letting the silence play between them.

Finally, David spoke again. "Mark needs him. Even if he's not what he hopes he is, and even if he doesn't respond the way Mark wants him to. Even if he's a bona fide jerk, Mark needs him. That's all there is to it. You can try to replace him, you can be there all you want, but when it comes right down to it, that relationship with his real dad is vital. If there's any way to salvage it, do it."

Steve clutched the steering wheel harder

as he navigated his way up the mountain toward Cathy's home. "Well, then, I'm not sure what my role is supposed to be as a stepfather. I want to be everything that I'm supposed to be, but how do I know when I'm overstepping my bounds?"

"If you start coming between Mark and his dad, or enabling Jerry to stay out of the picture," David said, "then you've overstepped your bounds. Your role as Cathy's husband will be to help *her* love her kids the best way she can. Just don't get in her way when you think she's doing it wrong. Don't try to control the way she loves them. I've seen too many blended families that have messed up that way. The stepparent gets in the way of the birth parent, interrupts the love relationship between the parent and the child— maybe disapproves of it somehow—and the next thing you know, the parent is full of resentment and confusion, and the kid is a mess. On the other hand, you can let the kids set the tone. When they need you, be there."

Steve let the silence fall between them as David's words sank into his mind. "That's good advice, David," he said finally. "I'll try to follow it."

"It won't be easy."

"Don't I know it." Steve had a lot to think about as he pulled into Cedar Circle.

Chapter Seventy-Two

Dear Mark,
  I know it's not like me to spend my time writing my kid brother when I could be out living it up with the Nicaraguan hunks, but the truth is I haven't met any. And even if I did, there wouldn't be time. Sylvia works me day and night, and I fall into bed exhausted. But like Mom said that day when we worked so hard at the fair to raise money for Joseph's heart, it's a good kind of tired.
  I've been thinking a lot about what you're going through, and in some ways

we're both in the same boat. I'm kind of stuck here, even if I decide I want to come home, and most of my time is structured for me. The thing is, I know that some day I'm going to look back, and it's going to be one of the best years of my life. Maybe you can't say the same thing, but who knows? I've been seeing God do some pretty amazing things.

There's this kid named Chico who came to Dr. Harry first because he had pneumonia and some kind of horrible rash on his legs. He was one of nine kids in his family, and none of them got much to eat. You could tell by their ribs—you could count every one just by looking. And he had crusty stuff under his nose, all raw and dirty. It made me just want to gather him up and take him inside and give him a bath. But his mother was with him, and I didn't want to insult her.

Dr. Harry got him going on antibiotics— a miracle of God, believe me—and then Sylvia started feeding him. His mother brought him back every day to Dr. Harry for two weeks, and every time he'd get his dose of medication, Dr. Harry would send him over to us and we would feed him.

*He's well now, and he comes around
every day asking if there's anything he
can do to help us. He couldn't be more
than seven years old. But Sylvia told him
about Jesus, and he understood. She
thinks telling him about Jesus is more important than filling his belly or making him
well. When I first got here, I didn't think so.
I thought we needed to do everything we
could to get these people well and keep
them from being hungry. But they're hun-
grier for God than anything I've ever seen.
One of the men came back the other day
after Dr. Harry had treated him and told
us he wanted to be a pastor because
there weren't enough churches around
here. Dr. Harry was so happy he cried.
Sylvia set to work right away finding
someone to train him to pastor a church.*

*I felt kind of bad because I should know
a lot more about the Bible than I do. But I
guess I'm taking it one day at a time and
learning just like these people are. Sylvia
surprises me every day by leaning on
God when we're almost out of supplies,
and all of a sudden somebody will show
up with some cash or some supplies.
Then we have enough for one more day.*

She says if she ever sells the house, she'll be set, but it doesn't look like the house is selling. I know Mom will be happy about that. But she wouldn't if she understood where the money was going to go.

Well, I hope all's well with you, and that you're not getting into any fights or getting yourself into any more trouble. Give Mom a hug for me when you see her. I'll send you pictures of little Chico as soon as I have time to take some.

Love, Annie

Mark folded the letter back neatly and put it in its envelope. He leaned against the table at the center of the room in Building A and thought about his sister down in Nicaragua, working with orphans and hungry children and not getting very much back. He'd never seen Annie that way before, and he had trouble imagining it now. It could only be considered a God thing, he thought. Annie on the mission field.

He looked around him at the inmates going about their own business in their free time. Steve had said that this, too, was a mission field, that God could use him here.

But he doubted that. God couldn't use him anywhere, not with his heart the way it was.

He reached into his locker and pulled out his Bible, got the letters out that Steve had sent him, and went over them again. The story about King David being a man after God's own heart, after he'd killed a man so he could steal his wife, really puzzled him. He turned back to it and studied it again, trying to figure out exactly how God's forgiveness had come. Was that whole story some great myth, or was it reality that applied to his life today? Could a repentant man really get the approval of God? Could someone weak and spoiled and tainted like him really ever become a man after God's own heart?

He envied Annie for knowing who she was. She had said that some day she'd look back on this year as one of the best of her life. What would *he* look back and remember?

The pensive thoughts stirred up his soul, disturbing him, but there was no comfort to be found. Not when he rejected the comfort that his mother and stepfather-to-be offered him. He wondered what advice his own father would give. He supposed he would never know.

He stuffed the letter back into his Bible

and returned it to his locker. Then, mentally, he tried to compose a list of questions he wanted to ask Steve the next time he saw him. A few things he wanted to clear up in his mind.

He just wanted things to make sense.

Chapter Seventy-Three

Tory was late for Spencer's T-ball game because it had taken her so long to prepare Hannah before she took her out in the hot sun. She had put a bonnet on her to keep the sun out of her eyes and a cool little sunsuit with brand-new sandals that matched. She brought Hannah in her stroller with the sun shield up and pulled a lawn chair up next to the bleachers.

Spencer saw her coming and yelled, "Hey, Mommy!" from the dugout. She laughed and waved, wondering how she could have stayed away for so long.

Hannah grew fussy, so Tory pulled her out

and set her up on her lap. Barry, who was standing at the fence next to the dugout, tore himself away from the field and came over to give Tory and Hannah a kiss.

"How's my girl?" he said, and lifted Hannah from Tory's lap.

Tory glanced around at the others on the bleachers. Everyone's eyes were on their children on the field. Two young children, around the ages of three and four, sat spooning up dirt. It reminded her of Spencer not so long ago.

Barry gave the baby back. "Has Spencer batted yet?" Tory asked.

"No, he's up next," Barry said. "You made it just in time."

She looked past him to her son, coming out to practice his swing next to the dugout.

"Mommy, look at me!" he shouted and demonstrated his prowess with the bat.

She clapped for him. She looked around and saw Brittany at the snow-cone stand. It was probably her second one of the night, and she had only been here half an hour.

"Look at the baby!" She heard the little four-year-old in the dirt and told herself not to get defensive. Little children loved babies.

They weren't staring at Hannah because she had Down's Syndrome.

The children got up and came running over to see Hannah. Hannah kicked her feet and shook her arms, delighted to have people around her. The little boy reached out to touch her with his dirty hands, and Tory resisted the urge to push him away.

Spencer walked over to the fence, forgetting the game. "That's my sister," he said proudly.

The boy turned around. "How come her tongue's hangin' out?"

Tory recognized the fulfillment of her worst fears, as some of the parents turned to look. The mother of the child looked more horrified than Tory. "Jonathan!"

The child ignored her and kept standing there. Tory tagged Hannah's tongue, and the baby pulled it in. But it only stayed for a second, and her mouth fell open again.

"It came back out," the kid said. "Does she have a stopped-up nose?"

Tory started to answer, but Spencer did it for her. "No, her nose ain't stopped up," Spencer said. "Her chin just doesn't work so good."

Tory wanted to tell Spencer to leave it alone, that he didn't have to defend his sister.

But Spencer didn't mind. "See, she's special," he said, leaning on the fence. "Not just anybody could get a baby like that."

"Why not?" the little boy asked, his eyes wide with fascination.

"'Cause," Spencer said. "God gave her to us because he knew she would need a lot of help. Doesn't she, Mom?"

Tory managed to smile. "That's right, Spence."

"But we take good care of her," he said, swinging his bat as he spoke. "And one day she'll keep that tongue in." He made a face at his sister. She recognized her brother and started kicking harder.

"I can't take you now, Hannah," he said. "I've got to bat." He turned back to the field and saw that it was almost his turn. Without another word, he headed back to his place. Tory looked up and met Barry's eyes. He gave her a wink.

She relaxed back in her lawn chair as Hannah kicked her arms and legs and watched her brother hit a double.

She couldn't express the pride that she felt in her little boy, but not because he'd been a good hitter. He was the best PR person Hannah could have had. Tory knew that, as long as he was around, Hannah was going to be just fine.

Chapter Seventy-Four

Mark woke up at two A.M. and stared at the ceiling. He knew better than to get up. The guards didn't look favorably on people wandering the floor in the middle of the night. They usually assumed you were trying to steal something.

He'd seen it happen a couple of times before. They'd put them in disciplinary for a week, and it only took one time in isolation for Mark to know he didn't want to go there again. These kids that he lived with now weren't his top choice in companions, but they were better than nothing. And in isolation, that was exactly what you got. Nothing.

A faint glow from the guard's station lit up the room. No wonder he couldn't sleep, he thought. Back home, he used to close his door and turn out the light and sleep in the pitch black. But there wasn't such a thing here, any more than there was privacy or choice. He just lay there on his back, staring up at the ceiling. He knew it by heart. He could have reproduced it himself if he'd been given the proper tools. He knew where every little hole was placed, every crack in the plaster, every place where the paint was thinning.

He thought about his father, who still hadn't been to see him. Mark had written him a couple of letters but hadn't mailed them. He figured his dad wouldn't open them anyway. He'd really blown it with him. He couldn't believe what a fool he'd been.

He wondered if anything would change when he got out of here. Would his dad act like nothing had ever happened and pick up where they'd left off? Or would he hold it against him for the rest of his life, passing the grudge down to his grandchildren? Would Mark forever be the black sheep of the family?

He started to cry, something he hadn't

done in a while, and he covered his face, trying to muffle the sounds that would give him
away in case anyone else lay awake tonight.

He thought back over the way things had
worked out since he'd been in here. If God
was trying to get his attention, he had certainly succeeded. Mark had been to every
chapel since the first week he'd been here
and had worked at every Bible study that
Steve had sent him.

He could tell from the way that God kept
getting in his face that he hadn't given up on
Mark. He had been there, knocking and
knocking on the door. Steve had shown him
a verse that said that Jesus stood at the
door and knocked, and if anyone opened it,
he would come in with them and dine with
them. Mark figured that was pretty cool.
Thinking about somebody as powerful as
God wanting to sit down with him over a
burger. That was pretty friendly. Not just anybody would do it, not with a kid who'd
messed up so badly and wound up in jail.

His heart melted at the thought of God
standing on the horizon, scanning it as he
waited for his child to come home. His problem before had always been that he'd assigned his dad's face to that father on the

horizon, and he couldn't picture it, not since his father had forgotten about him and left him in here to rot. But the Bible said that God would never leave or forsake him. If that was the case, then God was nothing like his dad. He wouldn't disappoint Mark, and he wouldn't just decide not to show up when Mark needed him. He wouldn't turn his back on Mark or hold onto his anger, refusing to forgive.

For the first time in his life, Mark got it. He understood about that father running to meet his son, kissing his face, bringing out a robe to put on him so that others could see him as royalty, putting a ring on his finger, restoring him in good standing to the family. He felt like that boy standing among the pigs, wishing he had what they were eating to fill his empty belly.

And then he remembered what Annie had said about their bellies not being the hungriest part. It was true with him. He had all he needed to eat, but his soul was so empty.

He began to weep harder, and as he did, he looked up at that ceiling again as if somewhere behind the tile he could see God's eyes on him, weeping and waiting with his arms spread wide. He pictured God running toward him, and his own feet falling into a trot, hurrying toward his home.

"I'm sorry, God," he whispered. "I shouldn't have been so stupid. If I had just done what you wanted . . ." He wept and felt his Father throwing his arms around him, lifting him off the ground, swinging him around, kissing his face and weeping with joy. He felt the love in that royal cloak being thrown around his shoulders, felt the authority and the inheritance of that ring as it slipped upon his finger. For the first time in his life he understood the love of Christ, that profound fill-up-your-heart kind of love that didn't go away or turn its back. It was the kind of love that would enable someone to lay his life down for someone else. The kind of love that could turn Mark into something useful, even in prison. The kind of love that could make this the best year of his life, just like Annie's, if he gave his life over to God.

"I'm yours, Jesus," he whispered into the night. "I'm yours a hundred percent. Do whatever you want with me. I just want to do what you say. I want to keep wearing the robe and the ring on my finger. I want to change. Please help me to change."

And as he wept into the night, he knew that it was an answered prayer already. God was already at work changing him. It was a done deal.

Chapter Seventy-Five

Mark was the first one in line for the telephone the next day. He dialed Steve's phone number at work, the number that had been printed on office letterhead Steve had used to write him. He called collect, hoping no one would refuse the charges before the call was routed to Steve.

"Steve Bennett."

Mark sighed with relief. "Steve," Mark said, "it's me, Mark."

"Mark, is everything okay?"

"Yeah," he said. "I just had a few minutes and a chance to use the telephone. I thought I'd call and tell you something."

"Okay," Steve said. "What is it?"

Mark hesitated for a moment. He looked around at the people standing near him, waiting to use the phone. Nobody was really paying attention.

"I just wanted to thank you. I mean for all the letters you've been writing and the Bible studies and all that."

"Well, you're welcome."

"'Cause I've been reading them and everything, you know," Mark said, "and I've been thinking about a lot of it. And I sort of woke up in the middle of the night last night. I kept thinking about the Prodigal Son, and I felt like that kid who wound up wallowing with the pigs and then came home. You know how his father was waiting for him with that robe and that ring? That was all pretty cool."

He could hear the emotion in Steve's voice. "Yeah, it was, Mark."

"I just sort of decided I was that kid coming home," he said, his voice wobbling. "And I sort of ran to God, told him I was sorry."

He heard Steve suck in a breath. "You did that?"

"Yeah. And, well, I realized what Jesus did for me and everything. And what a dope I've been, kind of throwing it back in his face the way I have. Running from it like there was something else I could get. I'm not gonna be like that anymore."

Steve's voice moved into a higher, emotional pitch. "Thank you for telling me, Mark. You don't know what this means to me."

"Well, I just thought you should know first," he said, "since you had so much to do with it."

"Are you going to tell your mom?"

"Yeah, the Bible says we're supposed to say it out loud, aren't we? Guess I need to do that. But I don't get another phone call, and besides, I want to tell her face-to-face."

"I'm going to let you tell her," Steve said. "It's the best thing you could give her, Mark. It's even better than Annie going to the mission field."

"No way," Mark said on a laugh. "You think?"

"Hey, I know. You tell your mom this and the jail, the drugs, all the rest of the stuff, she'll completely forget about it. She'll be so thrilled to know that you've got Jesus."

Mark swallowed the lump in his throat and blinked back the tears. "Well, I gotta go. There are people waiting to use the phone."

"Tell her, okay, Mark?"

"I will, next time I see her." He hung up the phone and stood there a moment, thinking of calling his mom right now, but those in line were growing impatient.

"Hey, man, move on. You've had your turn."

He turned around and saw Beef, and he handed him the phone. "Go ahead, man. I'm finished."

Beef grabbed the phone and pushed him out of the way, but Mark didn't react. He just hurried to the cafeteria to get started on his day's work.

Chapter Seventy-Six

Cathy noticed a change in Mark as soon as he walked into the room for visitation Wednesday night. His eyes were brighter than she had seen them in months, and he smiled as if he had a secret that he couldn't wait to share.

Pleasantly surprised by his new demeanor, she said, "You must have had a good day."

"It's been a good week," he said. He leaned up with his chin on his palm, fixing his eyes on her. "So what's going on with you? Have you heard from Annie?"

"I got a letter from her this week," she said.

"She's doing really well, Mark. I'm so proud of her."

"Me, too," Mark said.

The words surprised Cathy, and she lifted her eyebrows.

"What about the house?" he asked. "How far have they gotten?"

"Well, they've got the frame up, and the wiring's been done. They put the insulation in yesterday. They're starting on the drywall tomorrow. Once that's up, it shouldn't be that much longer."

"Three weeks? A month?"

"Maybe," she said. "They're working at it pretty hard. Steve got a good contractor, despite everything."

Mark leaned back in his chair and kept his smiling eyes on his mother. *He has a secret,* she thought. "What is it, Mark?" she asked, finally. "There's something going on."

He nodded, and his face got serious. "Mom, the other night I woke up in the middle of the night and I started thinking about the things Steve has sent me."

Her eyes widened, and she took his hand. "Really?"

He went on. "Mom, I called Steve the other morning, and I told him what had happened."

"What?" Cathy asked. "What happened? He didn't say anything."

His smile faded, and his eyes grew serious. "I gave my life to Christ," he said. "I finally got it about the Prodigal Son and that guy's dad standing there watching for his son. I finally realized about the robe and the ring, and I decided I didn't want to be going in the wrong direction anymore. I wanted to come home."

It was the first time he had said the word *home* without a plea behind it, and she knew that this wasn't another desperate attempt to make her get him out of here. Tears rushed into her eyes, and she covered her mouth.

"Mark, you're not just telling me what I want to hear, are you?"

"No, Mom. It's the truth." Tears glistened in his eyes, and he wiped them away and reached into his pocket for a folded piece of paper. Slowly, he opened it and ironed it out with his hand. "I drew this yesterday, when I was thinking about the son being like the father. I kept getting hung up on Dad, you know, and the way he's turned against me."

"Mark, he hasn't turned against you."

"Mom, the best you can say is that he just doesn't care one way or another. But that's okay. It's not so much about him. It's about God. I'm *his* son, too. And I want to be like my Father."

She looked down at the picture and saw the silhouette of a man, with a smaller silhouette of a boy just inside it.

"At first, this was Dad and me. We were both angry and disappointed. And then I realized it didn't have to be Dad and me. It could be God and me. And God had gotten over the disappointment. He could see some hope for me."

She reached out for her son and wept as he held her.

"I want you to have the picture, Mom," he said as he pulled back. "It's not great art or anything. But maybe it'll remind you that I'm not a lost cause."

She choked back her tears. "Thank you, Mark." She pondered the picture again. "So you gave your life to Christ, and you called *Steve?*"

"Well, I wanted to tell you in person. He sent me all those letters, and I saved them up, you know, and kept reading them and studying them, and even talking to God about them. When I finally did it, it seemed like he should know."

"And he didn't tell me?"

"He wanted you to hear it from me. He's a pretty good guy, Mom."

Cathy wiped the tears on her face with the fingertips of both hands. "I know he is, Mark."

"Then why won't you marry him?"

Her mouth fell open. "Mark, I was waiting for you."

"You don't have to wait for me, Mom," he said. "I think you need to go ahead and do it. I'm fine in here. And when I get out I'm going to need some stability in my life."

She started to laugh through her tears. "Stability? You?"

"Yes," he said. "You know, it's not always so great to have everything stay the same. I think he's going to be an improvement to our family. I can handle it. I'm a big boy."

She couldn't find words to answer him. Finally, she grabbed his hands and brought them both to her mouth. "Oh, Mark," she whispered.

"So you'll do it?" he asked. "You'll marry him?"

"Of course I will," she said. "I've been *wanting* to. But I thought it would be kind of a betrayal to you until you got out of here."

"Hey, you can videotape it, okay?" he said.

She shook her head. "I don't know what to say, Mark."

"Just say you'll do it," he said. "I don't have much to give you as a wedding gift, but you can take this."

She smiled and wept some more as she let the gift from her son sink in.

Chapter Seventy-Seven

Cathy almost ran two red lights trying to get to Steve's house when she left the prison that night. She left her car door open, bolted up the porch, and banged on the door. Tracy flung it open.

"Hi, Cathy," she said in that voice so full of enthusiasm.

"Tracy!" Cathy grabbed the girl and swung her around.

Steve came running into the foyer. "Cathy! What is it?"

Cathy set Tracy down and threw her arms around him. "You didn't tell me about Mark!"

He pulled back and looked down at her. "What did he tell you?"

"That heaven was having a celebration and I didn't even know about it!"

Steve's smile cut from ear to ear. "I wanted him to tell you himself. I figured if he did, that it must be true—not just something he felt for a few minutes."

"No, he meant it!" she cried. "He was excited, and he told me. And you'll never guess what else he said!"

"What?" Steve asked.

"He said we should go ahead and get married, that there was no point in waiting for him. He *wants* us to go ahead."

Steve caught his breath, and Tracy began jumping up and down, whooping with delight. "You can do it, Daddy! You can marry her now. We can move into the house as soon as it's finished, and . . ."

But Steve wasn't listening to Tracy. His eyes were focused on Cathy, and he touched her face with both hands. "Will you, Cathy?" he asked. "Will you marry me?"

"Yes!" she said. "Yes, I will. Let's set a date. How about . . . four weeks from now?"

He ran for a calendar and turned to September. "That would be the 26th."

"September 26," Cathy said. "Our anniversary will be September 26." She threw her arms around him, then embraced the bouncing girl. "Let's go home right now and open all those presents."

"Yeah!" Tracy said, and jumped even higher. "Come on, Daddy. Please, can we go?"

"Get in the car," he said. "I'll get my keys."

And together they all headed to Cathy's house to open the presents that had been sitting in her dining room for too long.

Chapter Seventy-Eight

The telephone connection between Breeze-wood and Leon, Nicaragua, seemed as close as if Annie was just in another house around the corner. "Mom, I checked into it, but I really don't think I can come home for the wedding and still afford to come back here. Would it upset you if I missed it?"

There wasn't much that could shake Cathy's joy now. "Well, no, honey. I know it's short notice."

"I want to come and everything, but right now we're so busy and I really don't think Sylvia can do without me. I know she did before, but now she's depending on me, you know?"

"I was hoping she could come, too."

"Well, she can't. We're just swamped. Besides, it costs a lot of money and she doesn't want to spend it on airfare when she could be spending that money on food. You know, they haven't sold their house yet. And until they do, we're just making it hand to mouth, giving the kids as much as we can each day. It's really hard to spread the food out among all of them. So neither one of us can come, Mom. So much wouldn't get done if I left."

"Honey, that's the best wedding gift you could give me. You just stay there and do your work. We'll be okay. Rick is going to be the best man and Tracy will be my little maid of honor."

"What about Mark?" Annie asked.

"Mark is great. In fact, I'm thinking about having the wedding in the chapel at River Ranch if I can work it out. That way Mark can be there."

"That's a great idea, Mom. And you have to videotape it, 'cause I really want to see it. Do Tracy's hair up real nice, with flowers in it and everything." Her voice cracked. "I wish I could be there."

"Don't worry. I'll send you pictures and tell you all about it. And I'll even videotape the house before we move Steve and Tracy in just so you can see all the changes as they take place."

"That's what life's about, Mom," she said. "I'm finding out it's all about change. You don't have to worry about me coming back and having everything different. It might sting for a minute, but it'll all be for the best. Won't it?"

Cathy couldn't swallow the tears down. "How'd you grow up into such a wonderful young lady, with a mother like me?"

"Mom, with a mother like you, how could I lose? You should see some of the kids here who don't have moms. It really makes a difference. It just breaks my heart. I wish they could all have a Cathy Flaherty in their lives."

Cathy wiped the tears from her face as she let those words seep into her heart.

Chapter Seventy-Nine

September flew by as Cathy took care of the wedding details, and when the 26th finally came, the wedding was everything they had hoped. It was small and brief, but beautiful. The singles' minister that Steve and Cathy had gotten to know at their church performed the wedding in the prison chapel, and Mark was allowed to attend.

When it was over, Cathy kissed her new husband, then his little girl, then turned to Rick and pulled him into a hug. Finally, she turned to Mark.

"Thank you, Mark," she whispered, touching his face. "You're turning into a very nice young man."

He smiled, teary eyed. He hugged his mom, then turned to his new stepfather and gave him an awkward hug. "I'm sorry I've disgraced everybody the way I have, but some day I'll make it up to you," he said. "I'll be even more useful than Annie. You'll see. Some day I'll make everybody proud of me. Even my dad."

Steve made the silent vow to be everything he could to fill in the blanks for this boy. But he would need God to help him discern where his boundaries were.

Rick stayed in Knoxville with his dad while Cathy and Steve honeymooned in Gatlinburg. Steve's parents kept Tracy, and the contractors had been given strict orders to finish the construction while they were gone.

Rick's visit with his dad was awkward, for Rick hadn't gotten over the fact that his dad had refused to communicate with Mark. But it was time to mend fences, he told himself, and if he could help mend fences between Mark and their dad, then it was worth the time.

Rick waited until Jerry was feeling good about a golf game with one of his partners. Jerry stood at the grill in his backyard while the steaks sizzled, describing the shot he'd made at the fourteenth hole that morning. Rick listened and pretended to be interested.

"It was beautiful," Jerry was saying. "You shoulda been there. I'm telling you, ESPN would have loved this."

"Too bad we don't have it on video," Rick said. "Mark would love it, too."

His dad got quiet and opened the grill and seemed to concentrate on moving the steaks off of the flames.

"You know, Dad, he's changed a lot since he's been in jail."

Jerry didn't look up.

"No kidding. He's a different person. You wouldn't believe it. He's made all these promises about when he gets out. He doesn't want to ever go near drugs again."

"You like T-bones, don't you?" Jerry asked. "Mary's been marinating them. Smell."

Rick slid his hands into his pockets and went to stand beside his dad. "Dad, he's become a Christian. He's been doing a Bible study and praying a lot, and I think he's able to look at his future now and see some hope."

He got a reaction then. Jerry closed the grill and stared at the top of it for a long moment. "Well, that's *something.*"

"Yeah, I thought so," Rick said. "I know you're not big on religion and stuff but, you know, it's really changed him. Oh, and I have some pictures of him at Mom's wedding."

Jerry rolled his eyes, as if the last thing he wanted to see was pictures of his ex-wife's wedding, but Rick pulled them out and showed him the ones of just Mark. "See how tall he's getting? And his hair's growing out a little. Did you know they shaved his head when he first got in there? But I think he looks pretty good right now. You wouldn't know him. He looks clean-cut, like he could actually get a job or something."

Jerry took the pictures and looked down at them, as if he didn't recognize his son. "They let him go to the wedding?"

"Well, Mom and Steve got married at the prison chapel. You know, it was actually Mark's idea that they go ahead and get married. They were holding off, waiting for him to get out, but that meant a whole year, and

Mark didn't think they should do that. I thought it was pretty mature of him."

Jerry looked up at him, pensive, and Rick wondered what was going through his mind. The fact that his dad even acknowledged what Rick was saying was a good sign.

"Dad, he'd really love to have a visit from you. I think every visitation on Wednesdays and Sundays he secretly hopes you're going to come."

Jerry opened the grill again, letting a puff of smoke escape. "I don't have any experience with this, Rick," he said. "Visiting my child in prison, knowing how to act toward somebody who's disgraced the family this way . . ."

"Well, it seems to me that it's Mom he's disgraced more than anybody," Rick said quietly. "I mean, the policeman came to tell *her* about it when she was at her own wedding shower. All the people who know him mostly are from Breezewood instead of Knoxville. A lot of people don't even know he has anything to do with you. But Mom hasn't turned her back on him."

Jerry turned around and gazed at Rick. "So what's it like in there? What are the other prisoners like? Are they a bunch of hoods from the ghetto or something?"

"Actually they're all pretty straight right now," Rick said. "When they're not on drugs they're pretty decent people. They all look clean-cut right now, except for those silly suits they make them wear. I think the whole experience has made Mark stronger. He's found out there are consequences to his actions and that those consequences can change his life. And he's learned about people of all different kinds and how to get along with them. Plus he's working in the cafeteria and studying, because they have classes during the day."

Jerry flipped the steaks over and stared down at them for a moment. Rick thought he was going to ask more about the prison, or maybe even about Mark. Instead, he said, "Go in and ask Mary for the pepper, would you?"

Let down, Rick took that as a dismissal of the conversation, and he knew his father wasn't going to engage any more. Well, Rick had said his piece, given his dad all the information he needed, even made a plea for Jerry to go visit Mark. But there was nothing more that he could do without straining his own relationship with his dad, and he wasn't sure that would accomplish anything.

"Yeah," he said, finally. "I'll get it." And as he did, he said a silent prayer that God would take care of the rest.

Chapter Eighty

Cathy and Steve spent the first day of their honeymoon lounging around the condo in Gatlinburg, and the next day they went rock climbing in Pigeon Forge. The day after that they traveled to North Carolina to a place called Horse Pasture Creek and spent the day playing in waterfalls that took their breath away.

Each night they ate in charming little restaurants and had romantic evenings in their condo. Cathy couldn't believe how blessed she was, how covered with God's grace, as she got used to Steve being her husband.

Steve and Tracy moved into the house the day they arrived back in Breezewood. Tracy seemed a little moody and emotional about all the changes in their life. Steve's parents helped them move in, and Cathy allowed his mother to help Tracy organize her room.

That night, when everything was in the house but not yet put away, and the grandparents had gone home, and everyone was exhausted, Cathy went to put Tracy to bed. She found her curled up on her new bedspread, leaned back against the wall, with tears rolling down her face.

"Oh, honey," Cathy said, and sat next to her on the bed. "What's the matter?"

"Nothing."

"Have we been ignoring you?"

"No, ma'am," she said.

"Then what's wrong?"

"I don't know."

She looked at the little girl and realized that, for the past few days, she'd been without her father. That, in itself, could have been slightly traumatic, especially since she anticipated so many changes coming upon their lives. Even though Tracy had wanted it, had looked forward to moving into her new room and having Cathy as her new mother, the whole thing was probably a little over-whelming.

"Do you want me to put you to bed?" she asked.

Tracy shrugged. "Where's Daddy?"

Cathy started to tell her that Daddy was busy hanging pictures in their room. But then she realized that Tracy wasn't ready to switch gears on her parent just yet.

"I'll go get him," she said. "Maybe you and Daddy need to spend a little time together, just the two of you. What do you think?"

Tracy's eyes lit up. Cathy reached down and hugged the little girl, then went back out and found Steve in the new master bedroom.

"How do you like this picture here?" he asked with a nail between his teeth.

She smiled. "It's perfect. But why don't you do it later?"

He turned back to her and grinned. "What have you got in mind?"

"Tracy," she said. "She needs a little time alone with her daddy. I think all the moving and all the changes are getting to her, and she's sitting in there in a new room feeling a little overwhelmed."

Concern instantly filled his eyes, and he took the nail out of his mouth. "Well, thanks," he said. "I needed to know that. I've been so busy I haven't paid attention."

"Just go in there and read her a story or something, lie down with her until she goes to sleep. I can take it from here."

He gave Cathy a sweet kiss, then headed back to the bedroom to be with his daughter. Cathy had plenty to keep her busy.

After a while, Cathy drifted back to Tracy's bedroom and saw the father and child lying together on the bed. He was reading to her from *The Lion, the Witch, and the Wardrobe,* making funny voices and talking in a British accent.

Tracy's tears had dried and all was well. Her eyes followed the words as he read. Cathy wished she had a camera ready to take a picture of that, but she wouldn't have interrupted it for the world. Her heart swelled to the point of bursting at the love that had been brought into this home.

If they were careful, if they nurtured it, if they did things right and didn't push too hard, some day the family would be one instead of two fractured pieces. Some day, with God's help, maybe they would all be comfortable and used to each other and think of each other as siblings and parents instead of steps. But she didn't want to hope for too much too soon. There were limitations, and she had to be aware of them and work around them. But those limitations weren't as great as the potential benefits. She couldn't be more thrilled with the new arrangement.

She only wished her children could have grown up with a father like Steve instead of a father like Jerry, but she supposed there was nothing she could do about it now. All they could do was pick up from this point and move on the best way they could.

Chapter Eighty-One

By the grace of God, Mark's incarceration went by more quickly than they could have expected. Though Jerry still kept his distance from Mark, Steve continued to disciple Mark through the mail and in his visits to River Ranch. As Cathy and Steve settled into their marriage, they saw a genuine maturity developing in Mark. Winter passed, then spring. As summer approached, Cathy began to look forward to Mark's homecoming with joy and almost painful anticipation. By the time June came and his sentence had ended, she had come to see the year of his incarceration as a blessing instead of a crisis. Never before had Mark been such a willing subject, listening to the things she wanted to teach him, puzzling over them, studying them, digging for them, and understanding.

Just last week, he had sent her a letter with a Scripture passage in it, and she had wept at the depth of his understanding. It was Proverbs 2:1–5. Mark had written, "Mom, look what the Lord showed me today." Then he'd quoted the verses: "My son, if you accept my words and store up my commands within you, turning your ear to wisdom and applying your heart to understanding, and if you call out for insight and cry aloud for understanding, and if you look for it as for silver and search for it as for hidden treasure, then you will understand the fear of the LORD and find the knowledge of God."

"It works, Mom," he wrote. "I tried to tell Lazzo. I think he's listening lately."

Just weeks before his release date, Steve had come up with an idea. "You remember the first letter I sent Mark with the Bible study in it, the one about the Prodigal Son?"

"How could I forget?" Cathy asked. "It wound up making such a difference in his life."

"Well, when he called me that night to tell me that he'd accepted Christ, he talked about the robe and ring. And I've just been thinking. What if we threw him a celebration when he gets out? We could do it here, in the house, and invite everybody we know, show him that we're not disgraced, that we're as proud of him as we can be."

Cathy threw her hands over her heart. "Oh, Steve, that's a fabulous idea. We could have a sport coat made for him, sort of like the robe the father gave to his son. And we could make him a ring."

"And that picture he drew for you. The one with the father's head and the son's head inside it? Maybe we could have it duplicated for some kind of insignia to put on the pocket and on the ring. He'd always remember what it meant."

"Yes! It could be even bigger than Annie's party. We could call it his Prodigal Son Celebration."

She threw her arms around her husband and almost danced a jig. "I'll get started on it right away. Boy, is Mark going to have something to come home to."

Chapter Eighty-Two

Not everyone was as excited about the Prodigal Son Celebration as Cathy was. A phone call from Jerry the night before Mark's release told her that *he* was anything but thrilled.

"What's this Rick tells me about some big party you're having?" he asked.

Cathy's hackles came up as she got ready to defend herself. "I'm throwing my son a party to welcome him home. We're calling it our Prodigal Son Celebration. Do you have a problem with that, Jerry?"

"Well, I have a problem with Steve doing it. He's not his father."

"And neither are you, last I heard," she

threw back. "You haven't visited Mark one time in a year. He's given up looking for you. Steve has been there at least once a week, sometimes twice. He's discipled him with Bible studies and patience. He's taught him things that will benefit him in life. What have you done, Jerry?" The passion in her words surprised her, and she realized that she hadn't dealt very well with the anger she had toward him.

"I don't care what you say," he told her. "I am still Mark's father, and I'm not going to have a party thrown where Steve steps into my shoes and pretends he's the conquering dad."

"Well, would you like to do it, instead?" she asked.

"No, I don't think we should throw a party for a kid who's spent the last year in prison. Welcome him home, Cathy, but for Pete's sake, he doesn't deserve a party."

"Well, he's changed, Jerry. You'd know that if you had visited him. And I'm throwing the party whether you like it or not. You're welcome to come if you want, but I'm not going to tell Steve to stay away from him. He's been too big a part of Mark's life in the last year. He's made a difference, and I'm grateful to him. Mark needed a positive male role model."

"Oh, thanks a lot," Jerry said. "Like I'm not one?"

"Figure it out for yourself, Jerry," she said. "Positive role models are there where people can look at them and imitate them. There's nothing that Mark's been able to imitate in you."

"I'm just saying that I don't think we should call more attention to the fact that he's been in prison. It just disgraces the family more."

"Not *my* family," Cathy said. "I'm proud of Mark. I'm proud of how far he's come. And you're missing it all, Jerry, every bit of it. Your occasional weekends with Rick aren't making up for what you're missing in their lives. They're all changing and growing and becoming adults. If you want to be part of their lives, if you want a say in what goes on around them, then you have to be there."

She hung up the phone and sat there beside it, realizing that forgiveness was much harder than she thought. How did one forgive someone who was so unrepentant? Still, she got down on her knees and turned it over to God, asking him to work in Jerry's heart for the good of her children. And she begged him to work in her own heart to help her forgive.

Chapter Eighty-Three

The long year was nearing its end, and Annie knew that it was time for her to go home. She had known it as soon as her mother told her about the Prodigal Son Celebration. But it would not be easy to leave the children she had come to think of as her own family.

Sylvia hadn't been feeling well and had been growing tired a lot more quickly than before. Dr. Harry was worried about her, Annie could tell, and arranged for Sylvia to accompany Annie home so that she could see a doctor in the States. Annie worried too, but Sylvia didn't have time to worry. She just tried to work around the fatigue and her limitations.

The day they were to head to the airport in Managua, Annie wept her heart out and said good-bye to each child individually, both the ones in the orphanage and the ones from the community who hung around waiting for handouts. She would come back and visit them someday, she promised, and when she did, she would bring them goodies from America. She would also see to it that others from Breezewood kept sending money so that the work could continue.

She wept throughout the flight home, but just as the plane landed in Houston, her heart began to lift. It was time to move ahead with her life, to make plans for her own future. Her time with Sylvia and Harry had given her a hunger for the Word, and now she realized that she wanted to major in Bible at a Christian college, then head to seminary. Someday, she hoped to return to the mission field. Whatever God's plan for her was, she wanted to make a difference. She didn't think she could ever return to a mundane, fruitless lifestyle again.

As they boarded the plane from Houston

to Breezewood, Sylvia grew faint and had to sit down in the jet bridge. She lowered her head, and a flight attendant got her some water. Annie tried to fan her off.

After a moment, Sylvia had gotten slowly back to her feet and boarded the plane. Annie prayed all the way home that the doctors would be able to quickly find whatever was wrong with Sylvia and cure it. There was so much work to be done. Maybe Sylvia just needed a rest. In a way, Annie was thankful that their house hadn't sold yet. Sylvia would be able to sleep in her own bedroom on her own mattress with her own linens, surrounded by her own things, with her neighbors fussing over her. Maybe within a week she'd be back to normal.

It had been good of Sylvia to come home to celebrate with Mark. Annie hoped that, when she got married and had a family of her own, she'd live in a neighborhood with friends who loved her and cared for her and celebrated her triumphs with her.

Yes, life held so much. Annie couldn't wait for whatever came next.

Chapter Eighty-Four

Mark woke up on the day of his release and realized that everything was different. Even before he climbed out of his bunk, he already felt free—and with a sudden grin he remembered how much he had to look forward to. When he'd first been told of the Prodigal Son party that his family had planned for him, he'd had to go into the bathroom to hide his weeping. He had immediately begun working on the speech his mother had asked him to give. He must have written it a hundred times in the days since then, adding things, deleting those things that sounded lame. He'd tried to organize it the way Brenda had taught him to write papers. He wanted everyone at the party to see that he had changed, that the experience of being in jail had not hardened him. Instead, he was a stronger person for it, a man of integrity and purpose.

But as he dressed that morning, Mark felt a sharp regret for leaving his prison friends behind. He went around to each of them, shaking hands and saying good-bye. He saved Lazzo till last. The boy couldn't meet his eyes as Mark shook his hand, and Mark knew that Lazzo was sorry to see him go.

"You'll come back and visit once in a while, won't you, man?" Lazzo asked, picking at a piece of lint on his blanket.

"Sure I will," Mark said.

Lazzo shook his head. "People say that all the time. They say they'll do it and then they don't."

"No, man. I'll really do it. And I was thinking I might write to you."

"Write to me?" Lazzo asked. "Yeah, right, like you're going to have time to sit around writing letters to your old pals in jail."

"No kidding. I will." He went to his locker, opened it, and pulled out all the papers Steve had sent him, with all the Bible studies and all of Mark's notes. He handed them to

Lazzo. "You can have these, if you want them. They're pretty cool, if you do them."

"That Bible study?" Lazzo asked.

"Yeah. If you don't want to do them, I'll take them, but if you want them—"

Lazzo took them out of his hands. "I'll take 'em," he said. "Might fill up some time."

"Worked for me." He cleared his throat and took in a deep breath. "You know, if you ever wanted to do more, well, uh . . . I could send you stuff . . . or bring it by."

"Yeah, man. Thanks."

He packed the few things that he had been allowed to keep and dressed in a new pair of khakis and a button-down shirt that his mother had brought him. Then he met her in the visitation room where they'd talked across the table so many times before. She wept as soon as she saw him come through the door.

Though he had seen her twice a week for the past year, he held her in a crushing embrace, a hello hug. But he couldn't help looking over her shoulder to see if his father had come. There was no one there, but Mark wasn't surprised. He had grown numb to that kind of disappointment months ago. At least, he told himself he had.

"So what time does the party start?" he asked his mother.

She wiped her face. "We're going straight there," she said. "I hope you're ready."

He nodded. "So who's going to be there?"

"Everybody."

She smiled and began to roll his suitcase toward the front door. He took it out of her hands and carried it as he walked out the door, an inmate no longer.

"Just brace yourself," she said as they drove home. "You're not going to believe this party."

When they pulled into the driveway, the house looked exactly the same from the outside as it had when he left, except for the cars parked along the cul de sac and pulled up into the empty lot between the Dodds and the Sullivans. He got out and dusted off his pants and realized he was pretty nervous. He wondered if he would remember his speech and if he would embarrass anybody.

But as his mother walked him into the room, his breath caught in his throat. The room was full of friends, old and new, kids he'd gone to junior high school with, kids from the youth group, relatives from his mother's side of the family, some of Steve's relatives he'd met briefly, and the chaplains he'd worked with at River Ranch.

His mouth shook with the emotion rising up inside him, and he told himself that he had to be a man, had to keep his eyes dry and his hands steady, at least until he was alone in his own room tonight.

"Mark?"

He heard his mother's voice at the front of the room. She was holding a navy blue sport coat with an insignia on the lapel. He studied it—the insignia was the picture he had drawn months ago of the father and his son. He had almost forgotten it, though it was packed with meaning for him—about his new heavenly father, and the fact that Mark was growing in his image, and was always on his mind.

"Come on," she said. "Put it on."

It was the robe, he realized. The robe from the Prodigal Son. He wove through the crowd to the front of the room and slipped his arms into the sleeves of the new coat. It fit him perfectly.

Everyone got quiet. His mother turned to the crowd, her eyes full of tears. "This coat represents something really special," she said. "It represents Mark putting on Christ and the life that comes with that choice. And it represents his right standing in our family. In the parable of the Prodigal Son, the father brought out a robe and put it on his son so that everyone would know that he was an heir."

She smiled. "I don't have much of an inheritance to leave." Everyone chuckled. "But I have a family to give Mark, and he's one of us. And I just wanted him to know that he's welcome back."

And then she pulled out the ring that she had had carefully made for him with the same emblem carved in gold. "And I had this made for Mark, too," she said. "Whenever he wears it, he can look down at it and remember how much his Father in heaven loves him, how much he searched the horizon waiting for him to come home, and how clean his slate is."

Mark burst into tears, in spite of himself.

"Mark, you have so much ahead of you," she said, as she slipped the ring onto his shaking finger.

The crowd parted, and Annie pushed through. She looked thinner, taller, healthier than she had before. Her face was more mature, more full of purpose. He'd never seen her more beautiful.

He met her halfway, and she threw her

arms around him and began to cry. He buried his face in Annie's neck. Then Rick came up behind her, and he hugged his brother with the same crushing strength.

Then Sylvia came up, and Brenda and Tory, and their husbands, Barry and David. One by one, he hugged Daniel and Joseph and Leah and Rachel, Spencer and Brittany. Even the baby Hannah, who was walking with the help of her parents, who each held a hand. He hugged Tracy, who was jumping up and down with excitement.

And then he came to Steve. He looked at him awkwardly. He had thanked him before, but he wanted to do it again. He just didn't know how. Steve shook his hand, then pulled him into a rough hug.

The moment was broken when someone began tinkling a bell to get their attention. It was Rick, standing on the hearth.

"We have a few people who want to say some things," Rick said. "The first one is from Dr. Harry. He sent it with Sylvia from Nicaragua. If everybody would listen, Mark, you especially . . . You need to hear what Dr. Harry has to say."

They turned on the video, and Mark listened as Dr. Harry gave him a blessing such as he'd never received before. And then Rick got up to speak and said things about Mark's childhood, how he used to skip and make everyone laugh. No one who spoke seemed to recall that Mark had once been arrested for stealing a car, for vandalism, for drugs, for distribution. No one seemed to remember his spending the past year in jail. Instead, you would have thought he was getting an award for feeding the homeless or saving souls.

He couldn't believe the grace of it all.

Steve hadn't yet spoken, but Cathy felt moved to say a few more words before he addressed the crowd.

"One more person has a few things to say," she called out, quieting the crowd. "But before he comes up, I just want to say how proud I am of my son." She met Mark's eyes. "I know that what you've been through in the last year has been really hard, Mark. And at the beginning, I was ashamed and upset, but today I couldn't be prouder of you if you had cured cancer or invented some kind of modern gadget that changes the whole world. I love you." She kissed her fingertips and blew it to Mark.

The door from the kitchen to the garage opened, and she glanced over to see who was coming in. She saw Jerry sticking his head slightly in, looking around with purpose . . . and anger.

Her heart crashed. How could he come here and make a scene, on Mark's day? How could he ignore the joy and dig up only the things that affected him? Was he going to heckle Steve's speech? Challenge his right to stand in the place of father?

Their friends and neighbors kept their eyes on her, as Mark did, so no one else saw Jerry. He backed out and closed the door. Great, Cathy thought—now he was out there like a ticking bomb, volatile and waiting to explode. Something was about to happen, and she couldn't predict what it was. Her eyes met Sylvia's in a moment of panic.

"But before we hear from Steve," she said, "I want Sylvia to come up and say a few words. Ladies and gentlemen, our resident missionary who's been mentoring my daughter for the last year—Sylvia Bryan."

Sylvia looked surprised, but she rose to the occasion and came forward, weak and pale. As the crowd applauded, Cathy whispered to Sylvia, "Jerry's in the garage. Stall while I calm him down." Sylvia nodded and started to speak. Cathy hurried through the crowd, grabbed Steve's hand, and pulled him toward the door.

"Jerry's here," she whispered. "He's going to ruin your speech. Come with me to talk to him."

They hurried out the side door.

Jerry was waiting in the garage, leaning against the wall, hands in his pockets. "What are you doing here?" Cathy asked.

Jerry stiffened. "I'm his father."

"So what are you going to do? Just come in here and tell everybody not to welcome Mark home, that he's an ex-con and he doesn't deserve any of this?"

The anger was clear on Jerry's face, and he took a step toward Cathy.

Steve stepped between them. "Cathy, let me handle it, okay? You go on back in. Mark's going to come looking for you, and we don't want to upset him."

Cathy drew in a deep breath, then lifted her chin. "All right," she said, "but so help me, Jerry, if you mess any of this up, you're going to pay. None of your children will ever forgive you." With that, she went back into the house.

She tried to act as if nothing was wrong, but her hands trembled. Sylvia's speech was heartfelt and spontaneous, and she realized that it was a God thing that she had let her friend get up. Sylvia kept talking until Steve stepped back in alone. Then she shot Cathy a questioning look. Cathy nodded grimly and started back to the front.

As Sylvia turned it back over to her, Cathy tried to swallow the tension in her throat. She drew in a deep breath, afraid of what was about to happen.

"There's one other person who'd like to speak," she said in a shaky voice. Everyone looked at Steve expectantly. He only looked down at the floor.

"He's someone who's had a huge impact in Mark's life, someone who's loved him and grieved over every step of this process. Someone who's celebrating now, just like God is in heaven."

She looked across the room at Steve and saw him shaking his head. She frowned and started to urge him to come on, when the door opened and Jerry stepped inside. He took a look around at the crowd, his face reddening.

She started to launch toward him, but Steve held up a hand to stop her. He nodded that it was okay.

Slowly, Jerry pushed through the crowd.

Chapter Eighty-Five

Mark slowly turned and saw Jerry moving to the front. His mouth came open, and his eyes looked so vulnerable Cathy thought they might shatter.

"Uh . . ." Jerry cleared his throat. "I feel kind of out of place in here." He coughed nervously and looked down at his son. "Mark . . . just look at you."

Mark slid his hands into his pants pockets and looked down at his new shoes.

"I'm not very proud . . ." He stopped and cleared his throat again. Mark brought his eyes back up, and Cathy moved next to Mark and touched his shoulder. "I'm not very proud of the way I've treated you over the last year," he said. "Even though I'm your dad, I was mad, and I didn't want you to think I would reward you for what you'd done. But I was wrong, Son."

Cathy covered her mouth against the muffled sob.

"I've missed a lot," Jerry went on. "I haven't been there for you. But tonight I've been standing outside the door listening to what the people said about you. To tell you the truth, I came here to confront your mother and Steve, who I thought was trying to fill my shoes. And standing out there, I heard all those great things that everybody's been saying, and I realized that I've missed an awful lot. Not just for the last year, but for your whole childhood."

Mark's mouth twitched at the corners, and Cathy could see the Herculean effort he was giving to not falling apart. But *Jerry* was falling apart.

"Mark, I hope you can forgive your old man," he said, "because when I look at you right now, I'm prouder of you than I've ever been in my life. I love you, Mark."

Before he had a chance to say another word, Mark bolted forward and embraced his father. Cathy saw Jerry dip his head down and kiss Mark's neck, just like the father had done to the Prodigal Son.

She watched father and son descend back into the crowd, watched the others patting his back and shaking his hand, watched Annie and Rick as they embraced their dad, celebrating the fact that he had come to do this thing for their brother.

Stunned, Cathy pulled back out of the crowd and stepped outside to calm herself. She leaned back against the garage wall, exactly where Jerry had been moments earlier. The door opened, and Steve slipped out.

He looked at her with worried eyes. "I hope you're not mad," he said.

"Mad? About what?"

"That I let him in, let him go talk in my place. Let him speak publicly like that to Mark."

"How could I be mad?" she asked, wiping her tears. "It was exactly what Mark needed. It's what he longed for all this time. Here I was thinking you were going to step up and make him feel so proud and bless him in a way that he needed so badly. But you did more than that. You gave him back his dad."

He held her as she wept with joy for what

her son had gained, when so many times before, she had wept over what he had lost.

And then the doors opened again, and David Dodd stepped out. They broke the embrace, and Steve whispered, "Why don't you go on back in? I need to talk to David."

Cathy went back inside to find her son.

David reached out to shake Steve's hand. "That was very moving," he said in a cracked voice. "I know it wasn't easy."

"It was your idea," Steve said. "I appreciate it."

"You know," David said, struggling to control his voice, "what happened in there . . . all the symbolism, the coat you had made for Mark, the ring on his finger, that little insignia, and then watching Mark and his father embrace the way they did. It was a real good picture to me, Steve."

"A picture of what?" Steve asked.

"A picture of God." He rubbed his jaw hard, trying to cover the trembling of his mouth. "I just need to think about all this for a while."

"I'll pray for you, man," Steve said.

David nodded. "You know, that didn't mean a whole lot to me a while back, but I think I'm starting to see that maybe there's some good to praying. It always seems to work."

"Every time. Not always the way we want. But I have no regrets."

David swallowed hard. "If Brenda comes looking for me, tell her I went home, okay? I have some thinking to do."

"Sure, I will."

And as David walked down the driveway and crossed the street, Steve prayed that David would see his own Father scanning the horizon, waiting for him to come home.

Chapter Eighty-Six

When the party was over and all the guests had gone home—and Cathy's kids had gone out for a bite with their father—Sylvia, Brenda, and Tory stayed behind to help Cathy clean up.

The kitchen was almost clean when Sylvia had to sit down. It was jetlag, Cathy thought, on the tail end of a couple of years of the hardest work of her life. Sylvia would rest, and they would take care of her, and by the time they put her back on the plane, she would be fine.

"You haven't been taking advantage of one of God's greatest gifts," she said, bringing Sylvia a mug of coffee and sitting down beside her.

Sylvia sipped, looking puzzled. "And which gift is that?"

"Rest," Cathy said, kicking off her shoes and pulling her feet up to the couch.

"You're right," Tory agreed. "Rest is a gift."

"One of many," Brenda said. She set her mug down on the coffee table. "Think where we were a year ago, when Cathy thought everything had come crashing down."

"But it hadn't," Cathy said. "Look what came of it."

"It's been a full year," Sylvia said. "A year with a lot of good moments. One of mine was when Annie got off the plane in Managua and saw the car I drive." She threw her head back and laughed. "You should have seen her face, Cathy. It was priceless. She was trying not to laugh, but then she fell against the car and laughed until she cried. Wish I'd gotten a picture of that." She sighed. "We loved having her there. It was a good time."

"But I'm glad you brought her back," Cathy said. "I missed her. But I have noticed that she's appreciated driving my little car. Not one complaint."

"That's just because it has real windows instead of duct tape."

"She said you were so tired from pedaling your car," Cathy said, and they all laughed again.

"So what was your best moment in the last year, Brenda?" Sylvia asked.

She thought a moment. "Mine was getting Daniel *his* car," Brenda said. "It's probably not a whole lot better than yours, Sylvia, but it suited him fine."

"Mine was the date with Barry," Tory said, "when he arranged the sitter and took me dancing."

"The wedding was nice," Cathy said, feeling that sense of well-being that comes in the wake of joy. "The marriage is even nicer. Best moment? When Mark told me he'd found Christ."

Sylvia nodded. "When Annie understood that Christ was better than food."

"When David was so moved today by the picture of the Prodigal Son," Brenda whispered.

Tory swallowed and drew in a cleansing breath. "When I understood that life's family joys are more important than my pride."

"Oh, yeah," Cathy said, relating too well.

"Or when Jerry understood that." She dropped her feet and leaned up, as if amazed all over again. "The look on Mark's face when his dad told him he loved him." Her heart ached with that sensitive joy that always comes with tears. "*That* was the best moment," Cathy whispered.

"You're right," Brenda whispered. "It was."

"Yeah," Tory said as tears rimmed her eyes. "I'll never forget it."

"Neither will he," Sylvia said. "What a precious gift."

Chapter Eighty-Seven

That night, Mark enjoyed settling back into his messiness, as he had not been allowed to do at River Ranch. He took his shirt off and threw it over the basketball hoop on his door, then pulled on a pair of jeans, relishing the feel of them in place of his Cat-in-the-Hat pants.

He plopped down onto his bed and stretched out on the thick mattress.

And then he thanked God that he was out of jail, that he wasn't the stupid, stubborn kid who went in, that his family had welcomed him back . . .

He had never expected to feel this sense

of well-being again, but tonight all seemed right with his life.

Cathy woke up in the middle of the night and reached over to touch Steve's chest. He slept soundly, with that rhythmic breathing she had come to depend on. Carefully, she slipped out of bed and walked barefoot across the plush carpet in their new bedroom. She went into the living room and down the hall to Tracy's room. The child slept with four stuffed animals and a nightlight on. Her hair lay like a blanket across her face, and Cathy pushed it back from her eyes.

Quietly, she slipped out of the room and went up the stairs. Rick's door was open, and she stopped in the doorway and saw him buried under his covers. He was almost too big for his bed, she thought. She hadn't noticed it before. But she supposed there was no point in getting him a bigger bed when he had such a small bed in his dorm. She stepped close to him and saw the perspiration on his face. He was too hot. She'd have to adjust the thermostat.

She went back out and stopped at Annie's room. Her daughter had already fallen into her habit of cluttering her room with clothes and shoes and makeup, as if she'd waited a solid year to spread out again. Photographs of the children in Leon were already framed and placed around her room. Cathy stepped close to the bed, where Annie lay like the little girl she had once been, all innocent and sweet and full of life. She was still that girl, Cathy thought with gratitude. Annie was tangled in her covers, with something clutched in her hands. Cathy looked to see what it was.

It was the picture of a tiny little girl Annie had come to love. Cathy swallowed back the emotion tightening her throat.

Then she went on to Mark's room and stepped inside. He was sound asleep on his bed, still wearing his jeans. He looked like the little skipping boy that Cathy had lost, with his bare chest and bare feet, and his arm carelessly flung over the side of the bed.

She went in and pulled his covers up over him. Love and unspeakable gratitude filled her heart so full that it almost hurt. She knew just whom to thank.

She looked up at the ceiling, as if she could see her Lord smiling down at her. "I owe you a big one," she whispered.

They had all turned out right. In spite of

her flawed mothering, in spite of their broken home, in spite of everything that had gone wrong in their lives . . . God had filled in the blanks.

He had raised her children right and had seen them all the way home.